BLESSED AND HIGHLY FAVORED

MELISSA BOWAN

Published by:
Blessed and Highly Favored Publications
7139 Highway 85 Suite # 272
Riverdale, Georgia 30274
678.662.1873
highlyfavored2006@hotmail.com

ISBN: 0-615-13143-3

Book Design by:
RJ Communications
51 East 42nd Street
New York, NY 10017
800.621.2556
jg@rjcom.com

Edited by: Edit 911
www.edit911.com

Printed in the United States of America

To order online, visit our website:
www.highly-favored.net

To order by phone, call:
678.662.1873

Send an email to Melissa Bowan:
melissabowan@hotmail.com

In loving memory of my niece and my namesake, Melissa Bowan, whose life was taken by a serial killer. I regret that I was unable to save you from the life that led you into the hands of such despicable evil. My hope is that this book will prevent other young girls like you and me from allowing the desires of the world to lead them to death.

Contents

Preface

I wrote this account of my life so that you can experience the wonders of God through my testimony. I have changed the names to protect the identities of the people that I have encountered and also for my own anonymity. The name Melissa Bowan is a fictional one; therefore, if you know someone with this name, rest assured that I have never met her nor is this an account of her life. In some instances, I have changed the locations of some events. In all instances, I have invented the places of employment. My brother does not work for the Texas Bureau of Investigation and never has, although he is in law enforcement. My sister has never worked for Xerox, although she does in fact work for a Fortune 500 company.

If by chance you recognize your character in these pages and you say, "I never said that," I apologize in advance. It is extremely difficult to remember every conversation thirty years after the fact. In those instances, I may have indeed invented dialogue to match the events as they occurred.

But make no mistake; this is a true and accurate account of my life. More importantly, it is a true and accurate account of God's love, His mercy, and His grace.

I say to you now it is the most incredible story you will ever read. It is the kind of story that only Hollywood movies are made of. It has drama, adventure, sex, passion, adultery, prostitution, drugs, homosexuals, orgies, drug dealers, gangsters, theft, cheating, abortion, and murder. It also has love, joy, sacrifice, compassion, grace, healing, mercy, and faith; but the greatest of these is love.

I have added the elements of spiritual warfare to my story, as I have been directed by the Holy Spirit. You will hear what Jesus has to say and, of course, you will hear from Satan as he plots to destroy me and those I love. My account of the conversations between God, the Heavenly Host, Satan, and his demons are also inspired and directed by the Holy Spirit.

Please do not interpret this account to mean that I think I possess favor from God that you do not have. God favors each and every one of us. This is simply my personal account of His favor, and I am sure that you have personal accounts also.

You have but to read these pages to know that God's love for us is as real as Satan's hate. My sole purpose for living is to tell this tale to you and for God to get the glory that I live to tell of it. The only way that I could have survived the events that you are about to read is through Divine Intervention. The only way to explain these extraordinary supernatural occurrences is to recognize the battle that is being fought between the Heavenly Host and the forces of Satan.

I pray that you are able to recognize the love that Jesus has for you before you spend your entire life, as I have, searching for that which has been with you every day since the moment of your conception.

Chapter One

But She Comes from Such a Good Family

My dad was an Air Force sergeant. As a result, we moved frequently. My mom was a clinical dietitian who worked for the state. I have two very pretty sisters and one very handsome brother. If you had happened by us, you would have undoubtedly said, "What a nice looking middle class family."

Although from all outward appearances we were a nice looking family, we were also a dysfunctional one. Dad was an alcoholic and Mom was a social drinker. I remember frequent arguments between my parents. Eventually they split entirely, resulting in a move from military life to civilian.

Through all of this, or in spite of it, we were raised Catholic, even though I'm not sure why as my mom was raised Southern Baptist. Somehow Mom always managed to get us to Mass every Sunday. She insisted on a Catholic school, which also included mass during the week. And then there was Catechism, during which we were frequently taught about hell and burning in hell. We were taught to fear God and given a long list of things that would ultimately land us in the fiery pit. I don't recall much about how to stay out of hell, though, and I certainly don't recall anything about God's mercy or grace or how his Son died so that we could be saved.

The one thing that disturbed me most was that the very people who supposedly represented those not going to hell seemed no better off than I was and at times were even worse. Our priest almost always had a cigarette and often a scotch. The nuns were meaner than rattlesnakes. One even slapped my sister Faith across the face. This remains as disturbing now as it did then. If you knew Faith, you would understand why. Faith was the one I always refer to as the perfect sister. She was the good sister and the sound of reason. She was the anchor, the mediator, and the diplomat. She was the one you could always count on then and even now forty years later. If anyone was to be slapped, it should have been me or my oldest sister, who would later run off to Vegas with her college beau. But not Faith. So in my mind, this was the proof that there was something terribly wrong with the entire lot of them. They were evil if they could not see her goodness. Frequently, I imagined meeting most of them when I arrived at hell's gates.

I was a rebellious sort, although I did not get into much trouble; so I graduated from high school with honors in 1974 at the age of eighteen. After graduation, I was still a good Catholic girl who believed that hell was around every corner and quite unavoidable. I was always told that I was quite pretty and thought that it was my ticket to modeling fame. The reality was that I was stuck in a dead-end job as a seamstress in a factory and attended a modeling school that told each and every girl she would be famous.

My journey started at that factory.

Chapter Two

I'm a Witness; You're a Witness

The floor supervisor walked by and dropped another bundle of sleeves on my sewing table and three bundles of collars on Sue Ellen's.

"I don't think she likes me very much," said Sue Ellen.

"She doesn't like anybody so why should you be an exception?" I asked.

"But I'm so nice to her," reasoned Sue Ellen.

"And I'm not nice? She doesn't acknowledge nice; as a matter of fact, it probably works the other way around for her."

"I'm not accustomed to people that don't acknowledge kindness."

"You live in a fairy tale world, Sue Ellen. In the real world, they don't give a shit," I said impatiently.

"I wish you wouldn't talk like that."

"Sue Ellen, you're such a goody-two-shoes."

"No, I'm a witness to the goodness of Jehovah God."

"Why do you call God Jehovah?"

"Because that's His name. It's in the Bible, you know."

"No, I didn't." *I think I'll look that up when I get home,* I thought to myself.

"Why don't you look it up when you get home," Sue Ellen said.

I rolled my eyes. "What are you, a mind reader?"

She smiled and quickly averted her eyes so that I would know the floor supervisor was approaching.

"If you two sewed as much as you talked, you'd be a lot more productive," said the Wicked Witch of the West.

I rolled my eyes again and Sue Ellen giggled.

The demon named Amducious flew as fast as he could. *This is it; this message will ensure my position as general. I will command legions of demons. I will cause those puny humans to bow to Master.* Amducious folded his wings and landed smoothly; then he walked through the guarded gates with his head held high with authority.

"I have an important message," he bellowed. "I must have an audience with the prince at once."

The gatekeeper smirked. "What makes you think you are important enough to be granted an audience with the prince?"

"I am Amducious the Destroyer, and I have a message of the utmost importance. Are you willing to bet your head that he does not wish to receive it?"

The gatekeeper's eyes flickered briefly with insecurity. "Wait here. I will announce your presence." Upon his return, he bowed. "The Master will see you now. Make haste; he loathes waiting."

Amducious preened his wings briefly and stepped into the great hall. He timidly approached the throne; the air was laden with the smell of sulfur. With his head bowed, he stole a fleeting glance at the one sitting upon the throne. His wings were massive and his beauty was astounding. He was adorned with every kind of jewel. Amducious was quite aware of how quickly his mood could change and his appearance with it. He knelt at the base of the throne.

"Master, Prince of Darkness and ruler of this world, I bring you worship and praise. Am I permitted to speak?"

"If you did not have my permission to speak, I would have severed your head before you had finished the first syllable," Satan replied.

"Very well, my king. I bring a message of great importance. This message was intercepted on its way to the golden warrior!"

Satan stood to his full height, his wings opened fully. As quick as the speed of light, he transformed into a ferocious beast and raised his sword. "You dare invent a story such as this? No one intercepts messages to the Archangel Michael!

Only Gabriel or I have the prowess to come into his presence undetected."

Amducious shrank back in fear and lay prostrate on the floor, knowing he was twenty seconds from having his head severed from his body.

"It is true, Master. Please spare me that I may give you a full report."

"Proceed, but if it is not to my liking, you will regret having the audacity to enter my presence."

"Yes, Master." Amducious's voice was barely audible. "The One Who Sits at the Right Hand of God summoned him to guide and protect a human on earth with the name Melissa. She is very important to him, and Michael was ordered to make haste. Because of the unusual request of the One at the Right Hand, Michael briefly let his guard down to ponder the request. At that brief moment, I was able to go undetected. Once he detected my presence, he decided his orders were too important to pursue me. Therefore, I escaped unharmed. Had it not been for his urgency to reach the Heavenly Throne, I would surely have lost my head."

"Hmmm, Michael summoned by The Morning Star to protect one human? This is most unusual. Michael has legions at his disposal for such a task. What is so important about this human that The One Who Sits at the Right Hand requires that she be guarded by Michael?"

Satan sat to ponder his question. Seeing that he had lowered his sword, Amducious lifted his head.

"It's quite strange, Master. I went to investigate this human and there is nothing of importance about her. She has no wealth or station. She possesses no land and nothing of value. She...she sews garments in a garment factory," he stammered.

Satan stood up again. "She sews garments in a garment factory?" he bellowed. "What sort of nonsense is this?"

"It is true, Master, I swear it. I saw it with my own eyes."

Satan threw balls of fire across the room.

"It had better be true, for if this is a trick of Michael's, I will see you at the guillotine. We must prepare an attack at once. This will require the utmost skill and cunning, for Michael is a worthy adversary. If this human is of such importance to The One Who Sits at the Right Hand, then she will belong to me. Assemble your best troops. Make no mistake. If you fail me, it will be your head."

Meanwhile, Michael the Archangel arrived at the Throne of the Most High God. He too was a work of beauty with shimmering gold and an array of jewels. His countenance was so bright that a human could not gaze upon him without becoming temporarily blind.

"Praise be to God the Father and the Son and the Holy Spirit," Michael said as he bowed before the Throne of God. "I am your humble servant."

"And you are my most trusted warrior," Jesus said. "Why are you troubled?"

"It is not my place to question He who made the Heavens and the earth," Michael replied.

"And yet you ponder the importance of my daughter Melissa." Without waiting for an answer, Jesus said, "She is one of my children and is predestined to reside with me in the Kingdom of Heaven. This alone warrants my intervention. She has a pure love for me, like that of a child. She also has many weaknesses, which Satan will exploit. However, that which Satan has planned for her demise, I will use for my glory. Her greatest threat is that of her own desires, and she will suffer much because of them. She will search for me to no avail, and she will be quick to accept defeat. The riches of the world will be a great temptation for her. She will pursue them with great longing, but they too will elude her. She will look for me again to no avail. Many will cry out, 'He is here. No, He is there,' but again she will not find me. However, they who search long and hard will not abandon the Truth once they have found it. Hers will be a long and arduous journey, but victory will be hers; and in the end, I will say to her, 'Well done, my good and faithful servant.' It is necessary for these things to take place, for I will use her plight as an example to the world that my grace and mercy are sufficient to sustain them through all, even death.

"I have summoned you, my most trusted warrior, for this

mission because it will require the utmost skill to protect her. Satan's attack will be a vicious one. You must exercise caution and be on your guard. Only through my grace will she be spared. You must protect her through a sea of sin and degradation. She will enter the sexual perversions of Sodom and Gomorrah and the drunken stupors of pharmaceuticals. She will escape the punishments of government authorities, the plagues of AIDS and cancer, and the blight of false religion. She will elude death by fire along with her male sibling and her first born. This she will see as a gift that was given to her and her sibling so that they may find salvation. Of you, I will require much. You must be prepared at a moment's notice to cross over to the earthly plane to take them back when I raise her and her male sibling from the dead."

Michael's wings fluttered ever so slightly at this command.

"I know, my faithful servant, rarely do I resurrect one from the dead; however, it is required to demonstrate that I hold the power over life and death.

"Like many women of her time, she will follow the world in the belief that my children who are unborn are not living souls. Four times she will murder her seed. You must be ready to protect them, for it is my wish that they do not suffer as a result. Shield them with your wings from the cut of the knife, for I will bring them unto me before the sting of death touches their bodies. Later she will suffer much because of what she has done of her own choosing. This lesson will cause her much pain, for she will know that I have spared her from death and yet four times she did not spare her own seed.

"When she finds the Truth, she and her male sibling and others will marvel at this gift of life that has been given to one so undeserving. This will help them to understand the real gift of Eternal Life that I give freely to those who do not deserve it. They have but to ask and it shall be given. Her first trial with false religion will be soon. She will seek me from within those who do not believe that the Father and I are one. This religion will appeal to her because they also do not believe in my wrath or the fiery gates of hell. You will be still during this time, for they are no threat to her. She will quickly grow weary when she repeatedly fails at keeping my commands. This time shall be of importance when she finds the Truth. Then it will be brought to her remembrance, and she will understand that salvation is not obtained by keeping my commands, for it is impossible to do so while within the confines of an imperfect and sinful body. Only through my death and resurrection can one be saved. Once Satan comes to realize that she is out of his reach and the second death has no power over her, he will then pursue her seed. However, I will make a covenant with her to protect her seed also, for she loves them as I love her and all of my children.

"Be on your guard, for an immediate threat is looming from within her own household. Go at once."

Michael bowed his head, "Praise be to God the Father, the Son, and the Holy Spirit." He then took flight.

Sue Ellen and I walked to the car, our feet dragging.

"Gosh, I'm tired."

"So am I," said Sue Ellen. We got into her car for the ride home together. "You know, Jimmy and me can come over and give you a Bible study about Jehovah God. You go home tonight and look up God's name and then let me know if you want to study tomorrow."

"Okay," I said, "you got a deal. If God's name is Jehovah, I'll let you and Jimmy come over and Bible study with me."

Sue Ellen dropped me off at my mom's house. I dreaded going in to face her and that sorry dude she had married. Jack Johnson was only after my mom's money. She couldn't see past his handsome face because he reminded her of Daddy. She was a sucker for a pretty face, Daddy's included. *I have got to get my own place,* I thought.

"Hello, anybody home in there?" I called.

"In here," Mom replied. They were both there, having a nightcap in the middle of the afternoon. Mom quickly turned her face from me. That seemed somewhat odd, so I moved to the far side of the room to get a better look. *She has a damned black eye. That bastard gave my mom a black eye.* She gave me the "please be quiet" look. *Well, I'll be damned if that's going to fly.* I threw down my purse.

"You are going to get the hell out of my mom's house right this minute!" I stormed into their bedroom and pulled out all of his drawers, grabbing up his clothes along the way. I stomped over to the front door and started flinging his clothes out of the door on to the front porch.

"Get out, get out, get out and stay out!" I flung another armload of his clothes out the door. He just stood there with his mouth open. Mom stood there also, but she looked terrified.

"You get my clothes off that porch right now and put them back where they belong!" he bellowed.

I was too mad to be afraid, so I pushed him, all 6' 4" of him. By the way, I'm 5'2" and a hundred pounds soaking wet. He glared at me. Then he grabbed me and started choking me. I saw stars. *He's going to kill me right here and right now.* Mom started screaming and ran to the phone. I knew she was calling the police, even though I couldn't see her.

The Archangel Michael drew his sword. The demon Balban was so intent on taunting Jack that he was unprepared for Michael's attack.

"Kill her, kill her," Balban taunted.

Michael thrust his sword completely through Balban, who vanished in a puff of smoke. Michael placed his wings on Jack's hands, which were around Melissa's throat. "Release her before the constables arrive," he whispered to Jack. "Release her; release her now before it is too late!"

Jack abruptly dropped his hands to his sides, as if he had been struck. I remember wondering, *Why did he let me go?* But rather than wait for him to change his mind, I grabbed a huge stereo speaker within my grasp and threw it at him. He screamed as it hit him squarely against his jaw.

"You crazy bitch," he screamed, as he staggered backwards.

"You haven't seen me as crazy as you will if you don't get out of my mother's house!" I yelled.

I picked up the matching speaker and threw it at his head. He yelped and ran like a scared rabbit out the front door. As he ran, I threw his keys and his stupid cowboy hat at him.

"And don't come back ever!" I yelled.

At that moment, the police arrived. Jack was gathering his clothing. "She's crazy!" he kept yelling. "She's crazy as a mad hatter. Look at my face!" he screamed.

My mom came to the door just as the police arrived. "He attacked my daughter and I want him off my property immediately."

"Do you want to press charges?" the other officer asked.

She glared at Jack. "No, not if he agrees to leave and not to come back."

"I got no problem with that 'cause you're both crazy!" and Jack stormed off, got in his truck, and sped away.

"Thank you," Mom said and I laughed and started singing. "Hit the road, Jack, and don't you come back no more, no more, no more, no more. Hit the road, Jack, and don't you come back no more."

Mom chimed in. "Hit the road, Jack, and don't you come back no more, no more, no more, no more. Hit the road, Jack, and don't you come back no more." She laughed and we went into the house.

As she closed the door, I said, "Why do you think he let me go?" I rubbed my neck.

"Perhaps he got an attack of conscience for once in his life."

"Now that would be the day," I laughed.

I plopped down on the bed, picked up the Bible, and lit a cigarette. I looked down at my cigarette; *I guess I shouldn't smoke while I'm reading the Bible*, so I put the cigarette out. *Hmmm, let's see if Jehovah is in here.* I looked in the index. *Wow, it's in here a bunch of times,* I thought. *Well, I guess Sue Ellen and Jimmy were right. I need to find out more about this Jehovah Witness thing. It sounds just like what the doctor ordered. Better yet, it sounds just like what God ordered.* I smiled at that, as I fell asleep.

Idiots, the entire lot of them, **Amducious thought.** *Had it not been for Michael's interference and Balban's incompetence the human Jack would have killed her and then she would have belonged to Master. I should have seen to it personally. Master will be furious when he finds out we had such a perfect opportunity and yet failed. Hmmm, given that Balban does not live to tell the tale, I think it is necessary to embellish the truth a bit.* **Amducious entered Satan's chamber and greeted him, as was the custom.**

"Master, Prince of Darkness and ruler of this world, I bring you worship and praise."

"What news do you have to report?" Satan asked.

Amducious hung his head and put on a face of deep sorrow. "My comrade Balban was slain by Michael in the line of duty;

however, his death was with great honor, for he devised a plot for the human Melissa to pursue a faith that is insidious to He Who Sits at the Right Hand."

"For what reason does The Morning Star have to despise this faith you speak of?"

Amducious snickered. "They do not believe He and the Father are one."

Satan threw his head back and roared with laughter.

"Remind me to ensure that they have the best accommodations when they arrive for their stay."

"Their group is in for many surprises, for they also do not believe the Father will banish them to hell."

This time Satan laughed so hard the room began to shake and sparks began to fly.

"What fun this will be. I must have a special reward for them when they deliver her to me. The smell of victory is sweet. What plot did Balban devise before his untimely death?"

"The human Melissa has an acquaintance that sews garments at the factory with her," Amducious responded. "This acquaintance transports the human to and from the factory, as Melissa does not own a transportation device. She will teach her faith to the human after the sun sets tomorrow. She will be putty in her hands, for she fears hell from prior teachings. The belief that hell does not exist greatly appeals to her."

"Excellent, excellent! You must ensure that she does not find out the truth about The One Who Sits at the Right Hand."

"Your wish is my command, Master." Amducious drew a sigh of relief. *That was close,* he thought, as he rubbed the spot where he had envisioned Satan's sword thrusting through him. *I must see to this plan personally, for future mistakes will be my own undoing.* He took flight and arrived just in time for Bible study.

After work on Friday, Sue Ellen arranged for her husband Jimmy and her to come over for Bible study at seven o'clock. "See you at seven," called Sue Ellen.

"I can't wait," I called over my shoulder. I glanced over at the car that was in our driveway. *Oh, for Pete's sake. Did she have to come over today? I certainly hope she's gone by seven.* "Hello, I'm home."

"Hey, turtledove, your Aunt Emma is here."

"Hi, Aunt Emma," I mumbled, as she squeezed me between two mammoth breasts.

"How's my favorite niece?"

"I doubt very much if I'm your favorite. That would be Faith, who's everyone's favorite."

"Now that is not true," Aunt Emma said without much sincerity.

At about seven, you will undoubtedly change that statement, I thought. I paced back and forth in the dining room, wishing Auntie Emma would tire of trivial conversation. She could talk incessantly about her numerous ailments. *Why doesn't she leave,* I thought, just as the doorbell rang. *Shit, that's Sue Ellen. Oops, I guess I shouldn't say shit right before a Bible study.*

"Hi, Sue Ellen. Hey, Jimmy."

"Hi," Jimmy replied with that infectious smile of his. Sue Ellen just smiled; she never said much when Jimmy was around. I seated them in the dining room and, just as I feared, Auntie Emma came snooping around the corner.

"Hello. Aren't you going to introduce me to your guests?"

"This is my co-worker, Sue Ellen, and this is her husband, Jimmy."

"What have you got there," Auntie asked, eyeing his Bible and Watchtower materials.

"We're about to have a Bible study. Melissa would like to know about Jehovah God."

"I think I'm going to need a cigarette," I sighed.

Amducious flitted around the room antagonizing everyone. "Tell them they are going to burn in hell," he hissed at Auntie Emma, while keeping a cautious eye out for Michael. "She hates your kind; get angry," he taunted Jimmy. "She believes that she is the only one who can worship God," he whispered to Melissa. "Show her that she is wrong."

Michael watched at a distance, careful not to interfere, as Jesus had instructed him to be still during this time.

"Jehovah's Witnesses. You're all going to burn in hell," Auntie Emma said under her breath.

Jimmy's breath quickened and his neck started to turn red. "There is no hell," he replied as calmly as he could.

"You keep right on believing that until your tail is on fire. Huh, all going to burn in hell, the whole lot of you." She then turned and stomped out of the room.

Jimmy inhaled deeply. "Well, why don't we start with hell, seeing as we are already on the subject?"

"Sorry, Jimmy. She thinks she's the only one who can worship God." *I'll show her,* I thought.

"Don't worry about it," Jimmy replied in his most persecuted voice. "Those of us who witness and teach the Word of God are destined to undergo persecution. It says so in the scripture." Our study lasted about two hours.

"Let's see if I've got this straight. There is no hell. When you die, you are dead and you know nothing, feel nothing, just dead. No burning, no torment, just dead. You do not go to heaven when you die; you sleep until Jesus resurrects you to live in Paradise here on earth. Jesus is God's Son, but that Trinity stuff the nuns taught us is also not true. I always thought that three people in one was sort of weird and I really got tired of hearing that I was going to burn in hell every day. If you ask me, they're more inclined to get to hell before I do."

Jimmy just chuckled. "Most people, including and especially priests, find it easier to judge others than to take a look at their own infirmities."

I just love to hear him talk, I thought. I marveled at how he seemed to know everything about God and the Bible. *I wish I could get Paul to believe in Jehovah.* Paul was my boyfriend. Even though he was much older than I, it seemed as if he didn't know much of anything. Not to mention that he hated the fact that I wanted to be a model and was actually going to school for something. He was a Vet and Uncle Sam would pay him to go to school, but he had no ambition to do anything but work in a factory all of his life. *If I could just get that man to do something constructive,* I thought.

"Earth to Melissa!"

"Huh," I responded, startled out of my reverie about Paul.

"Would you like to come to the Kingdom Hall with us Sunday?" Jimmy asked.

"Sure. Kingdom Hall, that has a nice ring to it."

We heard Auntie Emma mumbling as she passed the dining room.

"She ain't got no business messing with folk who don't know Jesus! Cults, that's what they are. Gonna burn in hell, sure as a pig is pork." She slammed the front door and I breathed a sigh of relief. *Thank goodness she's finally gone. How embarrassing!*

Later that night, I spent two hours talking to Paul on the phone. We frequently talked until we both fell asleep. Neither of our parents was very happy about our custom.

"I wish you would get an apartment. You're a bit old to be living with your mother, you know."

"I like living with Mama," Paul replied.

"I certainly don't like living with my mother and I plan on doing something about it. I'm getting sleepy. I'm gonna lay the phone down now. I love you." But I could tell he was already asleep.

The Kingdom Hall was very different from attending Mass. It was not stuffy and ritualistic and I liked it. Afterwards, Sue Ellen and I were chatting while Jimmy and the other deacons cleaned up.

"It's sort of hard having a relationship with a man who lives with his mother," I sighed.

Sue Ellen blushed. "You mean sex, don't you?"

"Well, yeah, I certainly don't mean Ring Around the Rosie."

"You know, sex outside of marriage is a sin against Jehovah God,"

"The good news is at least I won't burn in hell for it."

"No, but do you want to die and never wake up to live in Paradise?"

"Hmmm, I guess not, now that you mention it."

"If you really love Paul, then you need to get married."

"Married! Now that's a serious step."

"Not if you're in love. If you're in love and want to have sex, then marriage is the right way to do that."

"You're beginning to sound dangerously close to those nuns," I chided.

"I hate to admit it, but if that's what they told you, they were right."

"I had a feeling you were going to say that," I said as I rolled my eyes.

Jimmy had completed his cleaning chores by that time. "Ready, ladies?"

"Ready," we said in unison.

After I got home, I called Paul. *I think it's time to drop the bomb on him,* I thought. "Can you pick me up at around six? I don't want to stay out too late tonight."

"Six is sort of early, don't you think?" he responded.

"No, I have to get up and go to work."

"So do I, but I don't want to go out that early."

"Since we're only going out to grab a bite to eat, six is a perfect time."

"What do you mean 'only'? Aren't we going to the motel?"

"No, we are not going to the motel."

"And why aren't we?" he asked.

"Because if you want to have sex, then it's time you made a stop at the altar along the way."

"What?"

"You heard me. Altar as in marriage, as in bride and bridegroom."

"Whoa! Hold on! What have you been smoking?"

"I guess that settles that and I guess that means you don't need to pick me up either. Bye!" I slammed down the phone. *Let him stew on that for a while,* I thought as I lit a cigarette.

"I bring good news, Master," Amducious announced upon his arrival to the Satanic throne. **"The human Melissa has embraced the teachings of the Witnesses for Jehovah."**

"How exactly was this feat carried out? Did it require a legion of our troops?"

"No, Master, not one was lost in battle."

"What is the meaning of this? Did you not do battle with the Mighty One?"

"No, my lord, Michael did not show his face, nor did any of the Heavenly Host."

"How curious is this? Did you not report that Michael was to guard this human with a cloak of protection?"

"Yes, Master, the fact that Michael did not engage us in battle is quite puzzling."

"Hmmm," Satan pondered. **"Michael is up to something. Send out a squadron of scouts and see what scraps they can intercept. Be prepared for casualties, as Michael will no doubt be on his guard."**

"How am I supposed to plan a wedding in two weeks?" Mother

cried. "You're only nineteen. That's too young to be getting married, but what do I know. I'm only your mother." She paced about the room, wringing her hands. "Let's see, we can have it here in the front room. In view of the fact that your father is not here, and even if he was, he would probably be drunk anyway..."

"Mother!"

"Sorry, in view of the fact that your father is not here, your brother Michael will have to give you away. Are you sure you want to marry him? He doesn't seem at all like your type."

"You mean he's not your type, Mother."

"To be frank, he doesn't strike me as anybody's type, but it's your life, not mine."

"You were saying about the front room," I said as I rolled my eyes.

"Oh, yes, we can decorate the fireplace with roses and that's where you can say your vows. You aren't planning any of those idiotic poems that they're doing these days, are you?"

"No, Mother, no poems, just the usual till death do us part stuff."

"Good, a traditional wedding. Oh, my gosh, we've got to find a dress."

"I've already taken care of it." I held my breath for the response that was inevitable.

"What do mean you've taken care of it? You don't have that kind of money."

"Pamela is making the dress," I mumbled.

"So, you planned this behind my back. I should have known."

"It was not behind your back, Mother," I sighed. "I needed to give her a head start. Making a wedding dress is not exactly child's play, you know."

"Well, all right, little Melissa can be the flower girl and little Michael can be the ring bearer."

"And Faith can be my Maid of Honor." Faith was my older sister. I also had another older sister who had run off to Vegas with her college beau. She undoubtedly would not be here.

"There's so little time and so much to do," Mother wailed.

"What about the food? What should we serve?"

"We'll leave that up to Aunt Emma. That's her specialty."

Mom and I sat down at the table and continued with the wedding arrangements.

The next morning Sue Ellen was gushing with excitement. "Are you sure you don't want to have the wedding at the Kingdom Hall?"

"I'm sure. We need to be on neutral ground. My living room is as neutral as it gets. Auntie Emma and Paul's mother would have a stroke if we had it at the Kingdom Hall."

"Well, never you mind, it's still exciting. I can't believe you talked him into it."

"Actually, I didn't do any talking at all. It was the silent treatment that did it."

"Oh, I'll have to remember that trick."

"I'd doubt that that trick would work on Jimmy."

"You're probably right," Sue Ellen lamented.

Meanwhile, Satan preened his wings before entering the Gates of Heaven. I look forward to His discomfort, Satan thought. How distraught He must be about His precious human Melissa, whom he loves so tenderly. Satan approached the Throne of God.

"Where have you been, Satan?" Jesus inquired.

"Roaming to and fro throughout the earth," Satan replied.

"No doubt tormenting my children along the way?"

"Yes, yes, your precious humans. I so enjoy tormenting each and every one of them."

"We are well aware of your insidious plots, Satan. Your time is short, but your hate is long and far-reaching."

Satan whirled around to see who was speaking.

"Ah, it is you, my brother. The smell of defeat is most alluring," he snickered.

"Defeat belongs to you and your followers and it shall dwell with you when you enter the lake of fire," Michael replied.

"You have been allowed to torment my daughter Melissa for a short time, but this too shall pass," Jesus said. "Make no mistake, the second death shall have no power over her, for it is my will and mine alone which will be done."

Satan's wings flared to their full size and sparks flew from his nostrils. "I have been given the authority to rule over the earth. It is the Word and is so written," he yelled.

"I AM the Word and the Author of what is written," replied

Jesus. "Take leave now and go about your evil business, for your time grows shorter each time the sun sets upon the earth."

Satan took flight and cried out upon his departure. "Be forewarned, the one you favor shall suffer my wrath because of your insolence."

Michael bowed his head. "Praise be to God, forever and ever, Amen." He took flight to watch over Melissa.

"By the power invested in me, I now pronounce you man and wife," said the pastor. "You may kiss the bride." Paul kissed me and the crowd gathered in my mom's living room clapped and cheered.

"So, where are you guys going on your honeymoon?" Michael asked.

"Just down to Houston."

"Actually, Houston isn't close to Dallas, you know?"

"I know, but it doesn't cost that much to fly out of Love Field and that's about all we can afford."

"I hope you know what you've gotten yourself into?"

So do I.

Upon our return, everything went back to normal. We moved in with Paul's mother and sisters. What a drag. Every Saturday, she and Paul would give me grief about witnessing. Tonight, I was going to put my foot down.

"I found a cute apartment and I don't know about you, but I'm moving into it," I announced to Paul.

"So where is it located?"

"Don't worry, Mama's Boy; it's not far."

"Don't call me a mama's boy."

"If the shoe fits?"

"Not to change the subject, but you don't look so good."

"I'm fine, just some sort of bug going around." I wiped the sweat off my forehead.

"Maybe you should lie down awhile. We can talk about this later."

"Saved by the bed," I retorted and went to lie down. Something in my lower belly felt like it was on fire. I really needed a cigarette, but *Jehovah's Witnesses don't smoke,* I said, in my best Jimmy imitation. *I'll just rest a moment and then I'll go back and really let him have it,* then I drifted off to sleep. I slept until the next morning; everyone else had left for work or school. *I don't feel so good. I think I'll call in today.* And then I drifted off to sleep again.

Michael was surrounded by demons; however, they were no match for his sword. "Melissa, call for your mother," yelled Michael, as he cut off the head of one of Amducious's soldiers. "You must call your mother," he insisted, as he impaled five others with one stoke of his sword.

"Retreat," Amducious yelled. The demons scattered in all directions.

I woke up with a start; my entire bed was soaking with sweat. I was so very hot.

Michael was now able to wrap his wings around Melissa. "Melissa, call for your mother; she will help you."

I sat up and reached for the phone. "Mother, I'm sick. Come and get me." Somehow mothers know when you are in trouble.

"I'll be there in fifteen minutes," she said. When Mother arrived, she took one look at me. "You need a hospital."

The ER at Parkland was not anywhere you really wanted to be. But if it was good enough for Kennedy, why should I complain? They poked and prodded and took what seemed like every drop of blood in my body.

"I'm admitting you immediately," the doctor said.

"But I have to go to work before they fire me."

"You're not going anywhere. If you had waited much longer, this infection would have turned septic."

"What does that mean?"

"That, young lady, means you are very sick."

"Okay, what kind of infection is it?"

"PID–Pelvic Inflammatory Disease."

I pretended to know what that meant. "Well, can you fix it?"

"Yes, but it requires heavy doses of antibiotics delivered intravenously for about five days."

"Five days!" I cried.

"Need I remind you again how much sicker you could have been had it not been for your mother's insistence that you come to the ER? Speaking of which, would you prefer that I not tell your mother that you contracted PID?"

"Why should I care whether or not you tell her?" I asked, with a look of stupidity.

"Young lady," he said in his most condescending voice. "Do you know what PID is?"

Amducious flitted around the room, snickering. He was careful to keep a watchful eye out for Michael. The silly human had no idea that her lover had never severed his ties to the other female he lusted after.

"No, I don't," I admitted.

"It is a sexually transmitted disease."

"What? But I just got married!" I spluttered.

He looked at me over the top of his glasses. "You've had this infection for quite some time. Perhaps he contracted it before you were married." *If you believe that, I also have some swampland for sale,* the doctor thought to himself. "Are you allergic to any medications?" he asked.

"No, not that I'm aware of."

"Good, we'll start you on a round of penicillin immediately. Nurse!"

Sexually transmitted disease, five days, and slop for food. When I get my hands on that Paul, I should cut off his balls. The nurse came in about the same time as my mother.

"It's just one of those bugs going around, Mom."

I gave the nurse a scathing look. She winked at me. "This antibiotic will fix you up in no time. You already have an IV, so you won't feel a thing."

She pushed a full syringe of antibiotics into the IV port and then hurried out of the room with Mom close on her heels. I heard Mother ask about the cafeteria. I didn't hear the nurse's reply because they had traveled out of my range of hearing. All of a sudden, my arms felt itchy and my chest was heavy.

Amducious hovered over Melissa. "Soon you will be with my Master, my pretty," he laughed. At that moment there was a flash, and the three demons closest to him vanished in a puff of smoke as Michael severed their heads from their bodies. Amducious screeched and dived to avoid Michael's sword.

I lifted my arm to see why it felt like it was on fire. I couldn't believe my eyes. Both my arms were covered, every inch, with huge red welts the size of golf balls. I tried to scream, but whatever the things were on my arms were also growing in my mouth and my throat. No sound would come out. *I can't breathe; I can't breathe. Somebody help me,* I thought, *I can't breathe.*

"Melissa, reach for the red button," Michael coaxed. "You can do it, Melissa, reach out, there on the side of the bed."

My eyes frantically darted back and forth. *I need help; I need help. Somebody,* my mind was screaming, but I had no voice. *The button,* I thought, as my eyes darted about. *The red button, I need to push the red button.* I stretched my hand out, reached down the right side of the bed, and pressed the red button. A voice came over the speaker, "May I help you?"

Michael wrapped his wings around Melissa and gently blew breath into her throat to clear her airway. "Try to speak. You can do it, Melissa."

"Uh, uh, I...ugh, caa, uh...breee..." I heard footsteps running. *She's coming! Thank you, God; she's coming!*

The nurse took one look at me and grabbed the speakerphone. "Code Red, Code Red, Room 422. Anaphylactic Shock."

People were rushing about, screaming orders and grabbing this and grabbing that.

"Fifty cc's of Benadryl, stat," the doctor ordered. The nurse plunged another syringe into the IV port and, in twenty seconds, I could breathe again. Immediately the welts started to disappear.

"You gave us quite a start, young lady." This time there was compassion and concern in the doctor's eyes.

"I gave myself a start," I retorted.

"You certainly have a good sense of humor. The next time someone asks if you are allergic to any medications, I think it's safe to say that penicillin should be at the top of the list."

"What happened?" My mother was standing in the doorway holding a Styrofoam box, her mouth open, gaping at the multitude of healthcare personnel in my room.

"It's a long story," I said, as I smiled at the doctor. "Ask me tomorrow. Right now, I'm going to sleep."

"Pleasant dreams," Michael whispered, as he held Melissa in his wings.

I awoke with someone holding my hand. When I opened my eyes, Paul was looking down at me.

"Hey, how are you doing?" he asked.

I glared at him. "I'm alive, no thanks to you."

"What do you mean? You could have called me instead of your mother."

"I mean, I'm here because I have PID, Paul."

"What's that?" he asked.

"That is a sexually transmitted disease. Need I spell that out for you?"

"Oh, well, I can explain...," he blushed.

"I can't wait to hear this one," I said as I rolled my eyes and turned my back to him.

"Melissa, please, it happened before we were married."

I turned over to glare at him and then I turned my back again.

"I brought you some flowers." When I didn't respond, he got up and drifted to the door. "I'll be at home if you need me." Then he left.

Giving me flowers, as if that makes it all better. What a jerk!

Amducious and his cohorts had been outnumbered and outclassed by the Heavenly Host. Again, Amducious was forced to retreat in defeat. This time he wasn't going to be able to lie his way out of the guillotine. *I must be prepared with a new plan,* he thought. *Surely she has other weaknesses that can lead to her demise.*

The gatekeeper snickered as Amducious approached. "Master is in a foul mood and just recently had the guillotine prepared for you," he gloated. "Do you have a last request?" he laughed.

"You imbecile! Gatekeeper is a fitting occupation for one with a feeble mind such as yours. Announce me this instant or it will be your head in the guillotine."

Amducious attempted to gather his courage, but his wings trembled as he entered Satan's chamber. Immediately he lay prostrate in an attempt to prevent Satan from severing his head before he had a chance to speak.

"I know I have failed you, Master, but if you spare me the guillotine, I have a plan that is sure to work."

Satan was in rare form. He had taken the appearance of a ferocious beast, the likes of which no one had ever seen or imagined.

"You bumbling idiot, the entire lot of you are a disgrace, running with your tails between your legs like sniveling cowards. Why should I spare you another minute?"

"My scouts have good news, Master. The human constantly dreams of fortune, much more than most of her kind. This is a weakness that can surely lead to her demise. She longs to experience those things that are dangerous and exciting. This too will be useful when the time comes. She has tired of the spouse and also of the false religion. She will soon be ready for adventure. I have prepared for two who belong to you to cross her path. At such time, they will surely turn her from the Most High God and she will belong to you." Amducious closed his eyes and held his breath, anxiously awaiting a response.

"Very well. These two who belong to me, what sort of evil do they fancy?"

"Fornication, prostitution, and whoredom. They lust for the perversions of Sodom and Gomorrah."

"Excellent," Satan replied. "The One Who Sits at the Right Hand weeps for those who sin against their own bodies. To see her debased in this way gives me great pleasure. You may rise. Be off then, but make no mistake; you will not be spared again."

Amducious preened his wings as he strutted out to confront the gatekeeper.

"It appears you have the task of removing the guillotine. Be careful that you do not sever your own head." He then took flight without waiting for a reply.

I paced up and down in the kitchen. I had finally convinced Paul to move into a duplex my Aunt Jennie Mae had available. Jimmy and Sue Ellen had helped us install flooring and carpet, and Jimmy even blew some of that sparkling stuff into the ceiling. But even that didn't help.

I'm sick of him and I'm sick of trying to be perfect. Nobody can be this perfect. How can God even expect us to be? Doesn't He know that it's impossible? Witnesses don't do this and Witnesses don't do that. One thing is for sure; if I don't burn in hell, then I'm still toast either way. If I'm going to burn in hell, then I may as well enjoy the party while I'm alive. I jumped in my car and sped down to the 7-Eleven.

"Give me a pack of Virginia Slims Menthol, please." After I got home, I held the cigarettes in my hand for a while and then I lit one. As I put down the lighter, the doorbell rang. I took a drag from the cigarette and opened the door. To my horror, three of my Witness sisters stood there gaping at me.

"Melissa, is that a cigarette?" I looked down at my hand, as if I held a snake.

"Uh, yeah, I sort of needed one."

Janis, who was one of the more prominent members of the Kingdom Hall, looked at me with disappointment.

"You realize that you can be dis-fellowshipped for such an offense."

"Uh, what exactly does that mean?

"Kicked out," one of the younger women blurted. Janis poked her in the ribs.

"It means that if you do not repent and ask for forgiveness and vow never to do it again, you can be asked to leave the Kingdom Hall."

"Oh, well, in that case, I guess you had better ask me to leave now." I closed the door. "Good riddance!" I went to the kitchen drawer and got out a piece of stationery and began writing.

Dear Paul,

I'm sorry, but this is not working out. You're a nice guy and everything, but I have things that I want to do and places that I want to go. I'm taking the car and my clothes. You can have the motorcycle and the furniture. If you want, you can keep the duplex. I'm sure Auntie won't mind, as long as you pay on time. Good luck to you and don't try and find me because I'm not coming back.

Sorry, Melissa

Thank goodness I never changed my last name, I thought.

Chapter Three

Dillon's Deal

I picked up the phone and dialed the number from memory. Pamela was a true friend and also my sister-in-law. Even though she and my brother Michael were divorced, she would always be my sister-in-law. "Hey, Pamela, what's happening?"

"Oh, nothing much. What's happening with the newlyweds?"

"The newlyweds are about to be newly divorced."

"After six months and the most beautiful dress on earth, you're kidding?" she whined.

"Nope, I'm not kidding. You did make me the most beautiful dress in the world, if it's any consolation."

"No, it's not," she retorted. "Do you know how much work I put into that dress?"

"I know! That's one of the reasons I didn't get divorced six days after the wedding!"

She giggled. "You're a mess, girl!"

"I know that too. Can I come and hang out on your couch?"

"Sure, come on over."

I grabbed my clothes and threw them in the trunk of the car and smiled. *I hope hell isn't as hot as they say.*

I arrived at Pamela's later that evening. In addition to Pamela, there were also her sister Rachel, Michael Junior, little Melissa, and Rachel's son Alex. Even a house full of kids was better than my mom's endless rules and regulations.

"So, what's the plan?" Pamela asked.

"Tomorrow I'm going to apply at American Airlines. They're

hiring stewardesses. Don't you think that sounds exciting and adven-
turous?"

"Sounds like trouble to me," Pamela retorted.

"You know, Pam, you can be ever so ultra boring!"

"Ultra boring and ultra safe and sound; something you won't
understand until you're forty."

"Probably not even then," Rachel said.

I just laughed. "You two are such old fuddy-duddies."

**Amducious flitted around Candy's head. "You need to find
a new toy for Dillon," he coaxed. His cohorts chimed in.**

"A new toy, new toy," they chanted.

"A new girl will mean less work for you and more money."

"More money, more money," they chimed.

*Hmmm, there are bound to be some pretty girls there tomorrow. Girls
with dreams of becoming stewardesses. How stupid they are with their
dreams of working as waitresses on airplanes. But it is a brilliant way to
meet johns. I wonder how long it will take me to get bumped up to first
class once I'm hired. Then I will have access to the rich ones with money
to spend. Dillon is so smart about such things. I should have thought of
it long ago. While I'm there, I'll see if I can bring him a new toy. The
more girls I find to work for him, the less work I will have to do myself.
More girls mean more money,* thought Candy as she drifted to sleep.

"What do you mean I'm too short?" I cried. "What does that have
to do with being a stewardess?"

"Height and weight have everything to do with appearance," the
lady replied in a smug tone. "I'm sorry; you do not meet the requirements."

"Well, of all the stupid requirements," I said as I stomped down
the hall.

"What requirements?" asked the girl who seemed to come out of
nowhere.

"They require that you are at least 5-foot-3," I replied.

"Oh, no, I'm only 5-foot-2."

"Well, join the club. I'm 5'2" and a half and that wasn't good
enough for them."

"You mean they really won't let you apply if you're not tall
enough?"

"No, they really won't."

"But I was depending on this job."

"So was I and now I don't know what I'm going to do next."

"I've got an idea! Delta!"

"Delta Airlines? Aren't they in Atlanta?"

"Yeah, but so what? It's only a twelve-hour drive. With two people, it's only six hours each."

"You mean us, as in we, drive to Atlanta?"

"Yeah, we drive to Atlanta and apply at Delta."

"Hmmm, I do so despise Dallas. When do you want to go?"

"Soon. My name's Candy, by the way, and here's my number. You give me yours and we'll plan it for the next week or so. Deal?"

"Deal,"

After I got back to Pamela's, I described my depressing day to her and Rachel, and I could tell what they wanted to say. Wake up and get a real job in the real world, but neither of them had the heart to say it. I moped around for the next few days and then Candy called.

"Want to take a trip?" She sounded really excited.

"To Atlanta?" I asked.

"No, to Montreal."

That sounds exciting. Isn't that another country? But because I didn't want to sound stupid, I agreed to go without question.

"Me and my boyfriend of the month will pick you up tonight. He has some business there and he said you could come along if you like."

"Boyfriend of the month? Is that like flavor of the week?"

"Sort of. If he annoys me, then I get a new flavor."

I giggled. I liked this girl.

Candy and Dillon picked me up around nine.

"Change of plans," Candy said as I jumped in the back seat.

"The deal in Montreal fell through. I need to see someone in Monroe. Are you game? By the way, I'm Dillon." He extended his hand.

"Sure, I'm game. Where is Monroe?"

"Louisiana," he replied.

"Okay, but wait just a minute. I'll be right back." I jumped out without waiting for a reply.

I returned a short time later and Candy said, "What was that about?"

"I needed to let Pamela know where I'd be in case my brother asked. I wrote down your name and number for her. My brother is a little paranoid; you know the type."

"Yeah, the kind that can be a drag."

"Yeah, that kind."

"Let's roll," said Dillon.

I awoke as the car finally stopped. "Where are we?" I asked groggily.

"We're in Louisiana."

"Already?"

"Yeah, Dillon went in to get a room."

"You mean two rooms."

"Yeah, sure, two rooms."

Amducious flitted around the car. "It's time to turn her!" "Turn her, turn her," the other demons sang.

Dillon returned with a look of disgust on his face. "There's a convention in town and I could only get one room. I couldn't even convince him with a C-note."

"C-note?" I asked.

"Hundred dollars," Candy said with a condescending smile.

"You were going to pay an extra hundred dollars for two rooms?" I said in disbelief.

"Sure, no big deal. Anything for you, doll," Dillon replied.

"One room is okay. Does it have two beds?"

"Sorry." He shrugged his shoulders.

"Well, it's no big deal. I can sleep on the floor and you love birds can have the bed. Let's roll. I'm really tired." I jumped out of the car.

Dillon gave Candy a look that I could not interpret and he too got out. "First dibs on the bathroom," I called as I ran for it.

When I came out, they were rolling around on the bed in an intimate embrace.

"Oh, for heaven's sake, cut it out you two."

They laughed and Candy ran for the bath.

"So, Melissa, are you from Dallas?" Dillon asked.

"No, actually I'm an Air Force brat."

"So, you like lived in a lot of places?"

"Yeah, I was born in France."

"Wow, a French girl; I like it."

"You better not like it too much, or Candy will beat you on and about the head," I laughed.

He laughed too. "Candy's cool."

Before I could contemplate that, Candy reappeared. "Okay, your turn, Dillon."

"Excuse me, ladies, while I make myself more beautiful."

After he closed the bathroom door, Candy whispered, "Isn't he just yummy?"

"He is scrumptious," I giggled.

Amducious and his demonic clan flitted around the room. "Turn her, turn her," they chanted.

I grabbed a pillow and a blanket and made my way to the floor. "I'm pooped. I bid you farewell and goodnight."

Candy giggled again. "What are you now, a poet?"

"I have my moments," I replied and drifted to sleep. I awoke with a start, as I felt someone's hand rubbing my thigh. At first I thought I was dreaming, and then I realized it was Dillon.

"What the hell are you doing?" I screeched and jumped up from the floor. I expected Candy to chime in, but she remained silent.

"Relax," Dillon said. "Candy's cool."

"What do you mean she's cool? Candy, what the hell is this shit?"

They looked at each other, silently speaking in some sort of code I did not understand.

"Dillon has a crush on you. I told him you weren't into that freaky shit, but I guess he had to see for himself," Candy said.

"And you are into that freaky shit?"

"No, but I am into Dillon, so you know...." Her voice trailed off as she shrugged her shoulders.

"No, I don't know and you," I pointed at Dillon, "get away from me now!"

"Come on, Melissa," he reached out and tried to pull my top up.

I slapped his hand and grabbed my purse and coat. "Listen up, freakazoid, if you touch me again, I'm walking out that door and going to the desk to call my brother."

"Oh, I'm so scared," Dillon sneered. "The little girl is going to call her big brother to beat me up."

"No, I'm going to call my big brother to lock your ass up. He's TBI and he would lock up his own mother for spitting on the sidewalk, not to mention a creep messing around with his baby sister."

"TBI? What the hell is that?"

"Texas Bureau of Investigation, dumb ass," I retorted.

Dillon looked at me and then at Candy in disbelief. "TBI? Your brother is TBI?"

"Yeah, that's what I said. Do you need a hearing aid?"

"I didn't know her brother was TBI, I swear!" Candy said, a little tremor in her voice.

"It's cool, Melissa. I don't want no trouble with Five-O. You just chill and I ain't gonna bother you, okay?"

"Okay, but I want to go home right now!"

After dropping Melissa off, Dillon turned and slapped Candy across the face. "You stupid bitch," he yelled. "TBI is almost as bad as FBI. Do you realize what kind of trouble you almost got me into?"

"How was I supposed to know," she whimpered. "I can fix it; I promise. Tomorrow I'll call and apologize to her and make her think that I'm mad at you. Better yet, I'll tell her I dumped you. Then we'll go to Atlanta and I'll hook up with you there. Once we get there, we'll stay with that doctor. You know, the one who has the hots for me. It will be a sweet deal. He always lays a bunch of cash on me. I guarantee, when she finds herself stuck in Atlanta with no money, she'll come around."

"She better." He glared at her and slammed the accelerator.

Amducious drew his sword and cut off the soldier's head. "You fools, idiots," he ranted. "You had a perfect opportunity to turn her and you failed."

The demon on his left trembled. "Please, Master, spare us. We will follow them on their next journey and she will surely be ours." Amducious roared and took flight. The other demons watched until he was out of sight.

"Spare us, spare us," they mocked.

"You would not be so quick to mock me had it been your head," the demon replied. "Poor Pan, he lost his head and he was not to blame. Oh, how I wish we had not been summoned to entice this human Melissa," the demon lamented.

The next afternoon Candy called.

"Melissa, I'm so sorry about Dillon. He's such a creep. I don't know what I ever saw in him. I threw him out last night and I'm not going to see him anymore. Still friends?"

"Sure, it's not your fault he's such a jerk."

"Are you ready to hit the road?"

"You mean to Atlanta?"

"Yep, Delta here we come."

The demon named Kali flitted about as the girls drove down I-20. "Sodom and Gomorrah, turn her, turn her. You must have a plan or Dillon will surely be angry," he whispered to Candy.

"Turn her, turn her," the other demons chanted.

"I am so glad to be out of Dallas, Texas. I hate that place with a passion. Do you know where we are?

"Yeah, we just got on I-285. I think Doc's exit is coming up, but I can't remember the name of it. Let's stop at that filling station and call him."

"Cool, a doctor no less. Why would you even think of taking Dillon over him? Never mind, I don't want to know."

Candy giggled and jumped out to call Doc. "Okay, we need to take the Greenbriar exit," she said when she returned.

"Uh, what is Doc's name?"

"His name is Tim."

"Is he as cute as Dillon?"

"Not even," she replied.

"I guess that answers my previous question."

"Okay, the name of the apartments is Crooked Branch," Candy said as she read the signs.

"What kind of stupid name is that?"

"I'm not exactly in charge of what to name things in Atlanta, Missy."

"You're such a wise ass."

"So, what did your brother say about you coming to Atlanta?"

"He said that I'm going to wind up with my butt in the pokey hanging out with people I don't know. That means you, by the way."

"Yeah, I kinda got the impression that he was not too fond of me."

"For heaven's sake, he's not fond of anyone. He sees crooks in his sleep, has a gun under his pillow, and drinks orange juice at a bar."

"Well, here we are."

"He does know you're bringing a friend, right?"

"Yeah, he knows."

"And none of that freaky stuff, like with Dillon?"

"Doc freaky? Not a chance."

"Great, let's go." We knocked on the door. Doc answered with a huge smile.

"Hey, Doc, how have you been?"

"Candy, can you please not call me Doc."

"Sure, Doc." She kissed him on the mouth, long and hard.

"Well, with a kiss like that, I guess you can call me whatever you want," he grinned. "So, you must be Melissa," he said and shook my hand.

"Pleasure to meet you; I appreciate you putting me up."

"Not a problem; any friend of Candy's is a friend of mine," he said with a warm smile.

Chapter Four

Derek's Dames

Amducious flitted around the apartment of Doc's neighbor Derek Davis. Derek stood in front of his mirror, admiring his own reflection. "You look good," Amducious chanted. "Really, really good. You should go to meet that female who resides at your neighbor's abode. She is not his mate, and you could fornicate with her. She is quite the naïve one; she will be unable to resist you. You look good."

I look so good that I can't stand it, Derek laughed to himself. *I think it's time I introduced myself to that little chicky next door. She is so fine, even though she walks around all the time with no shoes on. How country can you get? I look good,* he thought again.

We've only been here three weeks and they are arguing already. Why can't Candy stay in instead of going out every night? What a nice man Doc is and she only takes advantage of him. If I had a guy like that, I wouldn't mess it up like she's doing. She's gonna get us both kicked out. I think the next time she stays out all night, he really will do it. I wonder who that can be, I thought as the doorbell chimed.

"Who is it?" I called

"It's Derek from next door."

My heart immediately skipped a beat. *Oh, my gosh! It's that really cute guy who looks just like Superfly.*

"Just a minute." I ran and put on lipstick, ran a comb through my hair, and then opened the door. "Hi," I said in the sexiest voice I had.

"Hello, I'm a friend of Doc's." He took my hand and kissed it.

"When I saw you the other day, I just had to know if you were Doc's girlfriend. I was really happy when he told me you weren't. Are you anybody's girlfriend?" he asked, with the most gorgeous smile.

"No, actually I'm new here and quite unattached."

"A beautiful girl like you unattached? Obviously by choice."

"Obviously," I replied. "I swear you look just like Superfly."

"I know. I get a lot of that."

"It's a compliment, you know. Ron O'Neal is a gorgeous actor."

"Yeah, thanks." He said it with such modesty that I had to admire the fact that he wasn't conceited about his looks. And that hair! It was prettier than mine.

Amducious began his instigations. "Invite her to your abode. She will be putty in your hands. She desires you. You can have her along with the other two. She will make a good addition to your harem. The other two are getting older. This one is young and ripe for the picking. You can have any girl you want."

"Hey, you want to come next door for a glass of wine?"

"Sure." We walked over to his place and, after he poured the wine, I decided I had forgotten to ask an important question. "We have established that I'm unattached, but what about you?"

"I have friends, but no one special."

"By choice, I'm sure," I laughed, and so did he. *What a laugh! Everything about him is sexy.*

The demons Amducious, Kali, and Uphir danced about the room. "You lust, you want, you need each other. Touch her, touch her, touch her. You lust, you lust, you lust," they cried.

I spent the night with Derek. Later that evening, when I lit a cigarette, he lit a joint. He passed it to me, but I shook my head. "You smoke cigarettes, but not pot?" he asked.

"It makes me paranoid, but I do smoke it sometimes," I lied.

"You know, those things will kill you."

"Yeah, and pot won't?" I retorted.

"Pot is an herb and can be quite therapeutic."

"Yeah, right; remind me to ask Doc about that."

"It's true," he said as he rubbed my back.

The next day all hell was breaking loose when I went back across the hall.

"What is going on with you guys?" I asked as I closed the door.

"I want you guys out," Doc replied.

"What? What do you mean out? We don't have anywhere else to go."

"Sorry, Melissa, I know it's not your fault, but I'm not putting up with anymore of Candy's shit. Staying out all night whoring around and I'm just supposed to ignore it? I don't think so."

"Candy, say something," I said under my breath.

"Say something like what?"

"Where are we supposed to go?"

"Dillon is picking me up in a few minutes; you're welcome to come with us."

I just stood there in shock. "Dillon! Did she say Dillon?"

"That's exactly what she said," Doc replied.

"Candy, do you mean to tell me that you've been seeing Dillon all along?"

"Melissa, she's a hooker and Dillon is her pimp," Doc sighed.

I just stood there with my mouth gaping open.

"Don't feel bad; she suckered me too."

"Melissa, grow up. Are you coming or not?"

"I wouldn't go anywhere with Dillon, even if there was a nuclear explosion and he owned the only cave on the planet."

"Come on, Melissa, let's go."

"No way, Candy. You can go with that creep if you want, but I'm not."

"Well, what are you going to do?"

"That's a good question, Melissa. I'm not your father and you don't have a job. I can't continue supporting you. You need to call your family and go back home," Doc said solemnly.

"You hate Texas. At least with Dillon and me, you can stay here in Atlanta. I promise he won't bother you."

"Fat chance. You go ahead, Candy; I'm going home."

Candy looked at me with disdain. "You're such a goody-two-shoes. Go on and run back home to your mama." She then stormed out and slammed the door.

I tried calling my brother, but he wasn't home yet. "I'll be out by the end of the week, Doc."

"No problem. The end of the week is fine and again I'm sorry,

Melissa. I know you like it here."

"Yeah, I do. I think I'll go and tell Derek that I'm leaving. I'll be back a little later. My brother gets in about six. I'll call him and he'll wire me some money by tomorrow."

"Okay, tell Derek I said hello."

I knocked on Derek's door. When he opened it, I guess he could read the disappointment in my face. "Melissa, what's wrong?"

I burst into tears. "Candy and Doc broke up. She's a hooker and she left with a pimp! I'm being kicked out and tomorrow I'm going home to Texas," I sobbed.

"Whoa! Slow down, baby. You aren't going anywhere."

"Doc's kicking me out; I have nowhere else to go but home."

"You can move in with me."

I blinked. "What did you say?"

"You can move in with me," he repeated.

"I can? Just like that?"

"Yep, just like that."

"But, but..."

"No buts; go get your stuff."

"You're serious?"

"As a heart attack," he replied.

"You're sure. You barely know me."

"I know you well enough to know that I'm not letting you leave after what happened last night."

"You are so wonderful," I exclaimed and ran to get my stuff.

Amducious roared with glee. *I did it; she traded Dillon for a wolf in sheep's clothing. Little does she know what lies ahead for her. The other female is unstable. When she returns from her journey, I will entice her into killing Melissa. I will be crowned a general and many will bow to me.*

When I returned, he was tidying up the apartment.

"Let me help you with that," I said. I was walking on clouds. *I'm living in Atlanta with the dreamiest hunk of man I have ever laid eyes on.*

"Can you cook?" he asked.

"Of course, what self-respecting woman doesn't know how to cook?"

"Well, you'd be surprised. By the way, you need to know about Jackie."

"Who's Jackie?" I asked cautiously.

"Just another chick that lives here too."

My mouth must have been hanging open because he quickly ran over to me.

"It's not like that. She's just a friend who needed a place to crash."

"Like me?"

"No, nothing like you, Melissa. I swear she's just a friend, baby. Don't go all nutty on me, okay?"

"Okay, you're sure?"

"Yes, I'm sure."

The Archangel Michael's wings fluttered ever so gently. "He's lying, Melissa, go home. Call your male sibling."

Something in the back of my mind kept telling me this was a lie and I should call my brother Michael, but I didn't want to come down from the cloud.

I awoke to screaming. *Who the hell is that woman screaming,* I thought groggily. Derek lived in a loft, so I got up and walked to the railing and looked from the bedroom down into the living room. There was this woman in a Delta Airlines uniform ranting and raving at Derek.

"I want her out of here now!" she yelled.

"She's not going anywhere," he replied calmly.

"I live here and no bitch is coming in here taking over," she screeched.

I watched as the realization hit me. *He's sleeping with her too. I can't believe it. He lied to me.* I walked down the stairs. "You know what? You can stop arguing because I'm leaving and going home to Texas today anyway. He's all yours, Miss...whoever you are."

"Jackie, my name is Jackie and you had better be gone by today," she hissed.

"You, shut the hell up now!" He stuck his finger in her face. "She is not going anywhere. You can get the hell out of my house right now!"

"What? You're kidding, right?"

"Do I look like I'm kidding? Your bags are already packed. I'll just call you a cab and you can go back the way you came."

"But, but you, but I..."

"But what? You want somebody gone? Well, that somebody is you."

I just stood there in disbelief and so did she.

"I'm sorry," she whispered.

"What did you say?" he asked.

"I'm sorry. It's just that...I was surprised, that's all."

I still couldn't believe my ears. *First Candy and Dillon and now Derek and Jackie. Where do I find these freaky people? They want to use me for a sex toy. Well, two can play this game, or should I say three. This is my chance to stay in Atlanta and I'm taking it no matter what.*

At the Throne of the Most High God, Jesus spoke. "Be still during this time. This path is of her own choosing. This will be a painful lesson for her; however, she is led by the desires of the world and with those desires there can never be fulfillment. Make no mistake; Satan has planned her demise. Be on your guard, for you will be required to protect her physical body from harm."

"Praise be to the Father, the Son, and the Holy Spirit, Amen," replied Michael and he took flight.

"So, I guess that means we're stuck with each other. Not to worry. Derek has a guestroom. I'll pretend to be a guest when you're here. Judging from your uniform, that is not very often."

She glared at me and then at Derek. "I don't want her walking around here in that," she replied, pointing to the towel I had grabbed when the shouting started.

"Get a grip! As big as that thing is, it covers more than you see at the beach." He then politely turned and left the room.

"So, how long have you worked for Delta?" I asked. She glared at me again. "We may as well be cordial and make the best of this. You don't want me here and I don't want you here, but Derek seems to want his cake and eat it too. There is no point in being at each other's throats about it. Believe me; I will not be here very long."

"Fifteen years. I've been flying for fifteen years."

"Is it as cool as they say? I guess if it wasn't, you wouldn't have stayed with it fifteen years."

"It has its moments, but don't believe everything you hear. It's a lot of work."

"My friend and I have applied at American and Delta, but we don't meet the height requirement. Being tall seems to have its advantages."

She grunted. I could tell that she was merely going through the motions and she would have preferred to scratch my eyes out instead of having a cordial conversation, but that was cool.

Amducious could not believe his good fortune. In addition to the obvious trouble that was brewing between the two females, there was much more trouble to come. The male human also had another female with whom he cohabited, and he also indulged in pharmaceuticals. "So many sins and so little time," he laughed. The human Melissa was in for the time of her life. Too bad her young life would be a brief one. He roared again with laughter and glee. "Come to me, my pretty," he whispered. He flitted around Derek's head. "Give her the pharmaceuticals; addiction runs in her bloodline. She cannot resist them."

After three weeks of dealing with Jackie, the situation was growing tiring. Jackie was on a trip and Derek and I were playing the happy couple while she was away.

"I've got some coke. Want to try it?"

"You mean cocaine?"

"I certainly don't mean Coca-Cola."

"Sure, I'll try it."

He took out a one-dollar bill and rolled it into a tube. He then poured the white powder on top of a small hand mirror and took a razor blade and separated the white powder into lines. He used the tube to snort it. When it was my turn, I followed suit. In a matter of seconds, I was on cloud nine.

"Now that's what I call a buzz."

"Yeah, this stuff is top of the line."

"How much does a little bag like that cost?" I inquired.

"A gram is about a hundred dollars."

"A hundred dollars! You have got to be kidding me?"

"Nope! I told you this is top of the line stuff."

"How can you afford to pay for something like that?"

"I have my ways." At that moment, the doorbell rang. "Well, here comes one of my ways right now." He grabbed his pants and pulled them on while making his way to the door. I took in a couple of more lines and threw on a pair of shorts and a tube top. I slowly made my way down the stairs. There was a handsomely dressed man talking to Derek. He had an air of authority, his clothes tailored and quite expensive.

"Hi, I'm Melissa."

"Ah, so you're what all the fuss is about."

"Fuss?"

"Yeah, the young addition to the group."

"Group? Group of what?"

Derek gave him a look that I could not interpret.

"Never mind. I'm Jim and it's a pleasure to finally meet you." Again I was puzzled by his references to me.

"So, Jim, what exactly do you do?" Again, there was that look.

"I'm a broker of sorts."

"Hmmm, broker...that sounds exciting."

"Never a dull moment," he quipped.

Derek went to the kitchen and returned with what appeared to be a set of scales.

"What do you have for me today?" he asked, as he set the scales on the dining room table. Jim gave him another strange look.

"She's cool."

Jim opened his duffle bag and pulled out several very large bags of marijuana. Derek put them on the scales and they negotiated a price. Afterward Jim left and Derek brought out a stack of small baggies and weighed a small amount of pot for each bag.

So he sells marijuana! It just gets wilder and wilder by the minute around here. My brother would have a heart attack about this. At that moment the bell rang again. *What next?* I opened the door and there was a woman standing there holding several plates covered with foil. Whatever was on the plates smelled wonderful.

"Hi, I'm Jessica, I brought you guys some food." She walked past me and put the plates on the table and, to my horror, kissed Derek on the mouth.

"Hey," Derek mumbled as he avoided my eyes. "Jessie lives down the hill. She's the apartment manager here," he said, as if that explained why she kissed him on the mouth.

She went to the kitchen and proceeded to fetch silverware. By that time, I had closed my mouth and the front door and had taken a seat, even though I didn't remember doing it. *You have got to be kidding me! I traded that creep Dillon for the creep of the universe. So this is where he spends his nights when he doesn't come home.*

"Melissa, how do you like Atlanta so far?" Jessie asked.

I actually had to laugh at that. "It's more than I could have possibly dreamed of."

Derek still refused to look at me. He cleaned up his mess of pot and bags and scales so we could eat.

"Well, it's a great place to live. If you want, I can see if my company has any job openings for leasing agents?"

"That would be great," I responded without much enthusiasm.

"Jessie's a wonderful cook, don't you think?"

"Yes, quite wonderful," I said dryly as I chewed.

Jessie cleaned up the table and kissed Derek. Then she left us alone, like a dutiful sex slave and servant. *Well, I guess I now have a good definition of what the word 'group' entails.*

"What the hell do you have here, some kind of harem?" I asked in disbelief.

"It's not like that, Melissa. Grow up! This is the big city."

"I know you think people in Texas spend their days shoveling cow shit, but contrary to popular belief, we are not stupid shit kickers!" I yelled.

"Hey, that was your description, not mine. And you know what? I've got work to do and I don't have time for this shit right now." He walked out and slammed the door.

Good riddance, I thought. *What in the world have I gotten myself into? Reality check, girl, this is not worth it. What the hell is wrong with these crazy women? He's using them, treats them like shit, and they just keep coming back for more. They both have good jobs. Jessie has her own place and Jackie could have her own, too, if she wanted one. I get it! They put up with him because he's drop dead gorgeous. Sorry, pretty boy, you just found yourself a pretty girl and I'm not taking this shit much longer.*

Around midnight, I heard Derek put his key in the door. For some reason, he was having difficulty opening it. *I bet he's drunk. If he thinks I'm coming down to help him, he's got another thought coming.* Somehow he managed to open the door and it sounded as if he fell into the living room.

"Melissa," he groaned. "Melissa, please help me." Something about his voice sounded strange but not drunk. I jumped up and ran down the stairs.

"Oh, my God! Derek, you're bleeding!"

"I've been shot, Melissa."

"What? Like with a gun?"

"Melissa, this is no time to be stupid."

"Okay, okay, I should drive you to the hospital."

"No!"

"Why not? Are you crazy? You've been shot and you're bleeding like crazy!"

"I said no. Go and get Doc and hurry."

"Okay, okay." I ran across the hall and pounded on Doc's door.

"All right, all right, I'm coming," he shouted. "This better be good, waking me up in the middle of the damn night," he complained as he opened the door. "Melissa, what the hell is going on? Do you know what time it is?"

"Derek's been shot," I whispered.

"What? Like with a gun?"

"That's what I said and he told me not to be stupid."

"Yeah, okay, let me get my bag."

Doc came over and tended to Derek.

"Man, you need a hospital."

"No! Doc, you know as well as I do that they report gunshot wounds to the police."

"Yeah, but you could get an infection or have any number of complications that I cannot address in your living room."

"If that happens, then I promise I'll go to the hospital. Please, just patch me up."

"The good news is it's a through and through. The bad news is it's going to hurt like hell. Here take these." He poured a couple of pills into Derek's hand and I got him a glass of water. "This is Percodan; you'll be in la la land in no time. Then I'll fix you right up." After he patched up the wound, Doc helped me get Derek up to the bedroom and then he left.

Derek was sound asleep in five minutes. I watched him lying there. *Women coming out of the woodwork, cocaine snorting, pot dealing, and shots at the OK Corral. I have got to get out of this zoo. But he is so gorgeous. What are you stupid?* I slapped myself in the face. *Wake up, girl! You're Alice and Wonderland is not cool.*

Because Jackie spent most of her time out of town and Jessie was working, I had been elected to take care of Derek. It seemed as if I had been waiting on him hand and foot for an eternity.

Derek was well enough to start doing business again and had just come in and pulled out his scales to weigh his pot. After bagging it, he went out to sell his wares. He hadn't learned anything from being shot. *I think it's time I took Jessie up on that job offer.*

"It's time," Amducious said as he prepared his troops. "The unstable female is primed and ready to strike. We must be prepared to push her over the edge. You have your assignments."

"Yes, Master," they replied.

Kali and Uphir and the others flocked around Jackie's head. "You hate her, you hate her, you hate her," they chanted. "Hurt her, hurt her, hurt her," they chanted. "Look at her; she thinks that she is so pretty. He likes her more than you. Look at her; she does not need to paint her face because she is young. Look at her body; yours is no longer appealing to him. You hate her, you hate her, you hate her. Hurt her, hurt her, hurt her," they chanted.

Jackie was home for two days. Man, I hated it when she was home. It was like being locked up with a demon. I hated being in the house with her when Derek wasn't around. But going home to Texas was not an option I wanted to explore.

I went to the kitchen to get a drink. "Hey, Jackie, would you pass me a glass?" I asked politely. Her back was to me. She reached for something, but instead of a glass, when she turned, she had a butcher knife.

"Cut her, cut her, cut her," the demons chanted. All of a sudden, there was a whoosh and Michael appeared, severing Uphir's head from his body, which vanished in a puff of smoke.

"You think you're so cute, don't you?" Jackie said. Her eyes were glassy. "You bitch! You think you can come in here and take what's mine! I'm going to carve you up like a Christmas turkey."

Oh, my God! This chick has lost it and she's going to kill me. "Whoa, Jackie! You can't own someone, especially someone like Derek. He didn't belong to you even before I got here. You've been sharing him with Jessie and heaven only knows who else he has on the side. So you kill me and end up in jail over what? Someone who treats you like shit? What sense does that make?"

"Cut her, cut her, cut her," Kali cried.

"Jessie doesn't live here with us and she doesn't count because he just uses her to cook for him. The sex isn't even good for him. He told me he doesn't even like her. But you, he told me to get out because of you!" She reached out and slashed me across the bridge of my nose. Blood gushed from my face and I screamed.

Michael pivoted in midair and struck Kali and the three others. With one strike, they all vanished.

"Put down the knife, Jackie," Michael coaxed. "You do not want to hurt anyone. What would your Grandma Jennie think of you, if you kill her? Put it down, Jackie."

Amducious had been smart enough to maintain his distance this time and ordered six others to take the place of their fallen comrades. It was suicidal, but they charged Michael as they were instructed.

"Cut her, cut her," they shouted as they charged.

"No, Jackie, do not!" Michael yelled, as he severed the heads of the first two.

"Cut her, cut her."

Whoosh! Michael swung his powerful sword and the remaining four vanished. He touched the knife with his wing and nudged it toward the counter. "Put it down, Jackie. Put it down. That is the way. Put it down. Go now and sit there.

"You cut me!" I screeched. "You crazy nutcase, you cut me!" I held my hands over the cut, as blood spurted out. And then the strangest thing happened. She put the knife on the counter and walked over to the sofa and sat down. *She has truly lost it. Look at her. She needs to be locked up in a loony bin. Look at her eyes. She's just sitting there, staring straight ahead, looking at nothing.*

"Melissa, run. Now!" Michael said. "Go to Jessie's; she will not hurt you."

I ran for the door, turning back one last time. She was still sitting there, staring. I slammed the door and ran down the steps. At the bottom, I realized I had nowhere to go. *Jessie's,* I thought. *She's in love with Derek, but she's also a class act.* I walked down the hill, holding my face. When I got to Jessie's, I used my foot to knock on the door. Jessie opened the door; her smile vanished.

"Melissa! Oh, my God! What happened?" She led me to the sofa and ran and got towels and a bowl of water. Then she started dabbing at my face.

"She cut me. That loony-tune woman actually cut me with a butcher knife."

"Jackie? Jackie cut you? You're kidding!"

"Not to be a smart-ass, Jessie, but do I look like I'm kidding."

She smiled. "At least you still have a sense of humor and the cut is not so bad. You were really lucky; it's only a nick. I don't think you need stitches. Let me get a bandage for it. Hold this towel on it while I go upstairs." She returned and bandaged my face.

"Jessie, you should have seen her. She was like something out of a zombie movie. She got all glassy eyed, cut me, and then just as calmly put the knife on the counter like she had cut a tomato. Then she went and sat down on the sofa like she was a normal person. I mean, it was Twilight Zone weird."

"I've always thought that Jackie was a bit unstable," Jessie replied. "You really need to be careful, Melissa. I'm not kidding."

"Yeah, I know. I think it's time I concede and go home. Living with a crazy woman is not exactly what I had in mind when I came here."

About an hour later, Derek showed up at Jessie's. His eyes got big when he saw the bandage and he was furious.

"She actually cut you? I can't believe she cut you. The bitch is really crazy. I'm gonna knock her ass into next week."

I just rolled my eyes. "I've decided to go home, Derek. This is not working for me"

"Come on, Melissa, you can't really mean that?"

"You're kidding, right?" I said as I rolled my eyes again. "You have two, not one but two, other girlfriends. No offense, Jessie. One of which tried to kill me! You sell marijuana for a living and you snort cocaine. You frequently get shot at and you think that I don't really mean it?" I yelled. "You have been smoking too much of that wacky weed of yours. Yes, Derek, I really mean it. I'm going home. Now if you can control Jackie, I'm going to pack and get some sleep. I have a twelve-hour drive tomorrow. Jessie, it's actually been a pleasure meeting you, considering the bizarre and extreme circumstances."

She just smiled that smile of hers. "The pleasure was all mine. Be careful on the way home."

"I will and thanks for the bandage."

The next morning, I got up and decided I would go to the gas station, fill up the car and come back, seeing as I had been too tired to pack the night before. I snuck out of the house, so as not to wake Derek and that witch. When I got outside, I just stood there. The loft was at the top of the hill with parking all along the hill, but to get up or down the hill, you had to wait for approaching cars to pass, just as one was doing now. After it passed, I looked at the spot where I had parked my car. I blinked and I looked again. *It's gone. I don't believe this shit. You have got to be kidding me! Someone stole my car!* I ran back inside.

"Derek!"

"What are you yelling about?" he asked, as he looked over the banister. His hair was tousled and he was rubbing the sleep from his eyes.

"What is it?" I heard Jackie say from his bed.

"When you came in last night, did you see my car?"

"Melissa, what are you talking about? Of course, I saw your car; it's parked on the hill."

"It is not on the hill," I wailed.

He ran down the stairs and out the door with Jackie and me in tow. We all stood there looking at the empty spot. "It's gone," he said.

"No shit, Sherlock," I retorted.

"Don't be a smart-ass, Melissa."

I turned and walked into the house and sat down. "How the hell am I supposed to get home?" I said out loud.

"Well, I guess you'll be my guest for a little while longer," Derek snickered.

You! You arranged for someone to steal my car, I thought. *That sneaky bastard. He really thinks I'm too stupid to think that he did it.*

Later that evening, Jackie had to fly out, so I walked down the hill to give Jessie the news about my car.

"Someone was actually brave enough to drive that car down the hill, knowing that if another car was coming up and you happened to walk out, they would have had no escape?" Jessie asked.

"Yeah, that's exactly right. Who would have that much nerve?"

Neither of us said anything, even though we knew the answer.

"So, how about that leasing agent job I told you about? I have an application right here, if you want to fill it out."

"Cool, but if I don't have a job soon, I'm going to ask my brother to come and get me."

I actually got an interview and was waiting to hear back from the leasing company that Friday. That Thursday, Jackie had come home while Derek was out. I was furious. *I know he knows her schedule and I told him not to leave me in the house with her.* I went to my room and closed and locked the door. *The crazy witch won't be carving on my face today,* I thought. *Was that the doorbell?* I heard Jackie open the door. *Did I hear that right? Did I just hear someone say 'FBI'?* I opened the door a crack and there were two men standing in the living room.

"Excuse me, miss, can you step in here, please? I'm Agent Samuels and this is Agent Scott. We're with the FBI."

I was so scared that I just stood there with my mouth gaping open.

"Miss," he said again with authority this time. "Can you please step in here?"

I walked into the living room without a word.

"We're looking for a female named Maria Spalding." He flipped open a book and read from it. "She is described as 5'4," a hundred and twenty pounds, with shoulder length brown hair."

They all looked at me because that was my general description.

"She's wanted for forgery, larceny, fraud, and money laundering. Ms. Blaylock, you were seen with her shopping at a Davidson's store on January 10. You, miss, fit Ms. Spalding's description, even though Ms. Blaylock says your name is Melissa. Do you have ID, miss?"

I was still too terrified to speak and just stood there with my mouth open.

"Miss, do you have ID?"

"Yes, it's in my room."

"Agent Scott, will you accompany this young lady to retrieve her ID?" Agent Scott nodded toward the room and walked behind me.

"Please point to the location, miss, and do not pick up the bag."

I pointed to my purse and he picked it up.

"Let's go back to the living room."

He opened my purse and pulled out my license. "Melissa Bowan from Dallas, Texas. Born June 19, 1956," he announced with disappointment.

Now that I did not fear federal prison, I began to recover my voice. "Not to mention the fact that I weigh a hundred pounds soaking wet," I retorted. They ignored my response.

"Ms. Blaylock, when was the last time you spoke with Ms. Spalding?" asked Agent Samuels.

"Two weeks ago when we went to Davidson's."

"And you have not seen or spoken with her since?"

"No, I have not!"

"If you hear from her, I suggest that you inform us immediately," even though it sounded nothing like a suggestion. He handed Jackie his card and the two of them turned toward the door.

Agent Scott turned to me. "I suggest you leave here and go back to Texas before you find yourself in trouble." And then they left.

I hurried back to my room and slammed the door, locking it before Jackie could utter a word. *Agent Scott, you don't have to tell me twice. First Candy turns out to be a hooker working for Dillon. Doc takes us in and then throws us out. Derek has two girlfriends, one of whom is a psycho with a knife. He sells pot for a living, gets shot at, and snorts cocaine. The psycho girlfriend shops with people wanted by the FBI, and car thieves just happen to steal my car the night before I leave. This just takes the cake.* I picked up the phone and dialed my brother.

"Texas Bureau of Investigation. How may I help you?"

"Agent Bowan, please?"

"One moment," she put me on hold a moment and then a voice came on the line.

"This is Agent Johnson. May I help you?"

"Is Agent Bowan in, please?"

"No, can I help you?"

"I'm Michael's sister. Can you tell him I called?" I sighed.

"Sure, no problem. Does he have your number?"

"No, I'll just try him back later, thanks."

Amducious flew around in circles like an angry bee. *She's leaving; I must do something before Master finds out what a debacle this has become.* **He called his scouts that were out gathering intel on every human connected to Melissa. "Report**

your findings. We must find a way to prevent the human Melissa from leaving this city. It is has all of the elements of Sodom and Gomorrah, and we must keep her here in order to lead her to her demise."

The first demon reported. "The disturbed female is too afraid of the male human and has abandoned her plan to inflict harm upon the human Melissa. The other female has befriended her and cannot be swayed, although this is highly irregular and improbable. The female Candy is involved in prostitution but has given up on recruiting our subject."

"Idiot! You have three females to exploit and you cannot persuade one of them to impose harm upon the subject? You," Amducious pointed to the second demon. "What is your report?"

"The human who spoke to her regarding employment is undecided. There are two candidates for the position for which our human Melissa has applied. The other candidate is favored because her employment list shows prior experience performing the duties that are expected."

"Excellent," Amducious replied. "This is the fork in the road to her demise. Gather intel on the human that has the power to decide employment. Find a weakness that will sway his decision in favor of the human Melissa. All of you, go at once and do not fail or it shall be your heads!" The flock of demons took flight.

Derek arrived home twenty minutes later. I heard him yelling at Jackie. I opened my door and went into the living room.

"What are you yelling about? I should be the one yelling, considering all that's happened."

"You two let the FBI into the apartment without a warrant!" he yelled.

"Don't yell at me. I didn't let anybody in."

"You ought to know better. How stupid can you be? I told you not to hang with that bitch," he yelled at Jackie.

They began a verbal sparring match that I was not in the mood for. "I'm going to walk down the hill," I said and stormed out of the house. *I have got to get out of this zoo.* I walked down the hill to the leasing office to see Jessie. She seemed the only sane one in the group, even though I could not fathom why she put up with Derek.

"Hey, Jessie," I called as I entered the leasing office.

"Melissa, what a pleasant surprise. I was just about to call you." Instead of Jessie, it was the Human Resources Manager, Mr. Eckles, who greeted me.

"Mr. Eckles, I wasn't expecting to see you. I came by to see Jessie. How are you?" I shook his hand and apologized profusely for my manner of dress.

"Don't worry about that," he said, as he ogled me in my tight jeans. "Since you are here, I can give you the good news. I've decided to take a chance on you, even though my other candidate has more experience. Don't disappoint me." He smiled again, leering at me.

"I won't, Mr. Eckles," and I sashayed into Jessie's office.

He followed me. "I have arranged for you to visit the property where you will be stationed. It's in College Park near Riverdale Road. You will receive a two-bedroom apartment as part of your salary. They will give you your keys tomorrow. There will be some additional paperwork for you to fill out and good luck. I will come out to do a follow-up on you some time next month." He then shook my hand and left.

I looked at Jessie and giggled. "I just bet you will and, if you thought you could get away with it, your follow-up would be between the sheets."

Jessie giggled too. "He's harmless. We're used to it; he leers at anything in a skirt."

"Men are sleezeballs in general." Then it dawned on me that I had just been given a way to stay in Atlanta! "Jessie, do you realize it's a gift from God? Halleluiah!"

Immediately Jessie started planning all of the household items she could spare for me. I couldn't wait to get back to the apartment and tell the happy couple that I was leaving them and good riddance. When I got back, I could not believe that they were still arguing. This time it was about me again.

Finally, I began shouting. "May I have your attention please? I have a job and an apartment! You can stop arguing about me. I will be gone as soon as I get a bed, a fork, and a plate."

Derek stood there gawking at first, and then he went into his usual planning mode. "You'll need some furniture, and Jessie has lots of pots and pans and also some dishes that she can give you. She has a bed and some other items in storage. What complex did you get?"

"Jefferson Heights in College Park. Do you know where that is?"

"Yeah, sure, it's off of I-285 and Riverdale Road."

Jackie even perked up when she realized I would be leaving. "I know that place too. A lot of stews and pilots live there because it's close to the airport."

"Great! I have to be there in the morning. Will you drive me, Derek?"

"Sure. What time?"

"Ten, but I thought you had to take Jackie to the airport?"

"Yeah, I do, but that's at five in the morning, so I'll be back in plenty of time."

Later that night, I called my brother. "Hey, how are you?" he asked. "Johnson said you sounded upset when you called."

"No, I'm fine. I'm just excited about the job and the apartment I just got."

"That's great! Anything else going on that I should know about?" he said suspiciously.

"No," I lied. "Everything is hunky dory."

The next morning, I was dressed and ready at nine. Derek was back from taking Jackie to the airport and was sipping a cup of coffee.

"You know, this is great, you having an apartment. It will be another place for me to lay, so be sure to get me a key. And when you get your paycheck, I'll take care of it and it will go into the pot with the others. Of course, I'll give you spending money and all."

I just sat there with my mouth open, staring at him, and then I laughed. "You've got to be kidding me! You are joking, right?"

He looked at me and didn't smile. "No, Melissa, I'm not joking. Jessie and Jackie both give me their paychecks. I manage the money and take care of things."

This time I laughed so hard I was crying. "They give you their paychecks? It's bad enough that they knowingly put up with each other. But they give you their paychecks? You cannot be serious!"

"Yes, I am serious and I have a key to Jessie's. It's just another apartment of mine." He said the last word with emphasis. "And yours will be another apartment of mine, too. You owe me. I am the one

who took you in. I am the one that had Jessie get you the job. I am
the reason you even have an apartment."

I laughed again. "I am so sorry to disappoint you. But nobody
gets a paycheck that I work for and nobody is going to have a key to
my apartment but me. And it's too bad Jessie and Jackie don't have
better sense than to give someone their hard earned money. But I am
not Jessie and I am not Jackie, and you will not be getting my
money. On the other hand, I do thank you for putting me up. I also
thank you for almost getting me killed by your psycho girlfriend.
And by the way, I was the one who interviewed for the job. I am the
reason I am employed, and Jessie was the one who gave me an application, not you! If you feel like I owe you rent, then I'll be glad to give
you something when I'm able. But I do not owe you my life, my pay,
and my apartment."

**Amducious and his demons swarmed around Derek.
"Strike her, strike her," they chanted. Even though Michael was
not present, the Heavenly Host evenly matched the demons.**

**"Do not do it, Derek," the Heavenly Host said. "Her brother
is a constable and will come for you. You cannot afford the
trouble."**

"Strike her, strike her," the demons chanted.

**"Do not," the Heavenly Host whispered. Michael watched
from a distance. He knew that Derek was swayed by self-preser-
vation and would not strike Melissa.**

He just sat there staring at me. I just knew he was going to hit me,
but instead he crossed his legs and frantically started bouncing the
top one up and down as he often did when he was agitated. *If her
brother weren't a cop, I'd slap the shit out of her. But I don't need Five-
O breathing down my neck. Let's see what she does out there with no
furniture, no food, no bed, and not even a fork for two weeks. She'll come
crawling back and I'll make her beg,* he thought.

"Okay," he replied. "You need to get on out then. I ain't taking you
nowhere and Jessie ain't giving you nothing. What are you gonna do
now, Smart-ass."

"I'll manage, thanks." I grabbed my bags. "By the way, thanks
again for everything. I'm sorry you think I owe you blood for a favor.
In the future, it's probably best not to help people if you expect
payment with two hundred and fifty percent interest." I slammed the

door on the way out, as I wondered how in the world I would get to the apartment and what I would do when I got there.

Chapter Five

On My Own

Michael watched Melissa walk down the hill. He flew into an apartment several buildings down from Derek. In the apartment lived twins, Steven and Stephan.

"Steven," Michael whispered. "You desire to go out to find that fishing rod you have been planning to buy. They have one on Riverdale Road. It is time to go out."

As I walked down the hill, I knew he would call Jessie and forbid her to help me. Besides Jessie didn't own a car anyway. As I drudged down the hill, I heard someone say, "Hey, Melissa!"

"Hey, Steven," I called. Steven was one of the twins who lived two buildings down from Derek.

"Melissa! Where in the world are you going with those suitcases? They look bigger than you are."

"Oh, Steven, I need to get to Jefferson Apartments off of Riverdale Road," I said as I read from the paper I had pulled from my pocket.

"Shoot, girl, it's your lucky day. I'm on my way to Riverdale Road."

"Steven, you have got to be kidding me! You're making that up because you're such a nice guy."

"No, really," he insisted. "There's a sporting goods store on Riverdale Road that has a fishing rod I want and I just decided to go and get it. Hop in."

As Steven drove, I told him about my plight. "Shoot, girl, I knew Derek was a player, but that's taking the game to a whole new level. You know, we got a bunch of house stuff from when Stephan had his own apartment. After I get that rod, we'll bring you some stuff to sleep on and some stuff to eat with. You got money?"

"No," I lamented. "But I can't ask you to do that. You've already gone above and beyond the call of duty."

"Shoot, girl, when somebody's tryin' to help you, shut up and take it."

I laughed. "The last time somebody tried to help me, I got cut by his girlfriend and now he wants blood as payment."

He looked serious for a moment. "I ain't no player dude like Derek and, even if I was, I wouldn't do no woman like that."

I smiled. "A knight in shining armor is what you are, Steven."

"Yeah, girl, that's me and I got a sword, too," he laughed.

Michael smiled. "Melissa, my child, if only you knew. You have better than a knight, for a knight is mere flesh and blood. You have the Father, the Son, and the Holy Spirit; and it is the Trinity that will be needed for the battle to come."

Amducious knew that he had lost a crucial battle and had no hope of preparing another attack before Master would summon him. He flew around in circles as he often did when he was excited or angry. "What am I to do? What am I to do?" As he watched Melissa, he became angrier and angrier. *She's so pleased with herself. If it were not for Michael, I would be on my way back to a parade, complete with a crowning.* But now, instead of a crown on his head, he would surely lose it to the guillotine or to Satan's sword. "Oh, what am I to do," he moaned.

At that very moment, a messenger appeared. "You have been summoned to appear before the prince," he announced. "Make haste; he is in a foul mood."

Amducious could not bring to his remembrance a time when he was more frightened. He preened his wings with extra care in the hope that it would make a difference.

The gatekeeper greeted him with a look of pity instead of the usual banter. *This is not a good sign,* he thought.

"Do you have a new plan?" the gatekeeper inquired.

"I do not, and I fear that this time I am surely doomed," Amducious replied.

"But you always have a plan," he whined. "You have

managed to elude Master's sword more times than any other. Your exploits are legendary."

"Not this time," Amducious replied solemnly.

The gatekeeper sighed. "Very well, I will announce you," giving him one last look of pity.

At that moment, one of Amducious's scouts, panting, landed at the gates. "Master, wait. I have a report."

The gatekeeper turned with a look of hope, as did Amducious.

"Make your report with haste, as any delay will prolong my torture."

"There is a male human that resides near the human Melissa. He fancies her and is a great threat."

"What evil is this male human capable of?"

"He is of a dual personality when he consumes wine. During those times, he cannot control his desire to inflict harm upon his female companions."

Amducious smiled. "This is excellent and quite expeditious. If I return with my head intact, you will be greatly rewarded." Amducious puffed himself up with his usual pride. "Gatekeeper! Stop dallying. Do you think I have a millennium? Announce me at once!"

The gatekeeper smirked. "With pleasure," he said as he bowed. He too was pleased that his verbal sparring partner might return with his head intact.

I spent the day filling out papers and learning my way around the apartment complex I had been assigned. Leasing Associates Inc. owned several apartment complexes in Atlanta, and Jefferson Heights was one of the largest. The Resident Manager, who was my boss, seemed nice enough, although I suspected she was a tad lazy. The maintenance man, Ben, showed me around the complex and took me to pick out an apartment of my choosing. As Jackie had indicated, there were mostly professionals living there: stewardesses, pilots, and some doctors from Southern Regional Hospital.

"This complex is gorgeous, Ben."

He blushed with pride. "Yep, I'm responsible for everything you see, and I keep the maintenance and yard staff on their toes. We don't do no sleepin' on the job 'round here, miss."

We arrived at building two and went up to the second level. Ben unlocked the door, and I couldn't believe my eyes.

"This here is a two-bedroom, miss; but if you don't like the color of the carpet, I got another one ready in building five." The apartment was enormous with brown shag carpet, a sunken living room, and a huge kitchen with all new appliances.

"Ben, this is wonderful and I'll take it."

Later that evening, Steven and Stephan brought over numerous household items along with a mattress and dinner. Stephan opened one of the bags and extracted three bottles of Champale. "I would like to propose a toast. To you, girl."

"Not to me, Steven, to my apartment." We all touched our bottles, one to the other.

"To Melissa's apartment!" Steven said.

"To my apartment!"

"Ditto!" Stephan said.

After dinner, Steven attempted to give me twenty dollars, but I wouldn't hear of it. "You've done enough, Steven. I called my brother this afternoon and he's going to wire me enough money to last until payday."

"Shoot, girl, twenty dollars ain't no big thing."

"I appreciate it, Steven; you are a Godsend for sure, but I'll be fine."

"Okay, I tell you what. Tomorrow I'll stop by and take you to the Western Union and you can run your errands, too."

"I think I'll take you up on that, Steven."

After they left, I put a sheet on the mattress and settled in for the night. *This is so cool,* I thought as I drifted off to sleep.

The next morning, I jumped right into my new job. *I'm going to be the best Leasing Agent they have ever seen, so that I can get my own property. How cool would that be? Melissa Bowan, Resident Manager. I like the sound of that.* I smiled to myself. I spent the next year diligently working and was promoted to Assistant Manager.

"You want, you need, a new beau. This one has eyes for you. He is the right one for you. Do not let his vows stand in the way of your happiness," Amducious coaxed.

During this time, I started dating a guy who resided in the complex, even though I was fully aware that he was married. As we lay in my bed, I marveled at how men always wanted sex and yet they were never any good at it. *Much ado about nothing. I get more satisfaction from reading a book than from having sex,* I thought in disgust.

"Ah, my pretty, adultery is sweet, is it not? So many sins, so little time. There is so much more awaiting you, my dear," laughed Amducious.

"So, Larry, what exactly do you do?"

"I manage a Lincoln Mercury car dealership," he said with satisfaction.

I perked up at that information. "Cool. I wish I had a car, but they don't make a car that I can afford," I said ruefully.

"Not true," he replied. "When I get to work tomorrow, I'll find you something you can afford and I'll find financing for you, too. Now don't expect it to be something fancy."

"Beggars can't be choosers. I'll take whatever you can come up with."

True to his word, by the end of the week, I was driving a little Toyota Corolla. It was a base model with no air, no power steering, and no radio. But it was new and it was mine.

At least men are good for something besides being jerks. They chase you and when they get you, all they want is sex and none of them are any good at it. Why is everyone so fired up about sex anyway? I just don't get it. I wonder if his wife knows he runs around on her. Why can't these guys ever see that I'm an intelligent person and not just someone to have sex with, I thought as I completed my daily reports. *These people at Leasing Associates Inc. work you like a dog, but when it's time for a promotion, they always bring in someone else and I end up doing all of the work.* Just like magic, the Resident Manager walked in and announced that the end of next week would be her last day.

"You're leaving, too?"

"Yes, I've been reassigned to another property," she responded.

"But you're the third manager I've had."

"Perhaps it's time they gave you this property. It's not like you don't know it like the back of your hand."

At that moment, Mr. Teasdale, one of the owners, walked up behind her. "When you talk about putting a property worth millions of dollars in the hands of a twenty-two-year-old, investors get really nervous," he said.

Before I had time to think about it, I blurted out, "That would be understandable if the twenty-two-year-old was someone they knew nothing about. On the other hand, because we're talking about a twenty-two-year-old who has proven herself, that's not an acceptable response. And quite frankly, if you bring in another person for the third time instead of promoting me, I will be forced to seek employment elsewhere."

Immediately after I spoke, I thought I would kick myself for saying the first thought that came to mind, as I often did. But instead of firing me on the spot, Mr. Teasdale smiled.

"My, aren't we feisty. Okay, Missy, the property is yours. Don't make me regret it." He turned and walked out.

Rebecca smiled. "I don't think he has ever had anyone talk to him that way. You, girl, are brave. Good job and good luck."

I'm not your girl, I thought, but this time I kept my mouth shut. *I did it! Melissa Bowan, Resident Manager. Oh, how I like the sound of that!*

Chapter Six

But He's a Mild-Mannered School Teacher

As always, the first five days of the month were hectic. Today, more so; everyone was scrambling to get their rent in before they would be charged late fees. *Oh, no, here he comes again!* Mr. Morgan was driving up in his Corvette. Oh, how I loved that car. Mr. Morgan was not my type, but unfortunately, I seemed to be his.

"Hello, beautiful," he said as he entered the leasing office.

"Hello, Mr. Morgan."

"I told you to call me Joe."

"Yes, I know Mr. Morgan."

"Miss Bowan, when, pray tell, will you grace me with your lovely presence on a date?"

"Pray tell, Mr. Morgan, that would be never."

"Miss Bowan, my dear woman, never is a relative term and not one to be used loosely. Tell me, there must be something that I can do to convince you of my undying devotion."

"If I went out on a date with you and you actually talked to me instead of trying to have sex with me, that might do it."

He was momentarily taken aback but recovered quickly. "I can see how one of the male persuasion would find talking to you without pondering such illicit thoughts to be quite difficult. But I, my lady, am a gentleman and a scholar and I assure you that any such activity would be by your request and yours alone. With that being said, I bid you farewell to ponder my request."

He then left me with my mouth open. *By my request only. Like a rat's ass,* I thought. But I was quite intrigued by the thought.

Amducious swarmed over Melissa. "If you go out with him, perhaps he will cease to annoy you on a continuing basis. Besides, he has such a lovely vocabulary. He's a scholar and a gentleman."

The next week Mr. Morgan returned to my office. I fully expected him to ask me out again, but this time he only requested maintenance on his apartment. Again, I was intrigued. He was a man of his word. So, on his next visit, I took him up on the offer. "Mr. Morgan, I have pondered your request and agree to a date, but only under the circumstances that we discussed last week."

He bowed. "I am your humble servant. What time shall I pick you up?"

"Seven."

He bowed again and left in that gorgeous Vette. *That is a car to die for. I wonder how fast it goes.* That night he picked me up and he took me to a club on Campbellton Road. We actually had a wonderful time. I found out that he was a school teacher. *That explains the vocabulary and how well versed he is.*

"Melissa, you are a very intelligent woman and I find it surprising that no on else has noticed it before now," he replied.

"No one else has bothered to look past the sheets," I retorted. *And you won't be able to keep your commitment either. As soon as we are within two inches of a bed, you'll forget all about that 'at my request' bullshit.* Joe walked me to the door, kissed me goodnight, and never asked to come in.

Joe and I continued to date and to my surprise he was again a man of his word. Not once did he ever make advances of a sexual nature. After the fourth week, I was quite intrigued. *I have finally met a man who doesn't try to get me in the sack. Now that's a first.*

Amducious laughed at the human's bewilderment. "Perhaps you are not as pretty as you think. They have all wanted sex, except this one. Is it because he does not find you alluring enough?"

After six months of dating Joe, I found out that looks weren't everything. This man was smart, funny, sensitive, and charming. I really liked him, even though he wasn't gorgeous like Derek.

That night we were having dinner at one of the nicer restaurants in Atlanta. This time when he walked me to the door, I invited him in.

"Joe, you are a man of your word and that is a rare commodity," I said as he took off his jacket.

"Your word is your bond," he said with a smile.

After sex, we smoked, and he turned and asked, "Why did you do that?"

"Why did I do what?"

"Fake it," he said.

I was so surprised that I choked on my cigarette smoke. "How...how did you know that I...." My voice trailed off.

"That you faked an orgasm? A real man always knows. Why didn't you just tell me you weren't satisfied?"

Again, I choked. "Well, I...I don't know. It's not exactly information that men want to hear, you know."

"What do mean? Why would we not want to know what you like?"

"Because you guys always act as if you've just moved the moon and the stars and I just don't have the heart to say that I didn't feel anything."

"So you mean you've never had an orgasm?

"Well, no, I haven't."

"Let's see if we can fix that, shall we."

You have got to be kidding me! Am I in heaven or what?

Amducious and his crew flitted around the room. "So many sins, so little time," they all chanted.

"Excellent," Amducious exclaimed. "She is hooked like one of God's best sea creatures."

For the next couple of months, Joe rarely went home.

"You know, it's a waste of money for you to keep your apartment; you're never there. Why don't you move in with me?"

"That's a fabulous idea," Joe replied. "Let's do it before rent is due next month."

"Yes, that is a fabulous idea." Amducious laughed so hard that he almost lost his ability to fly. "Come to me, my pretty," he hissed. "You will pay for bringing me so close to the guillotine."

Joe and I had been living together for about two months when the unbelievable happened. "What do you mean I'm pregnant?" I wailed.

"I mean the rabbit died," the doctor said dryly.

"But...but...I can't have a baby! I'm only twenty-two!"

"If you don't want to have it, I can refer you to an abortion clinic that I recommend."

"But I can't do that either," I stammered. I was so upset after I left the doctor's office, I didn't even remember driving home.

Amducious was so excited he flew around in circles. "Kill your seed, kill your seed. So many sins, so little time. It's not a real child. Kill it, kill it. Kill your seed, my pretty."

When Joe got home that night, I broke the news.

"Pregnant" was all he could say. "Pregnant," he said again. "Are you going to have it?"

"I don't know. An abortion seems so...wrong."

"It's a fetus; it's not a baby. There's a difference."

"Really? How do you know that?"

"I just know. I read a lot. I'm a teacher, remember. If it was a baby, then it would be murder to have an abortion. Abortion is legal, right?"

"Yeah, it is."

"Well, then, it can't be a baby or it would be murder."

"I guess that makes sense. Okay, I'll call the doctor and get the clinic number tomorrow." The next day I made an appointment for the abortion. It was to take place on Friday. That would give me the weekend to recover.

That Friday I was terrified, but I was also determined to go through with it. Joe waited for me in the lounge. The staff at the clinic was top notch and put me at ease. After they prepped me for surgery, they wheeled me into a small operating room.

"Now, Miss Bowan, I want you to count backwards from one hundred."

"One hundred, ninety-nine, ninety-eight...."

Michael hovered over the operating table. He swooped down into Melissa's womb. "Do not be afraid, little one; we shall journey together to the Kingdom of Heaven. There are no tears and no pain there. It is a far better place to be than here where the Prince of Darkness rules. You will see your mother again one joyous day and you will be together forever. Forgive her,

**little one, for she knows not what she is about to do. Praise be
to the Father, the Son, and the Holy Spirit."**

**Whoosh! Right before the scalpel touched the baby, Michael
covered him with his wings and whisked his soul away,
returning him to heaven from whence he came.**

"Scalpel!" The nurse placed a scalpel in the doctor's hand and,
with no more thought than I had given the child, he cut him and
removed him from the womb, as if he were a growing cancer and not
a living baby. After it was over, I went home, back to my life, as if
nothing had happened at all.

**"How delicious and sweet victory is. Woe to Michael the
Archangel, for he has been defeated by me, Amducious the
Destroyer. I, Amducious, have enticed the human favored by
the One Who Sits at the Right Hand to murder her own seed.
This prize has been worth the arduous journey."**

"This is awesome. I can't wait to see you!" I yelled into the phone.
My sister Faith was graduating from college and coming to live with
me.

"You know Joe lives with me, but he's a sweetie. How is your car
holding up? Will you be able to drive it?"

"Of course. It's in wonderful shape and I'm ready to hit the road,"
Faith replied. "I'll be there this Saturday."

"Cool. That gives me a couple of days to get things ready for you."

"This is so great! You and me in Atlanta. Now all we need is Big
Sis, too."

"That would be the day. Prying her away from that creep she
ran off with is not going to happen soon."

"Yeah, I know. I think he hits her, don't you?" Faith asked.

"Yeah, he strikes me as that type. What does Mom think about you
coming down here?"

"You know Mom. She was not too thrilled about it, but she sort of
likes the idea of me being there to keep an eye on you."

"As if that would do any good. So, drive safe and I'll see you on
Saturday. Love you."

"Love you too. Bye."

That Saturday Faith arrived on schedule. When we saw each
other, we jumped up and down and screamed like idiots.

"So what do you want to do first?" I asked Faith.

"Monday I have an interview with Xerox. It's nothing exciting, nor does it have anything to do with my major, but it will allow me to get my foot in the door."

"Cool. Do you have the address?"

"Yeah, do you know where Cobb Parkway is?"

"Sure, it's about a thirty-minute drive from here. Why don't I show you how to get to I-285 later on today? From there, it's a straight shot, and then Monday you won't get lost."

"Great. Where's this Joe person you talked about on the phone?"

"Oh, he went to see his daughter."

"His daughter?"

"Yeah, he has the cutest little girl from his previous marriage."

"And that doesn't bother you?"

"No, why should it?"

"Man plus child plus ex-wife always means trouble."

"That's why I'm glad that all my ex's live in Texas," I sang.

"I'm serious," Faith replied.

"I know, but really, it's no big deal. She's really nice and the little girl is too."

"If you say so."

"Oh, there he is now. He's not a cutie, like Derek, but he is the sweetest guy I know and he loves me."

"Looks aren't everything and they usually mean trouble," Faith replied.

"Hey, babe. Hi, you must be Faith. I'm Joe. I take it that your trip was uneventful?"

"It was, thank goodness. It's a pleasure to meet you."

"The pleasure is all mine, I assure you," Joe said, complete with a bow.

That Monday, Faith went on her interview with Xerox and sure enough she got the job two days later. True to form, she would remain there for the next twenty-five years.

Life went on at a much slower pace until the leasing company decided to hold its annual managers' meeting at Crooked Branch Apartments. That was where Derek lived and where Jessica was the Resident Manager. Yet I didn't give that a moment's thought, given that I had not heard or spoken to either of them in over a year. After our meeting, there was no time for me to go to my office, so I went straight home. Both Faith and Joe were already there and both had eaten dinner. Faith had gone to her room and, after a quick snack, I too retired and was lying across the bed talking to Joe about my day when all hell broke loose.

Amducious could not believe his good fortune. He swarmed around Melissa's room in circles. "The male human is primed and ready. It has taken an entire earth cycle, but now it is time. His duel personality is ready to emerge."

"What is the significance of the human's duality?" Hodi asked.

"The other side of the male human is vicious and desires to inflict harm upon the female that he loves. This side has no logic, as he truly loves the human female and yet he is compelled to do her harm when this side emerges," Amducious answered.

"What is the catalyst for the emergence of the vicious side?"

"The vicious side only emerges when the male human consumes wine. Before he arrived at their abode, he consumed more than two liters. That is more than enough to allow the emergence of the violent one. In addition, the female is unaware that he possesses an insanely jealous nature. These two elements are about to collide the moment he realizes that she spent her day near the abode of her previous lover. Watch and learn, young one," Amducious sneered.

"So how was your meeting?" Joe asked.

"It was awesome; they served us lunch and everything. Since it was at Crooked Branch, I even saw Jessie." Joe had the strangest look that I could not interpret.

"She spent the day with her lover," Amducious chanted. "She is cheating on you. Kill her; she deserves to die. She is cheating on you with that pretty one that she loves so. She never loved you. How could anyone love you? You are ugly, ugly, ugly. She loves the pretty one. Kill her!"

This assignment was as distasteful as the journey to escort the unborns to the other side. Michael had to allow Melissa to be struck in order to save her from the male human at a later time. This would be brought to her remembrance and she would not allow it to happen again. This would save her, for

the next time would be a deathblow.

"You spent the entire day at Crooked Branch?" he asked.

"Yeah, so?" That's the last thing I remembered.

Michael swung his sword and stuck Hodi broadside. Amducious charged Michael while his sword was still engaged with Hodi, thus insuring his survival. Michael pivoted and struck Amducious with his shield. Amducious knew better than to attempt to attack Michael when there was no obstacle between them, so he immediately retreated when he regained his balance. Michael was just in time to put his wing between Joe and Melissa to prevent him from killing her. Even with Michael's intervention, both blows to Melissa were savage and vicious.

Joe had hit me twice, once in each eye, and I had lost consciousness. When I awoke briefly, Faith was screaming at Joe. We were all three in the car. Joe was driving and Faith and I were in the back seat. My head was in her lap. The next thing I remembered was talking to a doctor in the emergency room.

"Miss Bowan, can you hear me?"

"Yes, who are you?"

"I'm a doctor in the ER. Do you remember what happened to you?"

"No, what...what happened?" I asked.

"Miss Bowan, did someone hit you?"

"Hit me? No, why would anyone do that?"

And then I remembered! Joe! Joe had hit me! But that was impossible. Joe was the nicest, most caring guy on earth. Joe and I had been together for over a year and he had never so much as raised his voice. *What the hell is going on?*

"Miss Bowan, please, did someone hit you? Are you afraid of anyone? Have you been threatened?"

"No, I'm sorry. I was just out of it for a minute. I remember. I slipped and fell down the stairs."

"Miss Bowan, your injuries could not have been sustained by a fall down the stairs."

"As I stated, doctor, I fell down the stairs. Once you have completed my treatment, I would like to go home."

"As you wish, but you are making a mistake. If he hit you once, he will hit you again."

"Thank you. I'll keep that in mind."

"Very well, once I've written your prescription and write your recovery instructions, you may go."

When I came out, Joe was crying like a baby and Faith was still furious and continued to yell at him. Faith's screaming seemed to make him cry more. When he saw me, I thought that he was having a stroke. He got down on his knees and begged me to forgive him, as he sobbed.

I've heard of this sort of thing. A man beats a woman and each time he promises not to do it again. I've always said that it seemed like the most stupid thing I had ever heard. But Joe? He's never hit me before and, for heaven's sake, he's a mild-mannered school teacher! Look at him; he's about to have a nervous breakdown. He loves me and could not possibly want to hurt me. This has to be some sort of stress induced fluke. Look how long we've been together. It's as if he's been invaded by the body snatchers. How could I have known that his personality flipped to the violent side after consuming just the right amount of alcohol?

"It's all right, Joe; get up. It's all right; don't cry."

"All right! All right! You're kidding! Look at you!" Faith cried. "Have you seen your face? You have two black eyes and you have no white left in your eyes at all. Both are entirely red. If you let him come home with you, you're crazy and I'm leaving."

"Faith, come on, you don't mean it."

"Oh, yes, I do. Because if you want to be stupid, I refuse to assist you with it and I cannot do this again."

True to her word, a week later Faith got her own apartment in a gorgeous complex in Riverdale. I missed Faith, but life went on and so did ours.

"Hey, babe," Joe called as he came through the door three months later.

"Hey, yourself. How was your day?"

"Long and tedious," he replied with a look that I could not interpret.

I know that look, but I can't put my finger on it.

"Have you seen my school papers, the ones I graded?" he asked.

"No, I don't think so." And again, there was that look.

"It is the look he had when he hurt you, Melissa," Michael

whispered.

Oh, my God! That's the look he had when he hit me. I remember now! Crooked Branch Apartments set him off because Derek lived there. I've got to be careful not to set him off. God help me! I'm not sure what will set him off this time. He's been drinking, just like when he hit me. It's the alcohol! He's an alcoholic, just like Daddy! Only when Daddy reached that magic number of drinks, he would cry. When Joe reaches that magic number of drinks, he hits. How could I have been so stupid?

"He had help hiding it, Melissa. He was very careful not to consume the amount that he knew would get him into trouble. Now that you have seen it, he will not be so careful in the future. You must get away from him."

I need to get him into the bed and asleep. I have got to get away from him. Lord, where do I find these people? Tomorrow I will go to Faith's and give him time to find a place of his own. If only I can keep him sane until the alcohol wears off.

After Joe got in bed, I climbed in. *Oh, no, he wants sex. If I fake it, he'll know. Oh, I pray he's too drunk to know. I just don't think I can do this otherwise. I'm just too scared.*

After sex, he lit a cigarette. "You want some herb tea?" he asked, again with that look.

I didn't dare refuse. "Sure, I'd like that."

"Well, then, get your ass up and fix it."

"Sure, Joe," I smiled. Joe had never talked to me that way and I knew he was going to hurt me.

"Melissa, do not go into the kitchen naked. Put on your robe; your robe, Melissa, put on your robe," Michael cautioned.

On my way to the kitchen, I reached behind the door and put on my robe before leaving the room. I prepared the tea and brought two cups into the bedroom. I walked over and smiled at Joe and handed him one of the cups of steaming hot tea.

This was his last chance. Hodi had recovered from his earlier wound and now he had another chance to prove that he was worthy to assist the Destroyer Amducious. "Throw it on her. She knows you are ugly, you know. Your brother, now he is the handsome one. You are ugly and you will always be ugly, and she will never really love you because you are ugly.

Throw it; throw the tea on her."

Whoosh! Michael severed Hodi's head with a single blow before he could utter another word.

Joe sneered at me and then threw the cup of hot tea all over me.

"Run, Melissa, run now," Michael shouted. "Run to the constable's abode."

I dropped the cup I was holding and ran to the front door. I unlocked it and flew down the steps. In my robe and bare feet, I ran to Melvin's apartment. Melvin was with the state police and also worked apartment security. I pounded on Melvin's door.

"In a minute, in a minute," he yelled. Melvin opened the door a crack. "Melissa, what in the world? Come in, come in. Are you hurt?"

"No, but I should have been. It's Joe; he goes crazy when he drinks. He threw a cup of hot tea on me and I ran before he could hit me. Three months ago he gave me those two black eyes. I lied to everyone about it."

"Yeah, we knew you were lying, Melissa. How can I help? Do you want me to throw him out?"

Melvin was 6'4." I knew throwing Joe out was not an issue for him. "No, I just want you to go with me to get my things. I was the one who asked him to move in with me. It's only fair that I give him thirty days to find a place of his own. I'll stay with my sister for thirty days. If he's not out by then, I definitely want you to throw him out."

Melvin and I went back to my apartment. Joe was sitting on the sofa sobbing. "Melissa, I'm sorry, babe. You know I didn't mean to hurt you."

"Yes, Joe, I do know you don't mean to. But I also know that you will. And you won't stop until I leave or I'm dead. That's why your wife left you, isn't it?" He just hung his head and cried.

"You have thirty days to find a place," I said sadly. "I'm going to Faith's and do not even think about coming near me. Leave a message at the office when you're out, and if you're not out in thirty days, Melvin will be forced to remove you."

"And make no mistake, Joe; I will remove you," Melvin said.

What are the odds? I finally find someone who really cares for me and he's a psycho alcoholic. Has the whole world gone bonkers or do I just attract psychos, I thought as I completed my paperwork. *I'm sick of men. I'm sick of this job. They work me like a slave. Alone again.* And with that thought I locked the office. *I need a bite to eat; maybe I'll stop at that new place that just opened on Old National.*

Amducious buzzed around Derek's head as he drove down Old National. "You wish to visit that new banquet hall, the one your friend spoke of yesterday. I am so saddened by Hodi's unfortunate demise. Good help is so hard to find," he laughed.

I walked up to the counter and had the strangest sensation on the back of my neck. I whirled around. Derek was standing right behind me.

"Hello, Melissa," he whispered.

"Hello, Derek. How have you been?"

"Not too bad and you?"

"Just hunky dory. So, are you still not speaking to me?"

"What exactly do you call what we're doing now, telepathy?"

"Now that you mentioned it, that's exactly what I call it."

"What do you mean?"

"I was thinking about you, not more than ten seconds before you walked up behind me. Not only that, I knew you were there."

"Melissa, that's freaky."

"I'll say."

"Are you here alone?"

"Yeah, are you?"

"Yeah, will you have dinner with me?"

"Sure, why not?" After dinner we exchanged numbers. *I wonder if he found a replacement for his harem.* I smiled.

"You, Missy, are of a feeble mind. You know that he has no good will toward you and yet you desire him still. Feeble-minded humans, the entire lot of you," Amducious sneered.

The next week, my cousin Dee Dee arrived in Atlanta. I had rented a car because mine was in the shop. "So, Dee Dee, how do you like Atlanta so far?" I asked as we made our way to the shopping mall.

"It's great. I can't believe the trees."

"Yeah, Texas just can't compare to this." At that moment, a car came out of nowhere, in the wrong lane, heading straight for us.

Michael enveloped the entire transportation device with his wings and jerked it right, then left, then right, then left.

Without thought, I jerked the wheel to the right. As soon as I did that, we were on a collision course with a huge tree. I jerked the wheel again, this time to the left. That put us into the lane of oncoming traffic. I jerked the wheel to the right and again to the left to straighten it out.

"Oh, my God! How did you do that?" Dee Dee yelled.

"I don't know! It was as if some other force was carrying this car!" I marveled.

"That was unbelievable! You should be a race car driver."

I just looked at her. "Dee Dee, even if I was a race car driver, a Ford Escort cannot take turns like that. I was not driving this car!"

Dee Dee just looked at me. "That was really strange."

"Dee Dee, that is what you call Divine Intervention."

"Yeah, well, I guess you have a Guardian Angel," she replied.

"That I do, Dee Dee; that I do."

One afternoon, as I posted rent checks to the office ledger, the phone in my office rang. "Jefferson Heights Apartments. This is Melissa; may I help you?"

"Yes, Melissa, you may," the voice said.

I know that voice. "Sybil, is that you?"

"Wow! I can't believe you recognize my voice, "Sybil said.

"Are you kidding? I'd know your voice anywhere. Where are you? Are you in Atlanta?"

"No, I'm in Dallas, but I've got to get out of here. I hate Texas."

"Yeah, so do I. What are you doing in Dallas?"

"I left my husband. He gave me a black eye, several to be exact."

"Oh, I know a little something about that too. You know Faith is here too."

"Yeah, I know. Is she living with you?"

"No, she has her own place. Hey, why don't you come down? You can live with me as long as you need to."

"Really? Are you sure?"

"Yeah, I'm sure. Do you have enough money for a ticket?"

"Yeah, I've got a small stash. I'll check the flights and call you back."

"Great, I can't wait to see you. I haven't seen you in years."

"I know. Do you remember when we went to that party? You were sixteen and you got drunk on the spiked punch."

"Yeah, don't remind me. I was drunk as a skunk and sick as a dog," I laughed.

"Yeah, you were a mess. Well, let me call the airlines and find out how soon I can get a flight out."

"Okay, call me back as soon as you make the arrangements."

After Sybil rang off, I sat there awhile. This was great. Me and Sybil, the dastardly duo. She and I were two of a kind. Like fire and kindling wood, and we were about to start a towering inferno.

Amducious was spinning round and round in circles, laughing and spinning. *I may have lost Hodi, but the future is as bright as a shining star. This human Sybil is the bridge I need to lead little Missy to the gates of hell. She thinks so highly of herself. She regards herself with such high esteem. You murdered your own seed and that was the beginning of the end for you. When will they learn? Each unrepented sin opens the door for the next. When the door is widened, many more of us will enter! It's been two thousand earth years and, thanks to the prince, many remain ignorant of the Word, even though it is within their grasp.* **He snickered.** *The Word sits in every bed table in every inn, and yet these are the same abodes they go to commit their acts of fornication, adultery, and prostitution.* **He laughed as he dived through the clouds.** *So many sins, so little time, so many humans to perform them.*

Sybil booked a flight for Atlanta and would arrive in two weeks. *What a drag it will be when Sybil gets here and I have to go to work every day,* **I thought.**

"Get rid of the boring employment. They work you like a slave girl. Sybil is coming. She will find your employment tedious. You must develop a plan to alleviate this obstacle. I will help you, my pretty."

That Friday I locked up the office. It was the fifth of the month and I had thousands of dollars in rental revenue that needed to be deposited. The procedure was all rental revenue must be deposited immediately after closing at the nearby bank drop. Instead of following the procedure, I went home and put the money in my bedroom dresser drawer. Later that evening I called Derek.

"I have those items that we discussed."

"Okay, I'll be right over."

After Derek left, I locked up and went to bed. Saturday morning I got up and went shopping. Upon my return I went into my bedroom and immediately called the police.

"Nine-one-one. What is your emergency?" the officer inquired.

"I've been robbed," I wailed. "They stole the money, my coats, my stereo, and my TV."

"What is your name, miss?"

"Melissa, my name is Melissa Bowan."

"Miss Bowan, are you in any immediate danger?"

"No, they're gone now. But my stuff! They stole everything."

"It's okay, Miss Bowan; an officer will be there in ten minutes."

When the officer arrived, he surveyed the damage and noted that all of the cash that should have been deposited was gone and the checks were scattered all over the bedroom floor. Also missing were two leather coats, a stereo, and a television. One of the coats belonged to my sister Faith and she was going to be furious. The officer took the report and noted that the point of entry was probably the patio door, which was unlocked.

"Miss Bowan, leaving your patio door unlocked is not a very wise course of action. Especially knowing that you have large sums of money that you are responsible for. I advise you to be more careful in the future. The perpetrator was aware that you are the Resident Manager and knew just when to strike and on what day. You were lucky that you weren't home."

After the officer left, I sighed. *I'm glad that's over.*

Later that night Derek came over. "I hear that you're in need of a TV, a stereo, and perhaps a couple of leather coats," he snickered.

"Wow, you must be psychic," I laughed. "Faith will be so happy that you just happened by them at the right time." After we had sex, Derek left me a stereo, a TV, and two leather coats. *Tomorrow I'll call Faith and tell her that Derek found our stuff at a pawnshop.*

Amducious watched the two humans with delight. *What a wonderful pair you make. Come to me, my pretty. Now that you have crossed to the dark side, you will be delivered to my master. The crown that I covet shall be mine.*

The next day Mr. Teasdale paid me a visit. "Melissa, I am very disappointed in you. You not only failed to follow procedure, but you were grossly negligent by leaving your patio door open with my money inside instead of at the bank where it belonged. I'm sorry, Melissa, but I have no choice but to fire you."

"Of course. I'm really sorry about your money, Mr. Teasdale. I'll get my things."

"You will be allowed to remain in your apartment rent free for sixty days. After that you will be required to sign a lease and pay rent or vacate the premises. Is that clear?"

"Yes, thank you; that is very generous."

"Yes, it is. I should throw you out on your ear," he snapped. He turned and stormed out of the office.

And good riddance to you too, I thought. *It's party time.* I smiled as I cleaned out my office.

Sybil arrived the next week. When we saw each other, we yelled so loudly that everyone in the airport turned to look at us.

"You look wonderful," I exclaimed.

"So do you."

"I have some bad news," I said solemnly.

"What could possibly be bad now that I'm here in Atlanta?"

"I got fired and I have sixty days to pay rent or vacate my apartment."

"Sixty days. Well, that's a lifetime. So what's the bad news?"

I just laughed. "Girl, you're a mess!"

"You don't know the half of it," she laughed.

After a week, Sybil was bored out of her mind. I picked up the phone and called Derek.

"I've got someone I'd like you to meet. She's here visiting me from Texas by way of California. Do you think you could fix her up with Jim?"

"I don't know. Jim is sort of paranoid about meeting people."

"Sybil's not people," I snapped. "Strangers on the street are people."

"Is she cute?"

"Am I cute?" I asked.

"Yeah."

"Then that would make her gorgeous."

"Okay, you guys come by at eight and I'll work on getting him over here."

Later that evening we went over to visit Derek. He had convinced

Jim to come by and he and Sybil hit it off immediately. As a matter of fact, they left together. Neither Derek nor I saw either of them until the next day. Jackie was on a trip, so I spent the night at Derek's. The next afternoon Jim and Sybil showed up.

"I take it that you two like each other somewhat?"

"I guess you could say that," they replied in unison.

"Oh, brother, they're like newlyweds," I said disgustedly.

"You were the one who thought to introduce us," Sybil replied coyly.

"Yeah, I guess I did," I laughed.

Chapter Seven

My Prince Charming Is a Toad

For the next week Sybil and Jim spent every available minute together. The next thing I knew, he was inviting her on out-of-town trips. First to Detroit, then New York, then Chicago, then LA. Boy, did I feel left out. Sixty days was fast approaching and Sybil was jet setting all over the country. *How did I get myself into this mess?* Then the phone rang.

"Where are you guys this time?" I asked Sybil. I didn't really want to hear what a good time she was having without me.

"We're in the Bahamas."

"You have got to be kidding me! I introduced you to a dreamboat who has taken you all over the country and now to the Bahamas! And I'm stuck here with the likes of Derek," I wailed.

"Just a minute. Jim wants to talk to you."

"Hey, Melissa."

"Hey, Jim. Don't rub it in. Sun, sand, and surf and I'm stuck here."

"Well, you don't have to be."

"What do you mean?"

"My business partner is here too and he would like to meet you."

"Meet me? And how do you propose to do that?"

"Why don't I let you talk to him and you guys can work it out. His name is Allen."

"Adventure, intrigue, sun, fun, and the beach. You must go, Melissa. Sybil is there and having all the fun! It is not fair." Furfur was young, but he too had something to prove. Since

Hodi's untimely demise, Amducious needed an assistant and
Furfur was determined to win the prize. "You should be the
one on the beach, not her. Do not let anything get in your
way. It is your turn to have fun."

Jim passed the phone to someone; the voice on the other end
was deep and sexy.

"Hi, I'm Allen. I'm stuck here with these two lovebirds and I'm
lonely. I tell you what. Why don't I send you a ticket, and you can
fly out here? Have you ever been to the Bahamas?" he asked.

"No, I haven't, but what if I fly out there and despise you," I
retorted.

"I'll make it a round trip ticket, and if you despise me, which I
doubt, then you can get on the next plane back to Atlanta."

"Now that will work."

"Give me that phone!" Sybil yelled. "Melissa, don't do it."

"A man invites me to come to the Bahamas on a round trip ticket,
and if I don't like him, I can turn around and go home! Are you
crazy? What do you mean don't do it? What is your problem?"

"There is more here than meets the eye, Melissa. You have no
idea what you're getting into."

"Whatever it is, you're in it and I'm not passing this up. I don't
care what you have to say about it. So, is he cute?"

"Yeah, he's cute. As a matter of fact, he's just your type."

"Really? Well, I plan to find out. I'm on my way to the airport
and I'll see you soon."

The Bahamas! Someone really likes me up there, I thought dreamily.
I packed in record time and headed to Hartsfield. When I got to the
ticket counter, I found that a round trip ticket in my name had indeed
been paid for. And it was in first class, no less. *First class! Wow! This
guy is really something.*

The two-hour wait passed quickly and we boarded the plane. I
had never flown first class before; it was unbelievable. *Now this is the
life.* I noticed the lusty stares of the men on the flight as I walked by
them. *Jerks! All men think about is sex. I'm sure that's all Allen has on
his mind. But two can play this game. I want to spend time in the
Bahamas, so this could turn out to be a mutually gratifying relationship
in more ways than one.*

The flight to Miami was quick and then we took a smaller craft to Freeport. As I walked down the ramp, it was just like on TV. And then I saw him standing with Jim and Sybil. He was drop dead gorgeous! He was a little short, but I'm only 5'2," so that wasn't a big deal. *Has Sybil lost her mind trying to convince me not to come?*

Sybil was jumping up and down and waving her fool head off. "Melissa, Melissa," she kept yelling, as everyone turned their heads. When I reached them, Allen stepped up and took both my hands.

"Hello, Melissa. I'm Allen."

"Hi, it's a pleasure to meet you."

"The pleasure is all mine, I assure you. So, would you like to use that return ticket?" he asked with a gleam in his eye.

"Not on your life."

"Well, then, shall we?" Allen looked at Jim and Sybil and they looked at each other.

Sybil said, "Oh, brother!" under her breath.

"I heard that," I chided.

"I knew he was your type," she sighed.

"Melissa, be careful! He is not what he seems. He is using you," Michael whispered.

Something told me I should be careful, but I pushed that thought to the back of my mind.

When we got to the hotel, I couldn't believe my eyes. The Zanadu was the most gorgeous structure I had ever laid eyes on. We had the suite at the top, complete with two bedrooms, living room, and dining area. The living room had sliding glass doors, from ceiling to floor, with a balcony and a view of the entire island. It was breathtaking. I looked at Sybil, who just shrugged her shoulders.

"This is the only way they travel," she said, as if it were the most normal thing in the world. That evening they took us to a five-star restaurant and it was like a fairy tale.

"Melissa, you realize that you can't continue to see Derek," Allen stated, as a matter of fact.

I was stunned. "You know about Derek?" I asked.

"Of course, it's my business to know everything about my subordinates."

"Subordinates? What do you mean?"

"Derek works for us. He's at the bottom of the food chain, so to speak."

"How dumb would I be to want someone at the bottom of the food chain when I can have the one at the top?" I asked coyly.

"She's a smart lady," replied Jim.

"Yeah, pretty and smart. I like that," Allen mused, as he poured me another glass of Pouilly Fuissé.

When we got back to the hotel, the guys exchanged some sort of look I could not interpret. *Here we go again. I don't like those looks; they always mean trouble.*

"So, Melissa, what do think about…you know…dual relationships?" Jim asked.

"Define 'dual relationships'?"

"He means that he wants us all to get into one bed," Sybil stated, as if it was a normal thing to do.

"In that case, I'd say it's time for me to use the other half of that ticket," I snapped.

Allen abruptly jumped up from the sofa. "That won't be necessary. I'm not willing to share you with anybody. Sorry, partner, this one's off limits."

He then put his hand in the small of my back and led me to one of the bedrooms and closed the door. *Jim and Sybil too. Freaky people! Is everyone in the world except me into dual relationships?*

We spent the entire week in the Bahamas. The guys had a wealthy business associate on the island who took us around the island to see the sights. I felt like Cinderella! By the end of the week, I was head over heels about Allen and he knew it.

When we got to the airport, Allen pulled a bag of white powder out of his suitcase. "Melissa, stick this in your pantyhose. Don't worry; they won't search you. You don't fit the profile."

I looked at Sybil who just shrugged her shoulders at me.

"You're sure they won't search me?" I asked. "Sybil, have you ever been searched?"

"No, I haven't, not yet anyway."

Michael approached the throne of The Most High God. "Praise be to the Father, the Son, and the Holy Spirit," he said as he bowed to the One True God.

"You are concerned for her, Mighty Warrior. Do not be dismayed. I will not allow permanent harm to come to her. However, she will follow her heart and it shall forever be

broken until I send her the proper mate. This one she fancies will be the catalyst that will cause her to sin against her body. When she realizes that he does not love her, she will then set out to punish all men for what he has done. She will make a decision to barter that which is precious, her body. But first, she will be used by this one to transport his wares from port to port. You must protect her and her female companion from the government authorities, for the penalties for this activity can be as many as twenty-five of their years. Dispatch a squadron from the Heavenly Host to guard her female companion, for their destinies are intertwined. Also, increase the protection for my daughter Melissa's earthly father and her male sibling. Satan wishes to devour them also, yet their names too are written in The Book of Life. Her earthly father is afflicted with a desire for wine. This disease is a scourge upon the earth and has devoured many. His drunken stupors frequently put him in harm's way. In addition, her male sibling's chosen profession is an admirable one; however, danger is its bedfellow. When Satan is unsuccessful at using his profession to orchestrate his demise, he will then insinuate himself into his chosen recreation. When that time is upon us, it will require skills that only you and Gabriel possess. Go now, for the authorities have positioned several canines to detect that which the females carry."

"As you wish, my King. Praise be to the Father, the Son, and the Holy Spirit," Michael said as he took flight.

"Uh, how much cocaine is this? It sure looks like a lot."

"That's a quarter of a key," Allen said with pride.

"A key?"

"Yeah, a kilo. Once we cut it, it will triple in value and then we'll sell it an ounce at a time. In the end it will net us about two thousand an ounce for thirty-two ounces."

"Cut it?" I asked with stupidity.

"Add a filler to it."

"Two thousand dollars times thirty-two is seventy thousand dollars!" I said incredulously.

"Yeah, that's about right."

I whistled. "That's a lot of money."

"Yeah, plenty to take care of you in style, my dear."

He knew exactly the right thing to say. I put the cocaine in my pantyhose. Sybil put an equal amount in hers and we entered the airport. We went up to the counter and asked for our tickets. The guys stayed a good distance from us. As I was occupied at the counter, the police drug dogs were busily sniffing the luggage as it was deposited onto the baggage carousel. I watched them from the corner of my eye. *Dogs? Why do they have dogs in the airport? They're sniffing out drugs! Oh, my God! I'm going to jail for the rest of my life!*

Michael swarmed above the canines.

Amducious too was there. "Attack," he yelled. Furfur and the other demons descended upon Michael, who had brought reinforcements. The demons engaged the Heavenly Host in battle. Michael severed the heads of two demons with one stroke.

When Furfur saw this, he was terrified. But he knew if he retreated without being ordered, he would surely lose his head anyway. *Oh, what good will it do to be a headless assistant?* At that moment, Amducious called for the retreat. *Oh, I would much rather be assigned a safe duty away from a warrior such as Michael.* "Oh, what was I thinking," he wailed, as he dived to avoid Michael's sword.

As the demons fled, Michael covered himself in a cloak with the scent of cocaine and flew away from Melissa. The dogs immediately picked up his scent and proceeded to chase Michael, although they could not see him.

"We got something!" the DEA agent yelled. The undercover agents followed the dogs as they ran. "Go get 'em, boys!" the agent yelled. The dogs ran to the opposite end of the airport.

At the other end of the airport, Michael shed the cloak and the dogs stopped in their tracks. Michael reached down and petted one of the dogs; he whined. He knew Michael was there, but he could not see him. "Do not be afraid," Michael whispered, and the dog stopped whining.

The DEA agent looked around. "What, boy? Where is he, boy?" The dog just walked in circles. "I don't get it; this canine has a one hundred percent detection rate."

"It looks like he just went down to ninety percent," the other agent sighed with disgust.

We boarded the plane without further incident, although I was terrified. The dogs and nearly a dozen DEA agents had run to the other end of the airport.

"Can you believe people actually smuggle drugs through the airport?" the guy in front of us asked.

"Drug dealers are the scum of the earth," one lady replied.

"I told you it was cool," Allen said. "They always have the dogs sniff the bags. Some dumb slob must have put it in his suitcase. We never put product in our bags."

"Oh," I sighed with relief, as if this was the most logical thing I had ever heard as I sipped my champagne in first class.

We stayed in Miami another week and again we stayed in the best hotel and ate at the best restaurants. Allen treated me like a queen. Anything I asked for, he would buy. *Now this is the way to live.*

"I can't believe you tried to keep all of this to yourself," I chided Sybil.

"This wasn't the part that I was keeping to myself," she retorted. "It was the part where you transport drugs across state lines and get twenty to life."

"I'm a big girl and it's not like he hid it on my person and I wasn't aware of it."

"Yeah, well, this is only the tip of the iceberg. You realize that you'll be expected to carry drugs every trip?"

"It's cool; it's a small price to pay to live like this."

"I doubt that you'll think so when you're sitting in a jail cell until age fifty."

"Oh, you worry too much. Besides, I don't see you bailing out."

"I'm responsible for myself. In your case, I sucked you into this when I allowed them to call you."

"You didn't suck me into anything. I could have said no at the airport. That relinquishes you of all responsibility."

"Doubtful. I knew once you laid eyes on him you would be putty in his hands and I was right."

"Yeah, he is scrumptious, isn't he," I said with dreamy eyes.

"Oh, brother," Sybil said. "It's one thing for you to do this for the lifestyle, but it's another if you think he gives a damn about you."

"Are you kidding me? He's crazy about me! Have you seen the way he looks at me?"

Sybil didn't have the heart to tell me that he had other mules and he looked at each of them the same way.

We spent another week in the Bahamas and then another week in Miami. When it was time to return to Atlanta, again Sybil and I both carried cocaine in our pantyhose.

Michael hovered over Melissa and Sybil, keeping them from harm's way.

Once we arrived, Allen made sure Sybil and I had enough money to live on. "I guess you were right about sixty days being a lifetime. We have rent money with thirty days to spare."

"Men live for one thing," Sybil stated. "My motto is if they want it, make 'em pay. When I was in LA, I would park my car and put the hood up. I then walked down the street wearing a business suit and carrying a briefcase. Guys would think I was stranded and pick me up. I charged them a hundred bucks and it worked like a charm every time."

"Sybil! That's disgusting."

"Yeah, but true."

She is right about men, I guess. But Allen is different. Two weeks later it was time for another trip. This time it was Detroit. We had a suite at the Renaissance Hotel. It too was breathtaking and came with the same hefty price–transporting drugs across state lines.

This pattern continued for the next year. We transported drugs every two weeks to New York, LA, and Detroit. Sometimes we carried drugs and sometimes a suitcase full of cash. In addition, we counted the money that went into the bags, as much as fifty thousand dollars; and sometimes I carried the money to Detroit without Allen. *He certainly must trust me to allow me out of his sight with fifty thousand dollars. How does he know that I won't just take off? I guess that's part of being in love. He really does love me.*

Boy, was I stupid! I found out he had a wife and a baby, but that didn't change my mind about him. Of course, he told me that he didn't love her and only stayed with her because of the baby!

In addition to his home in Decatur, Allen had a penthouse apartment in downtown Atlanta on Peachtree Street. This is where we spent most of our time together.

"Melissa, you look so good tonight. Where do you want to go?"

It was my birthday and he was taking me out on town. "How about the Mansion? I heard it's one of the oldest and best restaurants in Atlanta."

"Anything for you, Melissa." After dinner he pulled out a fabulous diamond ring.

"Oh, my goodness! It's beautiful, Allen!"

"Nothing but the best for you. It's a flawless stone," he said with pride. Then we went back to spend the night at the penthouse.

"So how do you reconcile staying out all night to your wife?" I asked as I snorted a line of cocaine.

"She's used to it. She did find out about you, though."

I sat up in the bed. "What! How?"

"She has short hair and you left yours in the sink in the bathroom."

"You mean she was here? At the penthouse?"

"Of course. Who do you think cleans it?"

"I just thought you had a maid," I sputtered.

"I do and she's it."

"That's a mean thing to say."

"Yeah, but it's true."

"What did she say about my hair?"

"She wanted to know who it belonged to, so I told her."

"What!"

"I told her it's Melissa's," he replied, as if that was a sane thing to do.

"Are you crazy?"

"No. She knows that I only stay with her because of the baby, so it's no big deal."

"Not until she shoots the two of us," I snapped. *Where do I find these people*, I thought as I drifted to sleep.

The next morning I had a trip to make to Detroit. This time it was pot instead of cocaine and I was to go by car. As the guys packed the trunk with marijuana, I noticed that the marijuana was compressed into bricks. Usually it was packaged in plastic bags.

"Is that a good idea? You know, to put it in the suitcases without the baggies? I can smell it even though the suitcases are closed."

"You worry too much, Melissa. Nobody is going to be close enough to smell it but you," Allen replied.

As I traveled down I-75, I noticed that all of the surrounding cars were traveling about ten or twelve miles over the speed limit. Allen had always cautioned me never to go over the speed limit.

Amducious buzzed in circles around Melissa's car. "Faster, my pretty. The authorities cannot detain all of you. Go faster, faster, like the others."

Everyone is doing it; they can't very well stop all of us. Five miles down the road there was a white car in the ditch. About eight cars going over the speed limit passed it. As soon as we rounded the curve, there was a roadblock in the middle of the freeway. *This is it; I'm going to jail. It's so hot outside that the pot smells as if I'm actually smoking it. There's no way in hell that he won't smell it.*

I pulled over to the side of the road, as did the other eight cars. *So much for being a smart-ass and thinking that they can't get everyone at the same time,* I thought in disgust as I waited to be handcuffed.

Amducious spotted Michael only a second before he struck. He dived just in time to avoid death, but his right wing was partially severed. Luckily for him, Michael's priority was to save Melissa; therefore, Amducious was able to escape again with his life.

The state trooper cautiously approached the side window, as he did with every traffic stop. "Driver's license and registration, please." As I handed him the documents he requested, I watched as he proceeded to the back of the car to record the tag number.

"Lord, I know I don't deserve it, but please don't let him smell that pot," I prayed.

As the officer approached the rear of the vehicle, Michael enveloped the car with the sent of ragweed to which the officer was allergic.

As soon as the officer reached the back of the car, he began sneezing and immediately backed away from the trunk. His sneezing stopped. "Ragweed," he muttered. "She must have driven through some of it." He backed up a few more steps and then wrote the tag number on the ticket, walked back around to my window, and held the ticket out to me from a few steps away. I quickly signed it and handed it back.

"Slow down, miss," he said, as he almost ran from my car.

I looked to heaven. "Oh, thank you, God." I got back on the freeway and dutifully drove fifty-five the rest of the way. *Allen is going to have a fit, but then so am I. I will never allow them to pack that stuff without putting it in the bags again. I don't care what he says. It's not his ass on the line.*

"Where are we going?" I asked, as Allen drove down I-285.

"It's a surprise." He took the Glenwood exit and began smiling. "Close your eyes; we're almost there."

"What is it?"

"Hold your horses and keep those eyes closed. We're almost there." He stopped the car. "Keep 'em closed."

He got out of the car and came around and opened my door. "Watch your step."

"Can I open them now?"

"Not yet. A little further...now. Open your eyes."

I opened my eyes and my mouth must have dropped open twenty feet.

"A house! You bought me a house?"

"Yep. I can't have my Melissa living in just any old thing."

"Allen, it's beautiful."

"Yeah, well, Sybil will live here too."

"You have got to be kidding me! Of course, I want Sybil to live with me. This place is huge and we've been living in a two-bedroom apartment. Besides there are only two women in the world that I would live in the same house with. Sybil is one and Faith is the other."

"Cool. I just wanted to be sure that it was no big deal."

"No big deal? This is fabulous!"

"You just wait, my pretty. Once you discover that he has shared his bed with the human Sybil, you will not be so happy to share your new abode with her." Amducious laughed as he flitted around the new house.

That night I decided to call my brother Michael.

"Hey, little sister. I haven't heard from you in a while. What's happening?"

"Same old stuff, Michael. How's everything with you?" I asked.

"I wrecked my Corvette and my cover got blown. I ended up in a shootout with a bunch of drug dealers."

"Michael, you have got to be more careful! That's the third Vette that you've wrecked. And shootouts? That's just crazy!" *My brother is getting shot at by the same people I'm in bed with. This is really not good!*

"Yeah, I know, but I got a Guardian Angel, you know."

"I know. I think I have the same one. You know, there has been some strange stuff going on."

"What kind of strange stuff?"

"I don't know exactly, but it's almost as if there's some kind of force that sends weird people to me."

"You know, you make your own destiny, Melissa. Just because weird people show up doesn't mean you have to get involved with them."

"Yeah, I guess you're right. Faith is here and she never seems to be affected by it."

"That's because Faith chooses to do the right thing. We, on the other hand, are different. I like fast cars and fast women and I get shot at for a living. You, you just like danger, so you attract it."

"Yeah, I guess, but somehow I think there's more to it than that. So you be careful."

"I'm always careful, little sister. Always."

We rang off as Sybil arrived home. Sybil had just returned from a trip and was unpacking as I lay across the bed.

"Where did you go this time?"

"LA and the Bonaventure."

"I love that hotel," I sighed.

"Yeah, me too. It was a blast. Allen is such a fool sometimes."

"Allen? Allen was on your trip?"

"Uh, yeah. You didn't know he was with us?"

"So let me get this straight. You, Jim, and Allen went on a trip without me. And when it came time for sex, who was Allen with?"

"Uh, well, you know Allen. Sex is no big deal to these guys."

"Sybil, stop stalling! Who did he sleep with?"

"He has a girl named Sky in LA," she sighed.

"Allen has another girl?"

"Melissa, don't be stupid. I told you none of this is real. He's a jerk. They both are. We do this for one reason, the lifestyle."

"You do it for one reason. I do it for another," I sighed.

"Melissa, you can't really believe that he ever loved you. We've all been having parties since the day he met you."

"What did you say? We? You mean you...and Allen and Jim and that Sky girl? You've been sleeping with Allen?"

"Me and half of LA. Melissa, grow up. This is the big city."

"That sounds familiar. First Candy and Dillon, then the Derek-Jackie-Jessie trio, and now there's Allen, Jim and Sybil." I got up from the bed and went to my room.

This is it! This shit stops here. That bastard will pay. I swear he will pay. He could have had anyone he wanted, but no, he had to have Sybil. Two can play this game, Allen; and now that I know the rules, I hope you're ready.

I never let on to Allen that I knew about his duplicity. I just sat back and waited for my opportunity. Three weeks later it arrived. My next trip was with Jim because Allen was detained in LA. *Detained, my ass; he's with that Sky chick. What's good for the goose is also good for the gander!* After Jim and I checked into the Plaza in New York, we went out to dinner. Jim had realized very early on that I was a one-man woman. As we were seated, instead of sitting across from him, I chose the seat next to him. Sometime during dessert, I put my hand on his thigh

"Does that mean what I think it means?" he asked.

"Yes, sir, that's exactly what it means."

"Hmmm, what's up, Melissa? I'm not stupid; I know you're in love with Allen and you have never been into the dual relationship bit. Why the change of heart now after all this time?"

"Things change, Jim. Do you want me or not?"

"That was never the problem. First you were Derek's girl and then you were Allen's."

"Now I'm Melissa's girl and I sleep with whom I want, when I want; and at the moment I want you. Isn't that how everyone else is playing this game?"

"Yeah, I guess it is. But somehow I have a feeling this particular play is going to mean more than everyone thinks."

"Maybe and maybe not."

"I'm not complaining, regardless of what your motivations are."

"Well, then, shall we?" and I got up from the table.

"Yes, we shall," he responded.

The next week the four of us went out to dinner. *I'm really looking forward to this. Payback is hell.*

"Sybil, now I see why you and Jim rarely come up for air. He absolutely positively knows how to please women. I don't think we left the room in New York once except when we had to deliver the product." *I would have gotten more out of reading a book, but they don't need to know that.*

Allen spit his drink out. Sybil's mouth dropped twenty feet. Jim just shook his head.

"You...you had sex with Jim?" Allen whispered.

"Yeah, so what's the big deal? You guys have been sleeping together from the get go. Not to mention Sky or Moon, and do you have one called Sun too? Hey, none of it means anything, right? We're just mules, so who really gives a shit about who sleeps with whom."

Allen just looked at me. Sybil also looked at me with hurt and disappointment.

"My, my, did I just hurt both your feelings? Surely not? What, you didn't think it would bother you when the shoe was on the other foot, did you? Oh, grow up! This is how it's done in the big city, right? Jim, I guess you were right about this play. Now that the ball is in my court, nobody seems to want to play anymore. What poor sports you guys are." I laughed and sipped my glass of Dom Perignon.

Allen put down his glass and just stared at me. Sybil stared at Jim and Jim just continued to shake his head.

"Bravo, my pretty! That was absolutely magnificent. You are becoming a master at the art of sin." Amducious surveyed the damage that Melissa had caused. He swooped up and down and all around the table with glee. "Revenge is so sweet, is it not, my pretty? Hah, hah, hah!"

We all rode home in silence. After the guys dropped us off, Sybil let me have it with both barrels.

"Melissa, how could you do this? That was just plain ugly."

"Yeah, it was, wasn't it," I laughed.

"I can't believe you slept with Jim and then threw it in our faces," Sybil wailed.

"You have got to be kidding me!" I yelled. "If I recall, this is what you described as living in the big city."

"That was different," she said under her breath.

"How, Sybil? How was it different? I was in love with Allen and you knew it and yet the two of you had sex anyway. Tell me, Sybil. How exactly is that different from me having sex with Jim, huh? Please explain it to me because I must be totally stupid."

"I don't know," she mumbled. "I just don't know. It...it just feels different."

"You mean it hurts! It just plain hurts like a knife being stuck in your heart. Yeah, Sybil, it's different when the heart belongs to you!"

"I'm sorry, Melissa. I'm really sorry."

"Yeah, so am I, but neither of us can undo what has been done. So, now we stick together and we don't let those jackasses come between us, deal?"

"Deal," she replied reluctantly.

Allen usually called me every day even when he was out of town. Three days had passed without a peep. On the eighth day Jim came by.

"Hey, Jim, what's up with Allen? I can't believe he's still brooding. Come on, isn't it time to get back to work and get over it?"

"Melissa, I don't think you realize what you have done."

"What do you mean? What have I done? I didn't do anything different than the rest of you."

"I know that. And you know that, but I guess Allen doesn't know that."

"So he's still mad?"

"Melissa, Allen is gone."

"What do you mean gone?"

"Gone, as in disappeared. He took the last shipment and disappeared. His wife doesn't know where he is. I don't know where he is, and you don't know where he is. He's gone Melissa, and he's not coming back because he can't. He knows he can't come back."

"But...but I didn't really mean anything to him. I was just one of his mules that he had sex with along with the others. Why would he throw away everything you guys have worked for because I had sex with you?"

"I told you that it was going to mean more than you thought, and quite frankly, I think you knew it too. You set out to hurt him and you did. And regardless of how he acted, he loved you too in his own way.

"I beg to differ. I don't know what your definition of love is, but mine doesn't include any of this dual relationship shit."

"I guess you're right about that, but not in his mind. He was totally unprepared for your retaliation and he didn't know how to handle it, so he left."

I just stood there stunned. "So what do we do now?" I sighed.

"I'm not sure. I'll help you as much as I can, but you need to face the fact that you're pretty much on your own. The fact that he took the last shipment puts an undue financial burden on the entire organization. The people I took the shipment from still require payment. It's going to take a real magic trick for me to bail out from under this fiasco."

So revenge is not so sweet after all, I thought. *How could he be so stupid? He's the one that made sex into some kind of game. And as soon as the game was played on him, he couldn't take it. I can't believe this! I have just disrupted an entire drug smuggling organization. That's just ridiculous! The DEA spends millions of dollars trying to dismantle these types of organizations. Little did they know that all they needed was a little sex to do it! You have got to be kidding me! I still cannot believe this. What the hell am I supposed to do now? This is just plain stupid!*

Jim had just dropped me off. He had given me a trip so that I would at least have living expenses for a while. He also acquired an apartment downtown for Sybil. *I need to decide what to do next; this is not going to last long,* I thought as the phone rang.

"Hello."

"Hello, is this Melissa?"

"Yes, this is Melissa. Who am I speaking with?"

"This is Rebecca, Allen's wife."

Oh, my! Why would Allen's wife be calling me?

"I suppose Jim has informed you that Allen has disappeared."

"Yes, as a matter of fact he has," I replied.

"Well, now that he's gone, that property you're living in belongs to me."

"What did you say?"

"You heard me. He's not here to take care of you anymore and I want you out of my house."

She can't be serious?

"Did you hear me, Melissa?"

"I heard you, Rebecca, but I have no intention of leaving my house."

"Is the house in your name, Melissa?"

I was quiet because I knew that it wasn't.

"No, I didn't think so," she replied. "You know how I know it's not in your name? Because I pay the mortgage. I want you out by the end of the week." And just like that she hung up.

Oh, it just keeps getting better and better. I guess that means this little fairy tale is over and my Prince Charming is a toad. If she thinks I'm just going to leave, she's got another thought coming.

On Friday I went out to run my errands. When I arrived home, it was after dark and I fumbled with my keys. *Damn, why isn't this key turning?* I set my bags down on the porch. I tried to put my key in the lock again, but it wouldn't fit. I tried four more times. Suddenly a face appeared at the window. I heard a voice on the other side of my door.

"I told you that you had until the end of the week. Did you really think that I didn't have keys to my husband's property?" she asked in a smug tone. "Now that the shoe is on the other foot, how does it feel, Melissa?"

"Rebecca, I know for a fact that you and Allen are not legally married. You live together. Technically this property does not belong to you. I think I'll see what the authorities have to say about your latest real estate venture. To be honest I don't want anything else to do with Allen and that includes his house. But the stuff in it belongs to me. To be frank I don't think you really want the police sniffing around, so why don't you just open the door and I'll take my belongings."

"I don't think so. You thought you were so smart, leaving your stuff all around his apartment. Leaving your hair in the sink for me to clean up. Well, now I run this show and I'm not giving you nothing."

"Suit yourself," I replied and I stormed back to my car. I rolled my eyes at the darkness. *You have got to be kidding me! It seems like I say that every other day. I knew there would be consequences for Allen flaunting his affair in her face. Too bad I'm the one paying the price.* I drove directly to the police station. *Well, isn't this just hunky dory. A drug dealer's mistress reports the drug dealer's wife to the police while he disappears with the other drug dealer's drugs. This is more interesting than Peyton Place. I think she knows where Allen is because he wouldn't just leave that baby. He's using her to get rid of me because he feels like the jackass that he is. He's a wimp and he's not man enough to do it himself. Running off with his little tail between his legs. I hope the two of you live happily ever after; you deserve one another.*

Michael surveyed the officers at the Dekalb Police Station. This would require just the right individual, one willing to offer assistance even when the outlook was a feeble one. "Detective Franks, you wish to handle the next case," Michael whispered.

I walked into the Dekalb Police Department and asked to see a detective. There were several milling about.

"Jenson, aren't you up next?" asked the desk sergeant.

"I'll help her," volunteered a very tall, well-dressed black man. "Hello, I'm Detective Franks. How may I help you?"

"My name is Melissa Bowan and it's a bit complicated."

"Miss Bowan, most police matters are. Why don't you have a seat and tell me all about it." So I did. I omitted the part about our illegal activities.

"Okay, let me see if I've got this straight. Your guy is also her guy. He lives in a house with her. He buys you a house in his name and then he vanishes. She finds the paperwork and the keys and has the locks changed on your house and now she won't let you in. You no longer want the house anyway; you just want your stuff, and she refuses to let you have that either."

"Exactly," I sighed.

"Okay, what's your phone number? I'm going to call her. If she doesn't know the law, I may be able to bluff her into allowing you to get your things. The bad news is possession is nine tenths of the law and she has possession. That gives her the upper hand. If she refuses and is not intimidated by me, there's not a lot that I can do and you'll end up fighting it out in court. That could take a while."

I gave him her name and the number.

"This is Detective Franks with the Dekalb Police Department. Is this Rebecca?" He paused. "Rebecca, I have just spoken with a Miss Melissa Bowan, who informs me that you are illegally in procession of items belonging to her." He listened for several minutes. "Rebecca, are you aware that it is illegal to withhold a tenant's processions in lieu of nonpayment of rent? If you are not prepared to go to jail, I suggest that you follow your legal recourse. Put the tenant's belongings out of the rental property so that they can be collected. You then have the right to sue her in civil court for the unpaid rent." He paused again. "That is sufficient. Good night." He hung up and smiled.

"She definitely didn't know Georgia law. She had no idea that the truth would have given her the legal upper hand. She made up a story about you being a tenant who did not pay the rent, so she was keeping your things until you did. And that, my dear, is against the law. She'll have your things outside by nine tonight."

He smiled again and so did I.

"Thank you so much, Detective Franks. You went above and beyond the call of duty on that one. You could have just said that there was nothing that you could do."

"There's always something you can do; you just have to put forth the effort," he replied.

"Well, thanks again. Your effort was a godsend."

Had I started to count the number of times God had sent me assistance perhaps I would have realized just how much he loved me. But it wasn't time for me yet. I was still trying my best to get to hell.

Chapter Eight

If Sex Is What They Want, Then Sex Is What They'll Get

After I collected my things, I was able to get an apartment near Buford Highway. It was fairly nice and very quiet and I was alone again. I still saw Sybil, but she spent a lot of time with Jim. She did say that trips were not as frequent as they once were and money didn't flow in an endless stream as it had before the Allen fiasco.

I too was falling on hard times and pondered how I would pay the rent. *I need a miracle. Like the way Allen invited me to the Bahamas. I can't believe he really just got up and vanished. What a wimp and a jerk. I must have been some kind of stupid to think a guy who would send me out to get locked up for twenty-five years could really love me. Not to mention the wife, the kid, and Sybil. What am I supposed to do?* I walked outside to get the mail and also pick up the huge phone book left on my doorstep.

Amducious hovered over the phone book. As it fell to the table, he blew the pages to Escort Services. "Now is the time, my pretty. Here is the miracle that you have requested. Your numerous sins have made you more receptive to that which was once unacceptable to you. The one you loved so betrayed you and bedded your female companion. You must make him pay. You must make them all pay. What better way than this? You must barter that for which they long. You sit on a mine of gold; it will bring you the riches you seek." He laughed as he watched Melissa. "Yes, my pretty, so many sins, so little

time," Amducious said as he blew the pages again.

As the phone book hit the table, it fell open and I read the page and then I read it again. I read page after page of ads for escort services. According to the advertisements, they sent girls to model in lingerie and in the nude for a fee. *Hmmm, that's all these guys have ever wanted is my body. Why not make them pay to see it? I could do that. I always wanted to be a model.* Again the pages fluttered as I flipped through the book, so I chose the escort service at the top of that page and called.

That night I put on an expensive dress suit that Allen had bought for me and went to the address that the girl had given me over the phone. It was an office building on Paces Ferry Road in Marietta.

Very nice, first class offices. That's a start, I thought. I went into the lobby and up to the suite. There was a waiting area with a television. Girls were sitting around eating, drinking, polishing their nails, reading books, and writing notes. Some were talking on telephones stationed around the room. They were all dressed to go out to dinner or a nightclub. The girls ranged in shape, size, and race, but none were fat and most were somewhat attractive. A receptionist handled a multitude of telephones, and there was also an office manager. I was escorted into the manager's office.

"Hi, I'm Patty Jo."

"Hello, my name is Melissa Bowan."

"So, Melissa, are you a police officer?"

"What?"

"Are you a police officer?"

"No, I'm not a police officer! What kind of crazy question is that?"

"Are you with the IRS?"

"IRS? These are awfully strange questions for a job interview. I'm not a cop. Far from it and I'm not with the IRS. And if it helps, I'm not with any government or law enforcement agency, okay?"

"Okay," Patty Jo replied. "That's what I needed to hear. Huh, Melissa, do you really know what we do here?"

"You send girls to guys and the girls pose in lingerie or in the nude for one hour, right?"

"And you're okay with that?"

"Yeah, I'm okay with it. Why all the weird police questions?"

"Because they want to shut us down. They send in undercovers to try to catch us in an unlawful act, which we don't do, by the way."

"If I were an undercover, why would I tell you that I was just because you asked?"

"If we ask, they have to tell us or it is considered entrapment."

"What sort of unlawful act do they think that you do that you don't do?"

"Sex for hire, prostitution. All of the girls are required to sign a statement indicating that they will not engage in any unlawful acts. Once the girls get in the room with the guy, we really have no way of knowing what they do or don't do," she said with a wink. "We charge a hundred dollars an hour. Half goes to the house and half goes to you. The guy also knows that he has to tip you. That amount is up to you."

Hmmm, fifty dollars an hour to stand around in my underwear. I can do that. The nude part might be a little embarrassing, but what the hell.

"The maximum time is three hours. After three hours there's no house charge and you can work on your own for tips. We take all major credit cards, and if they want, they can put your tip on the card also. We pay you once a week. When you take cash, you keep yours and turn in that which is owed to the house at the end of the night. You can work as many days or nights as you want. We're here from eleven in the morning until three in the morning. We take out taxes and we pay for medical, dental, and pharmacy insurance for the girls. You don't want trouble with the IRS, so I suggest you pay taxes on your cash portion. We have the IRS forms for that.

"We time you when you leave and we know what time you should arrive. You call immediately when you walk in the room. You also call when you leave. If you don't like the guy or you don't feel comfortable, you let us know and then you leave. When you enter a hotel room, you always check ID and their plane ticket while we're on the phone. If it's a residence, then we check the reverse phone directory to ensure that the address corresponds to the phone number. You always check ID there also. We take every precaution to ensure the safety of our girls.

"You'll make a fortune! You're gorgeous! You look like you stepped out of a fashion magazine in that suit. I really thought you were vice or IRS at the least. You'll breeze through the Plaza and all of the upscale hotels without a hitch. You will make a fortune," she repeated in excitement. "So, do you want to start tonight?"

"Sure."

"You are sure that you understand what you have to do?" she asked, in a voice that I read immediately.

"Yes, my pretty! You must sell your precious body. It is not really precious to any of those who have used you for their own gratification. You must make them pay. If they are determined to use you, make them pay for that which is so important to them. Why should you not profit from this commodity they seek. You can do it. You have no gold and silver; do it," Amducious whispered.

"Do not do this terrible thing," Michael said as he swung his sword at Amducious. Amducious dived just in time and scurried off into the clouds. Michael watched and was saddened by the choice that he knew Melissa was about to make of her own free will. He knew that he was not allowed to interfere with the human capacity to choose their own destinies, but he would protect her to the death when those choices brought her harm, which they inevitably would.

Oh, my goodness! She means that the girls do have sex for their tips. They're call girls, all of them! I thought about all the times I had been used for sex. I thought about Dillon, Derek, Jim, and Allen. I thought about the dual relationships. *No one has ever really loved me except maybe Joe, and his kind of love was to beat the shit out of me. I think it's time they paid for the only thing that they ever wanted anyway. Besides if I don't get anything out of it and it's the only thing they want, then why shouldn't I make them pay?*

"Melissa, do you really understand?"

"Yes, Patty Jo. I understand fully," I replied.

"Great. You'll need a stage name, so start thinking of what you want to be called. We never use real names."

"I'll use Michelle."

"Michelle it is. I like it."

"Be sure that the ones who choose her are to her liking. If she dislikes them, she will not continue. We must also send those who barter pharmaceuticals to her. Addiction runs in her bloodline. Once she becomes consumed by the pharmaceuticals, she will not be able to turn back. Do not fail me or it

will be your head," Amducious ordered his underlings.

That night I went on my first call. I was terrified but determined to go through with it. To my surprise he was drop dead gorgeous and a real gentleman. I followed all of the procedures and called the office. He paid by American Express. His name was Evan and I asked for a hundred dollars per hour for two hours. With my half of the agency fee that meant a hundred and fifty dollars an hour for me. We spent most of the evening talking and drinking a very good bottle of wine. He was delightful and charming and treated me like a queen. I couldn't believe it. When I asked for a hundred dollar tip per hour, he just said of course.

On the next call, I asked for two hundred. He too agreed. Like Evan he was a perfect gentleman and extremely handsome. We went to a fabulous restaurant and he too was everything you could ask for in a date. I couldn't believe it! Two hundred and fifty dollars an hour to have dinner with a gorgeous man! You have got to be kidding me!

"I told you that you would make a fortune, didn't I," Patty Jo said as I pondered the fate of the world.

"Yeah, you did. I just can't believe how many gorgeous guys call escort services."

"So, you really didn't know what was going on when you first came to me, did you?"

"No, I didn't," I admitted.

"You certainly are a fast study. These guys have money but don't really have time to chase women, so they call us."

Fast study, that's me. On the other hand, I'm not sure what I'll do when I don't like the guy.

"I know it's late, but I just got a party call and he's a regular. You'll love him and he will definitely love you," Patti Jo said with excitement.

"What's a party call?"

"Coke and cash," she said with a smile.

"Cool. Sounds like my kind of party."

The guy's name was Jake and he was at the Terrace Gardens on Lenox Road. When I went in, I saw cocaine, lots of it, on the table.

"Want a line?" he asked even before I had time to call in.

"Sure."

Jake was not just gorgeous; he was movie star gorgeous! He handed me a rolled hundred dollar bill and poured me a glass of Dom Perignon. I took the rolled bill and snorted the lines of cocaine spread out on the hand mirror. I then sipped my champagne. *Now this is the life.* He pulled a suitcase out from under the bed and opened it. It was full of money, wrapped with bands that said one thousand dollars! The entire suitcase was full of them. There had to be at least two hundred thousand dollars in the suitcase!

"You are beautiful, absolutely stunning. When you call Patty Jo, tell her you're out of the game for the rest of the night. As a matter of fact, for the next three days while I'm here."

He pulled five stacks of bills out of the suitcase and handed them to me. I just sat there and looked at them. *Five thousand dollars! Has this guy lost his ever-loving mind? Five thousand dollars and he looks better than Cary Grant! Is he kidding?*

"Is that enough?"

Before I could respond, he took out another bundle and handed it to me also.

"That is quite sufficient, thank you," I managed to whisper.

"Oh, I love it! A beautiful woman with class and smarts. Tell Patty Jo from now on I only see you."

"With pleasure, "I replied as I dialed the number.

For the next three days Jake and I rode around Atlanta in his Porch, snorting coke, drinking Dom Perignon, eating at the best restaurants, and shopping. I was having the best time of my life.

Amducious flitted around Melissa's head. "Are we having fun, my pretty?" **Fornication, prostitution, and adultery are just the beginning for you, my dear. The Mighty Warrior Michael cannot show his face as I, Amducious the Destroyer, have defeated him. His precious human has fallen to depths of depravity and is now on the brink of destruction. I have been summoned to receive my crown and soon, my pretty, you will allow me to become a general. "So many sins, so little time, ha, ha, ha," he laughed, as he dipped in and out of the clouds.**

I worked about three hours a night a few nights a week except when it was a party call. Those usually lasted several days and netted thousands of dollars. It was amazing how many drug dealers lived in or visited Atlanta. I continued on this path of destruction for more than two years. Now instead of snorting cocaine to make the job easier, I was doing the job so that I could snort cocaine. I was literally in hell right here on earth.

As Michael watched over Melissa, he lamented that Amducious no longer needed to entice her. She was her own worst enemy. As she went in and out of hotel rooms, it was his task to prevent her from encountering a human male who would inflict harm upon her. When she encountered those who carried the plague known as AIDS, Michael instilled fear in her, and each time she retreated without performing the task for which she had been summoned. Preventing an encounter with this insidious plague was an arduous task.

"My darling child, how far must you fall before you reach out to the King? He is within your grasp. He waits and He weeps for you. He knocks at your door, if only you would answer and let him in." Michael watched as Melissa walked into The Peachtree Plaza Hotel. Michael's wings drooped, and as he cried for her, his tears reached the crowd below. They looked up and thought how odd for it to rain only in this one spot.

I now had an abundance of money but not much common sense. My motto was "Spend it now for tomorrow you may die." And because I was certain that I would end up in hell, I needed to be sure that each and every act was worthy of the fiery pit. *This apartment stinks; I need a place worthy of the amount of money that I make.* I looked in the newspaper and there it was–Moonraker Apartments on Delk Road. The apartment featured a sunken living room with a fireplace, marble counter tops, and a Jacuzzi tub. There were tropical trees throughout the complex along with streams and brooks. *This is a fitting place for James Bond, as the name implies.* I moved in the next week. I also bought a new Cougar right off the showroom floor.

It seemed as if party calls were more and more frequent, but instead of waiting for a party call to do cocaine, I found a dealer and started buying once a week.

Amducious was ecstatic; the human Melissa had taken to buying more and more pharmaceuticals without enticement or prompting. "Woe to you, my pretty; you will be with the prince

very soon. That which you now desire will consume you even until death. You need it, you need it, you need it. More, more, more, my pretty."

"You better give me a quarter this time, Jazz. I get tired of running over here every other day."

"No problem, Melissa." He weighed out a quarter of an ounce of cocaine. "Anything for my best customer."

"Uh, you better give me twenty ludes too."

"Sure, no problem. Hey, you know there are other ways of paying than money."

"Yeah, I'm aware of that, but I don't think so."

"Well, you can't blame a guy for trying."

"No, I don't blame you at all, Jazz. I know you guys don't have any control over what's in your pants," I said as I paid him three hundred and fifty dollars. "I'll see you next week," I said as I slammed the door.

"Damn, she's fine" I heard him say.

I swear the only thing men think about is sex. Is there anyone in this stupid world that thinks about anything else? Lord, what a bunch of jerks your creation turned out to be. I'm surprised you don't just wipe us all off the face of the earth.

"I got a call for three girls. Who's up?" asked Patty Jo when I returned to the office.

"I'm up and so is Jan and Beth," I replied.

"Okay, here's the deal! They want three girls to fly on a Lear jet to Miami and back. It's a party call in the air, baby!"

"That's what I'm talking about!" I laughed.

"I already increased the regular fee, so you will all get a five hundred dollar modeling fee each for five hours plus your tip."

"Sounds good to me! You guys game?"

"We're game," the others replied.

When we got to the airport, we were directed to an exclusive area where the rich were escorted out to their Lears.

"This is beyond cool!" Jan cried.

"Hey, I must agree with you on that!" I yelled over the noise.

We were led onto the plane and introduced to Marty.

"So, girls, what's your poison?"

"Coke and cash, of course," I replied.

"Then coke and cash it is!" Marty yelled. "Let's get this party started!"

Upon our return, I turned and looked at Beth. "In the future, remind me never to agree to fly in a Lear jet with a bunch of drunken fools for any amount of money."

"Don't worry; I don't think you will need a reminder. But if you even think about it, I'll slap you first."

"Thanks. I'm counting on you."

The next night Beth and I went out again on a double. When we arrived, the guy appeared to be some kind of Arab sheik. He too had more money than he knew what to do with.

Amducious and Furfur had become accustomed to roaming to and fro without interference from Michael. *This is excellent; this one carries the plague and has infected every female he has encountered.* **"Come to me, my pretty; it is time. Michael has abandoned you, for you are hopeless," Amducious whispered.**

"Yes, she is hopeless, hope…" Whoosh! Before Furfur could finish his sentence, Michael severed his head from his body and Amducious was engaged in battle with one of the Heavenly Host.

As Amducious fought for his life, Michael flew to prevent Melissa from becoming intimate with the one who carried the plague, which would ultimately cause his demise. It would be a little more difficult to put fear in the other one. Melissa had become accustomed to listening to Michael when he spoke, even though she referred to him as her subconscious. Regardless of where she thought the voice came from, she always heeded it and acted accordingly. Many humans ignored the warnings given by the Heavenly Host and suffered dire consequences as a result.

"Melissa, Beth, do not stay with this one. Leave here at once."

"Beth, I got a bad vibe about this one. Let's go," I whispered.

"Melissa, get a grip. There are bodyguards everywhere and this is the Plaza for heaven's sake. What could possibly be wrong with him?"

"Okay, I guess you're right, but if he does anything creepy, I'm leaving you.

Beth was not one to listen, for she did not believe in that which she could not see. Michael lamented for her. He knew that he would not be able convince her not to touch the sheik.

Michael gravitated to the one called Ahmad. "The one called Michelle is considered to be of an inferior race in your country," whispered Michael. "What would be said if one of your bodyguards were to see one of her race lay hands upon you? One of your station and royalty must not allow her to touch you. Pay her to pose and gaze upon her."

Amducious dived through the clouds and flew at full speed as Pheus and the other angels chased him. *That was close,* he thought. Each time he manages to save her. We shall see, oh golden one! You cannot be there to save her on every occasion. We shall see what the future holds for my pretty and those she cares about.

Sheik Ahmad had a very thick accent and did not speak very good English. "You are Bith and you are Michill, is this not correct?"

"That is correct," I replied, as he mispronounced our names.

"Very well. You Bith shall come here and you Michill shall pose for me thare."

I looked at Beth and rolled my eyes. "Do you mean you want me to pose on the sofa?"

"Yis, this is correct; you do not touch." He pointed to Beth. "You may touch me."

I didn't know whether to be relieved or insulted, but I settled for relieved because I had no intention of getting anywhere near him. He gave me the creeps.

"No problem." I went and sat on the sofa. *Three hundred dollars for sitting on the sofa; sounds like a deal to me.* One thing was for sure; he could afford it. His bodyguards said he had taken over the entire floor for his entourage. As we were leaving, he pulled out another hundred dollar bill and handed it to me.

"As a token of my apologies. I do not wish to offend you," he replied.

I just smiled as I took the money.

"What the hell was that about?" I asked Beth as we left.

"He said that people of your race are considered inferior and therefore, as royalty, it would be inappropriate for him to be touched by one of your class."

"I'm so broken up about it. It worked out for the best because I wasn't going to let him touch me and I was five seconds from leaving you. If he had wanted me anywhere near him, I would have left you in a heartbeat. Didn't you feel that vibe when we walked in?"

"Melissa, you get creeped out about nothing. Nothing weird happened. I don't believe in that vibe crap. If I can't see it or touch it, then it doesn't exist. Besides you're too picky. I heard that you turn down a lot of calls because of that."

"You heard right. If I get a bad feeling, I'm outta there and I don't care if you guys think it's stupid or not. I can't see or touch God, but I know he exists."

"You can believe in that if you want to. The only gods I know are the ones I just put in my pocket."

Now, you girl, are scary and now that I know you don't believe in God, I'm making it my business to get as far from you as possible. I'm glad we came in separate cars because now you're creeping me out too. I may end up in hell, but it certainly won't be because I don't believe in God, I thought.

"Uh, I'll see ya. Bye," I said as I dashed to my car. *Whew, I'm glad I got away from her before she was struck by lightning.*

The next day I went to see Sybil. She was worried because she had not seen much of Jim and her rent was due.

"You can always come and work for the escort service," I said. This was the first time we had discussed my work.

"What! You, Miss Goody-Two-Shoes!"

"Yeah, well, somehow after Derek and Allen and Jim, the goody-two-shoes shit seemed moot. By the end of the week, you can blow this popsicle stand and move into Moonraker with me."

When Patty Jo saw Sybil, I thought she would have a coronary. "What are the odds of me having two girls with your looks? This is fabulous! You will make a fortune!" she told Sybil.

What you mean is you will make a fortune. But I'm not complaining; this is a mutually gratifying relationship, I thought.

Sybil chose the name Sandy and started working that night. And just as predicted, she was one of Patty Jo's stars. By the end of the week, she had moved into Moonraker.

Raphael and his squad hovered over Sybil. His instructions

were to ensure her safety. *This will require a multitude of the Heavenly Host. If we are to protect her from the scourge of that insidious plague, it will require our best maneuvers. In addition many of the male humans that she encounters wish to do harm to her. Michael is depending on me; I must not fail, for to fail him is to fail our King also.*

My next call was just as interesting. I called the guy, as was the procedure. I knew it would be a party call, even though he did not reveal it on the phone. When I arrived, sure enough, there appeared to be several kilos of cocaine in his hotel room. He also had several bottles of Dom Perignon, as was the custom among dealers. He too had a suitcase filled with cash and presented me with five thousand dollars. His name ironically was Dillon. *How can there be so many drug dealers running in and out of these hotels without the authorities knowing about them,* I wondered. *And these guys are absolutely stupid when it comes to money. I guess their motto is the same as mine; easy come, and easy go.*

"Hey, Michelle, let's go out and party," he yelled. Dillon called downstairs and ordered a limo. We spent the next few evenings bar hopping. He tipped one piano player a hundred dollars to play a song for me. A hundred dollars for a song! Again we were too high for sex, so we spent the entire time getting high and partying.

The next morning when I arrived home, I swallowed two Quaaludes so that I could sleep. When we ran out of Quaaludes, it was a nightmare because it was impossible to sleep and we would go into withdrawal, continuing to crave cocaine for hours. It was like riding a roller coaster–cocaine to go up and Quaaludes to come down.

Sybil and I had become highly requested. We were the agency's stars. That Thursday I took the night off and so did Sybil. *Is that ringing I hear?* I fought through a fog of sleep. *Who the hell is calling me?*

"Hello."

"Michelle? This is Patty Jo."

"Ah, come on, Patty Jo; I'm off tonight."

"I know, Michelle, but I got these two guys at the Peachtree Plaza and they don't like any of the girls I've sent them. I've already sent them six girls and they turned all of them away. Do you think you can talk Sandy into getting up too?"

"Yeah, all right, but this better be good."

"I promise, Michelle. They're two big shots from LA and they said that if I found the right girls they would triple the fee."

"Okay. Give me the info," I sighed.

I called the Plaza and asked for the room number Patty Jo had given me.

"Hello, this is Michelle; I'm from the escort service that you called."

"Hello, Michelle. I'm Brian. I've had three girls come over and so has my business partner. That's a total of six and none were even close to what we're looking for."

"What exactly are you looking for?"

"I'm looking for a ten, but I'd even settle for a seven at this rate."

"Well, in that case you're in luck. I'm a ten and so is Sandy."

"Yeah, right," he retorted. "So far tonight I haven't even seen a five."

"Trust me. You will be happy."

"Okay, Michelle. I'll give you a hundred dollars for every digit. That means if I think you're a seven, I'll give you seven hundred dollars. If you're a ten, I'll give you a thousand on top of the agency fee. And because I have a meeting tomorrow, you won't be here more than twenty minutes, deal?"

"Does that also apply to Sandy?"

"Of course."

"Then it's a deal. We'll see you in less than an hour."

When we arrived, we discovered that they had the penthouse suite.

"I didn't even know The Plaza had a penthouse suite," exclaimed Sybil.

"Neither did I."

We knocked and Brian opened the door.

"Hi, Brian. I'm Michelle and this is Sandy."

Brian looked at me and then Sandy. He then looked at his business associate. Without another word, he opened his wallet and extracted ten one hundred dollar bills and handed them to me along with the agency fee, which Patty Jo had tripled. His partner also opened his wallet and extracted the same for Sandy.

After I counted the money, I laughed. "I take it that means we're tens."

"You two are absolutely tens."

Exactly fifteen minutes later he said, "I don't mean to rush you, but I've got a meeting and so does Doug. You gals were great."

"No problem. Next time you're here, you know who to ask for."

"That I do, Michelle."

"This is the life, yes, my pretty. Pharmaceuticals and gold. You are so beautiful, yes. Finally your beauty is to your benefit. Vanity is Master's favorite sin because humans never see it coming. So many sins, so little time, and so many humans to perform them."

Sybil and I had been showered with so much money and attention that I imagine it was equivalent to what movie stars become accustomed to. No wonder they were all so screwed up in the head.

Even though I made a ridiculous amount of money, I began to spend the majority of it on cocaine. Sybil too had fallen into this trap.

It was a Tuesday night and Sybil and I were both working when Patty Jo received a call for two girls.

"Two girls for one guy?" I asked.

"Yeah, some of these guys think they are Superman," she chuckled. His name was Lenny and he fell head over heels for Sybil. Lenny had a thing for girls and hot tubs. He had installed a hot tub in the center of his recreation room. He also had a thing for freebasing and Quaaludes. Freebasing consisted of cooking the cocaine down to its purest crystallized form and then smoking it in a pipe. Sybil and I spent four days freebasing in the hot tub with Lenny. And freebasing became our method of choice; we did it every chance we got.

Lenny began to call Sybil outside of the agency, which was against the rules. She was so enthralled with him and the freebase that she wasn't putting in many agency hours. Four months after our first encounter with Lenny, he also fell for one of the other girls named Mandy. Mandy and Sybil would spend hours with Lenny. One Thursday Lenny and Mandy were freebasing and wanted Sybil to join them as usual.

Abigor flitted around Lenny's head. "They are coming for you. Get the guns; you must protect yourself. They want to kill

you," he whispered to Lenny. *Now that the male human is primed, I must get the human Sybil to join the festivities.* Abigor flew into Sybil's apartment and hovered near her head. *This one needs no prompting; her addiction to the pharmaceuticals will ensure her arrival just in time for the festivities.* Abigor flew off.

Raphael had watched Abigor from a distance. As soon as he left, Raphael dove down into Sybil's intestinal tract and deposited a small microbe. Sybil immediately felt nauseated. Within three minutes she was moaning. *This minor distress is necessary, for if the human Sybil were to reach her destination, it would surely cause her demise.*

"Ah, shit," Sybil moaned. "I'm coming down with something. I think I'm dying. I was supposed to go party with Lenny and Mandy and instead I'm puking my guts out."

"I'll call them and let them know you're not coming, and then I'll go and get you some ginger ale," I sighed. Sybil's intestinal bug lasted three days. That Monday we received shocking news. Sybil and I had just gotten home as the phone was ringing.

"Melissa will you get that," Sybil yelled.

"Hello!"

"Hey, Michelle, is that you?" Patty Jo asked.

"Yeah, what's up Patty Jo?"

"Is Sandy there?"

"Yeah, do you want to talk to her?"

"No, no...uh, are you sitting down?" she asked.

"Patty Jo, what's going on?"

"It's Lenny and Mandy."

"What about Lenny and Mandy?"

"Lenny's dead and Mandy's in the hospital with half her head blown off!"

"What! Patty Jo what happened to them?"

"Lenny shot Mandy in the head and then he killed himself. She's lucky to be alive, but she'll never be the same again. Personally I think I'd rather be dead."

"Patty Jo, you have got to be kidding me!"

"No, Michelle, and I don't want to be the one to tell Sandy, so I'm leaving it up to you."

"Yeah, okay, but you owe me and I won't let you forget it."

"Forget what?" Sybil asked.

"You must have a Guardian Angel just like me. Sybil, you better sit down."

"Why? Melissa, stop that shit. You're scaring me."

"Lenny's dead, Sybil, and you would be too, if you hadn't been sick."

"What are you talking about?" she screamed.

"You know how paranoid he was. He had two Dobermans and two guns because he thought people were after him. He lost it and shot Mandy in the head and then he killed himself."

"Oh, my God! Mandy? Is she all right?"

"No, not really. She's alive, but she won't ever be the same."

"It's just like with Jerry. I was supposed to be in the car with him, but I changed my mind at the very last minute and that truck obliterated his face."

"Yeah, I know," I sighed. Jerry had been one of her boyfriends in college. He had been killed on the way home from college. Sybil had planned to come home with him but had changed her mind at the last minute. Jerry had fallen asleep and had run his car into the back of a lumber truck. He had been killed instantly as the lumber impaled him.

After Lenny died, Sybil and I continued on our path of destruction: freebasing, unprotected sex, and meeting strangers in hotel rooms. It had been almost two years and we had made hundreds of thousands of dollars without a dime to show for it. Easy come, easy go.

Sybil and I had acquired a new regular. His name was Stevie and, strangely enough, this guy was a master chef who loved to cook for us. We spent most of our time sampling his exquisite gourmet dishes. He was also a wine connoisseur and, as a result, we had frequent wine tasting sessions. Go figure; two hundred dollars an hour to eat gourmet dinners and taste fine wine. He was such a gentleman that he also insisted on serving us and we were not allowed to assist with anything. He would then bring out the coke and we'd all get blasted.

After I left Stevie's, I realized that I needed to get gas, so I started looking for a station.

Amducious swooped down into Mark's car. "You want to get fuel now. Stop over there; they have a good price." *You are the*

**one that is needed to lead her to her demise. Master will be pleased
with this new development.**

I saw a station and pulled in. As I stood waiting for the tank to fill,
I heard someone say, "Hello, love." I turned and there stood the
most gorgeous guy next to a Cadillac Seville.

"Hi. My name is Mark."

"Hello, Mark. I'm Melissa."

"Melissa, you are the most beautiful woman I have ever laid eyes
on."

"Hmmm, I'm sure you say that to all the girls you meet," I mused.

"I assure you that I do not," he replied indignantly. "And I can
prove it."

"Oh, really, and how do you propose to do that?"

"In order for you to find out, you must have dinner with me
tonight."

Smooth. Very smooth indeed. That night I went out with Mark
and the next and the next. Soon we were inseparable and went out
each night that I was not working. I did not dare tell him what I did
for a living. We had been dating for six months and I thought he
thought there was something wrong with me. Frankly I was surprised
and shocked that a guy would actually date a girl for six months
without attempting to have sex with her. After dinner that night we
went back to my apartment and were snorting a few lines of coke.

"Melissa Bowan, do you ever plan to have sex with me?"

I almost choked on my cigarette smoke. "Why don't you just
come out and ask me?" I retorted.

"I just did."

"Mark, it's sort of complicated."

"Guy meets girl, guy dates girl for six months, guy is crazy about
girl, and guy wants to make love to girl. What's so complicated about
that, unless girl does not like guy?"

"I like you a lot, Mark."

"Well, then, what? Are you gay?"

I laughed so hard that I almost fell out of the chair. "No, Mark, I'm
not gay. I wish it was that simple."

"Melissa, just spit it out. It can't be that bad!"

"I'm a call girl and I only sleep with guys for money," I whispered.

"What did you say?"

"You heard me. I'm a call girl."

"Oh, my, that is complicated."

"Here. Have a line of coke." I couldn't think of anything else to say. He leaned over and snorted the coke off of the mirror.

"I don't care," he said, almost in a whisper.

"You're kidding, right?"

"No, Melissa, I'm not kidding. I care about you, and as long as you don't think of me in that way, I don't care what you do with them."

You have got to be kidding me! Where do I find these people? Has the whole world gone mad? Don't people have normal relationships anymore? Funny how I keep saying that, but I just keep on inviting them into my life. Stupid! So, needless to say, we stayed together. Not only that, we moved in together.

"Kill your seed, kill your seed, my pretty," Amducious screeched as he dipped up and down and around Melissa and Mark's apartment.

"This cannot be happening to me again," I wailed.

"What is it? What's wrong?"

"I'm pregnant! Damn! Damn! Damn! How can I be pregnant and on the pill?"

"Maybe it's a mistake," he said in bewilderment.

I just rolled my eyes at him. "I've got to have an abortion; I can't have this baby."

"Why not?"

"Are you crazy? I have sex with guys for a living. It's not like the baby's yours?"

"How do you know it's not mine?"

"I don't and I have no intention of finding out," I snapped.

"The time is again at hand," Michael whispered.

On Monday Mark took me to the clinic. "Are you sure you want to do this?"

"I'm quite sure." *This guy is a nut. This baby could be anybody's. How could he even consider keeping it?*

Michael watched and waited just as he did the first time. "You will be with your brother soon, little one. Fear not, for I am with you." He then whisked him away just before the scalpel touched his tiny body.

That weekend we were ready to party again. The baby was not given a second thought once its poor broken body had been discarded. Sybil had invited her ex-husband, Greg, to Atlanta, and he too was okay with our occupation. I had always thought Greg was a creep, but Sybil never seemed to see him that way. *What kind of men date call girls? Ones that don't give a damn about you, stupid!*

Mark and I had invited them over. We had cocaine, freebase, and Dom Perignon. I stood in front of the refrigerator and then slid down to the floor after I hit the freebase pipe. This was my signal that it was a good hit and I had reached the perfect high.

After I got up, I went into the bathroom, not knowing Mark was in there. I couldn't believe my eyes! He had a syringe sticking in his arm and Sybil was assisting him with an injection of cocaine! Greg walked up behind me, "You guys are busted!"

Amducious dived around the room with glee, keeping a sharp eye out for Michael. "Yes, my pretty, he has been hiding his nasty little habit from you. He allows you to bed the others to support his addiction to pharmaceuticals. Ha, ha, ha, you should try it. The euphoria that you seek is here. You want it, you need it; try it, my pretty."

"You have got to be kidding me! You guys have been doing this all along behind my back?"

"Michelle, I mean Melissa, chill out! You do not want to do this!" Sybil replied solemnly.

"Yeah, that's what you said about the Bahamas. That high looks wicked and I want to try it," I exclaimed. I was right! The high was more wicked than I could possibly have imagined. From then on I preferred the syringe to any other method of doing cocaine.

The syringe was so intense that it took over my life. On one occasion I decided to take a computer course. While I was in the class, I needed a hit so I left the room and spent the next two hours in the bathroom getting high. It was another one of those miracles that I was not caught. On another occasion, on a drive to Texas to see my mom, I spent two hours in a gas station bathroom near the highway getting high. Cocaine was the center of my life.

Michael watched and again his wings drooped, for he knew that Melissa was so very close to her death. *Only the King can save you now. He is the only one that can send you back once you*

have crossed over to the other side. And soon, my precious child, you will be the cause of your own demise.

For some strange reason, Mark became jealous of my work. We were fighting over one of my regulars. It seemed that he was okay if the guy was a stranger, but not okay if I knew the guy. What the hell difference did it make?

"You know what? I'm tired of this shit and I'm leaving. You can keep all of this stuff. I'm taking my clothes and my car and I'm getting the hell out of this freak show."

I slammed out of the apartment and went to Sybil's for a while, but I couldn't stand watching Greg and her with that lovey-dovey shit. I knew full well he didn't give a shit about her. He was just using her to get his fix, just like Mark. I decided to get an apartment of my own and moved to a complex near Lenox Mall.

I must ensure that she has a sufficient amount of pharmaceuticals to cause her demise. Ah, yes, this one will do nicely. **Amducious flitted around Ben's head. "You need, you want a pretty female. Call this one; they have the right girl for you."**

My next call was another cocaine dealer, Ben. He wasn't just any dealer; he was at the very top of the food chain. When I walked into his hotel room, I knew he didn't have just a kilo. He had access to a boatload! I stayed with him a week and he paid me eight thousand dollars. He never ran out of money or cocaine.

Ben also liked the syringe, but he couldn't do it himself. He had to have someone do it for him so I did. Whenever he took a hit with the syringe, he would get so high that he imagined he was having a heart attack and he would begin to pace around the room. He was a lot like Sybil in this regard.

I started to see Ben outside of the agency. He would come over and we would get high for a week at a time. I even shared with him my real name. His dramatics sometimes drove me crazy, but I liked to get high with him anyway because he had the best stuff and an endless supply of cocaine and cash.

Ben and I had gotten in the habit of doing cocaine with Sybil and Greg. We would snort it, freebase it, and inject it. We did everything but eat the stuff. Well, on second thought, we did that too sometimes.

Sybil and Ben were almost identical with their dramatics. Pacing and panting and taking their pulse. Greg and I had banished them to another room, and he and I were both using a syringe in the dining room. I had bought a box of five hundred syringes at the drugstore. I had told the idiot pharmacist that my dad was a diabetic, which was true. I had also told him we were going on a cruise for three months. Greg and I filled the syringes with cocaine and then injected ourselves repeatedly. We had already spent the entire weekend doing this and we were just getting started.

Amducious buzzed around with excitement. "You need more, more, more."

Greg was 6' 4" and two hundred pounds. Yet whatever amount of cocaine he put in his syringe, I also put in mine. This time he filled the syringe to its capacity and plunged the entire amount into his arm. Not be outdone, I did also. The last thing I heard him say was, "Is it good?"

"It's good," I replied, right before my heart stopped beating. I then fell out of the chair onto the floor.

Amducious grabbed onto Melissa. "I have you now, my pretty; you shall meet my master this day!" Satan himself came to meet Amducious. "I have her, Master!" Amducious cried. "She belongs to you, Master! I have her!" he repeated with glee. As he passed Melissa to Satan, Jesus stood up from his throne and struck Amducious with a bolt of lightning that caused him to evaporate in an instant. He then whisked Melissa from Satan's grasp and gave her to Michael.

"No!" Satan screamed. "She belongs to me! She has crossed to the other side! You have no right to her! She is mine!"

Whoosh! Michael cradled Melissa and whisked her back from whence she came.

"You have no right!" Satan wailed again.

"I have every right," Jesus calmly replied. "I alone hold the power over life and death. That which I have created belongs to me. All that is in the heavens and all that is on the earth belong to me. Where were you when I hung the moon and the stars? Do you hold the seas in their proper places? Can you make the sun cease to shine? You cannot, for you can do no more than that which I allow. Be gone, Satan, for your time is short."

"Melissa! Melissa!" Greg fell down on his knees and began to shake me. Sybil ran from the other room to see what the yelling was about.

"Oh, my God! Melissa! Is she dead? Is she dead?" she screeched.

Ben paced back and forth, "She's dead! She's dead!" he sobbed.

Michael hovered over Melissa's body, giving Greg instructions on how to bring her back. "Hit her with your fist. There. Her tongue. Put a spoon on her tongue; she must not be allowed to swallow it. Call for assistance. Breathe into her mouth: one, two, and three. Keep breathing; now push on her chest: one, two, three. Cold water. You need cold water."

Greg, who was an atheist, was the only one with the presence of mind to render aid. He felt for a pulse.

"Her heart has stopped! She's not breathing!" he yelled. He then hit me in the chest with his fist. He pulled my mouth open. "She's swallowing her tongue. Give me a spoon!" he yelled. "Sybil, dial 911 now! Ben, you get outta here. Go out the back." He then began to breathe into my mouth and push air into my chest. "Turn on the shower!" he shouted. "I need cold water now. Move, Sybil! Now!" Greg pushed and breathed and beat on my chest while holding me under cold water. "Sybil, get all the drugs and throw them into the woods. Now! Breathe, dammit!" He pushed and breathed some more. "Come on, Melissa. Don't do this to me," he yelled.

"She's dead! She's dead!" Sybil wailed.

"Sybil! I said throw out the drugs and the syringes! Put them in a bag and throw them into the woods!" He pushed and breathed as he yelled instructions.

Fifteen minutes later someone began pounding on the front door.

"They're here; the ambulance is here!" Sybil cried.

"Sybil, dispose of the container!" Raphael cried. "Sybil, the container!" But Sybil was too distraught and too high to listen to the voice.

Sybil ran to the door, but she forgot to throw the bag into the woods. She held it in her hand as she opened the door. Instead of an ambulance, the police were first to arrive.

"What's going on here, miss?"

"She's dead! She's dead! Oh, my God, she's dead!"

One officer ran to the bathroom to see who was dead and one

said, "What's in the bag, miss?"

Sybil then realized that she was holding the bag. The officer took the bag from her hand and opened it. He then placed her under arrest. The paramedics arrived and took over the CPR from Greg. The second officer placed him under arrest.

Once in the ambulance, the paramedic realized that Melissa still had no pulse. "That guy Greg gave her CPR for twenty minutes and we've been at it five. She's gone; let's call it," he sighed.

"No! You must stimulate her heart now!" Michael instructed.

"No!" his partner said. "Let's try and shock her." He grabbed the paddles. "Clear!" And then he shocked me. "Clear!" He shocked me again. "Ouch!" yelled the paramedic as he dropped the paddles. "I just caught a back current!"

Michael hovered over Melissa. As the paramedic shocked her the second time, he breached the earthly plane and delivered her back into her body. His countenance dimmed as he resurfaced to the Heavenly Realm and thousands of sparks flew about the sky. The people on the earth marveled at the multitude of shooting stars. He shook his wings and raised them to their full height to regain his composure. As he did so, his brilliance returned. Crossing to the other side took a tremendous amount of effort and concentration. He was happy to have completed the task. Because he had been occupied caring for Melissa, he had not been able to assist Raphael with Sybil. They must now find a way to save the females from the authorities.

"I got a pulse! Okay, go, go, go!"

"We got a female, approximately twenty-four or twenty-five. Cocaine overdose in transit!" he yelled into the radio. The paramedics arrived at the ER in record time.

"Have you ever seen a paddle malfunction like that?"

"No, never. It was extra weird. We better stop in supply and get another set."

I opened my eyes and looked up at four faces. *He was not at the coke party. She was not at the coke party and she was not at the coke party. Who are these people?*

"Miss, can you hear me?" the man in white asked.

"Yes."

"Do you know your name?"

"My name is Melissa Bowan."

"Do you know the date, Melissa?"

"It's May 19, 1979."

"She's okay," he said to someone behind him. "You can take her now." I too was placed under arrest.

When I got to the jail, Sybil was in the cell next to mine. I was black and blue all over from the CPR. My mouth was twice its normal size because Greg had forced the spoon into it to keep me from swallowing my tongue.

"Boy, are we in deep shit this time," I wailed.

"Yeah, and if it wasn't for that stupid bag, we wouldn't be here," Sybil lamented.

"What bag?"

"Greg told me to put all the drugs in a bag and throw it in the woods. I put the stuff in the bag but forgot I was holding it when I answered the door and the cops were on the other side."

"You forgot you were holding the bag?"

"Well, excuse me for being upset because you were dead!"

"Sorry, I guess you were entitled. Besides it's not your fault; I was the one who overdosed. So what happened to Greg and Ben? Are they in jail too?"

"Greg is, but he told Ben to run out the back, so Ben is free."

"Cool. In that case he'll get us out."

"Are you sure about that?"

"Yeah, I'm sure." Sure enough, Ben got us all out.

"So what do you think will happen when we go to court?" I asked Ben, as we got high the next night.

"Don't worry. I'll handle it. The cops erred when they took the bag out of Sybil's hand and opened it. The drugs were not in plain sight. They may argue that responding to an overdose is probable cause, but my attorney will handle it. He'll make mincemeat of them in court."

Michael and Raphael swarmed around the officers' heads. "You did not follow procedure. You took the container from her hand. You will look like fools when you appear before the one who judges. You must not show your faces there. There, on the listening device, 'Officer needs assistance.' You can respond with the others."

"Officer needs assistance! Officer needs assistance!" the radio blared. "Corner of Terrell Mill and Cob Parkway. Please respond."

"Let's take that!" Officer Reynolds yelled.

"But we have court," his partner reminded him.

"I know, but we had no probable cause to open the bag. We'll look stupid. This is more important."

When we went to court, neither of the officers showed up. After Ben's attorney shredded the DA's case, the charges were dropped.

Michael hovered over Melissa. "You must separate yourself from this life. Return to your home, my dear child. Your male sibling will help you."

After the overdose, things started to go downhill. Sybil and Greg started their own escort service and seemed to be living happily ever after. I needed to get away from them. I spent so much time getting high I was no longer a star at the agency. Even after all of the money I had made, I was low on cash.

"Lord, help me! I don't want to get high anymore!" I said out loud. *I need to leave here, but I'm not going home. Where shall I go,* I pondered. I ignored the voice that told me to go home and instead sat thinking of exotic locations.

Michael was required to take Melissa's request to the Throne of God. He flew at lightning speed. Her previous requests were for protection and he had already been authorized by the King to protect her; therefore there was no need to deliver those requests to the Throne. Finally she had asked for assistance from the King. "Ask and it shall be given," Michael whispered, as he made a smooth landing at the Gates of Heaven. Michael required no announcement as he approached the Throne.

"You fly with urgency, my most trusted servant," Jesus said. "She has made a request that you wish me to grant?"

"Yes, my King. She no longer desires to spend her days under the influence of pharmaceuticals."

"In due time, my valiant warrior, her request will indeed be granted."

"By your leave, oh, my King. In the name of the Father, the Son, and the Holy Spirit." Michael soared through the clouds.

Chapter Nine

Vegas, Here I Come

Valafar folded his wings as he entered the gates. Unlike Amducious, he was not one to banter with the gatekeeper and he was not skilled enough to think to preen his wings.

"State your business," the gatekeeper bellowed.

"I am here to see the prince," Valafar replied.

"This one will not remain until the sun sets thrice, for he is weak. Oh, how I miss Amducious," the gatekeeper lamented.

Valafar entered the great hall with great trepidation. He had never been this close to the prince and he was terrified. Word had spread of how the One Who Sits at the Right Hand had destroyed Amducious and returned the human to her body, even as Master had had her in his grasp. Upon Master's return, it was said that many faced the guillotine because of his wrath.

"You dare enter the great hall without the proper preparation!" Satan roared. Valafar trembled at Satan's roar. He dropped to the floor and closed his eyes. He had no idea what the proper preparation entailed.

"Wha...what preparation does the Master require of me?" Valafar stammered.

The gatekeeper snickered. "The fool went into the great hall without preening his wings."

"Even the humans groom themselves before a banquet," Satan bellowed.

My wings. I did not preen my wings. "Forgive me, Master. I was so anxious to pay homage to you, my great one, that I was distracted. It shall never happen again."

"If you wish to keep your head, see that it does not. What is your report?"

Valafar had now gathered enough courage to open his eyes. Satan's wings were massive, just as Amducious had described. His legendary beauty was not an exaggeration. Valafar was so captivated by Satan's beauty that he had not heard a word.

"Are you a babbling idiot?" Satan bellowed.

"No, Master. The human Melissa has tired of her surroundings and wishes to journey to another land. I will assist her in finding a location suited to our plans. I have located several that belong to you. They will ensure that she continues on the path leading to her demise."

I sold my car and sublet my apartment to my dad. Daddy's alcoholism had caused him to fall into the trap of drug addiction also. In his attempt to stay sober and avoid black outs and delirium tremens, he had substituted drugs. Being a diabetic made injecting cocaine seem easy. We would sit and get high together for hours. Poor Daddykins had just traded one demonic spirit for another.

I had decided on Las Vegas as my new destination. I bid Daddy farewell and took off for the airport.

As Melissa departed, Uriel hovered over the one she referred to as Daddykins. *It will require skill to protect him from himself,* Uriel thought. *I will need additional troops for this assignment.*

Daddykins spent the night getting high after Melissa left for Vegas. When he couldn't afford to buy another gram of coke, he reverted to alcohol. After Daddy had been in the bar for two hours, the bartender finally cut him off. He was so drunk that he didn't know his own name. Three guys followed him from the bar, recognizing an easy target. As soon as Daddy neared the corner, they jumped him and took what little money he had. The oldest of the three took out his knife.

"Let's do the old man," he said as he kicked him.

Uriel whispered to the younger one in the trio. "No, do not do this terrible thing. Think of your own father." He reached out with his wing and moved it over the younger man's hand.

The younger man reached out and knocked the knife from the older man's hand.

"What you do that fo'? You goin' soft on me now?"

"No, I just ain't down with killin' no old man. Let's go. You kill 'im and I ain't hangin' wit you no mo'."

"Okay, okay, whatever, softie," he laughed.

"I ain't no softie. Ain't you got no daddy?"

"Nah, my daddy run out on us when we was kids."

"Well, leave the old man be. He be somebody's daddy and I ain't doin' him and neither is you."

"I say okay. Let's go befo' the popo come by," said the older man.

The police discovered Daddy in the alley and he ended up in the drunk tank where he slept it off until morning. Eventually, Daddykins would make his way back to Dallas so that Michael could be there to bail him out when he ended up in the tank as he frequently did.

After the plane landed in Vegas, I was low on cash, so I put my things in a storage locker at the airport and decided to walk around. I had no idea where I was or where I was going. Too bad my sister had decided to move; it would have been great to have somewhere to go.

"Do not go with him, Melissa," Michael whispered.

As I walked from the airport, numerous guys had attempted to pick me up, but my subconscious kept telling me not to go with any of them.

Valafar dashed in and out of Frank's car. "You wish to go this way. Turn your transportation device around and go this way. You have business to discuss with your shopkeeper."

An hour later a guy drove up in a black Mercedes. "Hi. What is a gorgeous woman like you doing walking from the airport?" he asked.

"I just got in from Atlanta and wanted to walk around and see what's what." I gave him one of my sexiest smiles.

"Well, if you're tired of walking, I can give you a lift."

"Great. Exercise is not all it's cracked up to be. My name is Melissa," I said as I got into the car.

"Pleased to meet you, Melissa. I'm Frank. Are you hungry?"

"Yeah, I'm starved."

"I need to stop at one of my shops and then I'll take you to dinner. What's your favorite?"

"Japanese."

"Japanese it is then." We stopped at a lingerie shop and he spoke to the manager as I walked around.

"So, you own a lingerie store?"

"Actually I own several; lingerie is a hot commodity in Vegas."

Frank then took me to an awesome Japanese restaurant, complete with traditional costumes. After dinner he opened his wallet and searched through a stack of thousand dollar bills. Even the drug dealers with suitcases full of money had never had thousand dollar bills!

"I don't mean to sound ignorant, but I didn't know they made thousand dollar bills Can I hold one of them?"

"Sure, you can hold ten of them." He counted out ten bills, and I just sat there staring at them like an idiot. I handed the money back and we left the restaurant.

"You want to drive?"

"Oh, yeah! I always wanted to drive one of these. Where to?"

"My place, if that's all right with you?"

"Sure, just lead the way." His house was magnificent–five bedrooms and exquisite interior design.

"I had one of the best interior designers in Vegas decorate my home," he said with pride.

"It's gorgeous and awfully clean for a bachelor pad."

"To be honest it's not exactly a bachelor pad. I have a couple of girls that live here also."

"Need I ask why you have a couple of girls living with you?"

"My girls work the casinos. You know, call girls."

"You're a pimp?" I said incredulously.

"I prefer the term business manager."

At this point, I was just plain disgusted. "So, Mr. Business Manager, they give all of the money to you and you take care of things. Does that just about sum it up?"

"Yeah, that sums it up quite well."

"Okay, so you didn't give me a lift out of the goodness of your heart. You saw another girl to add to your stable."

"You make it sound so cheap and tawdry," he laughed.

"I take it that was your idea of a joke."

"You must admit it was a good one."

"Yeah, it was. So, tell me how it's done in Vegas and introduce me to the other ladies of the house."

"They're both at the casinos working right now, but there's Ming and then there's Shelia. Ming is Chinese obviously, and Sheila's white and blonde; and then there's you, some kind of gorgeous caramel mocha."

"Yeah, that's me all right, with the chewy filling," I replied sarcastically.

He laughed, but he didn't realize just how totally disgusted I was.

At least these girls cohabited in harmony. No knives and crazy shit going on. *If he thinks I'm giving him a dime, he's got another thought coming. I think that the player is just about to get played. These girls make thousand dollar bills and then give them to a pimp! How stupid is that! It's bad enough we do what we do, but to then give a jackass the money! I don't think so.*

Every evening I would go out and each time I would come back with a story of how no one was interested.

"I guess they just don't like black girls in Vegas," I sighed.

"I know that's not true, Melissa. There are plenty of black girls who don't look half as good as you do and they make a fortune. Look, Melissa, you've got to pull your weight or you've got to go."

"Okay, Frank, no problem. I'm sure I can do it," I said as I laughed to myself.

After three more weeks Frank finally threw in the towel. "Look, Melissa, the other girls are complaining and, to be honest, you eat like a horse to be so tiny. I can't keep supporting you. I tell you what. I'll buy you a ticket to anywhere you want to go and I'll give you some money for the trip, okay?"

"Okay, no problem. I'm sorry it didn't work out. I think I'd like to go to LA, if it's all the same to you."

"LA it is. Let's get your stuff ready."

Chapter Ten

Los Angeles, California

When I got to LA, the first thing I did was go to the beach. I sat there for about an hour, pondering what I would do next and looking at the ocean. *This is ridiculous! I've made thousands and thousands of dollars and I'm homeless.* I sat there a while longer and then moved down the street and sat on a bench at the bus stop. Again several guys had stopped, but the voice told me they were dangerous.

"Hey!"

I looked up and two guys were yelling at me through their car window.

"Hey, yourself," I called back. They got out and sat with me on the bench.

"I know it sounds cliché, but what's a girl like you doing in a place like this?" said the guy who sat on my right.

"I just got here from Vegas where this creep who mistook himself for a pimp tried to add me to his stable. When I work, I work for myself."

He laughed, "I could have told him you wouldn't fall for that and I just met you. Hi, I'm Josh and this is Elliot." Elliot was obviously gay and Josh was sort of a geek.

"Hi. I'm Melissa."

"Are you hungry, Melissa?" Josh asked.

"I'm starved."

"You haven't lived until you've had Johnny's Pastrami. You game?"

"Definitely. Pastrami is my all time favorite."

"So, Melissa, what's your plan?" asked Josh.

"I don't have the faintest idea."

"I have a friend who takes, you know, calls out of her house. In LA all you need is an advertisement in the *Free Press* and a place and you're in business. I'm sure she won't mind putting you up for a small fee."

Valafar swarmed around Melissa's head. "Yes, go and barter your precious body. Master will be so pleased. You need the money."

"Cool. Let's go meet this friend of yours." His friend also happened to be the mother of his child. Maria allowed me to take calls from her advertisement to get me started. She would only take calls in her house, so the ones that wanted someone to come to their location she gave to me.

I was on my way to see a guy named Brent Collins. Brent had asked me to pick up some Chinese food on the way and had given me the location of the Chinese restaurant near his home. When I picked up the food, the owner also gave me the credit card receipt, compete with a carbon copy.

Valafar again swarmed around Melissa's head. "Take it; it shall serve you well. You tire of the female who has given you shelter. Use this to acquire a temporary abode."

I stashed the carbon in my purse and gave Brent the credit card receipt. After I left Brent, I changed to jeans, a halter-top, and a ponytail. I looked like a cheerleader. I went to Hyatt and walked up to the counter.

"Hi. My name is Melissa Collins. Has my dad checked in yet? His name is Brent Collins."

The lady behind the counter looked the name up on the computer system.

"No, Miss Collins, he hasn't checked in."

"What am I supposed to do?" I wailed. "I'm supposed to meet him for spring break and I don't have enough money to check in. Can I use the phone to call my mom?"

"Sure. Step right over there."

I got on the phone and pretended to talk to my mom. I turned to the lady and said, "Can you take my mom's credit card?"

"Sure. What's the number?"

I whipped out the paper with Jake's credit card number and read it to the lady. I decided on a suite and I stayed for a week and ordered room service every day. I then went shopping at the boutique in the lobby.

"That was the most expensive date he ever had," I laughed. After living the way I had, stealing was easy.

I had been in LA for about two months and things were going fairly well. The money I was making was nothing close to that of the escort service in Atlanta, but I was in love with LA and was able to get an apartment in Hollywood. Working without the safety net of an escort service, however, was like playing Russian roulette. As with most things, I hadn't given it much thought.

Valafar navigated above Jason's head. "Choose this one; it is the right advertisement for you. You want, you need this one."

"This one looks good," Jason said, as he picked up the phone and dialed the number in the *Free Press* advertisement.

It was Friday night and my escort line was ringing. I picked it up.

"Hello. This is Michelle. How may I help you?"

"Hi. My name is Jason and I'm looking for a girl for a couple of hours. Michelle, are you pretty?"

"Pretty as a Georgia Peach," I said in a southern drawl.

"Cool. Is two hundred an hour okay?"

"Two hundred is good. What's the address?" It was an apartment building with indoor hallways.

"Do not visit this one; he is dangerous. Do not go," Michael whispered.

My subconscious was working overtime about this guy, but I really needed the money. *Melissa,* I said to myself, *you know your voice, whatever it is, is never wrong. Pass and wait for the next one. Four hundred dollars! I just can't pass this time. I'll be extra careful.*

"Do not go, Melissa!" Michael was louder this time.

I really have the heebie jeebies tonight. I shook my head and my shoulders, hoping that the inner voice would be quiet, but it just seemed to be more insistent.

When I arrived, I found that the elevator was out and his apartment was on the fourth floor.

Valafar and the other demons hovered above Jason's head. Valafar had been told of Pan, Kali, Hodi, and Uphir's fate. He

was determined not to make the same fatal mistake. For this mission, he had selected ten of his finest warriors.

"When she arrives, you must incapacitate her first. After you have forced yourself upon her, then you will kill her," Valafar hissed.

"You want, you need to kill her," they all chanted in unison.

Michael too was prepared. He possessed the ability to appear without warning. As the demons chanted, Valafar was astonished when Michael appeared and severed the heads of four warriors with one stoke. Valafar had never witnessed such prowess, nor had he ever seen another, other than Satan, with wings such as those. *He is even more magnificent than the legends his forefathers had told.* Valafar knew that his only option was to retreat.

"Retreat," he yelled and then he ran for his life. *It may be said that I am a coward, but at least I will live to fight another day,* he thought, as he dipped through the clouds.

"Melissa! Do not go into the stairwell!" Michael yelled.

I didn't want to go into the stairwell. It was dark and creepy. *You've had the creeps all night. Get a grip, girl; this is not a Jason movie. The guy's name is Jason, isn't it?* I giggled. I opened the door and entered the stairwell. As soon as I got to the second floor, I really had the creeps.

"Melissa, turn around now!" Michael screamed this time. He then blew at Melissa, just enough to make her lose her balance and miss a step as she turned.

I whirled around just in time to see a man holding a pillowcase above my head. I turned so fast that I missed a step and, instead of the case going over my head, he missed and plunged face first onto the metal stairs.

"Run, Melissa! Scream now!"

I ran down the stairs, out of the front door, screaming the entire way. Doors started to open as I ran and a woman yelled, "Shut up or I'm calling the cops right now!"

I kept right on yelling and running. By the time I got to my car, I already had my keys out and I opened the door with lightning speed. Having a brother for a cop paid off sometimes. He had told me to always have my keys readily available and never at the bottom of my purse. As I drove, I realized this had been the first time I hadn't heeded that inner voice. *Well, that was stupid. Has it ever been wrong before? No!*

Three more months went by without incident. Of course any normal person would have taken the hint and gotten out of the business after some madman had tried to put a bag over her head. But I'm far from normal. *Wow! Less money and crazy people with pillow-cases. I'm not sure why I'm putting up with this shit, but LA is so LA,* I thought as I dressed for my next call.

Valafar buzzed around Bill's head. "Sharpen your knife for this one."

"Cut her, cut her," they all chanted.

"This one is primed and ready. Let us visit the female to ensure her arrival," Valafar commanded. The demons fell into formation and arrived inside Melissa's apartment at exactly the same moment as Michael and the Heavenly Host. Valafar had no choice but to engage them in battle. "Attack!" he cried.

The demons were evenly matched, sword for sword; however not one of Valafar's demons could match the abilities of a warrior angel such as Michael. Michael decimated Valafar's finest warriors and forced Valafar to retreat. By the time Michael had completed the battle, Melissa was entering Bill's apartment.

I arrived at Bill's apartment and it seemed nice enough. At least the elevators were working. Bill answered the door wearing a robe.

"Hi. Would you like a drink?"

"Sure. What do you have?" I inquired.

"How about white wine?"

What I wouldn't give for some Dom Perignon, I thought. "White wine is great."

"So, Michelle, what do you charge?"

"Two hundred dollars."

"Two hundred dollars! You're kidding, right?"

"Thanks for the wine, Bill." I set the glass down on the table and started toward the door. Bill jumped in front of me; he was holding a knife.

"Lord, help me!" I prayed.

Michael arrived just as Bill put the knife to Melissa's throat.

He put his wing on Bill's hand. "You don't want to hurt her; she will give you what you want. Melissa, tell him you will give him what he wants. Smile and look at him with fondness. Do not be afraid; I will protect you." Michael then whispered to Bill, "Look at how she gazes upon you with fondness."

"Listen, Bill, you're a handsome man. Why would you want to pay for sex anyway when you can get it for free? Hey, you know, if we had met in a bar, I would have come home with you in a heartbeat." I looked up at him and smiled. "Come on, put down the knife and let's do this thing right, okay? I'll even give you a striptease. How about it?"

"You weren't so cooperative a few minutes ago," Bill sneered.

"Bill, let's face it; every now and then I do meet a guy that I want to be with. You are one of those guys. Come on, let's not waste anymore time."

"Okay, but if you're trying to trick me and you run, I'll hurt you," he hissed.

"I won't run. Come on. I promised you a striptease, remember?" I stayed with Bill for an hour. It was the longest hour of my life. He actually had the audacity to ask me if I would come back.

"Hi, Julie. Hi, Pam," I called. Julie and Pam were two girls who worked the street near my building.

"Hey, Michelle. What's happening?"

"Oh, it's the same old stuff," I replied. I hated to see these girls working the street. It was so much more dangerous than working in hotels, not to mention that pimp who beat the shit out of them every day. Maybe I could convince them to get off the street if I showed them how to work independently. We'd have to work on their manner of dress and their manner of speech, but I couldn't stand watching them do this any more. "You guys want to stop in for a visit?" I asked. I could tell that they were tired. "I got a pick me up." They knew that meant a couple of lines of cocaine.

After Julie and Pam snorted the coke, they prepared to leave. "What's the big rush?"

"You know Pete; he gets upset when we waste his time visiting." Julie sighed.

"Pete? He's your pimp, right?"

"Yeah, Michelle. You independent, right?"

"Yeah, I'm independent. Have you guys ever thought of going independent?"

"Pete, he'd whup our ass if we started talkin' independent."

"That's all the more reason to get away from Pete, don't you think?"

"How we 'pose to do that?"

How indeed! I told the girls exactly how they were going to dump old Pete. Since I had more calls than I could possibly take, I would charge the guy a fee just like the escort service did in Atlanta. I explained to them how it worked. I then showed them how they had to dress to enter an upscale hotel without being thrown out. It worked like a charm. In a week they dumped Pete and moved into my building. When Pete came lurking about trying to intimidate them, we called the cops and he never came back.

"Boy, Michelle, this ain't nothing like workin' the street. A hundred dollars! We ain't use to money like that." Pam exclaimed.

A hundred dollars is cheap, but one step at a time, I thought.

"Don't use the word 'ain't and get used to it. If you're going to do this job, then make them pay and never let a scumbag pimp beat you. When you work, you work for yourself or don't do it at all." I was really happy they were off the street and away from that pimp. "LA is a bit slow in comparison to Atlanta, but it will pick up."

"Hey, I got a call for three girls. It's a bachelor party." Since Julie and Pam had started, a couple of other girls had joined us also. "Who's up?"

"I'm up," Julie said. "And so are Pam and Lisa."

"Here's the deal. They want four hours and they're drunk already. I'll go with you and negotiate the best price I can. They're staying at the Bonaventure, so we have to be careful going in there. Wear those business suits."

Michael's wings drooped because he knew that he could not warn Melissa of the trouble that was to come. *This unfortunate event is necessary, for if you do not cease this activity, you will surely die.*

The guy that I spoke to on the phone had said his name was Bob and he also answered the door. He was so plastered he could barely stand up. I negotiated a fee of two hundred for the agency and four hundred for the girl. That came to six hundred per girl and there were three girls.

"So, Michelle, you make two hundred dollars just to hook us up with these girls?" asked Bob.

"Yeah, that's right. It beats having a pimp, no pun intended."

He laughed as he opened the door for me.

"Woe to you, little girl, for you have no idea the trouble that is to come. Where is Michael now that you really need him? Ha, ha, ha, I have a wonderful surprise for you." Valafar laughed.

Once I got to my car, I looked up and one of the guys from the bachelor party was in the parking garage. I thought his name was Roger. He was so drunk he was having trouble finding his car. "Hey, Roger, what are you doing down here? I thought you wanted to party with the girls?" Roger continued to stumble around and got closer to me at about the same time a car rounded the corner. "Be careful! There's a car coming, Roger!"

He finally stumbled his way over to my car, and I saw that the car had come to a stop. *I wonder if this fool can drive,* I thought. "Hey, Roger, what are you doing down here?" I repeated. At that instant Roger stood up straight, opened his jacket, and whipped out his badge.

"Arresting you," he replied. Two other undercover officers got out of the car and joined Roger. I was so stunned that all I could do was laugh. Roger, or what ever his name was, looked at me as if I had lost my mind.

"I'm arresting you and you're laughing? That's a first. Usually they cry."

I laughed again. "What's the point in crying? I'm laughing because I didn't have a clue. You guys are good. I can't believe that I didn't have a clue."

"Why is that so hard to believe?" Roger asked as he handcuffed me.

"I usually have an inner voice that tips me off when I'm in a bad situation, but this time it was on vacation. This was a very bad time for it to go quiet on me."

"Yeah, Michelle, considering the fact that pandering is a felony, I'd say it was a really bad time too. But on the other hand, maybe your little voice figures being in jail is better than being dead. You girls risk meeting a psycho every time you walk into a hotel room with a stranger."

"So what are you now? My father?"

"No, but if I was, I think I'd whip your ass. But since I'm just a cop, I'm gonna lock your ass up instead."

"Everybody's a comedian," I sighed.

I was held in Sybil Brand, the county jail, while I awaited trial. *What a name! Sybil, they actually named a jail after you. You should be flattered.* Sybil Brand was just like one great big dormitory. It was lined with beds, and next to every bed was a locker. The entire right side of the wall was lined with showers and bathroom stalls with toilets. In the middle was the guard booth, and the guards monitored everyone all of the time. When it was time to eat, we had to line up and face the front just like in grade school. Talking was not allowed in route to the dining hall. The food was terrible, there was no talking across tables, and of course we had to face the front. The girls would communicate with girls from other dorms by sending notes, referred to as kites. If we were caught, we ended up in solitary. The "girls" wore short mini skirt dresses and the "boys" wore long dresses below the knee; this let the "girls" know they were the male partners in lesbian relationships, even though the guard setup prevented them from acting out their desires. There was nothing we could do without the guards seeing us. Unlike prison, it was sort of like a big slumber party. We slept, we read, we watched TV, and we ate.

A boy in my dorm named Kit took a liking to me, as did several others. Kit was in for armed robbery and ultimately went to prison when her trial was over. Having Kit for a friend had some benefits. She always had cigarettes and commissary. If Kit had commissary, that meant I had commissary.

It also kept the other boys from constantly letting me know of their affections. It could be quite annoying at times. None of them seemed to care how many times I told them that I wasn't interested. Kit knew I wasn't interested in her, but she liked the idea of the other boys thinking that I was her girl. I just wanted all of them to leave me alone, so it worked for both of us.

While I waited for my trial, my relatives wrote to the judge, telling him what a wonderful person I used to be.

Michael hovered over Judge Stableton. "Look at the numerous correspondences. She comes from a good family.

To keep the other females from harm was of noble intent. What purpose does it serve to keep her here? Allow her to go home to her family; she has support there."

After serving almost five months, Judge Stapleton reduced my charges to several misdemeanors and gave me time served on one condition. I was to leave LA and go home to Texas. After five months in jail, even Texas sounded good.

Today was the day; I was finally getting out of this place. I was led down to a room and given my clothes, the ones I had on when I was arrested: a cashmere sweater, a pair of silk slacks, and my Louis Vuitton handbag. *Now this is more like it. Too bad about all of my other stuff; all of my clothes were gone in a flash. Well, easy come, easy go.*

My brother had sent me a one-way ticket to Dallas and I had it in my purse. The judge's instructions were for me to go straight to the airport and get on the plane. *What he doesn't know won't hurt him. The first thing I'm going to do is get a decent cigarette.* I walked outside and stood there for a minute, just breathing the air of freedom. I then hailed a cab.

"Where to, miss?" the driver asked.

"To the Tinderbox." The Tinderbox was a tobacco store that sold imported cigarettes. I had become accustomed to smoking Djarum, an Indonesian cigarette with spices. After acquiring the cigarettes, I then had the driver stop at Johnny's Pastrami. I arrived at the airport an hour later and caught the next flight to Dallas.

Chapter Eleven

"All My Ex's Live in Texas"

When I landed in Dallas, I found my brother's new wife waiting for me.

"Hi. Are you Melissa?"

"Yes, I am."

"I'm Shelly, Michael's wife."

"It's a pleasure to meet you, Shelly. Where's Michael?"

"He's working."

"At this time of night?"

"Yeah, you know Michael; he has numerous off duty jobs. This one is at the local pharmacy."

"Cool. Can we stop by there?"

"Sure. How was your flight?"

"I almost got rearrested for smoking an Indian cigarette, but other than that, it was hunky dory." She looked at me strangely. "Don't ask," I sighed.

When we got to the pharmacy, I ran and jumped up in Michael's arms and hugged him. He was as handsome as ever.

"Hey, little sis."

"Hey, yourself, you handsome hunk! If I wasn't your sister, I'd marry you."

"Yeah, well, you're not bad looking yourself. Of course, that's your problem."

"Yes, it is big brother. Yes, it is."

"So what are your plans?"

"Besides eating a steak, I haven't the faintest idea."

"That's your other problem."

"Yes, it is," I said again. "Yes, it is."

He shook his head, just like Faith always did, and laughed.

On the way home, I sang "All My Ex's Live in Texas" and hoped I wouldn't run into any of them.

Shelly laughed, "Well, as young as you are, you can't really have that many."

"No, I guess you're right. To be honest, there's only one and technically we're still married, so I guess he's not really an ex. I need to do something about that," I mused.

"Yeah, girl, you do," Shelly replied.

After I had been home for two days, I did. I signed the divorce papers and sent them back to Paul.

After spending a few days with Michael and Shelly, I decided that Shelly was a little too strange for my taste. *Michael won't stay married to her long.* Sure enough, Michael and Shelly lasted for about a year.

I left and went to Pamela's the next day. Of course, people find it strange that Pamela and I are like sisters, given that she and Michael are divorced. She'll always be my sister-in-law, and so will anyone else he marries.

"Hey, Pam. What's going on?"

"Hey, jail bird. How was prison life?" Pamela teased.

"I'll have you know that I was not in a prison. I was in jail; there's a difference," I admonished. "Besides, I was honored to be housed in a jail named after Sybil."

"I jail named after Sybil? You're joking?"

"No, I'm not. The name of the jail was Sybil Brand. She was some kind of philanthropist who decided she wanted to build a jail for women. Go figure."

"Sybil should be proud; it certainly is fitting," she chuckled. "So what is your next brilliant plan?"

"You don't have to be insulting. I shall ponder that and get back to you."

"While you ponder it, come and drive me to the store."

"No problem, but one of these days, you need to learn to drive. Come on, what are you now? Thirty-five years old and you still don't know how to drive?"

"Yeah, and when I get to forty-five, I won't know how then either," she retorted.

After I drove Pam to the store, she was kind enough to allow me to go visit my dad, who was working not far from where they lived. Pam and Rachel lived in Oak Cliff. I turned on Keist Blvd. and followed it to the theater where Daddy was a manager. When I arrived, he was cleaning the popcorn machine.

"Hey, Daddykins!"

"Hey, little girl! Come here and kiss your daddy."

I went over and hugged and kissed him. He looked a little pale but otherwise seemed okay. Daddy had numerous health problems from diabetes to pancreas, liver, and kidney problems.

"So how was prison life?"

"Daddy! I wish you guys would stop saying that. I was not in prison. You make me sound like some kind of axe murderer or something."

He laughed, "Well, I guess we are unaccustomed to family members being incarcerated."

"No doubt," I mumbled under my breath. At that moment one of the movies let out and Daddy was occupied with work.

"Daddykins, where are the restrooms?"

"Go around that corner and to your right." When I walked into the ladies' room, I immediately made an about-face and left.

"Daddykins! The bathroom is filthy and I really got to go."

Valafar buzzed in the earth father's ear. "Send her to use the facilities in the tavern owned by your friend. You have no time to clean the latrines now."

"Melissa, I don't have enough staff to send someone in there at the moment. Go next door and tell my friend McFarland to let you use his bathroom."

"You mean that nightclub? Is he open this early?"

"Yeah. He should be setting up his tills and liquor. Just knock on the door."

"Okay. I'll be back in minute."

I walked next door and knocked on the door of the nightclub. A heavyset gentleman of about forty came to the door. He was dressed to kill, wearing a five thousand-dollar suit and ostrich cowboy boots. *My, my, my! What have we here?* "Hi, Mr. McFarland. I'm Melissa. My dad says you might be kind enough to allow me to use your rest-room."

"Your dad?"

"Oh, sorry. I meant Michael from next door."

"Wow! Michael never told me he had a beautiful daughter. Come in; come in."

"Actually, he has three."

"And the other two? Do they look like you?"

"Almost identical," I replied.

"Michael is a lucky man to have not one but three beautiful daughters. The restroom is right there on your left."

After I came out, I sat on a barstool and watched in fascination as he prepared for the night crowd. "Mr. McFarland, what age group visits your club?"

"Call me Mick. I cater to the over-thirty set. And where are you coming from, Melissa?"

I laughed and said, "Jail."

"No, really. Where are you coming from?"

"Yes, really. I just got out of jail."

"What in heaven's name did a beautiful, tiny thing like you do to go to jail?"

"Pandering. Well, actually I was charged with pimping and pandering, although for the life of me, I can't figure out the difference."

His mouth dropped open. He closed it and said, "Come on, be for real. What were you in jail for?"

"I am for real. I was a madam and my girls were caught agreeing to perform sex acts for money and we all went to the pokey." He started laughing so hard that he was crying. I laughed too.

"Would you like a drink?" he asked.

"No, thanks. My taste in alcohol is a bit extreme."

"This is a bar, you know."

"Yeah, but most bars don't pour what I drink by the glass."

"And what, madam, would that be?" he inquired.

"That would be Dom Perignon."

"My, we do have expensive taste."

"And judging by that suit, so do you." *And I'll bet a hundred dollars that you can't resist showing off by opening a bottle of Dom Perignon.*

"Hold that thought. I'll be right back," he replied. He returned with a bottle in his hand. "Dom Perignon, my lady," and he held out the bottle with an elaborate bow and a flourish of his hands. *Too bad I'm not in Vegas because I'm definitely on a winning streak.* He poured two glasses and I sipped mine.

"So, Melissa, what do you plan to do, besides sip one hundred dollar champagne?"

"Offer her employment. You can then spend time with her. Later you must offer her pharmaceuticals; she cannot resist, for addiction runs in her bloodline. She will be putty in your hands. Too bad Amducious is not here to see your new beau, my dear. He would be proud of your selection," Valafar laughed.

"Get a job, I guess," I said without much enthusiasm.

"I need waitresses. Would you like to come and work for me?" he asked.

I immediately perked up. "That would be awesome! When I can I start?"

"How about tonight? There is one hitch."

"What kind of hitch?" I asked.

"You have to wear a uniform, and let's just say that your dad might not approve."

"Daddykins? You've got to be kidding! Daddykins wouldn't care if it was topless. Now my brother Michael, that's a different story. I just got out of jail, remember. It can't be that risqué. Let's see it."

He went to the back and returned with what looked like a playboy bunny outfit, only black instead of pink.

"That's it? That's what you're worried about? No problem. What time should I be here?"

"Be here at eight."

"Eight it is. Thanks for the Dom," I called as I went out.

"The pleasure was all mine, I assure you," he whispered.

When I got back to Pamela's, I was ecstatic.

"What are you all fired up about?" she asked.

"I just got a job and I've only been here a day."

"Now that's what I call progress! Wait a minute. What's that you're holding?"

"It's my uniform. Want to see it?"

"I'm not sure. Do I?" I held it up. "Where is the rest of it? What kind of job has a uniform like that?"

"There is no 'rest of it.' It's a waitress job at the nightclub next door to the theater."

"You mean McFarland's club?"

"Yeah. You know him?"

"No, and I don't want to know him. I hear he's trouble with a capital T."

"Sounds like my kind of guy," I called as I ran to the bathroom to try on my new uniform.

"Michael is going to have a fit," Pamela sighed.

That night I worked my tail off, but the tips were good when compared to other waitress jobs. After I changed into street clothes and started for the door, McFarland called to me. "So, how was your first day?"

"It was great."

"Would you like to come over to my condominium for a nightcap?"

"Sure."

Mick's condo was near N. Hampton Road. It was small but very nice and featured a very tall privacy fence. Knowing Dom Perignon was my preference, Mick was prepared. He also had a large quantity of cocaine. I stayed with him well into the next day.

I stopped at Pamela's to grab the few items Michael had bought for me the day before.

"Girl, where have you been all night?" Pam asked.

"I spent the night at Mick's."

"You know, when Michael finds out about this, he's going to have a fit."

"Michael is overprotective. He sleeps with a gun, and dreams about crooks.

"Well, you do have a point there, but he's still going to have a fit."

"I'm a big girl."

"You're a mess!"

"Yeah, that too," I laughed.

I went back to the club for my shift and then back to Mick's condo. As a matter of fact, I never spent another night at Pamela's.

I spent the next few weeks dodging my brother Michael; however, I knew that it was short lived. That Friday he finally caught up with me. Michael scowled, "So, you're hanging out with that crook."

"Michael, he is not a crook," I retorted.

"Melissa, he is definitely a crook and a gangster. The only reason we haven't locked him up is because he's smart and we haven't been able to catch him in the act."

"No, the only reason you haven't locked him up is because he's not a crook. If you want to know the truth about it, everybody I know is a crook by your definition. Doing recreational drugs, in and of itself, does not make one a crook."

"Melissa, doing recreational drugs will get you locked up and, therefore, does in fact make you a crook," Michael said as he rolled his eyes.

"Look at it this way; at least I have a job."

"Yeah, until we raid the place," he snapped.

Of course, I refused to listen to Michael and by the end of the third week, I had permanently moved in with Mick.

Mick and I spent all day and all night together. The other girls at the club were furious. Many of them had spent months attempting to get close to Mick to no avail. After the fifth month, I was receiving ugly phone calls from women on a regular basis.

Wednesday night was my night off. When Mick came home from the club that Wednesday, he was carrying two very large black garbage bags and went back to his car for two more. Even though it was two in the morning, I was still up.

"What size are you?"

"I'm a five."

"I think I have a six. Will that do?"

"Yeah. What is it?"

He reached into one of the bags and pulled out several mink coats. "Try this one on."

"Oh, my goodness! You have got to be kidding me!"

"No, really, try this one." I put on the black mink coat. "No, that's not a good color. Try this one." Next, I tried a light brown one. "That's perfect. Do you like it?"

"Are you kidding me? You mean I can keep it?"

"Of course, you can keep it."

I ran to the mirror. "It's beautiful, absolutely beautiful."

"Not as beautiful as you, but the two of you together are stunning."

A month later, on a Wednesday afternoon, there was a knock at the door. Mick was quick to answer it. He walked out and conferred at length with the man who had knocked. When he returned, he asked me to step outside. Right there in front of the condo was a huge semi-trailer. "Come on. I want to show you something."

Mick took me by the hand and led me up a ramp attached to the back of the trailer. When we got inside the truck, I couldn't believe my eyes. There were racks and racks and racks of every kind of clothing you could imagine. "Take your pick."

"What do you mean?" I asked

"Pick anything you want and as many as you want."

"You're kidding, right?"

"No, Melissa, I'm not kidding. I own this entire truck of clothes and you can have whatever you want."

It took me two hours to reach the end of the truck. When I finished, I had an entire wardrobe. I was in awe, just like the last time a man put the world at my feet. And, just like last time, Melissa Bowan plus cocaine equaled trouble.

After awhile, I began to take Mick's stash of cocaine without his permission. He was furious. "Melissa, I owe people money for this stuff! You can't just go into my stash and snort as much as you want. Every time you do this, it costs me hundreds of dollars!"

"It's only money. What's the big deal anyway?"

He just sighed. "The next time we have this conversation, you are not going to like the outcome," he replied, as he walked away.

"Oh, don't be such a fuddy-duddy," I said under my breath.

Sometime in late August, I got a call from Michael. "Hey, Michael. What's going on?"

"Not me, Melissa. Daddy."

"What about Daddykins?"

"He's in the hospital."

"Is he having DTs again?"

"Yeah, but this time he almost drank himself to death. They can't control his sugar or his blood pressure and they said he has bigger problems. You better get down here."

When I arrived, I met the doctor; he had what I call the Dr. Kildare look. Dr. Kildare was the main character on my favorite TV show. Whenever he got that look on the show, you knew that the recipient only had two months to live. In Daddy's case, it turned out to be about two years.

"But he's not that old," I cried.

"Assuming I can get him stable and, to be honest, it doesn't look hopeful. Your dad has spent his entire life drinking. Giving him two years is a gift. His kidneys are failing, his liver function is almost nonexistent, and he has prostate cancer. If I can get him stable, I'm hoping to buy him some time with chemo."

I hugged Michael and we went in to see Daddykins.

"Hey, Daddykins," I whispered, as I kissed him.

"Hey, little girl," he said with a smile.

"You don't look so hot, sweetie."

"Yeah, little girl, I think I finally used up my nine lives." I didn't want him to see me cry, so I held it in until he went to surgery.

Uriel hovered over the operating table. He had been instructed to render assistance to the earthly physician. With the power of the Holy Spirit, he flew down into the body of the one called Daddykins. When he got to the left kidney, he restored its function, although he did not heal the right one. He then moved to the liver, where he healed it enough to add eighteen more years to the human's life span. He then watched as the physician removed the cancer. He made no attempt to restore his sexual function. He would leave that to the physician. He did, however, stop the spread of the cancer. He then stabilized his sugar levels and his blood pressure and navigated out of Daddy's body and made his way to the waiting area.

"Your earthly father is blessed and highly favored, as you are. His health has been restored. See to it that this gift is used wisely," whispered Uriel.

Michael paced back and forth around the waiting room.

"Michael, be still! You're driving me crazy! He's going to be fine and there's not a chance in hell that Daddykins is going to be done in by cancer or anything else for that matter. At the rate we're going, he might even outlive us both."

"I doubt that. Did you see how frail he is?" Michael replied.

"Well, maybe outliving us is pushing it a bit, but I assure you he won't be dead in two years."

"You sound awfully sure about that."

"I am." I said as if it were fact.

Daddy went home after thirty days in the hospital. His sugar and his blood pressure had stabilized during surgery. After dialysis, one of his kidneys began to function on its own. His liver function improved so much that the doctors found this to be quite puzzling. Daddy received chemotherapy and his cancer never returned. Because Daddy fancied himself a ladies' man, he had a penile implant to restore his sexual function. He and I had a good laugh about that. But, after his recovery, he returned to his old drinking habits. Even though he didn't put his gift to good use, God still allowed him to live eighteen more years.

Things went okay for a while and then Z showed up. That's right; her name was simply Z, as in the last letter of the alphabet. Z was an Asian girl Mick took a liking to after she came into the club.

"Melissa, I've invited Z to come by after closing."

Here we go again! A dual relationship. I was wondering when it would rear its ugly head.

"I want Z to, you know, join us."

"Join us for what? Dinner?"

"Melissa, don't be a smart-ass. You know exactly what I mean."

"I sure do and she might join you, but she's not joining me for anything. You guys go at it. Just make sure you leave my cocaine on the table. I'll still be here when you get back."

"Come on, Melissa. Considering your past profession, I would think it's not that big of a deal."

"You can kiss my ass. I assure you that I don't care if you want to have sex with Q or Z or any other letter of the alphabet, but I'm not going to participate!" Actually, I did care a lot, but I wasn't about to give him the satisfaction of knowing it.

"You know, I do everything for you. This is the least you could do for me!" he yelled.

"Everything? Like what? Besides screw me every chance you get. Oh, sorry, I forgot. You do feed me and give me a place to live. What do you think would happen if I went walking around asking every guy I met if I could go home with him? Of the ones without wives, how many takers do you think I would get?"

He was silent.

"Exactly! Eight out of ten and the two holdouts are probably gay," I retorted. I turned on my heel and walked into the bedroom and slammed the door. I think Mick thought I might just kill him in his sleep if he had sex with Z while I was in the house, so he decided against it. He did continue to see her, however, when I was not around.

Next up was a girl named Indigo. *What is that? A color or something? Where do these people get these names anyway?* Again, Indigo was someone Mick picked up at the club and couldn't resist. She camped out in our spare bedroom and it was like a flashback to Derek and Jackie, except this time I was in Jackie's shoes. I'm sure every time I left the house, Mick was all over her. Of course, I could leave whenever I got ready, but I had no intention of working a job. And where else could I spend my life in a perpetual twenty-four-hour-a-day party?

And then Sybil came!

"Mick, remember me telling you about Sybil?"

"Yeah, I remember. She was your partner in crime, except she didn't get caught."

"That's not funny," I said as I rolled my eyes. "Sybil's coming here to Dallas, although I'm not sure why because we both hate Texas."

"You're here."

"Yeah, but I was forced to. By a judge."

Sybil arrived on Friday. When I got to the gate, Sybil was just coming out of the plane door. "Melissa! Melissa!" I ran over and we both jumped up and down and screamed the way we always did when we had been apart for a while. "It's party time!" we both yelled in unison.

Mick was mesmerized by Sybil. She had always had that effect on men. "Put your eyeballs back in your head, Mick. Sybil is off limits," I snapped. We took Sybil to the club that night and partied all night long. I was Mick's girl and no longer working as a waitress.

By the end of the week, Sybil was ready for something new. Mick's business partner, who also owned a club for the younger crowd, was a tall, dark, handsome guy.

"Mick, why don't we take Sybil to Benny's club tonight?"

"That's a great idea. You guys go ahead. I need to go to my club for a while and then I'll come over there when I'm done."

When we got to Benny's, the line was out the door and around the corner with people waiting to get in.

"Oh, man. This is the pits," Sybil wailed.

"You don't think we're going to wait in that line, do you?"

"We're not?"

"No way. I'm Mick's girl; we go to the front. Come on." I sauntered up to the front of the line with Sybil in tow. "Would you tell Benny that Melissa Bowman is here?"

"No need. Come on in, Miss Bowman. He already informed me that you were coming." He removed the rope and Sybil and I walked in.

"Now that was cool," Sybil yelled over the music.

"Being Mick's girl does have its benefits. Come on. I'll introduce you to Benny. He is some kind of scrumptious. If I had met him before Mick, all I can say is my, my, my."

I tapped on the door to Benny's office.

"Wait just a minute," he called. I knew that meant he was doing cocaine. In a few seconds, he opened the door. "Hey, Melissa, and hello, beautiful. You must be Sybil."

Sybil took his hand and curtsied. "The pleasure is all mine, I assure you," she replied.

Benny was a goner. He didn't take his eyes off of Sybil the entire time we were there.

"Benny, how about fixing us up?" I said as I winked.

"No problem." He locked the door, opened the drawer, and pulled out a hand mirror, complete with lines of coke. He then produced a small straw to snort it with.

"What would you ladies like to drink?"

"I'll have a piña colada."

"I'll have a Courvoisier," said Sybil.

He put his hand on his chest. "A woman after my own heart."
Oh, brother, is he done for.

Later on, Mick met us at Benny's club and we partied the rest of the night.

When we left, we all came back to the condo. We couldn't go to Benny's because he was married. But, of course, Sybil and I wouldn't let a little thing like that get in our way, would we? Mick pulled out more cocaine and the Dom Perignon.

"Now that's more like it," I said.

"This woman really has expensive tastes," Mick sighed.

"And so do you; that's why you love me," I laughed.

"You must admit she's got you on that one," Benny laughed. Benny then whispered something in Mick's ear and he and Sybil went into the spare bedroom.

"That didn't take long," I said as we went to our own bedroom.

Later we came out to get another drink and Sybil and Benny too had come up for air. We all sat down and Mick laid out more cocaine. The guys exchanged that look.

Here we go again. More of that dual relationship shit. I watched them. I wasn't as stupid as I used to be, so I knew what was coming next. *I am just so sick of this. Why can't I find a normal relationship with normal people?* Sure enough, Mick had Benny broach the subject. He wanted to sleep with Sybil so badly that he was actually willing to give me to Benny! *Where do I find these people? He's just like Allen. I'm going to stop this shit, right here and now.*

"No problem, Mick. You can sleep with Sybil, but I get Benny alone. You guys go that way and we go this way, deal?"

Mick stopped dead in his tracks. "But I thought..."

"No buts. The only way I do this is in separate bedrooms."

Mick agreed reluctantly.

When we got to the bedroom, Benny looked at me. "You don't really like this, do you?"

"Benny, I'm a one man woman. Always have been and always will be, but for some reason I can't seem to find a man that appreciates that."

"That is because you are choosing your mate from within the confines of Sodom and Gomorrah," Michael whispered.

"You are some kind of gorgeous man and if I had met you first, I would have been all over you. Besides, I have a feeling this will be the last time Mick decides to do this. So let's do this thing."

When we came out, Mick never took his eyes off of me for a second.

"Now that was well worth the wait," I said with a smile.

Mick's eyes got big and his mouth opened, but no sound came out. I would have preferred chocolate to sleeping with Benny, but I wasn't going to let Mick have the satisfaction of knowing it.

"You know, you really should be careful who you let your woman sleep with because you never know how good the guy might be," I said as I kissed Benny on the cheek.

Mick looked at me again and again he opened his mouth, but he was too upset to speak. From then on, Mick never brought another girl to our home and he never asked for any more of that dual relationship crap. Funny how these men can dish it out, but they never can take it when the shoe is on the other foot.

The next night we went to Jimmy Ray's club in Fort Worth and had a spectacular time. Sybil stayed for a few more weeks before she became bored and then she was gone.

After Sybil left, I stopped by to see Pamela and the kids. Pam was busy sewing as she often did.

"Pam, what are you making?"

"I'm making a dress to wear to church tomorrow. Why don't you come with us?"

"Me? In a church? I don't think so."

"Why not?"

"Because I fear God and I don't play with Him."

"What does that mean?"

"I am wrong, I do wrong, and I live wrong. I have no intention of changing, so I'm not going to pretend that I am."

"Well, one thing is for sure, at least you're consistent."

"That I am my friend."

"My dear child, if only you knew, Jesus will take you just as you are. You'll never be good enough to enter into His house. It is only by His grace and His grace alone that you will enter into the Kingdom," whispered Michael.

For some reason, I felt as if I had missed something, but I couldn't put my finger on it. Sort of like the forgotten words to a song. I shook my head and shoulders in the hope that that feeling would go away.

That Tuesday, I received some familiar news. *What is it about living with a guy? It's not like we haven't been careful.*

"Melissa my child, this time you must make a sacrifice.

Your destiny and that of this unborn child are intertwined. At all cost, you must not allow this one to be cut from your womb. He is a living being and he must live, Melissa."

Mick was going to freak out when I told him. I waited until he was high on Hennessy and cocaine. When he passed me the cocaine, I shook my head.

"You don't want any coke! What in the world is going on?" He looked up and laughed. "I think lightning is going to strike any minute. No, really. Here." He shoved it at me again.

"No, Mick, I'm not doing any. I'm pregnant."

His mouth opened and his jaw dropped. "What did you say?"

"I said I'm pregnant and I'm not doing any coke."

"You're kidding, right? You're still mad about Indigo and Sybil and you're trying to get back at me, right?"

"Wrong. I'm not kidding."

"Okay, I'm sorry about Indigo and I'm really sorry about Sybil. I won't bring another girl home, okay? Now do a line of coke."

"You're not sorry. The only reason you stopped your shit is because you got jealous when you gave me to Benny, but that has nothing to do with it. I'm not mad; I'm pregnant."

"Okay, well, there's still time to...you know...have an abortion."

"I'm not having an abortion, Mick. So you may as well prepare yourself."

"Why, Melissa? Why won't you have an abortion? You told me you've done it before."

"I don't know why, but I'm not."

What an ass he is! Mick decided having a pregnant woman around who would not party was a drag, so he got me an apartment at Wood Hollow Apartments in Oak Cliff.

"That's okay, little one; it's just you and me and Mommy is going to take care of you," I said to my stomach. Nine months was a long time. It was sort of like being in Sybil Brand. My mother freaked and my brother freaked and no one else was happy about it either.

My phone was ringing. "Hello?"

"Hey, girl!"

"Sybil, is that you?"

"Of course, it's me. Who else would be calling you at this hour?"

"No one except maybe Mick and he's too busy banging Indigo or some other color."

"Oh, don't worry. As soon as you have that baby, you'll have him back in no time."

"Sybil, should I want a man back that stashes me on the back burner because I'm pregnant and no fun anymore."

"It's not like you didn't know what kind of guy he was."

"How right you are about that! So what's going on in my town? I really miss Atlanta. I hate Texas."

"I know, Melissa; I know. Guess what?"

"What? Don't keep me in suspense."

"I met a guy that I like."

"Really. And what's new about that?"

"I mean it, Melissa; I really like him, as in 'marry him' like him!"

"What!"

"Yeah, and guess what else?"

"I'm scared to ask."

"He's a cop."

"What!"

"You said that already," Sybil replied.

"Are you crazy? Have you lost your mind?"

"No, really; he's cool and he knows," she whispered.

"He knows? About everything?"

"Yep, about everything."

"He likes that freaky stuff like you do, doesn't he?"

"Well, yeah. I brought him a girl for his birthday."

"What does he think about the coke? Does he know about that too?"

"He knows everything."

"Whatever makes you happy, Sybil. Whatever makes you happy."

I continued to abstain from drugs, cigarettes, marijuana, and alcohol for five months.

"You need, you want, you need that euphoria again. It has been such a long time. Go ahead; it will not harm the child. You need it; you need it!" whispered Valafar.

I was so depressed, hidden away from all of the action. I picked up the phone and called Angie, a friend of Mick's. "Hey, Angie. What's going on?"

"Hey, pregnant one. How's that baby?"

"Angie, to tell the truth, I'm sick of being so good."

"What do you mean?"

"I mean I need a hit."

"Is it cool to do that, you know, while you're pregnant?"

"Sure it's okay. But you know Mick would have a fit, so you go and pick it up. He left me plenty of cash. Come by here and get the money and then go over there and get at least a couple of grams and we'll cook it up.

"Okay. If you think it's cool, then I'm game."

Michael hovered over Melissa. Right before she inhaled the freebase, he swooped down into her womb and wrapped his wings around the baby to protect him from the freebase. "Hello, little one. Do not be afraid. I will protect you." Each time Melissa freebased, Michael was there to protect little Mickey.

While I was in my eighth month, I had complications and my physician confined me to bed rest. "Is there anything wrong with the baby?"

"No, Melissa, the baby is fine. He's the perfect weight and has a strong heartbeat. Even his lungs are fully developed. Even if you had the baby now, he would be a good size. But I would prefer you carry him to term. That's why I'm ordering bed rest. It's not the baby I'm worried about; it's you," he replied.

Maybe he wasn't worried, but I was because I knew I had smoked cocaine. "You know, my friend is also pregnant and she won't stop smoking cocaine. What's that going to do to her baby?"

"For one thing, the baby will have a low birth weight. Second, he'll be born addicted and sick and will require incubation. It also causes undeveloped lungs and irregular heartbeat."

I had no idea that it could do all of those things and I was mortified! *I have got to stop smoking! How strange that the baby is not underweight and is already fully developed. The doctor has no idea I smoked cocaine. Even the baby's heartbeat is perfect. Maybe God is giving me a break, not that I deserve one. Maybe not me, but the baby. I guess I better quit while I'm ahead or at least while the baby's ahead. Even the baby seems to have a Guardian Angel.*

Because the doctor had confined me to bed rest, I was forced to return to Mick's so he could look after me. *Where the hell is he? I'm starving to death.* The doctor had told me that I could only get up to go to the bathroom, so it was Mick's job to bring me food. But every day, I would lie there waiting and starving. I finally picked up the phone and called Pamela.

"Hey, Pam. I know it's late, but I'm starving. Do you think Rachel could bring me something to eat?"

"Melissa, it's ten o'clock at night! Do you mean to tell me that jackass hasn't brought you anything to eat?"

"No, Pam, and I'm dying over here."

"We'll be there in fifteen minutes to get you."

"What do you mean 'get me'?"

"You are not staying there another minute. When I get there, I'll pack you a bag and you're coming home with me so that you can get the proper care."

I knew better than to argue with Pam, not that I really wanted to anyway. I left Mick a note.

After I had eaten, Mick called.

"Melissa, what the hell is going on? Why are you at Pamela's?"

"Well, let's see. It's eleven o'clock and you just arrived home. Do you really think babies eat on club time? I haven't had anything to eat in eleven hours, Mick. But I'm willing to bet that you had yourself a nice juicy steak while you were at the club."

"Ah, come on, Melissa. I got tied up; the club doesn't run by itself."

"Mick, you have flunkies at your beck and call. You could have sent someone over."

"I know, Melissa, but I just forgot. Give me a break; this is all new to me, okay?"

"I am giving you a break, Mick, a permanent one. I'm staying at Pamela's until the doctor says that I can get up. Goodnight." I slammed down the phone as Pamela continued to mumble slanderous things about Mick.

Once I was closer to my due date, I was able to get up, so I went back home to my apartment.

Chapter Twelve

Baby Makes Three

Oh, my goodness! My water broke! It was three in the morning and I was in labor. I picked up the phone and called Mick. No answer at the club or at home.

"He's out banging somebody," I sighed in disgust. I called Pamela. "Pam, it's Melissa."

"Melissa, are you in labor?"

"I think so. My water broke and I keep having these pains."

"Girl, that's labor! Rachel and I will be right over." They arrived in fifteen minutes. "Let's go. We're having a baby. Did you call the jackass?"

"Pamela, that's not nice," I said between breaths.

"No, but it's true."

"I tried to call him, but he's nowhere to be found."

"Like I said, jackass," Pamela replied. Pamela called my mom and Michael and they were both there in an hour. Mom never left my side. I had been in labor for ten hours before Mick showed up. He saw me get one labor pain and nearly passed out.

"Melissa, I really can't handle this. I'm going to the club," he said as he mopped the sweat from his forehead. *I'm the one in labor and he can't handle it.* "Call me at the club when he comes out," he said as he hurried from the room. *He really is a jackass.*

Then Michael had to go on duty, but he kept in constant radio contact with the nurse's station.

"Push, Miss Bowan, push," the doctor cried.

I yelled at the top of my lungs. "Shit!"

"Miss Bowan, it doesn't call for that kind of language"

"Have you ever had a baby?"

"No," he replied as if it were a stupid question.

"Then you need to shut up!"

I pushed and cursed and he shut up. Twenty-two hours after I went into labor Mickey was born.

Michael came back just in time and was the first one to hold Mickey. "He's beautiful and he…kind of looks like…Michael Jr."

All of a sudden, I remembered what the doctor had said about drug babies. "Is he…is he all right?"

"He's fabulous. I wish all the babies I delivered were this healthy."

"He really does have a Guardian Angel," I said under my breath.

To make amends for abandoning me while I was in labor, Mick picked Mickey and me up three days later in a limo, complete with flowers, Dom Perignon, and plenty of cigars.

Mick had decided that I should keep my apartment for a while. I think he was scared of having an infant around. Everything was quiet until six months after Mickey was born; he developed diarrhea, a routine illness for a baby. I just kept changing diapers every other minute, but I didn't think it was a big deal. On the fourth day, Mickey was having a fit. He kept crying and crying and crying. On the fifth day, he not only stopped crying but stopped doing everything.

"Melissa, call the doctor now!" Michael said urgently. "Little Mickey is gravely ill. Call the doctor, Melissa!"

Mickey seems awfully sluggish. He's always so active and tries to lift his head and see everything, but today he seems so listless. Maybe I should call the doctor, but he's going to think I'm stupid, one of those mothers that panics every time her baby gets a cold. I'm not going to bother him at this time of night; it's stupid.

"Melissa! Call him now! He's very sick!" Michael hovered near Melissa's heart and flapped his wings.

My little voice didn't seem to think it was stupid and for some reason my heart skipped a beat, as it did when I was frightened. *He's sick! He's really sick! I'm calling the doctor and I don't care if it's late.* I picked up the phone and called the doctor and left a message with his service. My son's doctor was a very close friend of Mick's. He called back within five minutes.

"Melissa, what's wrong with Mickey?" he asked, even before saying hello.

"I don't know, Dr. Moss. He doesn't move or try and lift his head as he usually does."

"Melissa, does he have any other symptoms?"

"He had a fever and diarrhea a few days ago."

Michael swarmed around Dr. Moss. "You need to see the baby. Sometimes it is good to be old fashioned. You like to make house calls, as physicians of old once did. Tell her you will come now."

"I'm coming over right now; I'm not too far from you."

"You would do that?" I asked.

"Of course. I'll be there in twenty minutes." Dr. Moss was true to his word. He took one look at Mickey. "He needs a hospital now!"

"Hospital? What's wrong with him?"

"He's dehydrated. He doesn't have an ounce of sodium in his body."

"Is that bad?" I asked in bewilderment.

"Yes, Melissa, that's very bad. Now let's go, now!"

I called Mick and he met us at the hospital.

"Miss Bowan, do you have insurance?" the lady at the desk asked.

"No, I don't," I said as I looked at Mick.

"I'll pay cash," Mick responded.

"Cash? Sir, do you realize that the cost of hospitalization is thousands of dollars?" the lady asked.

Mick reached into his pocket and extracted a money clip with a huge wad of cash and counted out three thousand dollars. "Will this be sufficient to start?" The lady's mouth fell open. "Well, will it?" Mick asked.

"Yeah...uh...sure. No problem."

"If little Mickey incurs more charges, then call me and I'll come down and take care of it. Understand?" he said as he handed her his card.

"Yes, sir. I understand, Mr. McFarland."

"Good. Now where is my son?"

"He's in Room 268, Mr. McFarland."

"Thank you, thank you very much," he replied.

"My, how interesting it is that you became Mr. McFarland after you paid three thousand dollars," I retorted.

"Money talks. Always has and always will."

We went into Mickey's room as Dr. Moss was giving his nurse instructions. "Guys, Mickey's going to be here at least a week. Mick, this could get to be very expensive."

"No problem. Whatever Mickey needs, Mickey gets."

"I want to stay in here with him. I'm not leaving here unless Mickey leaves with me."

"I knew you wouldn't leave him, so I have instructed housekeeping to bring you a cot."

"Dr. Moss, you are a godsend."

"No, I'm just old fashioned."

"Nonetheless, I'm grateful."

"I'll be back in the morning to check on Mickey. My nurses are top notch and will take good care of him. Don't worry."

Of course, Mick made excuses and left after an hour.

Mickey improved by the third day and at the end of the week he was released. I decided to move back in with Mick. I missed the action and taking care of a baby was a lot of work. I needed some fun.

As soon as I moved back in with Mick, I resumed all of my previous habits. Mick even encouraged it.

Valafar flew around in circles. "You need it; you want it! Tell her to use the injection device for the pharmaceuticals. She cannot resist it. It is in her bloodline."

"You need, you want, you need," the demons chanted.

Mick was cutting the cocaine with Mannitol, a baby laxative, so that he could bag it up. "Melissa, why don't you test this stuff for me before I cut it?"

"What do you mean test it? I just snorted some. It's okay."

"No, I mean, you know, shoot it."

"You want me to shoot up?"

"Yeah, that's the only true test."

"I would need a set of works."

"What's that?"

"A syringe, dummy."

"I got some in the back."

"You have a set of works here? Why, why do you have syringes here?"

"Because I need someone to test it. Someone who knows what they're doing."

"I don't know if that's a good idea. Once you start hitting this stuff, it's not easy to stop."

"It's cool; you can do it," he said.

"Okay. Where are the works?"

"Look in my travel bag." I went to the bedroom and came back with the syringes. "So how do you do it?" he asked.

"Give me a fourth of a gram."

"A fourth of a gram! Isn't that a lot?"

"We'll see in a minute." I took a tablespoon and poured the coke in the spoon. I then took the syringe and a cup of water and pulled a little of the water up into the syringe and squirted it into the spoon with the cocaine. I took the orange syringe cap and used it to mix and grind the cocaine with the water.

"You see that?"

"What?"

"That stuff floating in it, which looks like sugar."

"Yeah. What is that?"

"That is what the guy cut this stuff with before you got it. That is why I needed a fourth of a gram. This stuff is already cut pretty well."

I took a very small piece of cotton and rolled it into a ball and then I put it in the mixture of cocaine and water. I was then able to stick the tip of the syringe in the cotton and pull up the cocaine into the syringe. "Anything that is not cocaine will be caught in the cotton," I said. I rolled up my sleeve, put the needle in my vein, and pumped the coke straight into my bloodstream.

"Well? How is it?"

"It's okay, but I would need twice that amount for the kind of high I'm used to. This stuff is crap compared to what comes straight off the boat."

"But I paid top dollar for this stuff!"

"I'm sorry. You got played. It's been cut at least four or five times already. If you cut it again, it won't be worth a shit. And that was just a tease. Since you were the one that insisted I do this shit, you need to give me enough to get a good high."

"Ah, come on, Melissa. You just did a fourth of a gram."

"That's your problem," I snickered. "You shouldn't have started something you couldn't finish. Now pony up."

"Yeah, all right."

I continued to shoot up for the next hour. Mick had no idea what he had started because I continued to shoot cocaine for the next five months. Poor Mickey was stuck with a cocaine dealer for a daddy and a junkie for a mother.

While Mick was at the club, I decided to take the money he had given me to get some cocaine. I went to a house that I had heard about. They sold cocaine there; you could buy it and then cook it or shoot it—whatever your pleasure—and they provided all of the necessary dope and equipment. I couldn't find a sitter, so I took Mickey with me, knowing that it was a stupid thing to do.

When I walked in, the owner greeted me. "Are you sure you know where you are? You don't look like you belong here with that mink coat and all."

"I assure you I know exactly where I am."

"This ain't really no place for a kid either, you know?"

"What are you? My father? Do you want my money or not?"

"No problem, lady. What's your pleasure?"

"Give me two grams, a set of clean works, and a room. And don't give me any shit. I want the good stuff and I will know the difference!"

"Right this way."

He provided everything I asked for and then politely disappeared. After an hour, I ran out of money so I bartered my mink coat for three more grams of coke. Three grams of coke was worth three hundred dollars. My mink was worth at least two thousand. After two more hours, Mickey woke up and started to cry.

"Come on, Mickey. This is no time for crying. Mommy's busy."

"Melissa get little Mickey and leave this place immediately! Melissa, this is no place for Mickey! Think of him, not yourself. You have a baby now; you cannot keep up this sort of activity," Michael insisted.

"Oh, shut up! Shut up! Why do you always have to spoil my fun by telling me what to do?" I asked the little voice that seemed always to get in my head somehow.

"You must leave this place, Melissa! You must do it now!"

Michael briefly left Melissa's side because he knew trouble was brewing in the other room. He went through the wall to the other side where two men were arguing.

"You stole my rock. I ought a shoot your ass right now!" The man's name was Bobby and he thought that Hank had taken a rock of cocaine that the two of them had cooked into freebase.

"I want it back right now, Hank. I know you took it." Bobby's hand was on his gun and so was Hank's.

"Are you callin' me a thief?" Hank yelled.

What is all that shouting about? I better get Mickey out of here. My subconscious is right; this is no place for him. Oh, why did I ever listen to Mick and start this shit back up again? Stupid! Stupid! Stupid!

Michael saw the rock cocaine that Bobby was too high to see. He flapped his wings just a little and it rolled out far enough for Bobby and Hank to see it.

"I told you I didn't take it. See! You was wrong and you're blind as a bat too. The damn thing was right under your nose all the time."

"Shut up and put it in the pipe," Bobby said.

I packed Mickey up and got out of there as fast as I could.

After I got in the car, I had to turn around to get to the freeway. As soon as I had gone a block, I saw police cars pull up to the dope house. I missed being busted by only two minutes! I was forced to proceed down the street because it would have looked suspicious to turn around. An officer was standing in the street flagging every car that came down the block. Several of the occupants were being detained. *Oh, what do I do now?*

"Extract a parcel of writing paper from your satchel and request directions to the apothecary," Michael whispered.

I rolled down my window. "Officer, is there a twenty-four-hour drugstore near here?" I pulled a piece of paper from my purse. "I thought the pharmacist said Chapel Street. Is that right?"

"Miss, you're in the wrong area and this is no place for you and a baby. Make a right at the corner and go two blocks and get on I-75. This area is infested with drug dealers and we're about to make a major bust. I need to be sure you are as far away from here as possible."

"Yes, sir, right at the corner and two blocks, and thank you so much."

"Hey, lock your doors too!"

"Yes, sir, I will." I rolled up my window and high-tailed it out of there as fast as possible. I breathed a sigh of relief. "Okay, I'm sorry. You were right as usual and I will never tell you to shut up again," I said to the little voice.

I lied to Mick and told him that my coat had been stolen and voilà! He brought me another one, just like that.

"Melissa!"

"What the hell are you yelling about? Can't a woman get any sleep around here?" I walked into the living room. "What do you want and why are you yelling?"

"You did it again, didn't you?" he yelled.

"Did what Mick?"

"Went into my stash. I've had three calls and all of them say that their grams are short."

"Well, your scales must be off because I didn't mess with your stash," I lied.

"I know you did it! I checked my scales and they're fine! Do you know what you've done? People get killed for shit like this!"

"Stop yelling. You're going to wake the baby."

"Wake the baby! I don't give a shit about waking the baby. I give a shit about my reputation and you're ruining it!"

"Melissa get the baby and leave right now," Michael said. "He is very angry; take little Mickey and go now!"

Mick put his finger in my face. "This is going to cost me over a thousand dollars if all of those grams are short. Are they short, Melissa? I need to know, right now!"

"I don't know anything about your shit. Just leave me alone."

"Leave you alone! Leave you alone!" He was scaring me. He took one of his golf clubs out of his golf bag that was sitting next to the door. "You don't want to mess with me about my dope. Do you hear me!" he yelled, as he waved the golf club around.

"Go now," Michael yelled.

Mickey started crying and I scooped him up and ran out the front door. I didn't even stop to put on my shoes. I ran down to the end of the block. I saw an older gentleman, who lived around the corner. I flagged him down. "Sir, I need help."

"What's wrong, miss? Where are your shoes?"

"I just had a really bad argument with my husband and I ran out without them. Can you take me to the corner, so I can use the phone?"

"Sure, miss; get in." He dropped me at the 7-Eleven store. "Are you sure you'll be all right?"

"Yes, I'm fine. Thank you."

"Okay. Take care of that little one."

I picked up the phone and called the police. When they arrived, I asked them to escort me back so that I could get some things.

"Did he hit you, Miss Bowan?"

"No, we had an argument and I just want to get my stuff; that's all."

"Did he threaten you in any way?"

"No," I lied. "I just don't want any trouble."

"Okay. Let's go then."

When Mick opened the door, I could tell that he couldn't believe I had actually brought the police to his house. *Serves him right! This is all his fault in the first place.* The officer waited while I got my things. Mick was so nice it was as if he were a different person. I only took the stuff I needed. I left the mink and all of the jewelry and expensive stuff he had bought me and I went to Pamela's. I had been there ten minutes when he called.

"I can't believe you brought the police to the house. That was really stupid."

"And waving a golf club around is smart?" I snapped. "You better be glad I didn't call Michael! Because if he knew you waved a golf club at his sister, you would be better off dealing with the thugs who got short bags of coke than dealing with him."

"Melissa, you know I wouldn't have hit you with it."

"I know no such thing. All I know is that you waved it as you were screaming at the top of your lungs like a mad man."

"I would not have hit you, Melissa. I was only trying to scare you."

"Well, congratulations! It worked," and I slammed down the phone.

For the next few weeks, Mick made every attempt to woo me back. He sent flowers and gifts and he called every day. When I picked up the phone, I knew it would be him again.

"Melissa, you left your mink and your jewelry."

"It's not my mink or my jewelry; it's yours. You bought it and it belongs to you. I, on the other hand, do not belong to you."

"Melissa, I bought those things for you."

"No, you stole those things for me."

"I did not steal anything. I am not a thief."

"Okay, maybe you didn't, but somebody did before they sold it to you. That makes you no better than a thief."

"Melissa, give me a break here, okay? I'm really trying to make amends. I'm going to send Sarg over with your stuff because I want you to have it, even if you don't come back."

"Whatever! You can send whatever you want, but it won't change anything. Goodbye!" *Stew on that for a while.* Sarg came by and brought my mink and my jewelry.

"Mick asked me to give you this. It's for Mickey." He gave me a bear and an envelope. When I opened the envelope, there was three hundred dollars in it.

"Thanks, Sarg."

"If you need anything else, miss, just let me know."

"Sure, Sarg. Thanks."

While Mickey was sleeping in the room with Rachel, I took the money and went out to score some dope. When I got back, Pamela was cooking. I waved and quickly retreated to the bathroom.

Valafar buzzed around Melissa's head. "More, more, more. You need more, my dear."

"More, more, more," chanted the demons.

I filled the syringe and made the mistake of pumping it in my vein as I was standing in front of the sink.

"I guess this stuff is better than I thought," I said and I passed out. When I hit the sink, it came crashing off the wall.

Michael arrived just as Melissa hit the sink. When Valafar saw Michael, he dived to avoid his sword. Whoosh! Michael severed the heads of the two demons that were chanting. It was just enough time for Valafar to flee, for Michael needed to assist Melissa and didn't have time to chase him.

"What the hell was that crash? Melissa? Melissa, are you all right?" Pamela banged on the door but I didn't answer. She ran and got a screwdriver and started to take the bolts off the door. Rachel ran to help her.

As the girls attempted to get the door off its hinges, Michael hovered over Melissa. He swooped down into her chest and pumped her heart because there was no human for him to use for the task. "Melissa, you must awaken. What will happen to poor Mickey without his mother?" Michael reached out and nudged the edge of the sink and water began gushing all over Melissa.

"Ahhhhh...what happened?" Pam and Rachel got the door off just as I scooped the syringe up and put it in my pants. "Are you all right?" Pamela cried.

"I must have passed out. Oh, my gosh! Look what I did to your sink!"

"Don't worry about the sink! What happened?"

"I don't know. I was standing at the sink and I guess my blood sugar dropped and I passed out. It's happened before."

"Well, sit down. You need to eat and I better call a plumber."

"Don't worry. Mick will have it fixed for you."

I decided that I'd better get my own place if I wanted to get high. So that Friday I moved. The place was a really gorgeous duplex with two bedrooms and two baths. I saw Mick a couple of times a week. Of course, his main priority was sex and mine was cocaine. He would give me money for the rent and each time I would use it for cocaine.

One weekend I left Mickey with Pamela and went on a binge. I found my way to a hotel in Oak Cliff that housed nothing but small time dealers and street hookers. I hooked up with a Puerto Rican and got high for three days. When I finally surfaced, I had to come up with a plausible explanation for leaving Mickey for three straight days without so much as a phone call, so I told Pamela and Rachael that the guy had made we stay with him against my will. Then I made them promise not to tell Michael.

Six months after I moved out, I arrived home to find the locks changed. Again I ended up at Pamela's. When I called the property manager the next day, I was informed that my belongings were being held in lieu of nonpayment of rent, which is legal in parts of Texas. I owed over fifteen hundred dollars. Mick refused to pay it. All of my beautiful clothes and all of that expensive furniture–gone. Well, easy come, easy go, right?

The next day I received startling news. "What? You have got to be kidding me!" I slammed down the phone. *Well of all the stupid....* I couldn't even think of words to describe how stupid I felt at being pregnant again. *There is no way I'm bringing another baby into this hellish life.* I called Mick and told him.

"What!"

"Don't worry. I wouldn't have another baby with you for all the coke in Peru."

"Kill your seed; kill your seed," the demons chanted.

"You don't have to be insulting," he replied.

"You just be prepared to pay for my abortion. I'm making an appointment for this Friday. And you're taking me too."

"Whatever you say. No problem."

That Friday was like a rerun of a bad B-movie, starring Melissa Bowan.

"I don't know what kind of condoms they're making these days, but this is ridiculous," I said.

"To be honest, I knew that it broke, but I was hoping we would come out okay," Mick said sheepishly.

"You can thank me for that. I made sure you chose the container with the flawed contents," laughed Valafar. "Now, my pretty, you must kill your seed."

"Kill your seed; kill your seed," the demons chanted.

"You knew and you didn't tell me!" I yelled.

"I didn't really think you would get pregnant. I'm sorry."

"You're sorry!" I turned my back on him.

Even though the Lord had prepared Michael for the four times that he would be required to escort the unborns, each time seemed more difficult than the first. Michael cried as he wrapped the baby in his wings to be taken to Heaven.

Mick did everything he could to make amends, including propose.

"You want to do what!"

"You heard me. Let's get married. Nothing big. We can do it at the house."

"Are you serious?"

"Yes, Melissa. I love you and I want to marry you."

"Will your father do the ceremony?" Mick's father was a pastor and had his own church. Believe it or not, Mick too had gone to Bible

College with theology as his major.

"Uh...he won't be able to. He's really tied up right now, but I'll find someone, okay?"

"He's lying, Melissa."

I knew it made no sense that his dad would miss this opportunity to marry us, but I didn't want to hear it so I pushed the voice away and shook my shoulders.

"Okay," I replied.

"Does that mean you'll come home?"

I decided it was best to go back to Mick's anyway. Getting high around normal people wasn't a good idea. "Yeah. I'll come home."

Mick was ecstatic to get me back and I was ecstatic that we were getting married. I planned a small ceremony, but for some reason Mick didn't want to invite anyone. He said it was our private moment. Little Mickey thought it was a game; he was so cute!

I went back to freebasing and snorting cocaine. Mick and I got high almost every day. Little Mickey was two now and getting into everything. We were careful never to leave cocaine within his reach. But we didn't realize was how smart he was.

One day Mickey was walking around and playing. I was snorting cocaine, using the edge of a business card to scoop it up and put it to my nose. After I finished, I put the mirror on top of the refrigerator out of his reach. As I watched TV with Mickey, he got up and walked over to the table. He picked up the business card and went to the ashtray. He scooped up some of the ashes from the ashtray and put it to his nose, just as he had seen me do with the cocaine. I was flabbergasted! But I didn't stop and I didn't change. I just kept right on getting high.

That weekend, I received some more startling news. "Mom, please tell me you're kidding!"

"No, I'm not. Paul said he didn't file the papers, so you're not divorced. Melissa?"

"Yeah, Mom?"

"Don't sound so dejected. It will only take a couple of months, but you do have to sign the papers again."

"Yeah, okay. I'll pick them up." I hung up the phone and just stood there. "I'm a bigamist! I'm going to jail."

"You are not wed to the one you call McFarland. Ask him

again for the documents," responded Michael.

I had asked Mick several times for our marriage certificate, but each time he had an excuse. The last time he had said that the certificate was in the safe at the club. That Wednesday, I decided to play detective and went to the courthouse downtown to investigate. *He has a reason for stalling and I'm going to find out what it is.*

"Now, this book has all the documentation. First, we look in this column," said the clerk.

"What does the list in this column mean?"

"This list shows where you got your marriage license and blood test. See, there's your names."

"Okay. Now what?"

"Now we flip over here and look to see where the authorized individual sent the license back to be recorded after you were married."

"What happens if the authorized person doesn't send it back?"

"Then you are not legally married. Of course, if you were married by a judge or an ordained minister of any kind that would not happen."

"Indeed," I said as I thought about the guy Mick brought home to marry us.

"Let's see. Surely your names are here." She looked three times. "I'm sorry, I...I don't understand!" she exclaimed.

"I do. It's not your fault. Thanks for your help."

"You were not destined to be wed to the likes of such a man. Therefore, what Satan planned for your detriment, the Lord has used for His glory. You are not wed to the one you call McFarland; therefore, you are not a bigamist. Do not be dismayed. God will send you the proper mate in due time."

I walked out of the courthouse. *God, you always manage to come through, even though I do think you have a strange sense of humor.* I smiled nonetheless. *He'll never change. He tricked me to get me to come home. What a jackass!* I went home but never told him that I knew.

It was Saturday afternoon and we had spent Friday night getting high. I woke up with a hang over. Mickey was hungry and I was too tired to cook, so I made oatmeal and dozed while he ate. I woke up with a start.

"Melissa!" Michael knew it was time. He must get Melissa

to leave or she and the baby would surely die soon. "Melissa! Listen to me now! You must get up immediately and go. If you do not leave now, you and the baby will die! Call your male sibling! Think of little Mickey. Now, Melissa!!" Michael touched Melissa's heart with his wings.

"Oh, my God! I need to leave here!" I said out loud. My heart started to thump as it always did when I was frightened. *Little Mickey didn't ask for this. It's my responsibility to take care of him. I've got to get him away from this madness.* I picked up the phone and called my brother.

Thank you, God! Michael answered on the first ring. "This is Agent Bowan. May I help you?"

"Michael!"

"Melissa, what's wrong? Are you and Mickey all right?"

"Yes, Michael. I'm fine but I need to leave here and I'm not coming back this time. Mick is not going to be happy about this, if you know what I mean."

"Melissa, you sound strange. You're really serious, aren't you?"

"I'm serious as a heart attack, Michael."

"I'll be there in thirty minutes and you let me take care of Mick." Michael arrived in twenty-two minutes.

"Where is he?"

"He's at the club."

"Good. Are you packed?"

"Yep. This is it."

"Let's go. I'll call him from the car."

Michael was one of the few people at that time who owned a car phone. Michael dialed the club and Mick answered.

"Mick, this is Michael."

"Hi, Michael. How are you?" Mick knew that Michael would have been very happy to lock him up and throw away the key.

"I'm fine, Mick. Mick, I'm in the car with Melissa and I have you on speaker."

"Melissa? What's going on? Is Mickey all right?"

"Mickey is fine, Mick, but I'm leaving you and I'm not coming back–ever. I do not want you to come near me or call me. I'm going to Michael's."

"Mick, did you hear the part about not coming near my sister and not calling her?" Michael asked.

"Yeah, I heard it, Michael, but Melissa has my son."

"If you want to see Mickey, I'll bring him to you every Friday. If you want to talk to him, you call me, not Melissa! Do you understand, Mick?"

"Yeah, Michael, I understand."

"I'm not sure you do, Mick. So I'm going to spell it out for you. If you ever come near my sister again, I will hurt you. Are we clear?"

"We're crystal clear, Michael; I got no beef with you."

"That's good, Mick. That's really good because I'm the last person on earth you want to have a beef with. You have a good day, Mick."

"You too, Michael."

"Now that that's taken care of, let's get you guys settled in. I hear that babies are chick magnets. Hey, little nephew, are you a chick magnet?" Michael asked, as he tickled him. Mickey just giggled.

"You let her get away!" Satan roared. Never had Valafar heard a sound such as this. As he lay prostrate on the floor, he opened one eye to see from where the roar had come. As soon as he did, he wished that he had not done so. Satan had transformed himself into a horrific beast, the likes of which Valafar had never seen. His fangs were enormous and appeared to be dripping blood. *Oh, how I wish I had not been so ambitious. I could have had a safe assignment enticing the damned. But, no! I chose this human that has caused the demise of the best of our warriors. Oh, woe to me, for I shall be eaten by those horrible fangs!*

"Master, have mercy. I assure you that it is temporary. She will be back with the male human that you selected before the sun sets thrice. The pharmaceuticals will entice her again. I have assigned my best warriors to see to it." Again he opened one eye. He sighed in relief, for Satan had seated himself back on the throne and had returned to his beautiful angelic appearance.

"See to it that they do not fail, for I will see all of you at the guillotine."

"Yes, Master. Thank you, Master."

"Leave me before I ponder further and sever your head from your feeble body."

Valafar bowed. "As you wish, Prince of Darkness and ruler of this world; praise be unto you."

The gatekeeper snickered as Valafar left the great hall.

" 'Master, have mercy, have mercy,'" he mimicked.

"You dare to mock me, gatekeeper?" Valafar bellowed, as he drew his sword.

"You wouldn't dare engage me!" challenged the gatekeeper.

"Are you willing to bet your head on that?" Valafar smirked.

"I suggest you busy yourself with the task of keeping your own head. You have somewhere you need to be, do you not?" replied the gatekeeper.

"That I do, gatekeeper. Until next time," he yelled as he took flight.

The Archangel Michael approached the Throne of God. He bowed before the King and said, "Praise be to the Father, the Son, and the Holy Spirit."

"My trusted warrior, you have served me well," Jesus replied. "My daughter will now begin a new journey. It is now time for her to be cured of this sickness that plagues her and countless others. From this moment on, she will no longer desire the euphoria obtained from pharmaceuticals. Many have searched for this cure. It is a cure that has eluded physicians, counselors, and even the men of God. The sickness of drug addiction is Satan's plague and a scourge upon the earth. At the proper time, this too will be brought to her remembrance and she will marvel at how few upon the earth have ever been given a permanent cure for an illness such as this. Many have found temporary cures in clinics and in hospices, but each time they again seek to escape into the darkness of addiction. But that which I command shall be done and can never be revoked, neither in the spirit nor in the flesh. Go now and proclaim that which I have commanded."

"The Lord God has spoken. In the Name of the Father, the Son, and the Holy Spirit, Amen," the Archangel Michael responded as he took flight.

Michael hovered above Melissa. "You will no longer desire pharmaceuticals. The King has spoken. That which He commands cannot be revoked by that which is in heaven nor

upon the earth."

Living with Michael was wonderful. He and Shelly had divorced and she had gotten the house. As usual Michael ended up in an apartment, but he didn't seem to mind. I would cook for him and he would eat as if he hadn't seen food in twenty years. Our favorite show was *Miami Vice* and he and I would watch it together every week.

It was weird the way my life seemed to change in an instant. Not only did I stop using drugs, but I also had absolutely no desire for drugs of any kind!

Michael led an interesting lifestyle. He lived for danger. He would come home and tell me horror stories of his escapades. Almost daily he was in some kind of altercation that involved guns and crooks of every kind. He constantly wrecked cars. If he wasn't wrapping one of his Corvettes around a tree, then he was wrecking one of the TBI vehicles. He wrecked so many that he received a written reprimand! It was as if some force was at work.

"You know, you lead some kind of exciting life," I said to Michael. "I've been listening to you and counting. Do you realize how many near death experiences you've had?"

"Yeah, it's kinda freaky."

"You know, I keep thinking about how strange it is, the number of times we both have had near misses. I mean I was actually dead for all practical purposes, yet here I am. That little voice has something to do with it too."

"What little voice?" Michael asked.

"The one that always warns me and things just always, sort of, get fixed somehow, you know?"

"I'm actually scared to admit that I do know because I have a little voice too. Somehow I always know where to shoot and what direction the bad guy is going to shoot from next. The guys joke about it. They call it my third eye. The only thing is it's not just when it comes to guns and bad guys. When I wrecked all of those cars, I always knew when to zig instead of zag. If I had zagged any of those times, the outcome would have been very different."

"Yeah, I know what you mean." I thought about DeeDee and me and the Ford Escort zigging and zagging. "You know, something is going on but I just can't figure it out."

"Don't go all weird on me. This isn't the Twilight Zone. It's all just coincidental."

"Yeah, right," I said, although I wasn't convinced.

Yodi buzzed around Melissa's head, for he had been instructed to entice her into the euphoria of pharmaceuticals. "You want, you need..." He tried to say the words, but no sound would come out. He cleared his throat and tried again. "You want, you need...."Again nothing. "What manner of calamity has befallen me?" He tried three more times to no avail. *I must report this strange phenomenon to Master at once.*

He took flight and flew as fast as he could to Valafar's strong hold. Yodi was so flustered that his landing was uneven and he collided with several others waiting to report.

"Are you in need of flight instructions, you clumsy fool?"

"Pardon me, but I am under duress. I was unable to complete my assignment and I fear Master will have my head."

The others immediately felt sorry for Yodi, for they knew what the penalty for failure would be. They whispered about his fate among themselves.

When Yodi entered Valafar's chambers, he trembled with fear. "Master, have mercy. I was unable to complete my assignment." Even though Valafar had been in Yodi's shoes with Satan only moments ago, he raised his sword to cut off Yodi's head. "Master, please, it was not of my own doing. I attempted to utter the words, but each time my voice was taken from me."

"What manner of nonsense is this?"

"I swear it, Master. Please accompany me to the human and I will prove to you my plight."

"Very well, proceed; but if I find that it is of your own doing, I will make yours a painful death," Valafar replied.

As soon as Yodi and Valafar arrived above Melissa's head, Yodi again attempted to entice her. "You want, you need..." And again nothing further would come out. Valafar watched in amazement.

"What are you? Daft?" Valafar then attempted to speak the words. "You want, you need..." But each time he attempted to entice Melissa to do pharmaceuticals, no sound would come out. Valafar was furious; he had promised Satan that the female would return to her mate. Yodi waited for Valafar to speak and, when he did not, he timidly requested to take leave.

"Be gone, you fool. I must ponder this strange phenomenon." Yodi was ecstatic that his head was intact and he hurried off into the clouds.

"How can I return to the prince with nonsense such as this? He will have my head for sure. Perhaps I too can convince him that this is not of my doing." Valafar reluctantly flew to Satan's palace.

"Back so soon?" the gatekeeper asked in bewilderment.

"Announce me at once! I have an important development to report."

"Indeed," the gatekeeper replied.

Valafar was sure to preen his wings before entering the great hall.

"Why have you returned to me with such haste?" Satan inquired.

"I have a strange phenomenon to report, the likes of which I have never witnessed."

"What is this phenomenon of which you speak?"

"I sent one of my best warriors to entice the human Melissa into pharmaceuticals, but he returned to report that each attempt had failed. Right before I was to cut off his head, he begged me to accompany him, as the failure was not of his own doing. I went to witness this occurrence with my own eyes and I too suffered as a deaf mute each time I attempted to entice the human."

Satan stood up and roared, throwing his head back and levitating from the ground. Lightning and thunder bounced about the room. The floors and the walls shook and mortar fell from the ceiling. This time Satan had transformed into a cross between a lion and a bear. As he watched, Valafar feared the shaking would destroy them all if Satan did not stop soon.

"It is His doing! He Who Sits at the Right Hand has commanded it!" Satan roared. "He has no right! This is my domain! Mine! Mine! Mine! She shall pay for this! She and her male sibling! You, find a weakness to exploit at once! I want them dead! Do you hear me? Dead!"

"Yes, M...m...master; at once, my prince." Valafar took leave. Never had he been so relieved. *This is bad, very bad indeed. Once the One Who Sits at the Right Hand has made a command, nothing good could come of it.* "Oh, why me?" he wailed. *Does Master not know that attempts to entice this human will only bring more trouble? If anyone is to be dead, I think it will be me,* he feared. "Oh, why me?" he wailed again.

Michael had very few vices. He didn't smoke and he never took a drink. As a matter of fact, he deplored alcohol and drugs. His first weakness was women and his second was danger–lots and lots of women and lots and lots of danger. That Christmas he bought eight bottles of perfume.

"You have got to be kidding me! You have eight women?"

"Well, I have two girlfriends; the others are acquaintances."

"Acquaintances that you have sex with," I retorted.

"A man's gotta do what a man's gotta do," he laughed. "Can I help it that women love me?"

I laughed too. "You're incorrigible, and when they catch up with you, you're going to be dead meat."

"Catch me? Not a chance."

"You have been forewarned," I replied, as he got ready for his multiple dates.

"Hello?"

"Hello, Melissa."

"Mick, you know Michael told you not to call me."

"I wasn't calling you; I was calling him. I can't help it that you answered the phone."

"Don't be a smart-ass. That's why he gave you his car phone number."

"Well, he's not in his car."

"Mick, cut to the chase. What do you want?"

"I want to see Mickey this weekend."

"No problem. I'll have Michael bring him over."

"You know, Melissa, as long as you live in Dallas, no one will ever want you because they know better than to mess with what belongs to me. Not only that, I'll never give you a divorce."

"You are so full of shit, Mick. I don't want anyone who knows you anyway because if they know you, then they aren't worth a shit. And on the subject of divorce, I went to the courthouse. I know we are not legally married. I've known for months. You're a slimy jackass. Always were and always will be."

"You think you're hot shit now that you're with your brother, don't you?"

"Actually I do because if you even think about coming near me, he'll kick your ass into next week. And for the life of me, I fail to see what I ever saw in you. I think I was experiencing temporary insanity," I retorted. "The only good thing to come out of you and your shit is Mickey. I'm really glad I'm far away from you and I'm going to make it my business to get even farther. Because something very bad is going to happen, and when it does, I don't want to be anywhere in the vicinity."

I slammed down the phone. *What a jackass!*

Nearly every other day I left Mickey with Rachel and went in search of employment. After nearly a month, I struck gold.

"Seek employment at the shop which barters furniture. It is the employment that will send you away from this place," the Archangel Michael said.

I decided to apply at a national furniture chain that had advertised a need for store managers.

"Miss Bowan, this employment requires that you relocate," said the district manager. "Do you have a problem with that?"

"No, sir, I do not."

"Great. Here is the list of store locations where we need managers. You have five locations to choose from."

I took the sheet and went down the list: Houston, Phoenix, Miami, Baltimore and Atlanta. *Yes, Atlanta, here I come.*

"Sir, I would prefer Atlanta if possible."

"Atlanta it is then. Can you leave in two weeks?"

"Two weeks is great." I went to Atlanta without even telling Mick. *Boy, is he going to be pissed.*

Chapter Thirteen

Honey I'm Home

As soon as I got to Atlanta, I called Faith and Sybil. I immediately went to see Faith, who had married a manager she met at Xerox. She too was a manager now and doing quite well. She and her husband owned two properties: a condo in Smyrna and one at the Plantation at Lenox. Her home was so beautiful that I was scared to let Mickey near the furniture. Everything was done in white, but Faith could have cared less about the furniture. She never scolded him once.

"Her spouse is not what he appears to be."

I had a bad vibe about her husband, but I couldn't put my finger on it because everything about him was perfect. I figured I must be wrong, but of course the voice was never wrong and Faith found out that he wasn't as wonderful as we thought. They later divorced.

I then called Sybil. "Honey, I'm home," I laughed.

"Melissa, what are you talking about?" Sybil asked.

"I mean I'm in Atlanta."

"Really? Cool. Where are you?"

"I'm in Gwinnett. My store is located in Gwinnett Mall and I got a condo at Beaver Ruin."

"Wow! You are way out there."

"So where are you located?"

"I'm living with my cop friend right in the heart of Atlanta, near Martin Luther King."

"Isn't that the hood?"

"Yeah, but they did renovations over here and a lot of yuppies have bought in the neighborhood."

"How is that going with you and the cop?"

"We're getting married."

"Sybil, have you lost your mind? You and a cop!"

"I have a job too. I sell cars."

"You? Selling cars? That's funny, Sybil."

"No, I'm not kidding! And not only that, I'm good at it! I'm so good that I'm their number one sales person."

"Wow, I'm impressed!" Sybil was straight and marrying a cop and working. I was straight with a baby and working again as a manager. *What are the odds of two people who are addicted to cocaine and using with a needle going straight? What are the odds of two call girls going in and out of hotel rooms with strangers and never getting hurt? Not only that, they both switch to straight jobs. Strange! Twilight Zone strange!*

"My darling child, there are no limits to what the King can do." Michael said with a smile. Raphael smiled too, for it had been his task to guard Sybil. It had required a legion of angels to accomplish this task. How proud he was that he had had a part in that which the King had planned for the human females. To see each of them safe and heading down the proper path was reward in itself.

And then the strangest thought occurred to me. *This new life is not what is odd; it was the old life that was totally out of my character. The drugs, the escort service, the dealers with their dual relationships–none of that was ever me. What was I thinking? That little voice of mine–it's almost as if it's schizophrenic. One moment I'm going one way and the next moment it's the opposite. Somehow I've got to learn not to listen to the bad one. Get a grip, girl! You never needed any help to do wrong; you just did it because you wanted to.*

"That is not true. You are being led, my child. The other is the voice of Satan. Heed the warning. Do not listen when he calls for you," said Michael.

I had been in Atlanta six months when it happened.

Valafar flitted back and forth in the vehicle of the assassins. "Kill him dead. He is of no use to me anymore. Perhaps his death will cause the female pain and grief. You must ensure his demise. Target his head, as it is a sure way to inflict death upon a human."

McFarland drove into the condominium parking lot. He had had a long night and he was tired. He turned off the engine and opened the door to his Mercedes and put one foot on the ground. As he did so, he looked up. The car next to him rolled down the window, which was tinted black. Before he could get his gun from the side door, the assassin raised his shotgun and shot Mick in the head. He was dead in an instant.

Michael walked over to the body that was sprawled out on the pavement. The officer raised the sheet and he looked at what was left of McFarland.

"They wanted to be sure he was dead," Michael said.

"Yeah. It was a hit. Probably by his own people," said the officer.

"You live by the sword, you die by the sword," Michael sighed. "I'm just glad my sister got away from him when she did."

"Your sister was hooked up with this creep?"

"Yeah, and they got a kid too."

"She's lucky to be alive. If she and the baby had been here, they would have made sure that they were dead too."

"Yep, lucky is not the word for what she is." *I guess I better call her,* Michael thought. *She really does have the third eye. Somehow she knew he was going to die. This really is the Twilight Zone.*

I had to work late and I was so tired that I was seeing double. As I pulled off my shoes, the phone rang. *Who is calling me? Probably Sybil. She's the only one who stays up this late.* But it was Faith, not Sybil.

"Melissa?"

"What is it, Faith? You sound weird"

**"It is the one you call McFarland; he is gone, my child,"
Michael whispered.**

"Melissa, I think you better come over here. I need to talk to you about something."

"Faith, it's ten o'clock at night. What could you possibly want to talk about?"

"McFarland."

"Is he dead?"

"Melissa, why don't you come over?"

"Faith, I'm tired and I have to go to work tomorrow and so do you. There's only one reason you would want me to come to Smyrna at ten o'clock at night to talk about McFarland. So just tell me. Is he dead?"

"Yes, Melissa. He's dead."

"Okay. I knew it was just a matter of time," I sighed.

"Michael said it was a contract killing, probably by his own people. He also said that Benny was in jail for tax evasion. You don't sound too broken up about it."

"Faith, I was over him when I left. My only regret is that I didn't let Mickey see him one more time before he died. That wasn't fair."

"So you're cool then?"

"Yeah, Faith, I'm cool. Goodnight."

"Goodnight, Melissa."

Almost every person I know is either in jail or dead. I wonder why Sybil and I are so lucky. We certainly should have died or been locked up a multitude of times. I just don't get it.

It is not luck, my child. God knows all things. When He has placed a hedge about you, there is no weapon formed against you that shall prosper.

McFarland's was the first death call. However nothing could prepare us for the next two! About two months after McFarland was murdered, Pamela called. "Girl, guess who was on the news last night?"

"You mean someone we know was on the news?"

"Not someone I know, but someone you definitely know."

"Who?"

"Jimmy Ray!"

"What was Jimmy Ray doing on the news?"

"Girl, he ran what the FBI called a drug cartel! They had banquet tables lined up with cocaine and guns. And then there were tables full of money, and even one with just jewelry. They said that he had four or five mistresses and each of them had his children and a house. His organization made a million dollars a month!"

"Pamela, you need to stop kidding."

"Girl, I'm serious! That man was some kind of kingpin and he didn't even get bail. I thought only murderers were denied bail."

"A black man in Fort Worth, Texas, with banquet tables full of cocaine? Please! He's lucky he didn't accidentally get shot," I retorted.

"Are you sure you didn't know anything about this?" Pamela

asked suspiciously.

"No, Pamela. I didn't really know him; I only visited his club with Mick. I did have a feeling that McFarland was going to get killed, but I don't know why and I don't really care why. I'm just glad I got Mickey away from there before the shit hit the fan."

"Me too, Melissa; me too."

"Speaking of children, how are Michael Junior and little Melissa? I guess we should stop calling her little now that she's fifteen." Pam was silent. "Pam, what's wrong?"

"Melissa ran away. She's been gone now for over nine weeks."

"Pamela, why didn't you tell me? What does Michael say? Can't he find her?"

"He did find her. Every time he finds her and brings her back, she runs away again. This has been going on for over a year. Now that she knows he will come for her, she hides and each time it's harder to find her. Last time he found her she was working the streets. She's a...hooker."

I just stood there.

"Last time she was home, she said that if he makes her come back again she was going to become an emancipated minor. We can't make her stay, Melissa. She refuses to listen to anyone."

"Pam, I don't know what to say. Do you realize how dangerous that is?"

"I know that, Melissa, but what am I supposed to do? I have to go to work; I can't lock her up every time I leave the house. As soon as I go to work or she goes to school, she vanishes again."

My own niece–a hooker! Not only that, she's on the street! I went to jail because I tried to get two strangers off the street and now my own niece is out there. Why didn't Michael tell me? Poor little Melissa is out there on the street! She's in the middle of ten times more crap than even I can imagine. The street is nothing like working the Plaza, and I wouldn't wish the call girl life on anyone. What must working the street with a pimp be like? Oh, my God! What is going to happen to her?

As a manager, I had to work nights and weekends and I was always looking for sitters because Mickey was a challenging child. The store I worked in was really nice, though, and I worked with a lot of nice people. My district manager would come by only twice a month, so I pretty much ran things on my own. This was his week to visit and he and I discussed plans for the store.

"Melissa, how do you like your new place?"

"I love it. It's a two bedroom and it's really close by."

"Do you have renters' insurance?"

"What's that?"

"It's a very inexpensive insurance that will replace all of your personal possessions in case of flood, fire, or theft."

"I don't know. I don't think I can afford that."

"Melissa, it's twelve dollars and you cannot afford not to have it. Here. I brought you an application. Just fill it out and mail it in with a twelve-dollar check. Twelve dollars can save you a lot of grief in the long run."

"Okay, if you say so." After he left, I filled out the form and mailed it on the way home. Twelve dollars meant a lot these days. It was so hard making ends meet. Every month I would be two days from having the electricity shut off. And then it would start all over again. Just one party call could make all of the difference.

Yodi flitted around Melissa's head. "Escorts, escorts, call them; call them. So much gold you need; you need gold."

I went and picked up the phone book. I looked at several of the escort service numbers and then I closed the book.

"Melissa, you must not listen to Satan. Think of Mickey; he is only three earth years. Who will care for him when the authorities apprehend you?" Michael raised his voice this time. "That life is over for you. Do not return to Sodom!"

My subconscious would not let me get away with it. "Okay, I won't do it," I said out loud. I closed that chapter of my life for good, but there was one more chapter that required my attention. Perhaps I should rephrase that. God closed that chapter and would now close another that needed His attention.

That Saturday, I decided to go to the south side of Atlanta. I was thinking of moving back across town. I was so far out in Gwinnett County. After looking around at places, I decided to splurge on take-out. *It has to be cheap, but I need vegetables to take home to Mickey,* I thought, as I rode down Old National Highway.

"Excellent," the demon Yodi exclaimed. "I have an old acquaintance who longs to see you. Stop here at this one. I have arranged a meeting for you."

I decided on a cheap fish place that I had been to before. As I got out, I thought about the last time I was here with Derek. *I wonder how his harem thing is going.* I laughed out loud at the thought.

As soon as I entered the restaurant I had that creepy crawly feeling behind my back. I whirled around. *He's here! Derek is somewhere in this restaurant.* I followed the sensation to the back dining area and looked up and down the aisles. His eyes met mine and he smiled that drop dead gorgeous smile of his and I melted. He got up and walked over. "Looking for me?"

"Actually I was."

"I was just kidding. I haven't seen you in years. How did you know I was here?" he asked.

"It was that Twilight Zone thing I told you about. I knew you were here the moment I set foot in this restaurant. I just followed my... spider sense or whatever it is and there you were."

"You know, you really need to stop that shit; it's not funny."

"I can't help whether it's funny or not. I pulled into this parking lot and as I got out I thought about you. Then I walked in here and felt your presence behind me. The only thing behind me was this dining room. I walked back here to look for you and voilà! Here you are."

"In that case I think it means that we are destined to be together, don't you?"

"I don't know about all of that, but it is certainly freaky and quite frankly it scares the shit out of me."

"Jessie will be glad to see you. We have a house right down the street. Why don't you drop by?"

"Okay, I will. Did you get rid of Jackie?"

"Yeah, it was long overdue."

"I'll say," I retorted as we walked out.

Jessie and Derek had a modest but nice house. Jessie was just the same. She greeted me with the same warm smile, just as if I wasn't another woman after her man. *Jessie, what do you see in him, as if I didn't know. It's one thing to have a romp in the hay with him, but it's another to be in love with him and set up house. I'm a fine one to talk. Mick wasn't worth a shit and neither was Allen or Mark.*

"Jessie, can I put this stuff in the fridge? I left Mickey with a sitter and I bought take- out for him to eat when I pick him up."

"Who's Mickey?" they both asked in unison.

"Oh, Mickey is my baby; he's almost three."

"You have a baby?"

"Yeah, don't act so shocked. I've actually become a very good mother. Of course, it did take me a couple of years to get the hang of it, but now that I do, it's cool."

Derek looked up. "I think lightning is going to strike here any second. Melissa with a baby–that's some kind of strange phenomenon."

"Maybe, but I gave up a lot to give him the right kind of home, so don't make fun of me," I said.

"We really missed you, didn't we, Jessie?" Derek had that look.

After I left Derek and Jessie's, I decided that that was it. *Lord, I do not want to know any more of these people and, whatever this voodoo thing is I have with Derek, I want it stopped.*

Michael was ecstatic; finally, she had requested help to be released from her demonic ties. *Now, I can deliver her request to the King.* **"Do not worry, my child. He will help you. He is the only one who can." Michael took flight.**

That was the last time I ever saw Derek or Jessie. The only person that I continued to see who was–well–strange was Sybil. She would remain in my life forever, but even she had changed into a normal person. Well, normal is a relative term. Let's just say, she was as normal as she could be for Sybil.

Chapter Fourteen

Someone Wants Us Dead!

"Come on, guys, the last one down is a rotten crook," they all laughed. The joke was they were all Texas Bureau of Investigation agents, so being a crook would just not do at all. Michael, Steven, Andrew, and ten other agents were all on their annual skiing trip in Aspen, Colorado. No one wanted to be the last one down the slope. They were all expert skiers and skied on the most dangerous slopes in Aspen, the black slopes.

Michael was a dare devil in everything he did, including skiing. He pulled down his mask and took off. "I know a short cut. I'll cut their asses off at the pass," Michael laughed as he glided down the slope.

"It is time," Jesus said. "You will again be required to cross to the other side. This task will also require the assistance of Gabriel, as Satan has planned the male sibling's demise in a remote region and there will be no other humans to use for this task. Gabriel will be required to take the human form of a physician, who carries the proper device to perform what humans refer to as a tracheotomy. Instruct the Heavenly Host to stand guard. Do not allow Satan's cohorts to approach the male sibling. He is to be guarded at all cost. Go at once. Time is short."

Michael and Gabriel bowed. "Praise be to the Father, the Son, and the Holy Spirit," they said in unison as they lifted off into the clouds.

Now is the time we have prepared for. The male sibling

would soon be his to take to Master. Valafar had been there to witness the one who was responsible for caring for the gliding devices. As he prepared the male sibling's devices, Valafar made sure that he had been distracted and, as a result, the male sibling's gliding device would soon malfunction.

Michael was skiing at full speed. All of a sudden there was a pop and his right ski broke into two pieces. "Aaaahhhhhh!" Michael yelled, but there was nothing he could do. He was skiing down the slope at seventy miles per hour, headed straight for a tree. He hit the tree at full speed. The impact killed him instantly, as it had every other human who had ever had the misfortune of hitting a stationary object while traveling seventy miles per hour.

Valafar and his warriors watched and waited. As soon as the human Michael hit the tree, they knew he was dead. "We've got him! He is ours; he is ours!" the demons shouted as they approached, unaware of Michael and the Heavenly Host. By the time they realized they had been ambushed, half of their army had been decimated. Yodi and the hundred soldiers to his right were all gone.

"Retreat!" Valafar yelled.

As the Heavenly Host fought, Gabriel transformed himself into a physician and glided down the slope to the human Michael. Gabriel did not bother with a pulse, for he knew the human Michael was dead. He took the tracheotomy tube from his bag and, using a scalpel, he cut a hole in his throat. He then inserted the tube to allow air into his lungs and began CPR. Seeing that it was the proper time, the Archangel Michael crossed the earthly plane and delivered the human Michael back into his body. He gasped for air.

"Okay, guys, the rescue squad is here," Andrew yelled. "Michael should have been down by now. Let's go and get our man back." Andrew and Michael's fellow agents followed the rescue squad up the mountain. When they found him, they were devastated.

"Is he dead?" yelled Andrew. "Move! Let me see him! Michael!" Andrew began to cry, as did most of the others. Michael looked as if he were humpty dumpty–broken into pieces without any chance of ever being put back together again.

"What's that in his neck?"

"I got a pulse!" cried the paramedic.

"He's alive? Are you sure? Look at him! He can't be alive!" Steven said.

"Well, he his," replied the paramedic. "Somebody trached him."

"What?"

"The tube. Somebody cut a hole in his throat to give him an airway and then stuck a tracheotomy tube in his throat."

"Who skis around with a trach tube?" asked the other paramedic.

"I don't know, but the problem now is getting him down. In the shape he's in, he doesn't have a chance of making it."

"To be honest, there wasn't a chance in hell that he could have survived the impact, so let's get moving." They put Michael on the stretcher and began to cart him down the slope.

The Archangels Gabriel and Michael watched from a distance.

"Shall we, Brother?"

"We shall," the Archangel Michael replied with a smile.

Gabriel and Michael crossed back over to the other side. As they surfaced into the spirit world, Valafar and his cohorts were running away with their tails between their legs.

"I almost feel sorrow for the likes of them when they are forced to admit defeat to the Prince of Darkness," said Gabriel.

"Yes, I am quite sure that many will lose their heads this day," replied Michael.

"Thank you for your assistance, Brother. I must make haste now; he will need me before he reaches the physician."

The Archangel Michael took flight. He wrapped his wings around the human Michael as the rescue squad carted him down the mountain. In addition, Raguel who had been the one who always told the human Michael when to shoot and when to zag was there, and a legion of the Heavenly Host followed close behind.

"We must be on our guard," the Archangel Michael said to Raguel. "Valfar and his host of demons will not give up so easily. They will wait and try again when the time presents itself. Be watchful and ready."

"Yes, sir. We will be ready," replied Raguel.

When they arrived in the emergency room, everyone began speaking at once as emergency personnel flocked around Michael.

"Agents, you've got to step back now and let us do our jobs; he's in good hands," the doctor spoke firmly and then turned to the paramedic. "You trached him? Good job, Bill."

"I didn't trach him, Doctor."

"You didn't? Well, who did?"

"We don't know."

"What do you mean you don't know?"

"He was trached already when we found him."

"What? On a mountain slope? That would mean a healthcare professional who just happened to have a trach tube would have had to be skiing behind him just at the right time?"

"Yeah, that pretty much sums it up."

"I have been a physician for twenty-five years and never have I left my home with a trach tube, much less have I carried one skiing!"

"Yeah, its Twilight Zone weird."

"I'll say."

"What now, Doc?"

"I haven't the faintest idea. He should be dead and I have no idea why or how he can be alive, much less how to keep him that way. I doubt very seriously if he'll last through the night, and even if he does, with that head trauma, his brain will be mush. His spinal cord has sustained a massive amount of damage, which also means he'll be a quadriplegic." The doctor worked franticly while he spoke. "Let's set these fractures and try to get him stable. All we can do now is go through all of the motions, not that it will do any good. Nurse!"

Valafar was not only furious but also terrified. Master would know that the human Michael had crossed to the other side. He would demand to know what had taken place and the demons that survived would surely place the blame upon him. "I was not to blame," wailed Valafar. "Oh, why did I ever fancy myself a general?"

At that moment a messenger arrived. "You have been summoned by the prince. Make haste, as others will suffer his wrath due to your incompetence." He looked upon Valafar with disdain.

Valafar took flight and arrived all too soon for his taste.

He hesitated before gliding through the gate. The idiot gate-keeper was waiting, gloating over his discomfort.

"Perhaps if you placed a bonnet upon your head, it might save you," the gatekeeper snickered.

"Silence, you fool! Can you not see that I am in distress?"

The gatekeeper laughed. "Your distress is quite evident. I am quite sure that you are eager to be announced; therefore, I shall not dawdle."

After the gatekeeper returned, Valafar again preened his wings, although he had done so several times.

Satan stood up. "What is the meaning of this?" he bellowed. "I felt the human cross to the other side and then just as quickly his presence vanished. Why is he not in his proper place?"

"It...it was Michael and the Heavenly Host," he stammered. "We were ambushed as we attempted to seize him and Michael returned him to the other side."

"That is impossible! There were no humans to assist him with preparing the body! The region was remote. I made sure of it!"

"G-g-gabriel took the human form of a physician. He prepared the body and then Michael delivered him into it," stammered Valafar.

"Aaaahhhhh!" Satan's roar was so loud the beautiful stained glass surrounding the gatekeeper exploded and shards of glass flew about the palace. Satan's numerous statues of himself exploded into thousands of pieces. The gatekeeper did not know if it was better to levitate or fall to the ground to avoid the barrage of falling objects and breaking glass.

Valafar watched in horror as Satan lifted his sword. His last memory, before Satan severed his head from his body, was that of a beast, which was a cross between a behemoth and a leviathan.

"Two prostitutes, a constable, and a drunkard! Why? Why would the likes of such a motley crew be of such importance to He Who Sits at the Right Hand? He stood up for the likes of Steven, but he was one of his beloved prophets. He stands for this... this prostitute! And then he dispatches not only the

**Archangel Michael but also our brother Gabriel to cross to the
other side for her male sibling! I will discover what lies beneath
this mystery! Gatekeeper!"**

"Come on, Mickey; stop dawdling. These packages are heavy."
Mickey was busy playing with something and wasn't listening to a
word I said. As I unlocked the door, I could hear the phone ringing.
"Come on, Mickey. Mommy has to get the phone." I closed the door
and got to the phone just in time. "Hello?"

"Hello. Is this Miss Bowan?"

"Yes."

"My name is Janis Jenkins and I'm a nurse in the ER in Aspen,
Colorado."

"Aspen, Colorado? I don't know anyone in Colorado."

"Miss Bowan, it's your brother Michael Bowan."

"Michael?" *Oh, yeah, he goes skiing there every year,* and then my
heart dropped out of my chest because I knew he was hurt.

"Melissa, he's been hurt," whispered Michael.

"What's wrong with Michael?" I shouted.

"Miss Bowan, please try and remain calm. Do you have a family
member there with you?"

"You tell me what's wrong with Michael this instant?"

"Miss Bowan, he was skiing down the black slopes, which are
extremely dangerous."

"Dammit! Just tell me!"

"He hit a tree and we don't think he will make it through the
night," she whispered. "Can you come right away?"

"You mean he's going to die?"

"I'm sorry."

I slammed down the phone and fell to my knees. "Please, God!
Don't let my brother die! I will...I will do anything you ask. I'll be
good, I promise. I'll go to church. For heaven's sake, I'll be a nun if
that's what you want. Just please, please don't let him die."

**"The King knew your request even before you asked. It has
already been granted, my child. Your brother is safe in the
hands of the King, as you are also."**

I called my sisters and my mom after I regained my composure.
"He won't let him die, I just know it," I said to Faith.

"How do you know?" Faith wailed. "Even the nurse said he

wouldn't last through the night."

"She doesn't know what she's talking about. God won't let him die."

"How can you be so sure?"

"I don't know; I just am. The question is how am I going to get to Colorado; do you know what that will cost?"

"Yeah, I know."

"Let me call the airlines and I'll call you back." I just stood there for a moment and then I went to get the phone book.

"Even when all earthly things are not possible, the King will provide a way." Michael smiled, for he knew who was on the other end of the phone.

Before I could find the number, the phone rang again.

"Hello?"

"Hello. Is this Miss Bowan?"

"Yes, it is."

"This is Rex Tanner. I have been informed that your brother Michael has had a serious accident." *Rex Tanner? Rex Tanner the Texas oil billionaire? You have got to be kidding me!* "I have also been informed that you and your family need to get to Michael immediately. I must apologize because my larger jet is overseas, but I would like to offer you and your family my smaller jet to get to Colorado. I have it fueling as we speak. Since your mother and Michael's fiancée are here in Dallas, after they arrive at Love Field, the jet will then fly to Atlanta. You can pick up any other family members you deem necessary. It will remain at your disposal for as long as you need it."

I was speechless.

"Miss Bowan?"

"Mr. Tanner, I'm speechless. You are a godsend."

"Agent Bowan came to my aid when my life was in danger, so it is the least I can do for him."

"Thank you so much. This is so above and beyond..." my voice trailed off. I was truly speechless.

After I rang off, I called Mom and told her where to go to get to Mr. Tanner's jet.

"Did you just say that all I had to do was drive to Love Field and there's a jet waiting for me?" Mom asked incredulously.

"Yep, it belongs to Mr. Tanner. He is a real southern gentleman, complete with a real Texan accent. He just called me and gave us his jet to use. Not only that, he actually apologized because it was the small jet and not the large one. Can you believe it? Like I would actually have the audacity to complain about the size!"

"Well, you know, perhaps there are some people that are actually that ungrateful, but I didn't raise you girls that way. I'm grateful to him and I don't care what size it is."

"Me too, Mother, me too. Call me when you get to the airport."

"Okay. I love you."

"I love you too. Bye." I called my sisters and then I packed for the trip. *Only God could get a billionaire to send a jet! That's just so...God!* I thought, and even as upset as I was, I smiled. "I'm coming, Michael," I said out loud.

When I saw Michael, I only thought I was prepared. Michael's fiancée, Amy, was devastated. She had just purchased her wedding dress and the invitations had been printed. Mother seemed in a trance, and none of us could stop crying.

"Miss Bowan, we are not equipped for this sort of trauma. He needs a real trauma center. We need to transport him immediately. You must choose a location. Denver is the closest, but you must also consider the fact that you and your family need to be close by. Can you stay in Denver...indefinitely?"

"No, Doctor, we can't. What about Parkland? Do they have the necessary facilities?"

"Yes, but you must consider the distance. I doubt that he can make it to Denver, much less all the way to Parkland, and then there's the cost. The type of jet needed to maintain life support with this sort of trauma exceeds seventy thousand dollars." I just stood there and stared at him, as did the rest of us.

Andrew and the others refused to leave Michael. "We never leave a man down, no matter what," Andrew replied. "When he goes, we go. Where he goes, we go." They all nodded. The Blue wall was mighty high and mighty wide. They loved him too.

I went to the waiting area to ponder what the doctor had said and to smoke a cigarette. Where do you get a seventy thousand-dollar medical aircraft and then which hospital do you choose, assuming that you can get one? As we sat discussing everything, the doctor came scurrying around the corner.

"I have just been informed that a medical aircraft will be here within two hours."

"What? Who...where did it come from?" I was flabbergasted.

"A Mr. Tanner, I believe. Do you know him?" asked the doctor.

We all looked at each other. "Kinda...sorta...yes," I replied.

"Kinda sorta? You mean you don't really know him and he sent your brother a seventy thousand-dollar aircraft?"

I smiled. "What can I tell ya, Doc. Michael has friends in high places." I looked up. "Really high places," I said as I mouthed the words *thank you. How does that guy know everything that happens in Colorado?* I wondered, as we discussed which hospital to choose.

"Have faith, my child. The King did not bring him this far to leave him now," whispered Michael.

After tossing the options back and forth for nearly an hour, I decided on Parkland.

"Look, guys. I know it's a risk, but he's alive only because God is keeping him alive. He didn't do that just so that he could die on an airplane. Have a little faith; he'll make it."

"How can you be so sure?" Andrew asked.

"I have a third eye too; it runs in the family," I replied. The agents all looked at me and nodded. Faith and the rest of the family were clueless.

"What? What's a third eye?" Faith asked.

"It's a long story; he's going to make it."

Mother and Amy flew with Michael on the medical aircraft. The rest of us went in Mr. Tanner's jet. When we landed at Love Field, there were several cars waiting, complete with sirens, to get us to Parkland.

At the hospital, we were met by the Voice of Doom. That was the name we chose for Michael's doctor. She was young with an attitude. I guess that's the only way you make it as a doctor when you're female and you look like you're a high school cheerleader. "I know you all want him to make it, but honestly, I doubt very seriously if he'll make it through the night," she said.

"They said that last night and he's still here. They said the impact kills one hundred percent of all victims and he's here. They said bringing him down the slope would kill him and yet he's still here.

Pardon me if I put my faith in the One who has the last word."

"Well, I put my faith in science and, scientifically speaking, he won't last through the night." With that, she turned on her heel and walked away.

"That, my dear, is because you don't know God," I replied as I walked to the chapel.

I sat down in one of the pews and prayed. "God, I know I don't belong in your house, but please don't hold it against Michael because the person praying for him is evil. He's one of the good guys, like Faith. He never did anything bad in his life. His whole world is about saving other people, people that he doesn't even know. Please, God, please fix him. If anyone should be in that bed, it's me. I deserve it, but not Michael. Please let him wake up. Please."

We all camped out at the hospital and the next day Voice of Doom was back.

"What does science have to say today?"

"He's still holding on, but don't get your hopes up. He's lucky," she replied, as if she wanted him to die so that she could save face.

Luck has absolutely nothing to do with it, I thought.

The next day it was the same old song. "Have you conceded yet? He's not going to die just because you say so.

"You're right! I have no idea what's keeping him alive, but I do concede that he will probably remain that way. However, he will never come out of that coma. His brain has sustained too much damage. I'm sorry."

"No, you're not and we'll just see about that," I replied under my breath.

The agents had taken to sitting with me in shifts. I had but to ask for anything and they would get it for me. I told my boss that I didn't know when I would be back. Both my sisters were married and had to go back home, so I volunteered to stay with Michael. They used Mr. Tanner's jet to get back. When I was sure Michael was stable, I flew on Mr. Tanner's jet to Atlanta and packed up my entire apartment and put everything in storage. I packed as much as I thought feasible and loaded it on the jet. *Well, Mickey, it looks like we'll be in Texas awhile.* I so despised Texas, but Mickey didn't care as long as he could play with his Power Rangers.

The agents took me to Michael's apartment and I settled in.

"Andrew, there are so many guns! I've counted twenty-five, including a rifle with a scope."

"Michael was, I mean, is a sharp shooter. He's the best there is," he said with pride.

"Can you do something with them? I mean, it's dangerous for Mickey."

"Sure, Melissa. I'll take them to the Bureau and lock them up until...until Michael wakes up."

"Andrew?"

"Yeah, Melissa?"

"He's going to wake up."

"I know, Melissa, I know." But he didn't sound convinced.

Mickey and I went to the hospital every day.

"Melissa, you can't keep this up," my mother said after the third month. "You have a life."

"I can keep it up as long as I have to. My life is here with Michael until he wakes up."

"And what happens if he doesn't wake up?"

"Do not be dismayed; all things are possible through faith. All that is required is faith the size of a mustard seed and when you speak, 'mountain move,' the mountain will move," whispered Michael.

"He will, Mother; don't you worry, he will," I replied as if it were fact.

Every day I visited Michael. I had every member of the family record messages and each day I played them for Michael. The Voice of Doom came in one day after I had kept up this ritual for more than five months. "You know he can't hear you."

"Yeah, the same way he wouldn't last through the night, right?"

She smirked. "Well, he hasn't come out of the coma and he won't," she said as she walked away.

"You don't have the last say," I snapped, as I put the earphones on Michael's head.

The Archangel Michael had been summoned to the Throne. "It is time, my trusted servant," Jesus replied. "I will restore his mind and he will awaken from his sleep. Soon thereafter, Satan himself will set out to destroy them both. I will require that he acknowledge that he is a created being; therefore, I

wish him to be defeated by his own brethren, you and Gabriel. Be on your guard, as this attack will be soon."

"Yes, my King, we will be ready. Praise be to the Father, the Son, and the Holy Spirit," he replied.

On July 7, at seven, Michael's eyes opened. Seven, you know, is the number of completion.

"Michael! Michael! Can you hear me?" The nurse ran over to the bed. "It's a miracle," she said. "I'll call the doctor."

The Voice of Doom came strolling in thirty minutes later. She pulled out a flashlight and flicked it back and forth in front of Michael's eyes. "He's still in the coma," she stated with smug satisfaction.

"How can you say that? His eyes are open?"

"Yep, they are; but they are unresponsive, which means that it is an involuntary movement. He doesn't know that they are open."

"Yeah, right."

"Miss Bowan, your brother is in a coma. He is not going to come out of it. You need to accept that and get on with your life."

"Yeah, and you just wish you had a life," I said under my breath.

"He is awake, Melissa, and he can hear you. You must continue to speak to him," the Archangel Michael said.

I continued to come every day. Mickey and I talked to Michael constantly, as if he could hear us. Thirty days passed and then Michael's open eyes began to dart back and forth.

"Michael! Michael! Can you hear me?" I shouted. Again the nurse ran over and again she was as excited as I was. Of course, Doctor Doom refused to accept it. When she came in an hour later, she barely looked at him.

"Rapid eye movement, indicative of a dreamlike state, happens all the time to coma victims." She put emphasis on the word coma and then she walked away. I never said a word to her this time.

Two weeks went by and each day his open eyes darted back and forth without a discernable pattern. But the third week, when I walked into the room, his eyes stopped darting and landed on me. I just stood there with my mouth open.

"Hi, Michael. I know you can hear me." I walked over to the side of the bed and his eyes followed me. I started to cry as I walked to the other side and he continued to follow me everywhere I went.

"He's awake! Thank you, God. I knew you wouldn't let me down. He's awake."

The nurse ran over to the bed.

"Watch his eyes," I instructed. I walked to the other side of the bed and then back again. He never took his eyes off me.

"He is awake! You were right all along," she said. Even she was tired of Doctor Doom's snide remarks. "I'll call the doctor right now."

"Don't bother. I don't care what she thinks. My brother is awake because God has the last say in everything."

This time the doctor appeared in less than fifteen minutes. I didn't even acknowledge her presence. "Well, it does appear that he is coming out of the coma," she sighed with disappointment.

"No shit, Sherlock!"

"Well, you don't have to be insulting."

"Yes, I do! You have no compassion, nor do you care! You even sound as if you're disappointed because you weren't right."

"Miss Bowan, I do hope you prepare yourself for the fact that your brother will be a vegetable for the rest of his life."

"You haven't been right from the moment he arrived and you won't be right this time either!" I turned my back on her and started to talk to Michael.

Every day for another three weeks, Mickey and I sat and talked to Michael. Every day his eyes watched me and followed me each time I moved about the room. During week four, he started to grunt and make noises that I could not discern.

"Michael, do you hear me? If you understand, squeeze my hand." He did and I started to cry. "You can hear me! I knew you could all along!"

He can hear you and he will be fine, my dear; but you must prepare yourself, for he will not have the use of his legs.

"Vegetable, huh? My little voice is never wrong," I said out loud.

All of the medical personnel started coming by to see Michael. No one believed that he actually comprehended what we were saying, but each time I asked him to squeeze my hand, he complied. Doctor Doom avoided me for as long as she could, but eventually she had to show her face.

"So much for your vegetable theory. If it makes you feel any better, before you even say it, I already know that Michael won't walk out of here." She glared at me and turned and left the room. "It's nice to have the last word for a change," I said with satisfaction.

Two weeks after Michael started making noises, he began to articulate discernable words. He looked over at the table and said, "Comb."

I walked over to the table and realized that he meant "cup." I picked it up.

"This is a cup. Try and say it."

"Cup."

"Yep, you got it." I smiled and kissed him. *We've got a lot of work to do.*

As soon as Michael was able to sit up, he began rehab. He had to learn to use his upper body and he also had to learn the English language all over again, as that part of his brain had been wiped out. After therapy started, he and I actually had a conversation. Although it was somewhat one sided, he did seem to understand what I was saying. "Michael, do you know who I am?"

"My wife?"

My eyes opened wide and I laughed.

"No, sir! I am not your wife! I am your sister. Do you understand? Sister."

"Yes, my sister."

"Why did you think I was your wife?"

"You are here." Then he said, "Days." And then he sat there pondering the right words.

"You mean 'every day'?"

"Yes, every day."

"That's what sisters do."

"I have a wife?"

"No, you were supposed to get married to Amy, the one who was here yesterday."

"Pretty."

"Yes, Amy is very pretty," I said.

"The other one who was here is Pamela. You were married to her, but not now. She is Michael Junior and little Melissa's mother. Do you understand?"

"Yes. More sisters?"

"Yes! You remember you have two more sisters."

"Where?"

"They live in Atlanta, but they will be here soon. Mother was here yesterday. Do you understand 'mother'?"

"Yes, Mother."

Michael and I went on like that for hours every day and each day he remembered more and more. He progressed in leaps and bounds. He was literally a medical marvel, but I knew there was nothing medical about it.

Every day another female would come to the hospital claiming to be Michael's girlfriend. And every day, I would tell her that he had a fiancée and she would not be allowed to see him. It was a juggling act to keep the other women from bumping into Amy. Somehow, though, I knew Amy would not go through with the wedding. Mother was fit to be tied, but I knew what a responsibility this was, so I tried to make her understand.

"Mother, they are not married. There is no 'until death do us part.' You cannot expect her to go through with a tour of duty that she technically did not sign up for. And believe me, it's a tour of duty that is not for the faint of heart. I'm the one that has been going to rehab with him to find out what the caregiver can expect and let me tell you it is not going to be easy."

"Well, I don't have to like it," Mother replied indignantly.

"No, you don't; but until you walk a mile in her shoes, don't judge her either."

That afternoon in rehab, I tried to lift Michael using the waist belt, the way the instructor had showed me; but every time I tried, he was just too heavy.

"How are we going to manage this?" I wailed. "I'll never be able to help him from the chair to the sofa or the bed."

"In due time; in due time," the instructor would say. He was still saying, "In due time," a month later and Michael was closer and closer to being released.

Taking care of Michael's affairs while he had been in a coma had been a challenge. He lived way above his means, with a Mercedes, a car phone, and countless electronic toys. Each of his ex-wives had received a house in the divorce settlement so he had no real assets.

Michael's apartment was on the top floor and, of course, that would not do; so I set out to find one that was handicapped accessible. That was the challenge in 1986 because no one really cared about the handicapped. I finally settled for an apartment in north Dallas near Prestonwood. It was unique in that it had front and back doors. I had a ramp built from the back door to accommodate his chair. The apartment was roommate style with a bedroom and a bath on each side of the apartment. The living room, dining room, and kitchen were all in the center. I had my furniture shipped from the storage facility and all of Michael's friends helped move his bachelor stuff.

"Melissa, you really need to get some dead bolt locks for these doors," Michael kept repeating as the agents were moving the stuff into the apartment for me.

"Once a cop always a cop," I sighed.

"Damn right," they all said in unison.

"Oh, brother." But I loved the way the guys took care of their own.

"Do not worry about locking devices; they are of no importance," the Archangel Michael whispered.

Michael never wanted or needed for anything. If the agents didn't take care of it, then Mr. Tanner did. We had been in the apartment two weeks and things were going as well as could be expected. I still had problems getting Michael from the chair, so we avoided that unless one of the guys happened to be there. Nighttime was always a struggle, so the guys had taken to dropping by when they knew I would need help.

It was midnight on Saturday night and Mickey had built a tent in the living room, pretending that he was camping outside. We had stayed up late watching TV and eating popcorn. Michael had just taken a shower, so I left Mickey in the tent and went to Michael's room to help him with his bandages. It was easy for him to get sores on his legs because he was unable to move them. *Boy, it just can't get any worse. Look at his legs. They're covered in sores.*

"Ready, brother?"

"Yes, I am ready," Gabriel replied.

"Ready!" Michael yelled to the Heavenly Host.

"We are ready!" they replied in unison.

They dove down through the clouds at lightning speed–Michael, Gabriel, and an entire legion of angels. They arrived just in time to greet Satan himself, along with a legion of demons, inside Melissa and Michael's apartment.

"I have been expecting you," Satan replied.

"Hello, brother," Michael responded. "You have no juris-diction here. Take leave now without engagement."

"You are wrong, brother. All in this household belong to me. Even the child responds when I call. A prostitute and a forni-cating constable! Why does the One at the Right Hand build a hedge about the likes of these two? Has he none deserving of His affections? My, He has become quite desperate in His pursuits. You should know that you do not frighten me, brother. I am not one of the puny demons that you engaged upon the wintry slope."

Satan raised his hand and crossed only his arm over to the other side. As his hand appeared inside Melissa's bedroom, he released a single spark then retrieved his arm and brought it back into the spirit world. Melissa's bedroom erupted in flames.

"They shall all three burn this day," he laughed, as he then raised his sword and engaged Michael in battle.

As Michael fought Satan, the Heavenly Host fought against the demons and Gabriel flew to assist Melissa.

The smoke detectors suddenly started screeching. "What the hell is Mickey doing? Hold on, Michael; I'll be right back."

I walked into the living room and looked in the tent, but Mickey wasn't there. I continued through the dining area and down the hall to my bedroom. My bedroom was on fire. The entire room was engulfed in flames!

"Mickey! Mickey! Where are you?"

"In the closet, Mommy! Mommy!" The closet was on the other side of the room. I stood there for one brief moment. "God, help me!"

Go, Melissa. I will protect you," Gabriel shouted.

I ran through the burning room to the closet. Mickey was crouched down on the floor inside. "Okay, Sweetie. I'm going to take you though the fire. Do not move, okay?"

"Okay, Mommy, but I'm scared."

All is well, Melissa. I will protect you with the power of the Holy Spirit!" cried Gabriel.

"It's okay. Mommy won't let it burn you. Here we go!" I cried as

I scooped him up and ran back through the fire.

Gabriel covered Melissa and Mickey with his wings as she ran with Mickey in her arms.

I couldn't believe I had actually gone through a room engulfed in flames twice without so much as a blister. I don't think I even smelled like smoke. I ran out the front door, which was near my bedroom. I immediately crossed to the other side of the street, as the fire spread throughout the building.

"Mickey, you stay right here on this grass. Do not move! I've got to go back and get your Uncle Mike."

"No, Mommy, no! You burn up."

"I have to go, Mickey, and I will not burn up. Now stay."

"Go, Melissa.   All is well," Gabriel said. Just as Gabriel finished his sentence, Michael was struck a debilitating blow by Satan's sword and was flung backward twenty earthly feet. As he attempted to recover, Satan stuck Gabriel broadside. Gabriel too was temporarily incapacitated.

I ran back into the burning building. The fire had spread into the hallway, the kitchen, the dining room, and the living room. I remembered fire training in school, so I crouched down as low as I could to the floor and inched my way through the flames.

Satan flew behind Melissa. He was furious and raised his wings to their full height. Just as he was about to fan the flames with his wings to burn Melissa, the Archangel Michael struck him with his sword and sent him reeling backwards. As he did so, Gabriel covered Melissa with his wings, just as the flames licked out to grab her.

"Keep going, Melissa! You can save him! You can!" Gabriel shouted.

Raguel and three thousand angels built a wall between the flames and the human Michael's bedroom to give Melissa time to reach him. The others fought the demonic hosts.

I skirted around the last corner and was relieved to see that that the fire had not yet reached Michael's room. It was as if we were in another apartment, one that was not engulfed in flames. "Come on, Michael. We've got to get out of here. The apartment is on fire!"

Since the accident, Michael was a little slow to comprehend certain things, so instead of having the required urgency for such

an event, he replied calmly, "Okay, let me put on my clothes."
Michael was wearing a towel around his waist that was held by Velcro
and he was lying on the bed where I had left him when the smoke
detector went off.

"Michael, you don't have time to put your clothes on!" I shouted.
I reached out and scooped him up–all two hundred pounds of him.

**As Melissa reached out, Gabriel stretched his wings out,
put them under Michael, and then lifted him into the wheel
chair.**

When I put Michael into the wheel chair, he seemed as light as
a feather. "Okay, Michael, the fire is right outside the room, so don't
put your hands out."

**Satan tried his best to get to Melissa before she could reach
the back door, but he was no match for the Archangel Michael.**

"This way, Melissa," shouted Gabriel. **"No! Turn this way!
Good. Keep going. A little more. Now, there; reach for the
door!"**

I crouched down behind Michael's chair and pushed, following
my third eye. I couldn't see anything; the smoke was black and thick
as tar. *Thank God this apartment has a back door. We would never have
been able to get through to the front.* I was coughing and choking and
I couldn't see the door.

"There, Melissa. Reach up! More, more, now!"

I reached up and there it was, right where my voice said it would
be. I turned the knob and thanked God that I had been too lazy to get
the deadbolts. I opened the door.

**Satan hit Michael with another blow that sent him
sprawling. He pivoted and hit Gabriel as he covered Melissa
near the door. Satan reached out again with his wings to fan
the flames. A huge gust of wind came from under his right
wing.**

**At that moment, the Archangel Michael recovered and
pushed Melissa out the door and grabbed the ball of fire and
threw it backwards. Satan was so angry, he roared like a
wounded bear.**

I felt a gust of wind as I started to push the chair. It seemed as if
someone had shoved me. I flew into the chair and the chair flew
into the grass with Michael in it. I fell on top of Michael, and as I fell,

the wind roared, blowing a huge ball of fire out of the door behind me. All of the windows exploded, glass flying everywhere. The fireball was then sucked backwards into the flames. I got up and again lifted Michael like he was a small child and put him in the wheel chair.

As Melissa lifted the human Michael, Gabriel used his wings again to support him as she put him back into the chair. Now that Melissa was safe, Gabriel joined Michael in battle. They crossed their swords together, a sign to Satan that he would now have to engage them both. Satan looked from one to the other.

"You shall regret this day, brothers! You cannot protect them forever. My wrath is long and far-reaching," Satan roared.

"There will be no need to protect them forever, for salvation is near," Michael replied. "Once the second death has no power over them, your evil plots will be useless."

Satan threw his head back and roared with laughter. "You delude yourself, brother. The likes of these two seeking the One Who Sits at the Right Hand? A constable who is betrothed yet fornicates with other females and a prostitute who kills her own seed and fancies pharmaceuticals? Not in this millennium," he sneered.

"Why do you not say His name, brother? Your Creator, can you not bear to hear it?" asked Michael.

Satan appeared uncomfortable.

"Jesus," Michael and Gabriel said in unison.

Satan roared and immediately took flight.

"You cannot protect them forever, my brothers," he yelled.

"And you, Satan, cannot avoid the lake of fire," called Michael.

Satan's wings gleamed and shimmered as he flew into the clouds.

I wheeled Michael over to the other side of the street where Mickey sat waiting dutifully, just as I had instructed. He ran over and kissed me.

"Mommy, Mommy, you not burned up."

"Nope and Uncle Mike isn't either."

He began to jump up and down shouting, "Yeah! Yeah!"

"Yeah, indeed," I laughed.

I frantically replayed the events in my head. *If I had rented the other apartment in this same building–the one with no back door–we would have died. If I had installed the dead bolt locks, we would have died. If I had been afraid and not gone back for Michael, he would have died. How did I go through those flames without so much as a blister? How did I lift Michael twice? And how did I find my way to his bedroom and then to the back door through that black smoke? Why wasn't Michael's bedroom burning like the rest of the apartment and why didn't I drop dead from smoke inhalation? How in the world were those walls burning as if someone had poured gasoline on them? I must be losing my mind because I could have sworn someone pushed me out of the door. Michael has only been out of the hospital for two weeks; first the skiing accident and now this. What the hell is going on? There is something very wrong here, but also something very right.* The fire trucks began to arrive. The entire building was engulfed in flames, a five-alarm fire that totally destroyed the entire building.

The media came out in droves. Michael had already received an enormous amount of press because of his accident. *Here they come, like vultures, with their stupid questions!*

"Miss, miss, were you in this fire?"

"Yes, I was," I replied.

"You just lost everything you own. How do you feel?"

I looked at the reporter. *You are some kind of stupid!* "I feel wonderful. I didn't 'just lose everything.' I didn't lose my life and neither did anyone else and I can't buy another one of those at the mall," I retorted.

I don't think they played my clip on the news. But they did do a newspaper story on Michael and me. It too was amusing. They had to take my picture over because I looked too happy; I wasn't supposed to smile. The caption on the article read,

"Sister Taps Superhuman Strength." *Superhuman, no; supernatural, yes.*

The mayor also presented me with a commendation for saving my own brother! That too was some kind of stupid. What was I supposed to do? Let him burn alive?

After the fire we stayed with Amy until the complex prepared another unit for us. Then I found out why my boss in Atlanta had insisted that I get apartment insurance. *How strange that a man who didn't even know me would go to such lengths to be sure that I had renters' insurance!*

"It is not strange, my child. God knows all things and acts accordingly," whispered Michael.

Even though I had moved, my insurance had carried over to my new apartment. Allstate handed me a check for twenty-five thousand dollars that afternoon. In addition, Beth Tanner, Rex Tanner's sister, gave us a check for five hundred dollars.

It definitely wasn't "easy come, easy go" this time. Replacing everything with twenty-five thousand dollars wasn't as easy as it sounded, but I didn't complain. It was a blessing because none of the other renters in my building had insurance, so they had to depend on the Red Cross.

Things moved along slowly after that. No big surprises, no strange people, no fires, no accidents, and no excitement. I dated a few times, but I really hated it when guys pawed all over me and always expected sex, so I didn't go out much. I had been with Michael two years now and he had become dependent on me.

Abdiel had been instructed to find a weakness in Melissa. Satan's demons had not had much success with any of the sins with which they had enticed Melissa.

"Ah! This will do nicely. She feels burdened and has no gold. I see a crown in my future. It has been almost two earthly years and yet all others have been unsuccessful. So unsuccessful, in fact, that they lost their heads. I am determined to keep my head. You are resentful, my dear. Why should you be the one burdened with the one who is lame? Look at how everyone dotes on him. They have showered him with gifts and gold. You want, you need, to pay for your transportation device. The gold is rightfully yours. Take it! You need it. He will never know. Besides, you will not be taking from him; it was given to him in trust. He will never know that it is gone. Take it! Take it!"

I hated Texas and I was beginning to feel burdened. The money had run out and that meant I needed a job. I couldn't pay my car note and I was beginning to feel resentful. The bank and all of those people had taken care of all of Michael's bills but none of mine. *I*

*have no money and yet I do everything. I'll just slip the money out, using
one of the checks on the trust account. It's not as if it's stealing from
Michael; they donated the money and I need it to pay my car note.* So
later that day I took one of Michael's checks from the bottom of the
book and paid my car note.

I didn't know that he too was short on cash and the donations had
stopped coming in. I had stolen from his disability benefits! The
check I wrote caused Michael to be overdrawn, and he racked his
brain trying to figure out how he had bounced a check when it was
actually my fault!

Things went downhill from there, just as always. Michael found
out about the check. The bank sent him a copy and, because it went
to pay for my car, he knew I had stolen from him. I couldn't look him
in the eye. My guilt wouldn't let me get over the fact that I had stolen
from my own brother. Of all the things I had done, stealing two
hundred dollars from my brother was the worst. I had to get away
from him, so I moved out.

The doctors had said that I should have left a year ago, but I just
couldn't. Now, it was the guilt that drove me away. I got an apartment
down the street and went by to check on him, but it was never the
same. Losing my relationship with Michael was worse than divorce.

I was so messed up that I couldn't stay in Dallas. *I need to get
away. I can't stand to see him and not see him the way we used to be!* So
I transferred to a store in Atlanta. I still talked to Michael on the
phone, but again it was not the same. It was easier not seeing his
face or looking into his eyes, knowing he knew what I had done.

I realized later that moving out was probably better for him in the
long run, for as long as I was there he would never have become
independent. He did so well after I left that he was able to take a
desk job at the Bureau. Later he bought a new Mercedes, complete
with hand controls and a wheel chair that fit in the back.

Chapter Fifteen

It's Good to Be Home

It was good to be back in Atlanta. It had always felt like home to me.

Mickey was now eight and still a challenging child. I was summoned to the school every day. I lost sitters every week and I was losing my mind in the process. All I did was go to work and visit the principal. That was my life and it sucked.

I had decided to quite smoking when Mickey was three. I had never been much of a drinker, unless I was high on cocaine, so now my life did not include cigarettes, drugs, sex, or alcohol. I was tired and stressed. If I had to leave work one more time to go to Mickey's school, I thought I'd lose my job. Every month I struggled to pay the bills and each time I was one step and one payday from poverty. *I am so tired. This is it; they really are going to turn the electricity off this time. I have until five o'clock this afternoon to pay the bill. Payday is still eight days away,* I thought as I got up to go to the mailbox to get more bills.

"You of little faith," sighed Michael.

I dreaded opening the mail, as I did every day. *Hmmm, this is one I don't recognize. I don't have insurance with them anymore.* I opened the envelope and a check for two hundred and forty-five dollars fell out. The letter informed me that I had been overcharged on my premiums and that I was due a refund for the overpayments that I had made each month for the two years that they had insured my vehicle. I smiled and looked up and said, "Thank you." *That is so God!* I continued to struggle, but God always provided a way.

I didn't date much. I never really cared about sex because I didn't really like it. Even Joe's attempts to please me didn't change my mind about it. I preferred a good book and chocolate.

"That is because the gift of intimacy belongs with him who is to be your mate," Michael whispered.

After engineering the break from her male sibling, Abdiel had again been instructed to find a weakness to exploit in Melissa. "She has become a recluse. I must create a way to motivate her to sin."

"Fornication is always the easiest of sins to encourage," said Supay, Abdiel's assistant.

"Yes, however, this human female has no desire for fornication. Her previous fornications were motivated by her desire for gold, not sex."

"Perhaps we can change that, yes?"

"And how do you propose to do that? Pan, the demon of lust, was slain."

"How about Jesabeth? Is he not available? He is legendary for those he has destroyed; even the prophets of God have been susceptible to his suggestions."

"Summon this Jesabeth at once."

When Jesabeth arrived, he was only too happy to assist Abdiel.

"This human Melissa has not been susceptible to sexual desire and I wish you to entice her to fornicate with the male human that I have arranged to cross her path. You, Supay, are to distract her when it is time for her daily dose of contraceptive. When she is again with child, she will destroy her seed," laughed Abdiel.

As I was closing up my store, the manager of the shoe store next door came by. "Hey, Melissa. You want to stop for a drink?"

I was usually too tired and stressed to go out, so I surprised myself when I agreed to go out with David. After we had a couple of drinks, he walked me to my car. Before I could open my car door, he kissed me. I was so caught off guard that I didn't stop him. Then the strangest thing happened–I liked it!

"You want to go to my place for a nightcap?" Again I surprised myself by saying yes. Once we got to his place, before I sat down, he kissed me again. I was shocked at myself because I wanted to have sex. What made it even stranger was that I didn't really want to have sex with him; I just wanted to have sex. Period!

Abdiel was prepared for Michael; he was escorted by a legion of demons. While Michael was engaged in battle, Abdiel carried out his plan. After Jesabeth covered Melissa with a cloak of sexual desire, Abdiel was there to ensure that David's sperm reached its target.

The Heavenly Host arrived to assist Michael but too late to prevent Abdiel from carrying out his plan.

Supay had already distracted Melissa when she was to consume her contraceptive and she was a day late taking it. Unfortunately for him, it would be his last assignment, for Michael severed his head.

I didn't like this new development because I felt I was acting like the guys that I despised for only wanting sex with me. I didn't really like David and I certainly didn't want to ever see him again. He wasn't even my type. *What is happening to me? It's as if I'm in someone else's body, someone who wants sex. I don't like this; I don't like it at all!* Unfortunately, it was just the beginning. Two months later I went to the doctor with flu symptoms.

"Miss Bowan, you do not have the flu, my dear. You are pregnant." I just sat there and stared at him. *I haven't had sex in two years and I have sex once and get pregnant? This cannot be happening!*

"But...but...I'm on the pill."

"Yes, but it is a low dose contraceptive because of the many complications you've had with other contraceptives. A low dose isn't one hundred percent effective and, if you miss a pill, it can be even less effective."

I left the doctor's office in a daze. The first time was stupidity; but when I was with Mark, I got pregnant and I was also on the pill. When I was with Mick, I got pregnant using condoms. *What the hell is going on? No one in the world has this much bad luck.*

"Luck has nothing to do with it my dear," laughed Abdiel.

"Kill your seed; kill your seed," the demons chanted.

"Of all of the stupid..." my voice trailed off. *I can't even afford an abortion.*

That afternoon I paid a visit to David. He too was not happy, especially after I had avoided him for months. But because he had no desire to be a daddy, he agreed to pay for the abortion.

"Do not do this terrible thing again, my child," Michael whispered. But he knew Melissa would not listen, for the King knew all things and had warned him that she would kill her seed four times. He prepared for escorting her unborn child to Heaven before the knife touched his tiny body.

The sex thing continued; I could not shake it. I settled for staying away from situations where I was close enough to a guy to let him touch me. It seemed to work and again I abstained from sex. I thought about Sybil, who definitely had no control over her desire for sex. *Oh, my goodness! I've become Sybil!* I laughed at myself because that was really, really bad. Sybil was a nymphomaniac!

Sybil did in fact marry the cop and she too had a child. Sybil was so extreme when it came to motherhood. She was a cross between Betty Crocker, Donna Reed, and June Cleaver. I just didn't know what to think about the three hundred and sixty degree turn she had made. Even I wasn't that dedicated and I was pretty darn dedicated to Mickey. But making your own baby food from scratch? That was too extreme even for me. Besides, who had time? Sybil did because she was a stay-at-home mom. Sybil even went to church. Now that was scary!

Chapter Sixteen

Little Melissa

"It's getting chilly out here; I wish I had a coat," little Melissa said as she shivered.

"You know Danny don't allow that. He says they can't see the merchandise. It ain't him freezing his ass off out here, so why should he care," sighed Melissa's friend Janet. Little Melissa and Janet were standing on a corner in South Dallas waiting for a date to stop.

"Well, I'm not putting up with much more of this shit anyway. I'm gonna meet me somebody and he's gonna take me away from this."

"Melissa, you been sayin' that for two years now and you still here wit' me. You act like some prince is gonna ride up on a white horse and carry you away, like in the movies."

"You're laughing now, but when my prince comes, I'm gonna be laughing all the way to my mansion."

"Girl, get a grip. You better be tryin' to get a date befo' Danny come and whip both our asses. Hey, looks like I got a live one. Hey, baby, you want a date?" yelled Janet, as the man drove up beside her. Before he could respond, Janet opened his car door and jumped in the car. She waved at little Melissa as they rode off.

Little Melissa stood on the corner shivering and waiting. She began to dream about her Prince Charming who would take her away from the streets:

My prince is a dashing knight on a white stallion. He is dressed in fine garments. He is tall and handsome. He is fearless; he is blameless. He stands for truth and justice. He rescues the weak and punishes doers of evil. Even the fire-breathing dragon is no match for him. My prince is not only invincible but perfect in every way. He has no blemish and no faults. He is never selfish or demeaning. He is gentle. He is kind. His love is powerful. His love is true. He will never disappoint me. He will never hurt me. He will always be there for me. He knows my every need and my every desire and then fulfills those needs.

I am the damsel in distress. I face peril and destruction from a fire-breathing dragon. But my Prince Charming arrives in the nick of time. His eyes meet mine and in an instant I am mesmerized. He takes my breath away and in an instant I am madly, passionately, and helplessly in love with him. He sweeps me off my feet and gently lifts me up upon his stallion. He whisks me off to safety. Without even a word he says, "Everything will be all right. Don't be afraid. Stand still and wait for me and you will be saved, for I will slay the dragon. You have only to believe."

All of this transpires in an instant and he is off again on his valiant steed. He is magnificent. He is majestic. His hair flows behind him as he rides. His back is straight and he sits with authority and power. A bright light surrounds his continence. I watch in awe and wonder as he faces the dragon. The dragon is fierce and breathes fire and brimstone; however, the Prince is unafraid. He lifts his sword; it is adorned with ivory and gold and every precious gemstone. He swings his sword and the sky throws lightning and loud thunder erupts from the heavens. With but one blow the dragon is defeated. The handsome Prince turns to face me. His eyes are ablaze with fire, yet I am unafraid. He rides to me and again sweeps me off my feet onto his stallion. In an instant I am whisked away to his magnificent mansion in the clouds and we live happily ever after, forever and ever.

"My dear child, the Prince you seek was never meant to be a mere mortal man. That deeply rooted inner desire–that fairytale prince–is Jesus Christ, the Son of God, the Prince of Peace. Jesus is perfect. Jesus is blameless. Only He can come down from the clouds on a white stallion and take you to His kingdom which is everlasting.

Only Jesus is King of Kings, Lord of Lords. Only He can slay the fire-breathing dragon, who is the Devil, who is Satan. Only He can save you, if only you believe in Him.

Only the love of Jesus is an everlasting love, an unconditional love, an Agape love. A love so deep, so profound, that it changes you forever. His love is faithful; His love is true.

His love will never disappoint you. He will never leave or forsake you. His love is eternal," the angel whispered.

"Hey, hey, beautiful lady!" yelled the handsome man in the black sedan.

Oh, my, here comes my prince now. Maybe he's the one that will take me away from here, away from Danny. I can't believe I was stupid enough to think Danny was my prince. What a toad he turned out to be!

"Hey there, handsome, you want a date tonight?" Melissa asked the stranger in the black sedan.

"Sure, hop in. What's your name?"

I know I'm not supposed to tell him my real name, but this is the one. I just know it. He's the one who will be different than the others.

"My name is Melissa. I've got a room right down the street. Turn left at the corner and it's that motel on the right."

The stranger ignored her.

"Hey, you missed the turn! Where are you going? The motel's back that way!" Melissa heard a click as the locks engaged on the car, but her door had no handle.

"Nine-one-one. What is your emergency?"

"There's...there's a lady layin' by the side of the road. I was just drivin' by and there's a lady just layin' there. You better send somebody. Something ain't right. She's just layin' there...and she don't have no clothes."

When the officer arrived, he found little Melissa's nude body in the ditch by the side of the road, right where the serial killer in the black sedan had dumped her as if she wasn't even human. As if she wasn't someone's precious daughter; as if she wasn't my little niece. He dumped her like she was a piece of garbage to be used and discarded. He dumped her as he had done countless times to countless young girls who had left home looking for Prince Charming and instead found a killer who used them and then threw them away.

Little Melissa was twenty-two years old when her life was taken by a serial killer in 1995. Her killer was later apprehended but never stood trial for little Melissa's murder or for the other six women he was suspected of killing in four different cities. He did, however, stand trial for raping and sodomizing another sixteen-year-old prostitute who survived. Her testimony convicted him and he was sentenced to life in prison.

Pamela's heart was broken into a million pieces, as any mother's would be.

Chapter Seventeen

Coach

Instead of taking Mickey to church, I decided on involving him in sports. Mickey was ten when I took him to the recreation center to sign up for football.

"Forty-five dollars? Are you kidding me?"

"No, I'm not kidding. In order to sign your kid up, it costs forty-five dollars," replied the coach behind the desk.

"Well, it ought to be free. That's a lot of money to some people."

"I know. I'm sorry, but we do provide the uniforms."

"Okay, so are you the coach for his age group?"

"No, that would be Coach Jimmy Dawson."

"Okay, so where is he?"

"He's on the far side of the field. Just go down the path there and you'll run into him."

I took Mickey by the hand and we walked down the path to the far side of the field. When we got there, a group of mostly women was milling about. I walked up to one of the other mothers.

"Is this the ten-year-old group?"

"Yeah, are you new here?"

"Yes, and forty-five dollars is highway robbery just to play football," I complained.

At that moment, the coach turned in my direction, as if he wanted to see who was speaking.

"Is that Coach Jimmy?"

"Yeah, he's our coach."

"Hmmm, he is some kind of cute. Is he married?"

"No. As a matter of fact, he's the only coach who's not married."

"Nice legs," I mused. "Cute butt too."

"He is kind of cute. Do you like him?"

"He's definitely promising."

She laughed. "My name is Margaret."

"Pleased to meet you, Margaret. I'm Melissa."

After chatting a bit, I decided to meet the coach with the nice legs. *Hmmm, cute butt!* I walked up behind him. *Get a grip, girl. You sound like Sybil.*

"Hi. Are you Coach Jimmy?"

"Yes. Hi and hi. What's your name?" he asked as he glanced at Mickey.

"Mickey. It's Mickey Bowan."

"Hi, Mickey Bowan. Would you like to play football?"

"Yeah, sure."

"Have you ever played before?"

"No."

"That's okay. Come on over here and we'll get you started."

"You know, forty-five dollars is highway robbery," I complained again.

"So I've heard," he replied, as if that would make me shut up.

"They should be able to come here and play for free"

"Well, if it's any consolation, I come here and volunteer my time to teach these kids how to play football. The forty-five dollars only pays for the uniforms and keeps the lights on."

Hmmm, a man who volunteers his time to help kids. I like that.

"Excuse me. I need to round up these kids and see what I've got this year."

I watched him walk away. *Cute, very cute indeed.* Margaret walked up behind me.

"So, what do you think?"

"I think I came here to find my son a mentor and some of that male bonding, but I might want to bond a little myself."

Margaret laughed, "Down girl."

Mickey went with Coach Jim and the other boys. I sat with Margaret and we watched. This went on for two hours and then it was finally time to go. It was going to be tedious coming over here and having to sit and wait, but Mickey seemed to enjoy it. Practice was every Thursday, so the following Thursday we returned and Margaret was there also.

"Guess what?" she said with excitement.

"What? What gives?"

"Coach Jim."

"What about Coach Jim?"

"He likes you and wants your phone number."

"What? How do you know that?"

"I asked him."

"You asked him?" I said incredulously.

"Yeah. I told him one of the moms liked him and he wanted to know which one. I described you and, when I told him you had long hair, he wanted to know if it was real."

"What difference does that make?"

"He said he doesn't like fake hair."

"Hmmm. You know, Margaret, this sounds way too much like high school."

"Yeah, but isn't it fun?"

"I guess so. What else did he say?"

"He said that he's going to give you his phone number so that you could hook up."

"He did?"

"Yep, he did. Oh, here he comes now."

Coach Jim walked over. "Melissa, can I have your phone number?"

"Only if I can have yours too." He reached in his pocket and handed me a piece of paper with his number on it.

Margaret then whipped out a pen and paper and I wrote down my number for him. "Cool. I'll call you tomorrow."

"Oh, this is so exciting," Margaret said with way too much enthusiasm.

"How old do you think Coach Jim is?" I asked.

"He's about twenty-five or twenty-six."

"What? Have you lost your mind?"

"What? What's wrong with that?"

"Do you know how old I am?"

"Twenty-five? Twenty-six?" she said as if it were a question.

"No, I'm thirty-five!"

"What? You're thirty-five?"

"Yeah!"

"Oh, my, that would make Coach Jim a boy toy!"

"Girl, get a grip. I have no intention of going out with that...child."

"Oh, well, you never know. It could be very therapeutic. Besides, I would never have guessed your age and I'll bet he doesn't have a clue either. Girl, go for it! Get your groove back," she laughed.

"I don't think so, and thanks to you, I just gave him my number."

"You'll thank me one day," she laughed as she walked away.

You must go, Melissa; he is the one God has sent to be your spouse.

I have been praying that God send me a real man and not a creep like the ones I pick. What if this is the one he sent and I won't go out with him? "I guess I could at least go out with him. It's not like we're getting married," I said out loud.

Michael smiled, for he knew that that statement would prove to be inaccurate.

The coach and I became inseparable after just that one date. That first night I pounced on him like a cat. I was appalled at myself, but the sex was incredible. Since I'd met the coach, I had begun to like this sex thing. My coach didn't need to figure out what I liked; he just knew from the very beginning. It was as if we were meant to be together.

"He is the one that our King has sent to be your spouse," **Michael said again.**

Coach also seemed to like it because the three things he cared about most were sex, football, and computers, in that order. The first time I asked him to stay the night he said, "Let me get my clothes out of the car." *He knew I was going to ask him to stay! Can you believe that?*

I liked the fact that he didn't smoke, drink, or do any kind of drugs. I also liked the fact that I couldn't tell him what to do. I know that sounds strange, but I'm bossy and it was nice finally to meet a guy who didn't let me boss him around. Mickey seemed to like him, especially because one of Jim's other favorite pastimes was Nintendo. The only one who seemed bothered about our age difference was me.

Jim took me to meet his mother and the rest of the family. His mom accepted me as if I were part of the family, even though I was ten years his senior with a ten-year-old child. When I met his sister, I told her that I was going to marry her brother. She laughed.

Everything was absolutely wonderful! For a while.

Mickey continued to have problems at school. He would go to school and kick, hit, bite, and throw things–not just occasionally but every single day. After having tried various methods for the past ten years, including changing his diet and visiting psychologists and psychiatrists, I was willing to try anything. Jim and I had been dating two years and he was the closest thing Mickey had to a father figure. Jim seemed to think that Mickey lacked a strong disciplinarian and volunteered for the job. His solution to Mickey's behavior was to spank him. I had always hated spanking Mickey, even though he surely needed it. But six months of spankings hadn't done anything. I was still at the school two and three times a week. So I just continued to hope.

"Master is not pleased with our lack of progress. Master will not cease until she and her offspring are destroyed," Abdiel said to Supay.

"Perhaps we should proceed with her offspring. He listens to us and performs each and every act that we suggest to him. He is highly susceptible to our calling. What better way to wreak havoc than to use the child as a disruption?"

"Excellent! We shall proceed with this plan."

"Mickey, where are you?" I had just gotten out of the shower and Mickey was nowhere in sight. *He knows he's not allowed to go outside without permission.* Everyone said that I was overprotective because I wouldn't allow Mickey to ride the bus or come home alone after school. I refused to have a latch key kid, so I paid extra for Mickey to attend after school care. I also didn't allow him to go out after homework unless I was near the window to keep an eye on him. Even though he was almost eleven, I just wasn't comfortable because of the way the world was. The mothers of those murdered boys thought that their children had been safe walking from school and playing outside, but since the Atlanta child murders, people stopped calling me overprotective.

"Where is that child? Mickey? Where are you?" I went into Mickey's room and picked up the paper that was lying on the bed. He was running away from home! I ran to the phone to call Jim, although they weren't really getting along very well. "Hey, what's going on?"

"Jim, Mickey ran away from home!" I wailed. "He wrote a note and said he's tired of getting spankings! It's my fault; I should have never let you spank him!"

"Melissa, the boy goes to school and kicks the teacher, for Pete's sake! You have to let kids know that there are consequences for that kind of behavior. If he's tired of getting a spanking, then he needs to stop kicking grownups! Just calm down. We'll find him. I'll be there in ten minutes."

We lived in a duplex at the end of the cul-de-sac. When Jim arrived, we searched the entire neighborhood. The thought of Mickey leaving the confines of the cul-de-sac terrified me. *I never should have let Jim spank him. I don't care what he says. You shouldn't have to spank a child this much. Something is very wrong with that. I wish I knew what the hell was going on?*

"Melissa, he needs Jesus. He is the only one who can release him from the demons that torment him. It is the demons, Melissa! They want him because they cannot have you. Melissa, follow the cat."

Where the hell is Mickey's cat going? Why does he keep going in and out of the woods behind the house? I opened the back door and watched the cat. He turned back and looked at me and then he proceeded towards the woods again. *He wants me to follow him.* I watched the cat and then I followed him into the woods. He was hard to keep up with, but he was leading me somewhere, so I followed. *Well, I'll be! The cat is Lassie.*

"Mickey!" I ran over to Mickey, scooped him up, and hugged and kissed him. "Do you realize how frightened I was not knowing where you were? You scared me to death. Come on; let's go home. Don't worry; I won't let Jim spank you anymore, but you have got to stop kicking teachers and throwing books and chairs. You can't have it both ways." I looked up and mouthed the words *thank you.* "Sending a cat. That is so God!" I laughed. I had the sense that my subconscious had said something else that was important, but I was just happy to have Mickey back, so I didn't dwell on it.

Things did not really go very well after that. Jim was furious and thought I was being manipulated by a ten year old. We actually broke up about it.

"Melissa, he is right. The child is being used by Satan to manipulate you. This is the one God has sent to be your mate. You must mend your relationship."

Of course, our break up didn't last long and we got back together.

You have got to be kidding me! I've had a sexually transmitted disease twice, both times during supposedly monogamous relationships. The first time I was even married. *How do you get chlamydia using a condom anyway? I know there's something going on here. Pregnant using the pill and STDs while using condoms.*

"Yes, ha, ha, ha! And the joke is on you, my dear. Your beau has another female, just as your previous spouse did. You are of a feeble mind, my dear; male humans find faithfulness an impossibility," Abdiel laughed as he flitted around Melissa's head. **"This is why you should go back to your prior trade. Barter that which they seek from female to female. Think of the gold you long to possess again."**

I called Jim. When he arrived, I was furious. "Would you like to explain to me how I have chlamydia? I know for a fact I haven't slept with anyone but you for almost two years.

He just looked at me and then he sat down. "Melissa, I've had a girlfriend for almost five years."

"What! Five years! You have got to be kidding!"

"Melissa, if he loves you, he will choose you. Let him make his choice."

"You need to make a choice and you need to do it soon. You think about it and let me know. In the mean time, I suggest you tell her to get checked out because it appears that your girl has a guy."

A week later he called me. "Hi, how are you?"

"I'm fine." I just sat there holding the phone without another word.

"I'm no longer seeing Vanessa. I broke it off with her."

"So, does this mean it's just you and me now?"

"Yes, that's exactly what it means."

"He is telling the truth, Melissa; he has severed the ties to his other relationships," Michael said.

"Great! Why don't you stop by?"

"Master is furious. Instead of creating chaos, the male

human has ceased his duplicity. This is most unusual. Perhaps we can entice her to kill another seed. Master would be quite pleased with that development," Abdiel pondered.

During my next doctor visit, I was about to get some familiar news. I was pregnant. I walked out of the doctor's office in a state of shock. *This is a conspiracy. I don't know how it is I'm pregnant again. Nobody, and I mean nobody, gets pregnant this many times while using two different types of birth control.*

When I told Jim his mouth fell open. "That's impossible; the condom has never broken. This just doesn't happen." *Maybe not in your world, but it's become a ritual in mine,* I thought.

He never asked if I wanted to keep the baby. It wasn't even a question. It was our baby and we both wanted it. He never said a word about what we would do next, but I decided to let him stew on it awhile. In the meantime, we decided to visit his mom and give her the news.

Jim's mom lived in Fort Lauderdale so we drove to Florida. Mama had always treated me as a daughter from the first day we met. I loved her like my own mom. While we were there, we were able to steal an hour alone while everyone else was out.

"I guess there's no point in using a condom considering the fact that you're already pregnant."

"Yeah, I guess you're right."

We had been there two days when I started spotting and having stomach cramps. Mama decided that I should go to the emergency room.

"Miss Bowan, you are not pregnant," the doctor stated.

"What! But my doctor told me I was pregnant!"

"I'm sorry. False positives are rare, but they do happen."

It was strange. This time I really wanted this baby, but there was no baby.

"It looks like you're off the hook," I said sadly.

"Yeah, it does. Funny though, I'm not as happy as I thought I would be."

"Neither am I."

I was one of many women diagnosed with endometriosis. To prevent the growth of the endometriosis a monthly injection was required. The side effects were horrendous.

After returning to Atlanta, I decided that I wasn't prepared for the side effects of the drug so I discussed alternatives with my doctor. One of those alternatives was a hysterectomy. It was the only permanent fix for endometriosis. That evening I discussed it with Jim.

"You know, the pregnancy scare brings up a crucial decision that I need to make that also involves you. I need to have a hysterectomy, but you have no children. You would probably make a good dad and you need to consider where this is going so that I can get on with it. The clock is ticking and I mean that literally. I'm thirty-eight and I don't have five years for you to make up your mind. You get one shot at fatherhood and, if you want it, it needs to be soon. I'm in pain every day and I'm not prepared to do another shot or another laparoscopy. I want a permanent cure and the only one available is a hysterectomy."

"Melissa, I'm not sure I'm ready to get married," Jim sighed.

"No problem. That is exactly what I need to know. You aren't ready for a commitment. Fine, but I have no intention of sitting around in pain waiting for you to make up your mind. I'm going to call tomorrow and schedule that hysterectomy."

"You cannot change that which the Father has prepared for you," whispered Michael.

The following Monday I went to the hospital to meet with the anesthesiologist. My hysterectomy was scheduled for that Thursday. I had had numerous tubes of blood drawn. That Tuesday I received a call from the surgeon's office.

"Hello. This is Melissa Bowan."

"Hello, Miss Bowan. This is Lisa Green from Dr. Shin's office. I'm sorry, Miss Bowan, but we will be unable to perform your surgery."

"What! Why not?"

"Because you're pregnant." I just stood there with my mouth open.

"You cannot be serious! Do you realize that this is your fault?"

"What do you mean? How could it be our fault?"

"I mean we had unprotected sex because you people told me I was pregnant already and that's how I got pregnant for real." Rather than wait for an answer, I slammed down the phone. *I guess someone else decided that you're going to be a daddy.*

"Ha, ha, ha! It worked! She is with child again. Now she will

kill her seed," laughed Abdiel.

"Kill your seed; kill your seed. He does not want a child. Kill it; kill it," the demons chanted.

This time Jim just looked at me and never said a word.

"Well, say something and stop playing that blasted Nintendo," I cried. He looked up at me and then he looked down and continued playing. *That went well. What's the point in getting upset; it appears that even when we think we're in control of our lives we aren't.*

Mickey and Jim were still constantly at each other's throats, as if they were in some sort of contest. *Maybe if I take Mickey to church. It's not right that he doesn't even know the basic Bible stories.* That Sunday I dressed Mickey and we set out to find a church. When I arrived at the church on Old National Highway, the parking lot was filled to capacity and I noticed that people were starting to come out. *I guess they have early service here. Oh, well, we missed it; maybe I'll try next Sunday.*

"Melissa, look across the street."

Oh, there's another church over there. It looks like they have an afternoon service. I left the parking lot of the first church and drove across the street to the other church and Mickey and I went in. It was incredible. I remembered why I wanted to be a Jehovah's Witness so many years ago. I also remembered Auntie saying Jesus had to be in it. *How did I ever get so far away from God? This is what is missing in our lives.* When Pastor Bosley gave the offer to salvation, I grabbed Mickey by the hand and flew down the aisle. Too bad I didn't have a clue about what salvation entailed and, because I thought I knew everything, I wouldn't study to find out. Pastor Bosley preached the Word every Sunday and yet I never heard a word because I thought that I knew everything. The next month Pastor Bosley even baptized Mickey and me.

For the next few months everything was pretty quiet. My stomach was growing fat in leaps and bounds, yet my Jim was as evasive as ever about marriage. Jim didn't want to get married, but he didn't have a problem wanting sex. I informed Jim that now that Mickey and I were Christians, there would be no sex. I was going to be a perfect Christian. It didn't work the first time and it didn't work the second. *Why is it so hard to do the right thing and why won't anybody cooperate?*

During this time, Daddykins had joined a retreat of sorts. It was a Christian hospice for alcoholics and drug addicts. When we visited, it was so nice to be able to talk about God and marvel at how he had changed us. He too had become a Christian, but he seemed to understand what it meant, while I was still at a loss.

"Why is it so hard to be a Christian, Daddykins?"

"It's not hard, little girl. You're just not ready yet."

"But I took the call to salvation. I'm supposed to be different. I'm supposed to be a Christian."

"There's more to it than walking up and shaking the pastor's hand. You must study the Word and, when it's time, God will change you."

I just sighed. I still didn't get it.

Even Michael seemed to get it. I had realized long ago that I couldn't live with what I had done to Michael and had asked him to forgive me, which he had. It was that easy.

"Hey, little sis!" Michael had called.

"Hey, Michael."

"Guess what I did?" Michael asked.

"What? Did you wreck your car?"

"Nah, I haven't wrecked any cars lately. But I did take the call to salvation."

"You took the call to salvation?"

"Yeah. Why do you sound so surprised?"

"I don't know; it's just that you never really seemed interested in God."

"After all he did for me, I would be pretty stupid not to get interested."

"Yeah, you're right about that."

"You know it was an angel that trached me on the mountain," he replied in a whisper.

"I figured as much. Who skis with a trach tube and has the experience to use it? Do you get it?" I asked.

"Get what?"

"You know, how you are supposed to be this good person all of a sudden?"

"It's not supposed to be all of a sudden," he replied. "You can't change yourself overnight and furthermore you can't change yourself at all. God changes you as you grow in the Word. Do you study?"

"I've read the Bible, if that's what you mean."

"No, that's not what I mean because you obviously don't understand what you're reading."

"Of course, I do; I'm not stupid," I said indignantly.

"I didn't mean that you were stupid. There's more to it than just reading it. You must be led by the Holy Spirit."

"Oh," I said as if I knew what he meant. Since I didn't want to appear stupid again, I decided to change the subject. We said our goodbyes and I ended the call, not knowing any more than when it began.

"Melissa, I told you I'm not getting married until I have a home to put my family in," said Jim.

"Oh, really! Well, part of your family is going to pop out in about four months and I personally could care less where we live. And what exactly does that have to do with getting married anyway?"

"You wouldn't understand. Just chill out. I'm talking care of it."

"Yeah, right," I said under my breath. That Friday he came by and picked me up.

"Come on I want to show you something," Jim said with excitement.

"What?" I asked.

"Just hold your horses and get in the car."

He took me to Riverdale. There was this gorgeous property there with houses on a lake. We passed by it all the time and, several months ago, I had told him that he would buy me a house there one day. He had rolled his eyes at that. But it had been the little voice that told me, so I guess I wasn't surprised when I found out what he was about to do.

After we went into the house, we walked out onto the balcony to look at the lake.

"It's beautiful," I purred.

"Yeah, it is. Are you okay with this carpet?"

"Yeah, sure. Who cares about the carpet? We can always replace it. What's the price on this one?" I asked.

"It was ninety-five thousand, but the last buyer had financing problems and the deal fell apart at closing, so they dropped the price to eighty-nine thousand. They were the ones that chose fuchsia carpet."

"It is a crazy color. But for that price, it's worth it."

"Okay then; it's settled. I'll let her know, and as soon as we move in, we'll get married."

"Really?"

"Really," he replied.

And thirty days later that's exactly what we did. *A husband, a home, and two boys. Wow! This is too good to be true.*

Abdiel was furious. He had been unable to convince the female to kill her seed and now she had wed the male human. "This is terrible. We must destroy this union and with it the sanity of the female. Jesabeth, remove the cloak of sexual desire from the female," Abdiel commanded.

"Very well, as you wish." He removed the cloak from Melissa. "And do you wish that I remove it from the male also?" asked Jesabeth

"No, leave it intact. Perhaps his desire and her lack of it will send them further apart."

"Your wish is my command," Jesabeth laughed as he flew into the clouds.

Abdiel preened his wings before entering the great hall. The idiot gatekeeper had kept him waiting. I would like to see him lose his head before this millennium is concluded, he thought. He smiled as he envisioned the gatekeeper at the guillotine. He stole a furtive glance at the one on the throne. He was still quite unaccustomed to being in the presence of the prince. Even though he had the opportunity to gaze upon him frequently now that he was a lieutenant, the prince's beauty and the size of those massive wings always took him aback.

"Oh, I do hope he does not transform into one of those ferocious beasts that he fancies," Abdiel moaned.

"What is that insidious moaning and what is your report? Make haste as I loathe waiting."

"S...sorry, Master; I was taken aback by your beauty."

Satan puffed out his chest and raised his wings to their full height.

"Of course, you were; there is no one fairer than I, hmmm?"

"No, Master, none."

"Very well then, what do you have to report about the human female and why are she and the other female still alive? Must I do everything myself? And what has become of that horrendous constable and the drunkard earthly father? I want them dead. Do you hear me? Dead!"

"Yes, Master, of course. The female Melissa...uh...has wed the male human and instead of killing her seed they have had an offspring."

"What! What is the meaning of this...this incompetence?" he roared as he transformed into one of his infamous beasts.

"Do not be dismayed, Master; the firstborn and her mate despise one another. The firstborn and the mate are both susceptible to our calls and can be used to wreak havoc in their new dwelling. We shall drive the male away and then we will drive the female to the brink of insanity and push her over the edge."

Satan sat on the throne, as he often did when he contemplated the demise of a human. He reverted to his angelic form. Abdiel sighed in relief, as all of those had done before him.

"Excellent, excellent! Proceed with this plan and do not fail me, for the others before you have made that mistake and do not live to tell of it."

"Yes, Master, I...I...no, Master, I will not fail you."

Michael folded his wings as he approached the Throne of God. "Praise be to the Father, the Son, and the Holy Spirit," he said to Jesus.

"As always, you have served me well, my trusted warrior. Satan has indeed planned to destroy her by using her firstborn. When he fails at this attempt, he will then seek to destroy her using that which she and her mate find so alluring–gold and silver. When she realizes that happiness has eluded her in this too, it will cease to be of importance to her. True happiness and peace cannot be obtained through that which is on the earth, not even that which is born from your own flesh. This is the final test that will cause her to again seek me. Again she will search for me to no avail. But this time she will study my Word to find the Truth and, in the end, she will indeed find salvation, for she will ask and it shall be given

not only to her but also to her mate so that they do not remain
unequally yoked. Because of her faith, all that Satan takes
from her, I will give back threefold."

"Praise be to the Father, the Son, and the Holy Spirit,"
Michael said as he bowed and then took flight.

After little Jimmy was born, things just got worse. Asking a child
like Mickey to make such a huge adjustment in sharing me with a
husband and a new baby was more than he could handle. And given
that he was such a problem child, it wasn't as if I could tell he was
having problems with the adjustment because Mickey had problems
with everything.

I was able to stay at home with Jimmy and Mickey until Jimmy
was three. It just so happened that I was suited to motherhood. Little
Jimmy was growing bigger, and Mickey and Jim were growing further
apart. It was a constant battle every waking moment. They were
driving me insane. I needed to get out of the house for a while.

Things between Jim and me didn't seem much better. I noticed
that the sex thing that had plagued me for a time was gone. I thought
I'd be glad, but I actually loved having sex with Jim. I guess that's the
difference between having sex and making love. What was worse, I
realized that my husband was obsessed with sex, and because I was
back to my old self, we were drifting further and further apart.

I also hated the fact that Jim controlled all of the money. He was
a real tight wad, except when he wanted to buy something. I needed
to have my own money. What I needed was to go back to work. I
discussed it with Jim and we agreed. That Monday I started looking
for another retail management job.

I had been interviewing for two weeks when I hit the jackpot. A
popular ladies' clothing store chain hired me as a manager for their
South Lake Mall shop. The starting salary was twenty-eight thousand dollars. I was to start in one week. There was one
drawback–retail required working weekends, nights, and holidays. *I
wonder how Jim will handle spending that much time alone with Mickey.
Perhaps this is not such a good idea, given that I won't be here to be the
referee.*

"Look down, Melissa, into the trash. Look at the manuscript."

At that moment I looked at the newspaper that I had discarded.

Another advertisement in the classified section caught my eye. It read, "Can you teach?"

"Yeah," I answered out loud. "I can teach."

I took the newspaper out of the trash and read it in its entirety. The advertisement said that if you could teach you were to go to the address for an interview. There was no phone number for inquiries. *I bet it's a waste of time. One of those by commission only jobs. That's why there's no phone number for you to call to find out.*

"It is not a waste of time. You should go. It is not far. This is of great importance. You must go, Melissa," Michael encouraged.

"Oh, all right. I'll go," I said out loud.

"Go where?" Jim asked, as he walked up behind me.

"To this job interview." I showed him the newspaper.

"Well, you have a job, so it can't hurt. Go see what it's about. You would make a great teacher."

That was my Jim! Always encouraging me to do more and to be better. He had even insisted that I learn about computers, even though I hadn't been the least bit interested. "Computers are the future," he kept saying. Jim's major was in Computer Technology, so he could go on and on about them just like when he discussed football. And I had learned about that too.

I went to the location as instructed. When I got the there, I saw nearly a hundred other people waiting in a large room. First we were told to fill out a questionnaire. There were lots of questions about computers, so I went into the bathroom and called Jim on my cell phone.

They then had each person stand up and give a three minute introduction of himself or herself to the group. As we did this, some of us were sent to another room and some left altogether. There were about fifty of us remaining. We were then told to talk to the person next to us and gather enough information to introduce that person to the group. Then we went home.

I received a call that night and was invited to come back. The next day I was to give a fifteen-minute presentation on the topic on my choice. I was hired to teach at the same salary that I had been offered at the clothing store, but this job was nine to five with no weekends or holidays. What a blessing!

So I worked hard, Mickey and Jim fought like cats and dogs, little Jimmy grew like a weed, and it was total chaos.

After learning the ropes and everything I could about computers, I moved to a better position with another school. I then decided to check out working as a contractor. The girls who worked for the school as contractors made much more money than I did. I began to research agencies that found employment for contractors in the field of computer technology. There seemed to be hundreds of them. *How in the world do I choose?*

"Choose this one."

So I picked one and went on the interview. I was assigned an employment specialist, Betty, who would search for jobs that fit my qualifications. Then she would set up interviews for me.

"So, let's see, Melissa. What is your degree in?"

"I don't have a degree," I replied.

"Hmmm, we'll work around that because you have a good background. We'll use your experience instead of a degree. There's a job I would like to submit you for at a hospital on the north side. What rate are you asking?"

"Uh...I don't know? What about thirty-five dollars an hour?"

"Too low. I'll ask for forty-five."

I wondered how I could command such a rate with only a high school diploma, but I kept quiet. All of the other teachers I worked with had college degrees except me. It was a miracle that I had been hired to teach in the first place.

"You of little faith. Have you not learned that there is nothing that the Father cannot do?" asked Michael.

That Monday I got the job. *Forty-five dollars an hour to teach? This is unbelievable!* In addition to using the employment agency, I also searched for contracts using my own business name. I couldn't believe it when I procured a contract to teach for the State of Georgia.

Although things were great in the employment arena, it was just the opposite at home. Every facet of our lives was a problem. He and Mickey were still fighting. Now that Mickey was sixteen, he was six feet tall. They stood eye to eye and one day that was going to be a problem. I had stopped going to church long ago. It was just too hard. Jim wasn't at all fired up about it, and Mickey resented being dragged along while Jim watched football. I worked in North Atlanta and never got home before seven because of traffic. Jim went in early, so he got home before four and then spent the remainder of the evening in front of the TV. All he thought about was sex and football. The house was a mess; nothing was ever done and he didn't even take the food from the freezer or pick his clothes up from the floor. I would come in at seven, thaw out dinner, cook it, bathe Jimmy, get Mickey and Jimmy ready for school, do laundry, clean up, study for my class, and coordinate the classes for the state contract. I was exhausted and, when I finally fell into bed, he wanted sex. I was losing my mind.

All the wonderful blessings that had come from my employment opportunities were also adding more problems to our marriage. Because Jim had been the only income provider for so long, he held a tight rein on our finances. Everything was in his name and whenever I wanted to buy anything it was a major ordeal. I resented it. Now that I had an income, I spent as much money as I wanted. The bottom line was I was miserable.

"It is your gold and silver. Spend it. You earned it. Why should he have a say in that which is not his. Look at the mess he has made. He treats you as a servant girl. Leave him; leave him," the demons chanted.

I am so sick of this. Look at this house. His underwear is on the floor, his towel is on the floor, this bedroom is a pigsty, and then he has the nerve to tell me what to spend my money on after I work my butt off to make it! And everything is about sex, sex, sex! Even marriage is about sex. Is there anything in this world about love?

"The kind of love you seek can only be found in the love of Jesus Christ, our Lord and Savior. All others are conditional, even that from your spouse," Michael whispered. But Melissa was too angry to hear the voice.

"What do you mean you put your stuff in the basement?" Jim asked.

"I mean I have a room in the basement that is my personal space and I don't want any of you in it. If the rest of you want to live in a pigsty, then be my guest, but I'm not doing it anymore. We've had this conversation every day for five years and you will never change. I am not the maid. I'm not sleeping in the basement; I just want to have a space of my own." This arrangement went on for five months.

"Bravo, my dear! You are not a slave girl. You make a good income. You do not need him. Leave him; leave him," the demons chanted.

"Stop it. Stop it, both of you!" Jim and Mickey were at the top of the stairs arguing, as they did each and every day. Jim was furious this time. Mickey got right up to Jim's face and screamed an obscenity.

"Curse him," they yelled at Mickey.

"Strike him; strike him," the demons chanted at Jim.

I looked at Jim, and before I could utter another word, he reached out and hit Mickey, knocking him halfway down the stairs.

"Mickey!" I ran over to the stairs as Mickey got up. Again he began shouting; Jim was also shouting and now so was I. Poor little Jimmy just sat there on the floor crying.

I jumped in between the two of them. "Mickey, go to the car now. Now, Mickey! And do not say another word! And you! You cannot hit a seventeen-year-old child. I don't care how big he is or what stupid things he says; he's still a child."

"He stopped being a child when he got in my face and started cursing like man. If it walks like a man and talks like a man, it's a man."

"Leave him! Leave him! He struck your off spring. Leave him," the demons chanted.

"Well, I hope you're happy because this is it. I cannot do this any more. It is just not worth it. It is my responsibility to protect my children. You are a grown man; Mickey is a child and my responsibility and because you're making me choose between you and his welfare then I must choose the welfare of my children. This isn't any good for Jimmy either. Look at him. I'm going to take Mickey to a hotel for the night and then you need to decide how we are going to do this. One of you is leaving, either you or Mickey. The question is what's best for the children?"

The next day Jim decided that he would move out because it was best for the children. I made arrangements to be out of the house when Jim moved his stuff out. I didn't want to see it, so I took Jimmy to breakfast and took Mickey to a friend's house. After breakfast, I waited over an hour to give him plenty of time and then I started home.

"It's time to go now, Melissa," Michael whispered.

They're still moving; I thought they would be finished. My little voice is never wrong. Why aren't they done? I don't want to be here with him. As I sat in the basement, he and his friends were moving his stuff out of the bedroom.

"You still love him, Melissa; do not let him do this. God has joined you in matrimony. Do not let Satan come between you. If he leaves now, he will never return," Michael said softly.

I jumped up from the sofa and ran upstairs. Jim and his friend had just put the last item on the truck and his friend was sitting in the truck waiting for Jim to come out. Jim turned and looked at me and then started to walk out the door. I looked at him and tried to speak.

Supay fluttered around Melissa's chest and she began to hyperventilate before she could tell Jim not to go. "No, let him go you fool; he does..."

Whoosh! Michael severed Supay's head from his body and then Abdiel engaged Michael in battle.

"Don't go. I...I...." I tried to talk but my heart was beating so fast I was hyperventilating and gasping for air. Jim spun around and grabbed me as I was about to fall.

"I love you," I finally said.

"You do?"

"Yes, I do."

"I love you too, Melissa. Why don't we sit down. You're shaking," Jim replied.

"For some reason, I couldn't get the words out and then I couldn't breathe," I said as I gasped again for air. "So what do we do now?" I asked.

Abdiel was no match for Michael and within minutes Michael thrust his sword through Abdiel's heart and he vanished in a puff of black smoke.

"I don't know," Jim replied.

"You and Mickey aren't going to be able to live in the same house together just because we love each other. We've always loved each other and you fight like cats and dogs and that's only half of our problems. We just can't continue like this if we're going to stay married. You know you could have hurt him."

"Yeah, I know. So what do we do about it?" he asked. "Maybe we need to go to some kind of counseling."

"That's a fabulous idea!" I cried.

"I'll go ahead and live in the apartment while we all go to counseling."

"Great idea and when you're both cured of your male stupidity then you can move back," I retorted.

He smiled, "Yeah, I guess we do have some of that."

"What about the sex?" I asked.

"What do you mean?"

"I mean, for some reason, I can't keep up with you like I did when we first met. Wouldn't you be better off with a younger woman? Somebody who wants sex every day like you do?"

"I don't want another woman, Melissa. I want you."

"Okay, then it's settled. We go to counseling."

Mickey was furious and refused to go to counseling.

"He is manipulating you, Melissa. Satan is using him to keep you from your mate," said Michael.

Mickey had known what he was doing all along! He had provoked Jim into hitting him so that I would get a divorce. *Of all the sneaky....* "Let me tell you something, young man. Contrary to popular belief, everything is not all about Mickey. Since the day I left your father to give you a better life, everything has been about you. My entire life has been about you. Well, in about six months, you're going to graduate from high school and go off to college and not give me a second thought. My husband and I are going to counseling to figure out how to live together and if you plan to live here then so are you, so get in the car now!" We all got in the car and went off to family counseling. As soon as Jim parked the car, Mickey got out and walked across the street and refused to join us.

"Let him go. He'll come home when his stomach is empty," I replied.

Jim and Jimmy and I went in to the counselor's office. After we left the counselor, Jim looked at me and I looked at him and we both shook our heads. "This isn't going to work. She doesn't have a clue about what makes me tick," he sighed.

"Nope, I don't think she knows what makes me tick, much less what makes you tick."

"*What about the Prophet Bosley?*" *Michael coaxed.*

"We should go and see that pastor. The one at that church you wanted me to go to," said Jim.

"Pastor Bosley? What a wonderful idea! I'll call him tomorrow."

That Thursday we started counseling with Pastor Bosley. After he spoke to both of us and listened to all of the problems we had, he asked me to leave and he talked to Jim alone. I don't know what he said to him exactly, but my husband has never been the same man since.

Mickey did indeed come home, but he was resentful and angry. My refusal to take his side made him even angrier. He didn't understand that I couldn't take his side when he was wrong. Refusing to go to counseling the first time and having no respect for Jim was just not going to fly; however, he did agree to go to counseling with Pastor Bosley. Again I'm not sure what Pastor Bosley said to him, but he would remember it six years later when he became a father himself.

In the meantime, his grades weren't good, he continued to get into trouble at school every day, and he began to smoke pot. He liked being angry, so he continued on his path of destruction. He was me in a male body.

We began to go to Pastor Bosley's church every Sunday and Jim joined the church just as Mickey and I had done several years ago. Pastor Bosley baptized Jim and Jimmy just as he had Mickey and me. Sometimes I would just sit and stare at Jim, wondering who this new guy was and when it was going to wear off, but it never did.

"He has been changed by the Father and that which is of the Father endures forever," Michael replied.

There was one problem; I still didn't understand what salvation entailed.

Lucifuges had been summoned to the throne. *This is it, he thought. I shall lose my head this day.* "Oh, what have I done? I've tried to be an evil force to the humans. Oh, what have I done," he moaned, as he landed at the gates. He was so distraught that he stumbled into the gatekeeper. "Oh, pardon me. Are you the gatekeeper?"

"I am he. And who might you be and why are you stumbling about like a drunkard?" the gatekeeper bellowed.

"I am Lucifuges and I have been summoned by the prince," he whispered, as if it were a secret.

"Speak up, you fool! Are you of feeble mind?"

"No, sir, I am terrified that I will surely not see the morrow. A summons from the prince could only mean the guillotine," he cried.

"You are of feeble mind! You have been summoned to replace Abdiel. He was killed in the line of duty, as you undoubtedly will be," the gatekeeper mumbled under his breath.

"You...you mean I am to be promoted to lieutenant?"

"Where does Master find these bumbling idiots?" sighed the gatekeeper.

"Stand up straight, you fool, and preen your wings before entering the great hall. If you do not learn his ways quickly, you will lose your head for sure."

"Yes, yes, of course," Lucifuges sighed. "What other advice do you have for one such as myself?"

"Compliment his beauty and do not look up. Now I will announce you. Come along; he loathes waiting."

I lusted not only for more money but also for more stuff. I lusted for a two hundred and twenty thousand dollar, five-bedroom house in Fayette County and, to make me happy, Jim agreed against his better judgment.

Nothing I had was good enough; I had to have more and more.

Lucifuges flitted around Melissa's head. Satan was quite happy with his progress to date. He had enticed the humans to spend twice the gold that they earned and now they were to take a journey on a magnificent ship. "Yes, my dear, spend more, more, more," Lucifuges cried.

Instead of my income helping us, it hurt us because the more I made, the more I spent and the more debt I incurred. My husband had a plan to be debt free. That was a joke; as he paid a bill, I started another one. I even purchased a seven-day cruise for us. I also bought Mickey everything he wanted, with the hope that it would make him happy. Instead it just made an already hateful, angry child an ungrateful child as well because he thought he was supposed to get everything he wanted.

This was the beginning of our financial ruin. Six months after we purchased that fabulous house, my contract with the hospital ended abruptly.

Oh, my! This is not good. How are we going to pay all these bills? I'll just have to find another contract and fast. But the industry was in a slump. Contracts in our field were few and far between.

"You of little faith. Did the Father not give you your previous employment? And if he gave that to you, will he not give you another?" Michael sighed.

I used another employment agency, but this time I was sent on an interview for a fulltime job with the consulting firm of Jefferson Stanley and Waite. I interviewed with several people and it went fabulously. Although fulltime employment meant a thirty thousand dollar decrease in income, it was definitely better than nothing. As I prepared to leave, I knew I had the job and then came the other shoe.

"Melissa, take these forms with you and fill them out and fax them back to me this afternoon. We will make our decision by Friday."

"Thank you very much," I replied as I took the forms. When I got to the car, I looked at the forms and then I just sat there. *There is no way in hell I can pass a background check. Michael told me that my association with McFarland and his association with Jimmy Ray had landed me the prestigious honor of an FBI file. Well, back to the drawing board. I know I had that job! I could tell by their faces.*

"Have you not yet learned that anything is possible with the Father? My dear child, where is your faith?" said Michael in exasperation.

"Oh, all right, already! I get it! Sorry, that was stupid," I said out loud. I drove to the Office Max store, filled out the papers, and sent them back within the hour. That Friday, I got the job. That was the good news.

The bad news was Mickey decided to quit school. When I approached him about it he yelled at me and then he slammed his bedroom door in my face.

"This is it! You will not continue to disrespect me and my husband in our home!" Mickey was eighteen; he had quit school, he smoked pot and he refused to work. "Mickey, you need to leave now."

Mickey ignored me, as if I hadn't said a word, so I had the police remove him. The only thing I could do for him now was pray.

I had been working at Jefferson Stanley and Waite for three months. It was just a regular day at work and a regular drive home. **"Call your earthly father," Michael whispered.**

On the way home, I called Daddykins on my cell. We had been playing phone tag for three days.

"Hey, little girl!"

"Hey, Daddykins. How are you?"

"I'm fair to middlin'."

"I have yet to understand that expression."

"I talked to Michael today," he said.

"Oh, really? How is he?"

"He's good. We hadn't talked for a while, so it was good to hear from him."

"Yeah, I miss him like crazy." Daddykins and I talked for forty minutes.

"Well, I gotta go, little girl. Hold 'em in the road and don't take no wooden pesos." That was always Daddykins favorite parting line.

"Okay, Daddykins, I won't. I love you!"

"I love you too, little girl."

After dinner, the doorbell rang. Standing at my front door were Mom and my two sisters! "What are you guys doing here this time of night? What a pleasant surprise!" I yelled. And then I saw their faces. "What?"

No one said a word.

"Mickey? What happened to Mickey?" I cried.

"No! Not Mickey, Daddy!" Faith cried.

"I thought it was Mickey. He's out there in the street..." I then I realized what she had said. "Daddykins!"

"He's gone," Faith said as she burst into tears. "Had you talked to him lately?"

"Yeah, I did. He knew he was going home. That's why he kept calling me. And for some reason I knew I needed to call him back. He even talked to Michael for an hour today."

"He called us too," Faith said in tears.

We all cried. I was sad, but I knew that God had given him just enough time to find salvation, so I was really okay. I also knew that he had made sure that he spoke to each of us before he left. *That is so God!*

Daddykins was gone, but life went on. I had been working at Jefferson Stanley and Waite for nine months when I was summoned to the conference floor.

"Melissa, Jordan would like to see you in conference room B." Jordan was the office administrator, which made her everyone's boss. I went up to the thirty-first floor and into the conference room. There were two other people in the room with Jordan.

"Melissa, please have a seat." I sat and Jordan dropped a bombshell. "I'm sorry, Melissa, but because of the recent slump in the market we're experiencing cut backs."

"Does that mean I'm being laid off?"

"I'm afraid so. Your work has been exemplary and I'm really sorry."

"Of course. Well, it has been very slow. To be honest with you, it would be negligent to keep two people when one can do the job. I just appreciate the time I've had here and I thank you for the opportunity." I left the conference room, but it was too hard for me to say goodbye to the others without crying, so I left without packing my things.

Jim came home at four. "What are you doing home?"

"I got laid off, so I'm taking a nap."

"What?"

"Yep, I thought layoffs were inevitable, but my manager didn't think it would ever happen. I should have listened to my subconscious and looked for a job sooner."

Jim just stood there and continued to look at me in disbelief.

After taking a brief vacation, I decided to work independently under a new company name I had created. It was slow and we were in deep financial trouble. Then an American tragedy sent what little work I had down the drain.

I picked up the phone that was ringing incessantly. "Can't a woman get any sleep?"

"Melissa, turn on the TV," Jim said.

I turned on the TV. The reporters were talking about an airplane that had collided with one of the twin towers in New York.

"Melissa, I think they did it on purpose."

"What? How dumb is that? To run a plane into a building on purpose? It had to be a freak accident," I replied.

At that moment, I watched as another plane came out of nowhere and hit the other tower. "What the hell is going on? Another plane hit the towers and it was on purpose! Are you seeing this?"

"No, we don't have a TV, but I think we're under attack. That's what's going on," Jim cried.

"By whom?"

"I don't know and I don't think they know either," Jim replied solemnly.

Daddykins was gone, Mickey was out there in the street, I was laid off, we were bankrupt, and America was under attack!

The computer industry took a beating, along with lots of other industries, after September 11. Jim and I struggled to pay two fifteen hundred dollar mortgages, thirty thousand dollars in credit cards, and three car notes. And we owed the IRS ten thousand dollars.

We had rented our other house to a woman with five children, against warnings from everyone we knew. I had done what my subconscious told me to do. It had said that renting to her was the right thing to do. She destroyed our house and then stopped paying the rent.

I really hadn't seen Sybil much, so when I saw her after September 11, I was shocked. She had gained a tremendous amount of weight after having the baby and, fifteen years later, had still been more than forty pounds overweight. Now Sybil was a size six again! "Sybil, you look fabulous!" I cried.

"Yeah, I do, don't I?" she laughed.

"While we're on that subject, I hope you realize where that comes from."

"What subject is that?"

"The subject of vanity."

"What do you mean? What's wrong with wanting to look good?"

"Nothing, but you and I have a tendency to take it to a whole new level. Vanity is what got Satan kicked out of Heaven you know."

"Whatever, Melissa. I think you're putting way too much thought into it."

"Well, I think you need to put much more thought into it. Vanity is how we ended up in the mess we were in."

Sybil rolled her eyes and changed the subject.

I had a lot of free time on my hands so I read a lot. I couldn't afford to buy books anymore, so I went to one of those stores where you trade books.

"This one! Choose this one," the demons chanted.

Michael watched from a distance. He had been instructed to be still during this battle that Melissa would fight on her own.

I started a book by Ellen White about God and the history of the church. It was fascinating until she wrote that to worship God truly I had to keep all of His commandments, including the Sabbath. She also said that the Sabbath was Saturday, not Sunday!

I went to the library and read everything I could on religion, its origin, and the Sabbath. *Why do we worship on Sunday? The Ten Commandments are quite clear on the fact that you are to honor the Sabbath and keep it holy. I just don't get this. How can all of these people worshipping on Sunday be wrong and not realize it? Or perhaps they just decided to do their own thing?*

"They are all going to hell if they do not keep the Sabbath," the demons chanted. They were laughing so hard they had trouble staying in the air. "You cannot worship on such a day," they said to Jim. "This is very bad indeed. Tell her it is stupid. Tell her she is stupid."

"I don't care what it says; I'm not going to church on Saturday. That's just plain stupid and if there was something wrong with worshiping on Sunday, Pastor Bosley wouldn't be doing it."

"Even if I prove he's wrong, you wouldn't do it because you might miss your precious football game, as if that's more important than God. Let's hope you don't punt yourself all the way to hell," I said under my breath.

That Saturday I went to a Seventh Day Adventist church I had located from the newspaper. The people were wonderful. Little Jimmy had a ball there and so did I.

"Tell her it is her fault sin entered into the world because Eve was as gullible as she is. Ha, ha, ha!" The demons laughed and dipped around the room.

Jim and I began to fight about the Sabbath.

"You know, Pastor Bosley has a point. Why am I listening to Eve?

You all are the reason we're in this mess to begin with."

"So it's Eve's fault that Adam had no backbone?" I yelled.

"No, it's Eve's fault that she was gullible enough to listen to a snake," he retorted.

"You know, that sounds like something that would be said when you can't come up with a rational reason. And you have yet to explain to me why we do not honor the Sabbath and neither has Pastor Bosley. So until I get a logical reason, I'll be at church on Saturday."

I spoke to one of the elders at the Seventh Day Adventist Church about my dilemma at home. "Well, these things take time," he said. "You realize that he may never come around, but you must put God first. Taking a stand and worshiping on the true Sabbath is a great sacrifice that we all make for God. It is important to know that when the Great Tribulation starts, it will be revealed that Sunday worship is the mark of the beast. Worship on the true Sabbath will be against the law and when that happens, we will be forced to take a stand. At that time, everyone will realize that Sunday worship is not of God and each person will be required to make up his own mind."

I continued to study everything I could find. Jim and I began a ritual. I would find a Bible scripture that supported my stance and I would highlight it and leave it on his night table. Then Pastor Bosley would give him a scripture that supported his stance and he would highlight it and leave it on my night table. We were actually learning the Word by trying to prove each other wrong.

I began to put a lot of thought and study into the mark of the beast and that was the beginning of the turning point. I kept thinking about what the elder had said about the mark. That would mean that all of the millions of Christians would wake up one day and essentially God would say, "Sorry! Joke's on you. You have been worshipping on the wrong day for twenty years. Go directly to hell; do not pass go or collect two hundred dollars." *Would God do that?*

"You know that He would not!" Michael replied.

I don't think so. That would mean Pastor Bosley is not a true man of God and I know that that cannot be true. Test it by fire. Pastor Bosley passes the test. Even if he did call me Eve, I thought with a smile. Then my smile faded. *This is serious; my eternal life depends on this.* "Lord, help me. This is madness! What is going on? I'm just trying to do the right thing by You. Please tell me what that is?"

Chapter Eighteen

"I Once Was Lost but Now I'm Found, Was Blind but Now I See"

It is time. This madness is finished. She will begin a new journey now. **Michael smiled at the thought.**

"Come on, Jimmy; it's time to go," I called. We were on our way to Florida to visit Jim's mother in Fort Lauderdale for Christmas. It was an eight-hour drive, but with the van it wasn't a bad ride.

When we got to Mama's, Jim and I were actually behaving in a civil manner. We decided to go to Christmas service with Jim's brother. My brother-in-law and sister-in-law belonged to an awesome church. I had decided to call a truce on the Sabbath issue for the duration of the trip and had even gone to church with Jim on that previous Sunday.

The church was decorated beautifully. On the stage were living room furniture and a Christmas tree with lots of presents under it. Midway through his sermon, the pastor said, "Whoever believes that they have a gift, I want you to come up here and get your gift from under the tree."

Nobody moved. So he repeated his statement. "Whoever believes that they have a gift, I want you to come up here and get your gift from under the tree."

Again, nobody moved and again he repeated his statement. "Whoever believes that they have a gift, I want you to come up here and get your gift from under the tree."

This time a gentleman went up and took a gift from under the tree. And then a woman went and then another and another. Not to be left out, I got up and got one too.

"Now, those of you that got a gift, do you believe that Jesus is God and that he died to save you?"

We all said, "Yes." But even though I had responded yes, I didn't really have a clue why Jesus died.

"Well, that's how easy it is to get the best gift you could ever have, the gift of everlasting life! 'For whosoever believes in me, shall have everlasting life.' He didn't say 'might have everlasting life.' He didn't say 'for whosoever believes in me and keeps all ten commandments shall have everlasting life.' There is nothing that you can do to earn it! You will never be good enough to earn it!"

I just sat there and cried.

"That is the Word, Melissa. That is the Truth that you seek. That is the Truth that you have searched for all of your years. Now you must study to understand it better. I know you are still unsure, but this is the way, not the Sabbath. The Sabbath is the law and cannot lead you to salvation. Follow your husband. You have always known Pastor Bosley was a true prophet. Go back where you belong," whispered Michael.

"You were right all along, you know," I told Jim on our way home. "Let me rephrase that; Pastor Bosley was right all along. You just followed the one with the football."

"Yeah, sure, Melissa. You just hate it when I'm right."

"Yeah, actually I do. Thank goodness it's not that often," I retorted. He nudged me on the arm. "Ouch! That hurt." I laughed and he laughed too.

It seemed as if we resolved one problem only to find a line of others to take its place. I had been without permanent employment for almost two years now. Our credit cards were maxed out and our savings were depleted. I needed a job, so I decided to make a new resume. I took out the skills category and the technical jargon, which were probably making me over qualified, and created a basic resume for an administrative assistant.

"Not bad. I would hire me, except I can't type. Who hires an administrative assistant who can't type? Well, who hires a computer teacher with no computer skills and no degree? I'll let God worry about that part."

"Now you are beginning understand," Michael laughed.

I posted my resume on Monster.com and started to get calls right away.

Michael flitted around Steve's head. Steve was fretting about losing his reputation because he had no one to fill a temporary position with one of his clients, the CEO of an airline. "Look. There on the screen. Choose this one; she will serve you well and save your reputation."

The phone rang. "Hello."

"Hello. Are you Melissa Bowan Dawson?"

"Yes," I answered.

"Melissa, I'm Steve Dunn with Careers Temp Agency and I saw your resume on Monster. Your background is impressive. Are you available to work?"

"Yes, Mr. Dunn, I am. What sort of position is it?"

"It's executive administrative assistant to the CEO and CFO of a major airline company. The job is temporary, while his regular person is on maternity. There is one hitch, Melissa."

"Yes, and what is that, Mr. Dunn?"

"You must start tomorrow and it's near the airport."

"I can start tomorrow, Mr. Dunn, and I have no problem with the location."

"Excellent! Excellent! I will check your references and get back to you before the end of the day."

"Very well. I look forward to it."

"That is so God! An executive assistant to a CEO and a CFO without so much as an interview! And I can't type! God, what in the world did I ever do without You?"

"My dear child, you have never been without Him," Michael said.

The guys I worked for were Dutch and absolutely marvelous. The company had as many perks as Jefferson Stanley and Waite. They even fed us gourmet lunches every day for free! But even though the job was great, it paid a fourth of what my teaching jobs had paid. We were still in a financial mess and sinking in quicksand.

We gave the bank back the rental property. We also gave back one of the cars, the one we had bought for Mickey. We turned off Jim's cell phone. We got rid of the NFL package Jim loved so much.

We cut out the home security, eating out, beauty parlor, nail salon, and anything else we could live without. But it was still not enough; we were almost in foreclosure.

My temp job lasted four months and then I was right back in the fire. I went out searching for anything, including retail. At my last stop one day, the people were so nasty and mean that I got up and left before my interview.

"Lord, forgive me. I'm not being ungrateful, but that was just ridiculous. Please give me strength. I have got to have a job, any job. If You give me anything, I will be grateful." I buckled my seat belt and turned at the red light. As soon as I made it around the corner, my cell phone rang.

"Melissa?"

"Yes."

"This is Jennifer at Morgan Receivables Incorporated. I would like to offer you the position that you interviewed for this afternoon. Are you interested?"

"Of course!"

"When can you start?" she asked.

I looked up and mouthed the words *thank you*. "I can start tomorrow."

"Great! I'll see you then."

I started at Morgan Receivables the next day. I went from forty-five dollars an hour to ten, from a corporate trainer to a receptionist. The third day I was there, the office ran out of paper. How does a corporation run out of paper? The place was a disorganized mess. Instead of being grateful, I resented working for a company that had to run to Office Depot to buy paper. I wanted to find another position as soon as possible. After I had been there a week, I was able to get three interviews. Each one was for a teaching position similar to the one I had had at Jefferson Stanley and Waite.

"You must learn to honor your commitments to the Father. You are not grateful as you promised," Michael whispered. "To much that is given, much is required. You have much to learn, my dear child."

This is unbelievable! I had gone on three interviews and all three companies had called me back for second and third interviews; yet I was turned down for all three jobs. That had never happened before.

What is going on?

"You listen only to that which you want to hear," Michael chastised.

I stopped abruptly in the center of my bedroom.

"Oh, my God, and I mean that literally. You! You are my subconscious! All of this time it has been You speaking to me, not some corner of my mind. I know You saved Michael; he even told me that the doctor who trached him was an angel. But me? Why? Why would You help me all of those times and I was...I was evil. You have been with me from the beginning. Each and every time You saved me! You took away my addiction, kept me from going to jail and getting AIDS. You made my heart beat when I died, just like You did Michael. You saved all of us from the fire and gave Daddykins just enough time to find salvation. You saved Sybil too! Oh, my God! You saved me, so that I could be with You. But why? And after all that I have done? Why? And how can I hear You in my mind?"

"It is the Holy Spirit that speaks to you. I am merely a messenger and, as such, I take your petitions to the Throne of God. Satan has set out to destroy you; however, you are blessed and highly favored. I am the servant of God sent to protect you from Satan's insidious plots. My dear child, Jesus loves you. Do you not love your offspring even to the death, regardless of what evil they do? Would you not do for them what he has done for you?" Michael asked.

"Of course, I would die for them without hesitation," I replied out loud.

"Then that is your answer. He loves you as you love your offspring. You and all mankind are His children. And as such, He loves you even to the death. That is why He saved you in your physical body, so that you could also be saved in the spirit. His death on the Cross is the only way to salvation. Your salvation is at hand. You must study to show thyself approved," Michael concluded.

"You kept me from those jobs because You want me at that company for some reason, right?"

"Yes, He does and soon you shall find the cause. Be patient and grateful. Has He not always supplied your needs?"

"I know, but ten dollars an hour? You can't get blood from a turnip."

"Did He not put a tube in your male sibling's throat when there was no human present?"

"Yeah, all right. I should know better than to argue with God. He knows everything and I concede that He can do anything. So, this is what I'll do. I will go back to work and I'll whip that place into shape and I'll be the best receptionist ever until such time as You decide for me to leave there. I guess when You're ready You'll let me know, yes?"

"Yes, He will," Michael replied with a smile

"Okay, okay, God; I'm sorry. I said I would be grateful and I wasn't. I really am grateful. Grateful cannot begin to describe what I am today."

"He knows my child," Michael whispered.

"One more thing. The other side of the voice that makes God seem schizophrenic. That is not God, is it?

"No, my child, that is Satan and his cohorts. You must know when they are speaking to you. You have the power to banish them without my assistance. You have only to say, 'Flee now in the name of Jesus,' and they will depart from you, for they can not endure the Name."

"This is good to know, but it could take some getting used to."

"You are but an infant who needs milk at this time. The milk is the Word. As you study, you will grow. Soon you will be ready for meat and will be weaned as an infant is weaned from his mother's breast. Have patience; study is the key."

I did exactly as I promised. Within two weeks I had used my computer skills to organize the entire front office. The managers were amazed at how smoothly things could run. That week the VP decided to appoint an office manager and, needless to say, I was not chosen.

"Get angry! The position is rightfully yours. You were the one who worked hard. Curse, yell, and be angry! It is your position, not hers. You earned it!" the demons cried.

"Get out of my head, all of you, in the Name of Jesus!"

Lucifuges, Zagan, and Morax disappeared in a puff of smoke. When they reappeared, they were at Satan's palace.

"She...she banished us," they said in dismay.

The gatekeeper roared with laughter.

"You were banished by a prostitute who fancies pharmaceuticals! The prince will be furious. I hope you have a new plan. If you do not, I have a basket for each of you, each of your heads that is. Ha, ha, ha!" he laughed as he went in to announce them.

But instead of being resentful, I let the new manager know that I would be happy to help her in any way I could. Even though I had the computer skills, she was the right person for the job because I knew nothing about the collection business and she knew everything.

I continued to ponder how I would manage to attend Bible study. Pastor Bosley had Bible study Tuesday night at eight. That was so late, with Little Jimmy having school and our working the next day. "I know I need study, but eight o'clock at night! Come on, God!"

That Tuesday an amazing thing happened. I was manning my post when a very distinguished gentleman with an air of authority and a marvelous vocabulary entered the reception area.

"Good morning. I'm Mr. Carr and I have an interview with Mr. Scott."

"Of course. Please have a seat and I'll let him know you are here." I buzzed Mr. Scott. "He will be with you shortly, Mr. Carr. Would you like a cup of coffee?"

"No, thank you. You certainly have a pleasant personality."

"Thank you. It's hard not to be pleasant when you consider that you could be dead."

He laughed, "I couldn't have said it better myself."

"So, Mr. Carter, what's that book you're holding? It says *Corinthians*; isn't that one of the books of the Bible?"

"Yes, it is a study guide I use for my sermons."

"Sermons?"

"Yes, I'm a minister."

"Really? Do you have your own church?"

"No, not yet. I'm an associate pastor, which is like an assistant to the pastor."

"What denomination is your church?"

"Baptist."

"I'm a new Christian and I'm hoping that I can finally get it right this time."

"The only way to get it is through study," replied Mr. Carr.

"Yeah, I know, but my church has Bible study at eight o'clock Tuesday nights and that is so late."

At that moment, Mr. Scott walked in and we were unable to continue. I missed Mr. Carr when he left because I was at lunch. The next day I looked up from my desk to see him back again.

"Mr. Carr, how are you?"

"I'm blessed and highly favored," he replied.

"Oh, I like that. You know, I'm blessed and highly favored also, now that you mentioned it. So, did you get the job?"

"I most certainly did. How would you like to Bible study with me at noon every day?"

"Are you serious? You would do that?"

"Of course."

"Absolutely," I replied. *A Bible study with a minister and all I have to do is walk to the break room. That is so God! This is why He made me stay here, isn't it?*

"Yes, my dear child, it is," replied Michael.

Reverend Carr and I studied every afternoon at lunchtime. After our study, I would go home and share with Jim what I had learned.

Lucifuges was worried. "We must stop this insidious study of the Word before she discovers the truth about the One Who Sits at the Right Hand," he said to Zagan. "Gather intel on those who can assist us with this attack."

After we had been studying in the break room for two months, our company held a mandatory meeting on harassment in the workplace. Our speaker, Ms. Johnson, talked about sexual, racial, and religious harassment. During the presentation, one of the employees raised her hand

"Miss Johnson, isn't it harassment when some people make us listen to their religious nonsense when they study in the lunchroom?"

I held my breath in anticipation of the answer.

"Do they include you in their conversations?" she asked.

"Uh...no," the girl replied reluctantly.

"Do they ask you to participate?"

"No," she said in exasperation.

"Can you leave the lunchroom and go somewhere else?"

"Yes," she sighed.

"Is the study in any way tied to your employment here?"

"Oh, forget it," she snapped.

"I take that to be a no," Miss Johnson responded. "In that case, the Bible study in the lunchroom in no way constitutes harassment."

"Idiot! I instructed you to locate someone to assist us! This is of no use to me," Lucifuges cried, as he severed Zagan's head. "Morax! Entice the human female who despises the Word to antagonize the prophet during their study. Perhaps we can deter them in this way."

Our next study was quite interesting and even somewhat amusing. As Mr. Carr and I studied on Friday, the girl who attempted to stop our study came into the lunchroom with her friend.

Morax buzzed around the lunchroom tables. "Use profanity; then the prophet will be forced to study elsewhere. More, more, more profanity," Morax coaxed.

All of a sudden the girl said, "F**k, f**k, f**k! I hate this f**king lunchroom and I hate these f**king people. And that mother f**king customer gets on my God d**n nerves."

Mr. Carr and I were flabbergasted. Profanity wasn't unusual, but this was something altogether different. "Ignore it," Mr. Carr said. "It is merely one of Satan's minions attempting to disrupt the Word. That just let's me know that we are fast approaching our goal."

"What goal is that?" I asked.

"For you to understand salvation," he replied with a smile. "I know one sure way to get rid of Satan's little helpers. When I say ready, I want you to say 'Jesus,' as loud as you can. Ready?"

"Jesus," we said in unison.

"Again!"

"Jesus," we repeated.

"I'm sick of this sh*t. Let's go," she said to her friend.

Mr. Carr looked at me and smiled as they left the room. "Works every time. They can't stand the Name." We continued our study without further interruption.

Morax and Lucifuges flew out of the lunchroom and dipped through the clouds. "I hate the prophets of God," Lucifuges yelled as he fled the Name.

Things were looking up with my relationship with God, but our finances were still in poor shape. We had put our house up for sale months ago, but it was the only house in the neighborhood that just wouldn't sell.

"God has decided, now that it is no longer an idol for you, you may keep it."

"Yeah, well, when is He going to tell me exactly how to do that?" I retorted.

Michael smiled but did not answer.

"We're going to need an extra fifteen hundred dollars to stop the foreclosure," Jim sighed. "I already took the maximum I can get from my 401K when we bought this house. Our savings account is depleted and our cards are maxed out. We're too far in arrears. I received the foreclosure notice today while you were at work."

"What are we going to do? We can't sell it fast enough," I wailed.

"You call your female sibling. Swallow your pride and she will give you assistance. You offered assistance to a mother of five when all others warned against it. She abused your kindness and yet you knew it was the right thing to do. For this reason, He will not allow you to lose your home when you attempted to give a home to another."

"Excellent idea," I said out loud.

"What's an excellent idea?"

"I'll ask Faith to loan us the money and we'll pay her back in increments."

"I don't like borrowing from relatives."

"Well, neither do I; but unless you have a better idea, it's our only option. Swallow your pride; I'm the one that has to ask her. If I can swallow mine, then you can too." He just grunted. "I take that to be a yes."

As usual, Faith came to the rescue and did not even flinch. She loaned us the money and we avoided foreclosure by seven days.

"We need a plan to get out of this mess," I said. "We're bankrupt, not figuratively but literally. I know we have excellent credit, or we had excellent credit, but that is not the case anymore. Our credit went in the toilet when we gave the other house back to the bank and Mickey's car to the finance company. Let's face it; there is no way to recover from this except bankruptcy. Shelly tore that house up so bad that even when they sell it, we will owe them forty thousand dollars. We owe thirty thousand in credit cards. My car is leased and the lease runs out soon. That means we will continue to have two car notes until yours is paid off. And on top of that, there's the IRS. That's another ten thousand dollars."

I knew bankruptcy was not a good thing, but I figured that God would work it out somehow. So we filed for bankruptcy. It actually turned out to be a good thing, in a way. It forced us to buy only things that we could afford because we now had bad credit. It forced us to be humble and it forced us to budget. Jim created a budget, cutting out my cell phone and everything else we had not cut previously. When we finished, there was nothing left but the basic satellite service. The satellite itself belonged to us, so we only paid a small monthly fee. We had absolutely no other frills. I relinquished all control of our finances, given the fact that I had no discipline, but we barely had enough to make Jim's new budget.

That Monday afternoon I studied with Mr. Carr, as I always did.

"Whoa! Did you just say 'robbing God'?" I asked in shock.

"I didn't say anything. You read it for yourself; the Word said it." We had just read Malachi 3:6-12.

"Come on, Mr. Carter. We are broke! Busted! We have no tithes to give," I wailed.

"Has it occurred to you that you are busted, as you say, because you don't tithe?" he asked with a smile. "What did the scripture say? 'Test Him on this and see how He will pour out a blessing so great that you do not have room to hold it.' You will stay busted and broke until you give God what belongs to Him."

"He has not lied to you. He is a true prophet of God, just like Pastor Bosley. You have eyes and you saw. Where is your faith? Test God on this and make room for your blessing," Michael said.

"Easy for you to say; you don't live with Jim," I retorted.

Michael smiled, "You of little faith. God will deal with your spouse."

That evening I gingerly broached the subject with Jim.

"Are you crazy? Ten percent of what? Don't you get it! We can't even buy enough groceries!" he yelled.

"Yeah, well, the groceries you can buy are because He blessed me with a job. And technically, we should be out on the street. Do you realize that ten percent of what we make each payday won't even pay the light bill? Let's test Him on it. We're broke anyway. I'd rather be broke than to rob God."

"Why not try it? Do the test. When it fails, you can tell her that you were right and she was wrong again," Michael whispered to Jim.

"Whatever, Melissa! Okay, let's do that. Let's test Him and, when we are worse off, it will be your fault!" and he stormed out of the room.

My next Bible study proved even more enlightening. Mr. Carr was taking me down what he called the Roman Road. We were to study the entire book of *Romans*. When we got to chapter two about the Jews and the law, that's when I finally got it.

"Oh, my God! I get it!"

Mr. Carr smiled. "You have been taught all your life that it was about the Ten Commandments. Now you understand it's the blood."

"It's the blood! I get it! Mr. Carr, I could kiss you. You don't keep the commandments to get to heaven; you keep the commandments because you love God. Jesus is the reason you get to heaven and that's why you can't earn it. He took our place. We were the ones that sinned and deserved to die. But He loved us so much that He came down here and took our place, so that we could have eternal life. Oh, my God! I get it! The Seventh Day Adventists are trying to circumvent grace by insisting you must obey the Jewish Sabbath. They are like the Jews of Paul's day. They wanted to be Christians but continued to put the stipulations of the law on their brothers. It's the blood, stupid," I said as I hit myself in the head. *Auntie Emma was right. She said if Jesus ain't in it, it's a cult.*

Mr. Carr smiled again. "I do believe you've got it. Now all you have to do is believe."

"No problem. I've always believed. I just didn't know what or why. It's the blood of Jesus. I get it! I really get it!"

"Indeed she has," Michael said with a smile.

"No!" Satan cried. "Do you realize what your incompetence has done? She has found out the truth about the One Who Sits at the Right Hand! The second death no longer has power over her!" Whoosh! He severed the heads of Lucifuges and

Morax in one stoke. "No!" Satan roared so loudly that again the stained glass windows exploded into thousands of pieces.

The gatekeeper tried to comfort Satan. "Master, perhaps we can damn some other human?"

Satan turned to the gatekeeper and severed his head also. "I do not want another! I want her! First her earthly father, then that insidious constable, and now her! If I cannot have her, I will destroy her seed! Satan bellowed.

"You know, Mr. Carr, for the first time in my life I am truly content and at peace. The amazing thing about that is I'm bankrupt, without a dime to my name, and I'm content. My child is running around out there in the street and yet I am not worried. Imagine that! The thing I've been searching for all of my life was right under my nose. True love, peace, and contentment cannot be found in a mortal man or in money, and not even in your children. It can only come from your belief in Jesus. Amazing!"

"Amazing, indeed," said Mr. Carr.

The lease on my car was up and I started to look for another car. It had been so long since I had bought a car with bad credit that I had forgotten what it was like when no one would finance you. Not to mention the prices! My goodness, it was going to cost twenty thousand dollars for a standard midsized car. Of course, I had paid thirty-two thousand dollars for the van, but that was before I had common sense. It went to nine dealerships before I could find financing. I finally settled for a used car with ten thousand miles on it. At least it was a 2003 model.

"We really can't afford a four hundred and twenty-dollar car note," Jim sighed.

"Yeah, I know, but the van was four hundred and seventy five dollars. At least it's less."

"Yeah, there's that," he lamented.

That Monday I got a call from the dealership asking us to come down and resign some papers. When we got there, we found out the bank had denied the loan at the price the dealership had submitted but had approved us for five thousand dollars less. Rather than take the car back, the dealership dropped the price of the car that amount. That dropped our payment to three hundred and sixty dollars.

"You realize that God just poured you out a seventy dollar a month blessing."

"Yeah, I realize that, but I can hold seventy dollars just fine."

Michael smiled. "You have yet to see the glory of the Lord."

My next Bible study was a painful one. This time I had stayed up late to read a few passages of scripture. I read that God knew each of us in the womb at the moment of conception and even knew how many hairs we had on our heads.

"Oh, my God! The babies! They were living beings with a soul from the very beginning, weren't they? God, forgive me! What have I done?" I sat on the floor and I cried for the babies.

"It is all right, my dear child. There is nothing that you can do to lose His love. The babies are here with the King now. There is no better place for them to be. They do not blame you; they know that you did not know of that which you were about to do. Once a sin is forgiven, it is thrown into the lake of forgetfulness. God forgives all things if only you ask. God is not like man; His love is unconditional and there is nothing that you can do to earn entry into the Kingdom. Nor is there anything you can do to be denied entry, except grieve the Holy Spirit. You will continue to fall, but He will always be there to pick you up. Dry your tears. He is with you."

"I know, but it is still a terrible thing, a very terrible thing. Look at the many times You saved me and yet I did not spare them. I think I will name them and I look forward to seeing them one day."

"As you shall," Michael replied.

When I woke up the next morning, I had a terrible backache. My back and my right leg made it impossible for me to move; so I called in sick, took some medicine, and went back to sleep.

Abusing my body all those years had finally caught up with me. Over the years, I had developed arthritis, fybromyalgia, and chronic fatigue. I was no longer able to do all the things I had once done at home, and it was hard for Jim to accept that I was no longer super-woman. He was accustomed to me doing everything. When I couldn't do it anymore, it was a huge transition for both of us. I had realized during our counseling sessions that these diseases were the reason I was so exhausted and menopause hadn't helped my irritability.

The phone woke me.

"Hello."

"Hello, Melissa?"

"Yes, this is Melissa."

"Hi. This is Jordan Baker from Jefferson Stanley and Waite."

Jordan Baker from Jefferson Stanley and Waite? I haven't worked there for three years. What could she possibly want?

"To give you a blessing that you cannot hold," Michael replied.

She wants to ask me to come back!

"Hello, Jordan. How are you?"

"I'm fine; I'm calling to see if you would like to come back to work."

"Excuse me?"

"We would like to have you back, Melissa."

"Jordan, you laid me off. What is to prevent it from happening again?"

"We laid you off because we had two teachers and we needed only one. Now we have none."

"Oh, that does make a difference."

"So, will you come back?"

"Will all things be as they were in regards to compensation?"

"Yes. Is that enough?" I was silent. "Melissa, is that enough?"

"Yes, Jordan. It is quite sufficient."

"You're sure?"

"Yes, I'm quite sure."

"Good. When can you start?"

"I can start in two weeks."

"Okay. I'll send the offer letter and the paperwork by FedEx."

"Thank you, Jordan."

"No, thank you, Melissa. I remember how gracious you were when we laid you off. You were an asset to the company. The decision was based on seniority, not on your performance."

"As it should be," I replied.

"It will be good to have you back."

"Thank you. I'll see you in two weeks."

You kept me home with a backache, so that I would be here for Jordan's call, didn't You?

"Yes, He did." Michael responded.

God has a sense of humor. That is the best backache I ever had! I slid out of the bed onto my knees. "Thank you, Jesus. I know I keep saying it, but oh, my God, You are so God!"

"Yes, He is my child! Yes, He is!" Michael whispered.

When Jim came home, I just looked at him a moment.

"What? Why are you looking at me like that?"

"I have a question for you."

"Yeah, what?"

"I make what? About twenty thousand dollars?"

"Yeah, that's about right."

"If God would more than double my salary overnight, would you say that's a blessing that you can't hold?"

"Yeah, right. Nobody doubles their salary overnight without doing anything."

"No, nobody on earth could do it, but God did it."

"Melissa, what are you talking about?"

"Jordan from Jefferson Stanley and Waite called and asked me to come back to work–same salary, same vacation, and same benefits. I think your test has just been answered."

"You're kidding, right? You just want to see me squirm."

"Well, I have to admit, it is pleasurable watching you squirm; but I'm not kidding."

I told him the conversation I had had with Jordan.

"When Jordan asked if your previous salary was enough, why didn't you ask for five thousand dollars more? She would have given it to you, you know?"

"Yeah, I know, but think about it. She didn't give me anything. It was God. If I had asked for more, it would have been downright ungrateful."

"Yeah, you're right," Jim replied.

"Now you both are getting it," smiled Michael.

That was just the beginning. When I returned to work, I got two more calls about employment. One was from one of those interviews when I had first come to work for Morgan Receivables. The human resources manager told me that she had been impressed with me then, but I wasn't the right fit for the first job. I had to tell her that I had just accepted another position. More blessings than you can hold–that about sums it up. You can only accept one job at a time.

The next call was from Loretta, asking if I would come back and work on another project at the hospital for fifty dollars an hour! I had to tell her that I had just accepted a position, but I would be happy to consider working in the evenings and on weekends.

That night Jim just threw up his hands. "Okay, okay, you were right. The window is open and we can't hold the blessings. Tithing is good and you will never have to convince me again. Bible study is good too. From now on we're all going to Pastor Bosley's Bible study."

Is this my husband talking? Yes, it is! I am truly blessed and highly favored.

"Yes, my child, you are," said Michael.

When the head of the family takes his rightful position and leads the family the way they should go, everything begins to fall into place. When Daddy goes to church, everybody goes to church. When Daddy goes to Bible study, everybody goes to Bible study. When Daddy prays, everybody prays. And that is as it should be. To this day, Jim is the first to write the tithe check. Even when I forget to calculate tithes, he holds up his hand and says, "Wait! We need to tithe first." Jim's financial management has put us back on track. *I wonder where all of those demons went that were lurking about?*

When I went for my annual check up I discovered that the demons had not gone very far. When I went in, my doctor had that Dr. Kildare look. "What's wrong? You have that look."

"Nothing to be concerned about. I would like to rerun a test."

"Which test and what is it for?"

"Just a blood panel. Here. Take this down to the lab and I'll call you next week."

I wasn't happy to be kept in the dark, so I wrote down the name of the test from the lab slip. It was called serum protein electrophoresis. When I got back to the office, I went to the Internet and looked it up. I couldn't believe my eyes. Serum protein electrophoresis was used to diagnose multiple myeloma, a rare bone cancer with a survival rate of about two years. Five if you went to the best clinic in Switzerland.

"Ha, ha, ha! My pretty, you will soon be with Master. He has seen to it personally. Did you really think you could escape him? He is the ruler of this world, not the God you serve."

That night while I was in the shower, I was distraught. "Lord, I'm dying! Little Jimmy is only eight and Mickey is hanging out in the street. What will happen to them?"

"What did the Prophet Bosley teach you? You have the power to banish this sickness," Michael whispered.

Yes, that's it! Pastor Bosley taught us about the prophet of God who was told by the angel that he was to die that night. He prayed! That's what I will do.

I jumped out of the shower and ran and got my Bible and found the prophet. The angel had told him that he was going to die and he had asked God for fifteen more years and God had granted his request. *I don't need fifteen years; I only need ten. Mickey will be twenty-eight and Jimmy will be eighteen.* Pastor Bosley had also taught us about the lady who had touched Jesus' garment and was healed. So I prayed and I prayed. Every day I prayed.

When I went back to the doctor, the news wasn't good.

"Melissa, the test was the same."

"You mean multiple myeloma, don't you?"

"Yes, how did you know that?"

"The Internet. I'm sure you rue the day they invented it."

"Yes, it can be challenging. I'm sorry, but I need to send you to an oncologist. Your appointment is tomorrow."

The oncologist informed me that he would need to perform a bone marrow test and would have the nurse schedule my appointment. As the nurse stepped out, the doctor continued to examine me.

"Now, Melissa, hold still."

I was lying on my stomach and I felt a prick in my back. The next thing I knew he had stuck a needle into my back, all the way into the bone, and then pulled it out. It was the most excruciating pain I had ever experienced, including childbirth.

"Now, that wasn't so bad, was it?"

"You're kidding, right? I thought you were going to do it next time."

"That was just to set you at ease. If I had waited, you would have agonized over it the whole time. Now it's done."

"You're really sneaky," I replied.

"Yeah, I know," he laughed. "The test will take about a week. It will tell us what to do next. Now don't you worry?"

"Yeah, right."

That night I went into the bathroom and I prayed again.

"God, I know You can do anything. I've seen it with my own eyes. Please, God, I just need ten years for my boys. If the best clinic in Switzerland can give me five years, I know that You can give me ten. I don't care if I have to do chemo and I don't care if I don't have hair. I don't even care about the pain. I just need to raise my boys. You gave your prophet fifteen years and I'm standing on Your Word. I know if You did it for him, You will do it for me too. In the name of Jesus! Amen."

Michael landed at the gates of Heaven and approached the Throne of The Most High God. He bowed. "Praise be to the Father, the Son, and the Holy Spirit."

"You have a request, my brave warrior?"

"Not me, Lord, but she."

"I know. You may tell her that her request has been granted."

Michael bowed and took flight.

I stood there for a few minutes and then the most wonderful thing happened.

"He has answered your request, my child. He was given you that which you have asked," Michael said.

"He has?" I asked. "Yes, He has!" I said to my own question.

Michael smiled. "Now you are no longer an infant and you are ready for meat."

I never gave the test results another thought. As a matter of fact, I forgot about the appointment until the reminder popped up on my electronic calendar.

The appointment was at three. I had no idea how God was going to do it. I just assumed that He would make the chemo send the cancer into remission. After my hair fell out and all of the other stuff that goes with chemo, then I would get ten more years and then I would die. I had read that bone cancer was the most painful of all the others, so I also prepared about that.

"Melissa!" The doctor got up from his chair and took my hand. "Have a seat. Melissa, you do not have multiple myeloma."

"What? But what about the tests that kept coming back positive?"

"In essence, you carry a gene that can develop and become multiple myeloma. It may never develop or it may take it twenty years. There is no test to determine whether or not the gene will develop into multiple myeloma. The percentages are about thirty percent. So you have a seventy percent chance of not ever having multiple myeloma."

I just smiled. I had only asked for ten years. I thought I was getting ten years of cancer, pain, and chemo, and then I would die. Instead, He just made it go away. *Now that is so God! Thank you, Jesus!*

"Melissa?"

"Oh, sorry. I was somewhere else," I said with a smile.

"Well, you have a lot to smile about. So get out of here and go and celebrate."

What manner of God is this we serve? How could anyone serve a god other mine? My God can do anything. Why and how can You be so good to us when we don't deserve any of it? Thank You for allowing me to stay with my children. You could have let me die, knowing that I would now reside with You in the Kingdom. But instead, You've allowed me to stay with them. How do I begin to express to You the words that describe how grateful I am for all that You have done? All of those times You saved me and now this. I am truly blessed and highly favored, but for the life of me, I still don't understand why or how You could love me so much?

He knows, my child, what is in your heart and He feels the love that you have for Him. Even when you were led by the desires of the world, the love was there. Your offspring does not cease to love you, when he is disobedient. More often than not, disobedience is synonymous with youth. Once a child is chastised by his father, he then learns obedience. God loves all of His children. Nothing in creation can separate mankind from the love of God that is in Jesus Christ our Lord.

I've been at Jefferson Stanley and Waite almost six years now. Life is good. Sybil left her cop and ran off with her latest conquest. I have yet to understand it, after what God has done for us, but look how long it took me to get it. Perhaps she doesn't get it either. Faith, well, Faith is just that–steady as a rock. Michael and I are as close as ever now and I miss him terribly. I plan to visit him this summer. Daddykins is with the King and I will see him too in time. Mother too is a fine Christian woman. Too bad I didn't realize that she knew more than I did.

Mickey is twenty-two now and has a baby. It's hard to chastise him when I see myself in him. But, do you really think I'm worried? If you do, then you haven't been paying attention. God has a wonderful plan for him when it's time. Little Jimmy is eleven and a "know it all" just like his mom. He's also an honor roll student and a really good basketball player. He is a fine Christian young man.

And my Jim has grown into a wonderful Christian man and an awesome father. He is my heart and my soul. I couldn't have done it better if I had planned it myself. Well—now that I think about it—if I had planned it, it would have been a disaster

My granddaughter Jasmine is beautiful; she actually looks just like me. I have some future words of wisdom for her. Last month, Pastor Bosley dedicated her to God, just as he did when Jimmy was born. When Mickey introduced his family as he stood in front of the congregation, he referred to my husband as his father. Again Pastor Bosley had come through for me. Whatever he had said to Mickey six years ago stayed with him and changed his life. Pastor Bosley is a true prophet of God and such a gift to all of us. He has baptized all of us and dedicated the babies. What a blessing!

I have a very dear Christian friend here at Jefferson Stanley and Waite. Her name is Joan. A few months ago, Joan and I decided to have a study on our purpose in life. The author of the book that we used said something really important in the first chapter: If you want to know your purpose, you should ask the One who created you. I never read another chapter of the book; there was no need. I asked God my purpose and He told me. He told me that my purpose was to tell others what He had done for me.

Yeah, right. And how exactly am I supposed to do that? First my husband would divorce me, my employer would fire me, and no would have an ounce of respect for me again. I'm not really going to do that after all I've gone through to get this life. I can't go around telling people that I was a call girl and a drug addict. So I argued with God for a while, but I knew that I had to do it. I just didn't know how I would do it.

Then one day Joan brought me another book written by her friend Phillip Sacco. *Awaken the Warrior* explains how to be a warrior for God. His book talked to me in more ways than one. As I held it in my hand, the Holy Spirit began to speak.

"This is how you are to tell the world what God has done for you. You shall put the words to a manuscript and all shall see the Glory of the Lord," Michael whispered.

The next day I began writing. To let the world know what I was required the strength of those who fight on the front lines. Yes, a warrior attitude perfectly described what was needed to perform this task: A warrior goes into battle with the full knowledge that he may be killed and yet he goes without question.

It took me six months to complete the manuscript. I decided it was only fair to let Jim read it, so I held my breath and gave it to him. I told him that he needed to prepare himself because there were many things that he did not know about me and some were ugly. He said he wasn't worried about it, but he hadn't read the book. The next day he met me at the door, walked over, and laid the book on the table.

"I can't read any more of this," he whispered.

My heart fluttered and I started to hyperventilate. *This is it; he's leaving me.* "What chapter did you read?" I asked.

"I finished chapter seven, about Allen and the other Jim," he replied.

"If you are having a hard time with chapter seven, you need to know that it is merely a ripple. Chapter eight is a tidal wave."

"I don't care. I love you too much to read this." He hugged me and kissed me, a tear in his eyes. "I'm not married to the woman in these chapters. I'm married to the woman that I met. I will read the chapters that start the day we met, but I will not read these."

"And what happens when people start to talk about chapter eight and you haven't read it?"

"I already know what is in chapter eight. Jesus already said what you would do. I know the woman I'm married to and that's all that matters. I don't care what people say, but I don't need to read it, okay?"

"Okay," I replied.

"I love you," he whispered.

"I love you too."

He then went to bed as I sat there and marveled at what God had just done. The next day I went back and revised this book to include Jim's response.

I don't know why I haven't gotten used to this by now, but the things He does are just so incredible. "You knew he wouldn't read it, didn't You?"

"Yes, my child, He knew."

"I really thought he would and I really thought he would divorce me. This is where You are supposed to say, 'You of little faith.'"

"On the contrary, you have faith much more abundantly," said Michael.

"Really? Why do You say that?"

"Did you not write the manuscript fully expecting it to sever your bonds of matrimony? You did so because that is what God had commanded, yes?"

"Yes."

"You did so with the knowledge that your marriage was in the hands of God. That, my child, is faith."

"Yes, I guess it is."

"The time is yet young. Perhaps he will sever the marriage bond at a later time," said the demon. **He was cautious to stay a good distance from Michael.**

"You know, he could still divorce me after he hears what people say about chapter eight."

"You know that he will not," replied Michael.

"Yeah, I know. That's the voice of Satan."

"You have learned much since your conception."

"My conception?"

"Yes, the day of your rebirth."

"Yes, I have. I'm what you call 'a quick study.'"

Michael smiled.

"I will be fired."

"Are thou troubled?" asked Michael.

"No, He did not save me all of those times to teach others how to use a computer. He saved me to show others how to find Him!"

"As the Prophet Carr has said, now you understand. And because of your faith, your blessings have yet to begin."

"You know, He is so God!"

"Yes, He is, my child. Yes, He is."

"Well done, my good and faithful servant, well done," Jesus said from the Throne.

Epilogue

Before I speak to you concerning the ramifications of prostitution and drug addiction, I need to clarify the contents of this book. Please do not confuse my portrayal of the Holy Spirit and the warnings given by Michael as this new fangled nonsense "speaking to your spirit guide" or "talking to your guardian angel." I am a true born-again Christian and I do not believe in or speak to **spirit guides**. I do not believe in or participate in **WICCA** because the Scriptures are clear that witchcraft, speaking to the dead, and speaking to spirits are of Satan. My guide is the Father, the Son, and the Holy Spirit. If I did not make that clear when the Archangel Michael answered my question about hearing him in my mind, then let me make it crystal clear now. I do not talk to spirits. I listen to the Holy Spirit as He resides in me.

If you are offended by those statements, then I apologize. If you are a Jehovah's Witness or Seventh Day Adventist and you are offended by what has been said in this book, then I apologize to you also; but this is my God's book and, as such, I am obligated to follow the Holy Spirit as He dictates what is to be written.

Now that I have clarified that, let me also clarify one other facet of this book. Do not misconstrue what has been said as a glorification of the life that I led. If you are a young woman reading this book, as Sybil attempted to tell me on more than one occasion, **you do not want that life.** That life is a living hell for any woman who lives it. Five thousand dollars, ten thousand dollars, or a million dollars a night cannot repay what you will lose when you allow yourself to be degraded in this way.

I truly believe that, considering how many young women are led into the life that I lived, this book should be required reading for girls fifteen and older and maybe even for younger girls, considering the statistics. Many of you may say, "I'm not letting my daughter read this because she will never encounter people such as this." You probably believe that your status or your wealth or **her** intelligence will prevent her from encountering this type of madness. I beg to differ with you. Intelligence and street smarts are two different things. And then you may say, "My daughter will never encounter anyone on the streets like little Melissa did." I beg to differ with you again. The reality is that the hood has merged with Hollywood. That means that this filth is no longer confined to the streets.

If you recall, the very people who use escort services are educated, middle class to upper middle class white men with law degrees and doctorates. They make up the bulk of the clients. Drug dealers are only about thirty percent. The other seventy percent, for the most part, are your husbands, friends, colleagues, and neighbors.

You do not need to be an FBI profiler to know the profile of a serial killer. Go to the web and Google *serial killers* and look at their pictures. They are not black men in watch caps with their pants hanging down on their butts; they are white men between the ages of twenty-eight and fifty with above average intelligence. Most have had some college courses, if not a degree. That includes ninety percent of all the men that your daughter will meet every day when she steps out of the confines of your neighborhood. Unfortunately, the killer will more likely be your neighbor than anyone who lives in a ghetto.

Parents need to wake up and smell the coffee. Predators look just like you and me. My first encounter with a prostitute was applying for a job at American Airlines. My next encounter with a predator was Derek, who lived next door to a doctor. He preyed on professional girls and was no different from a pimp who had sex with them and then took their paychecks. Allen and his drug dealing crowd frequented hotels where their rooms cost in excess of five hundred dollars a night.

The drug dealers that prey on our daughters have millions of dollars at their disposal to lure our children away from us using the common sense that you think our children have. If you recall, one of my calls was on a Lear jet. Those guys were rich, smart, and educated. They were not drug dealers. They could have just as easily picked up three naïve college girls at a popular disco and lured them onto that jet. They could have drugged them, used them, and dumped them anywhere in the world, never to be seen or heard of again.

Even though I did not have perfect parents, I challenge you to find anyone who does. The statistics say that I should have left home and entered college just as my sister Faith did. Do not be misled by what the statistics say. Just because your daughters and grand-daughters come from stable middle class and upper middle class environments does not mean that they are not easy prey for the cunning predators waiting to pounce upon them the moment they are away from your prying eyes. I was raised to be a good Catholic girl. My dad was a twenty-year military man and my mother was a college graduate. I came from a good home and yet I was lured into the seedy world of drugs and prostitution.

Young women lack the maturity of always making the right deci-sion. Our daughters need to be anchored in the Word of God to deal with the new predators in our society today. I was raised in the church and yet I had no knowledge of the Word of God. It is our responsibility as parents to train our children up in the way that they should go. The real world has every element of Sodom and Gomorrah. It is our responsibility to educate our daughters about what is waiting for them when they enter that world looking for their Prince Charming, who in fact does not exist except though Jesus Christ our Lord and Savior. Our daughters need to be educated about what Sodom really entails, as Sodom can be very alluring to the naïve. It is also our responsibility to pray for them as they go about their daily lives.

But how can you ask God to protect your children when you yourself have no relationship with Him and do not who He is? How can you–as a man, as a husband, and as a father–ask God to protect your daughter when you are the predator who frequents an escort

service and uses someone else's daughter for your own sexual gratification?

As I wrote this book, I was required to go back and read it and
reread it to make edits. Each time I read it, I am unable to comprehend the fact that I was the woman in these first chapters. My sister
Faith and I decided together that it was necessary to edit some of
the harsh realities and, as a result, I have omitted some of the more
graphic details. As unbelievable as it may sound, I also omitted many
events because the reality was too sickening for me to relive.

Each time I read these pages, I want to vomit, hoping that I can
purge myself of the ugliness and the filth that is contained here. But
then I realize that it is not necessary, for the blood of Jesus performed
that task two thousand years ago. The blood of Jesus is what has
cleansed me of this ugliness, of this sin, and of this guilt.

Even so, I must find a way to make that life that I lived count for
something. I must make something good come from all of that ugliness. I replay each event in my mind, trying to find a way to make
sense of it. Yet, no matter how hard I try, I cannot.

So it is up to you, the reader, and the women who read these
pages. It is up to you to read this and refuse to allow yourself to be
degraded, to be used, to be abused, and to be manipulated by the
evil men that prey upon the naïve, that prey upon our daughters, that
prey upon our sisters, that prey upon our granddaughters. It is up to
you to refuse to allow Satan to take your desires, your wants, and
your needs and use them to lead you down a path of destruction. It
is up to you to look to Jesus to fulfill your every need rather than to
look to a mortal man, who is incapable of unconditional love. It is up
to you not to allow your heart to be broken into a million pieces and
scattered like dust and trampled upon. It is up to you to say no to the
temptations that the world has to offer you. It is up to you to make
the life that I led count for something by living yours the way God
intended.

If this book can prevent one girl, just one young woman, from
entering into the life that I lived, then that life was not in vain.

I dedicate this book to all of you

First and foremost I dedicate this book to the One who inspired me to write it. To the Father, the Son, and the Holy Spirit. Thank you, Jesus, for loving me unconditionally, for loving me, saving me, and dying for me even though I did not deserve it. Praise be to the Father, the Son, and the Holy Spirit.

To my Guardian Angel. Thank you for your diligence, dedication, and determination to keep me safe from harm. God entrusted me into your hands and you have performed this task, never once failing me for fifty years.

To my Mother, who dedicated her life to caring for four children, mostly alone. After experiencing raising one child alone, I have yet to understand how you accomplished this miraculous feat. I want everyone who reads these pages to know that I chose this life in spite of what I was taught. Thank you, Mom, and I love you.

In loving memory of Daddykins, who spent most of his life tormented by the disease of alcoholism. To you, Daddy, how happy I am that you are now with the King, never to be tormented again. I will see you again on resurrection day. Until that time, you will forever be my Daddykins.

To my Dearest Husband, I am truly sorry for any pain this book may cause you. You must know that the Father has ordained this book and as such I am obligated to obey His call. I love you and hope you can understand. You are my life, my love, my heart, and my soul. You are my one and only true love. Our union was planned and ordained by the Father and will forever remain until death do us part.

To my First Born, whom I would surely die for. May you find the One who truly did die for you. This is for you also. I pray that you do not think less of me but instead use my life as a map that shows the direction to where you wish to go, for I have already been there and at the end lies death. This is for you, with all of my love.

To my Second Born, whom I love as much as the first. You are the ray of light in my life. You too I would give my life for. I hope that one day you understand that the woman in these first chapters is not and never has been your mother.

In loving memory of my Unborn Children. Forgive me, for I took your lives and yet they were not mine to take. My only consolation is that I know that you are with the King and it is a far better place than here.

To my Brother, my Fallen Hero. In this book I named you Michael because you always protected me. You too loved me unconditionally.

To my Sister whom I named Faith. Without faith, it is impossible to please God. To you, Faith, the voice of reason to whom I never listened but will forever love, respect, and admire.

To the one I named Sybil. To you, in the hope that this account of our lives of sin and degradation will inspire you to find the only One who truly loves you, He who saved you and me even though we were surely undeserving. You, I love also, for you are merely a mirror reflection of myself.

To my Sister-in-Law, whom I named Pamela. Thank you for always giving me shelter and for never abandoning me, even when I disrespected your home, taking advantage of your kindness, your tolerance, and your love. To you, Pamela, for caring for me when I never repaid a penny and never even gave as much as a thank you. I thank you here and now in the presence of all who read these pages.

To Pastor Bosley, who has always given us the true unadulterated Word, even when it was unpopular and not what the world's itching ears preferred to hear. Thank you, Pastor, for saving my marriage and my sanity. You, Pastor, are a true prophet of God.

To Reverend Carr, my Mentor and my Friend. Thank you for

staying with me until I got it. It's the blood!

To my Friend, whom I named Joan, for your encouragement and support while I penned these pages. You are definitely a warrior, as your name implies.

In memory of him whom I named McFarland, the Father of my First Born. You lived by the sword and died by the sword. May you serve as a reminder to those who say, "I will wait until tomorrow," for tomorrow may never come.

To my Editor Sandy, for your wonderful insight in making this book the best it could be.